VARIATIONS

VARIATIONS

John Reeves

Anywhere But Here Publications

Toronto ~ Taipei

aBHp

2018

© John Reeves, 2018

ISBN 978-0-9948164-5-0 (paperback)
ISBN 978-0-9948164-6-7 (eBook)

Legal Deposit fourth quarter 2018
Library and Archives Canada

Published by Anywhere But Here Publications, 2018

Library and Archives Canada Cataloguing in Publication

Reeves, John (1926-)

[Fiction]
Variations

Issued in print format.

ISBN 978-0-9948164-5-0 (paperback). – ISBN 978-0-9948164-6-7 (eBook)

I. John Reeves, 1926–. II. Title. III. Title: Fiction.

CONTENTS

PREFACE

The three novellas in this book vary in setting, period, and manner; but they are technically related as fiction in dealing with crimes of one sort or another.

"Jane" is set in contemporary Toronto. It features a private eye, who is hired to investigate the perhaps wrongful conviction of a murder suspect, and thus to correct a miscarriage of justice of the kind sadly common in real life.

"Sargent," by contrast, is not a detective story at all. Set in England, in a time-span from the late nineteenth century to the early twenty-first, it has the form of a literary documentary: an enquiry into the life of a woman poet whose early years were marred by incestuous abuse, horribly present, then and now, in all ranks of society.

"Final Lap" is a police-procedural, also set in the Toronto of today. It features Inspector Coggin and Sargent Sump, of previous novels: it begins with a routine investigation of a homicide, but it expands into a more wide-ranging exploration of greed as a defect of modern life; the story's subplot addresses the related problem of sport corrupted by performance-enhancing drugs.

i

JANE
a quest

for Howard Engel
crime-writer, colleague

She called the first thing Monday morning, and asked for me in person.

"Speaking," I said.

There was a short pause.

I knew what that meant. What sort of one-horse outfit was Mark Ellis Ltd, if it couldn't afford a receptionist to answer the phone? I could hear doubt in the silence.

Then, all business but no warmth, she asked for an appointment, preferably tomorrow.

Summoning up an appropriately genuflective tone, along the lines of the-customer-is-always-right, I bade her hold the line while I consulted my day-book.

That was just a feint, suggesting a busy man who cannot be available at one day's notice. Actually, Tuesday was a total blank, and a new customer would be welcome in what looked like a rather lean month.

Coming back on the line, I said, "How would 10.00 am do, Miss...er?"

She hadn't said her name.

"Ms Smith," she said. "Jane Smith. Yes, ten would be fine. Just for a consultation, of course."

"Of course."

That was a good sign. She hadn't mentioned a fee. Either I'd be able to size her up in person, and figure out what the job might be worth. Or else, with luck, she had the kind of bank account where money was no object. The clue lay in the name. If you need an alias, surely you can do better than Jane Smith! But then, even someone self-assured – and she sounded that way – can figure details like that are unimportant. If she wanted to hide her identity, for some reason, so be it. In my business, such as it is, all in the end will he revealed.

"By the way," I added, "may I ask who recommended our firm?"

Our firm was a bit shy of the truth. Mark Ellis Ltd was just me, period. But she didn't have to know that. Yet.

"Let's just say, you came highly recommended," she replied. "By an aunt of mine, as it happens."

On that unforthcoming note, she said goodbye, and hung up.

There was nothing I could read into that. If some unnamed, and perhaps invented, aunt had steered her my way, that could mean any one of three things, because three quite different kinds of clients made use of my business, from time to time. First, there was the Mark Ellis who did the book-keeping for recent widows who were left sadly clueless about money-matters when their husbands died. Second, there was the Mark Ellis who ran what's bluntly called a vanity press, printing limited editions of books by would-be authors who couldn't make the grade with mainstream publishers. And third, there was the Mark Ellis, private detective, who investigated the sleazy and/or criminal side of life.

It may seem like an odd mix of jobs. But it suited me. The book-keeping part came easy. My Dad had his own accounting firm, and I had worked in it part-time to pay my way through university. After graduation I went freelance as a book-keeper, not out of any love for accountancy, but just to earn a basic living while doing other things on the side. The other things were literature and the Law.

An honours degree in English literature is no stepping-stone to employment, unless you have a vocation to teach it. I didn't. But during my third year, I sat in on a summer course in Creative Writing. It was an eye-opener in more ways than one. The instructors were a sorry pair, who came well short of being famous authors, and who needed to supplement their probably thin royalties; they may even have believed that creative writing actually can be taught. The students were a sincere but equally sorry lot: middle-aged, they clearly thought so; but their fictions were a dismal farrago of regurgitated self-reference. Even at twenty-one, enamoured of Jane Austen and Vladimir Nabokov, I knew that gifted writers have always taught themselves. But I also knew that the ungifted, after enough rejections slips, will gladly foot the bill to see themselves in print. It didn't take me long to figure out how to turn that fact into a paying proposition for me. It was quite simple, really. Part-time work for a major publisher, at a very low clerical level, gave me access to the stack of unsolicited manuscripts that arrived there every week. My job was to send them back unread, with a polite covering note, saying that only manuscripts would be considered which were submitted by an established agent. Sifting through them, I could quickly spot which ones, with a little editorial help from me, could make a reasonably presentable book – provided, of course, that the content was not libellous of anyone living. So the New Writers Press came into being. It never made me a fortune nor did it for the authors, but there was a fairly steady supply of disappointed scribes who paid to see their work issued in book form. It helped pay my rent.

Everything to do with that pseudo-publishing business was neatly housed in a single filing-cabinet, next to a matching one that housed all the accounting files. A third one, also identical, housed case-files, past and current, of the work I did as a private investigator.

That work had fallen into my lap almost fortuitously. Or anyway it does bear out the old axiom that good luck depends on who you know.

One of my friends at the university, Al Agostino, was studying Criminology, prior to following in his father's footsteps and becoming a policeman. Meanwhile, his father had retired from the Force and set up a detective agency, along with two fellow-retirees. They did well, and were looking to expand their business by hiring a trainee. Thanks to Al, I got the job.

Really, he talked me into trying out for it. One thing we had in common was an interest in crime. I'd come to it indirectly: there was a section of my own father's firm that specialized in forensic accounting, and I was fascinated by its investigations into pecuniary wrongdoing; and Al pointed out to me that investigations like that were parallel to the kind of literary research I was schooled in, which tracked down tricky clues in pursuit of proof. That seemed to me a bit of a stretch. But I had nothing to lose by taking a crack at it. Apparently my interview went well – this was just after I graduated – and Mr Agostino and his partners took me on.

The pay was meagre. Rightly so, for I was a complete novice, and they could only give me quite simple assignments while I was learning the trade, So I was glad to develop a couple of sidelines, in accounting and publishing, to pad my wage. But gradually I did catch on, and in due course became a fully licensed private investigator, complete with a firearms permit. Not that I've ever used a gun, and I hope I never have to. Mine, a .45 automatic, sits locked in my office safe, unloaded.

Most of the cases were civil rather than criminal. In the past there had been a lot of divorce cases, turning on evidence of adultery. That line of inquiry almost evaporated when the divorce laws were reformed. But there was still detective work to be done in connection with marital breakdown: there were battles over property and over child-custody; and in both areas there was nasty infighting, on both sides. It was sordid stuff, and I only reconciled myself to dealing with it because, sadly often there was one grievously wronged party (usually a woman, but not always), and it was gratifying to set the record straight.

Over time, however, I found a specialty which took me out of that morass of ex-marital spite. Cases started to come my way that addressed miscarriages of justice, where people had been wrongly convicted of serious crimes and were sent to prison, often for long terms. High-minded lawyers tried to have their convictions reversed and their sentences revoked. Either they would argue that the original investigation was irredeemably flawed and that the trial denied the defendant due process. Or else, more hopefully, they would conduct a new investigation, which would prove the defendant's innocence and even, perhaps, point to someone else as the probable perpetrator. For the latter purpose, they would need a skilled detective, necessarily a private one: the police could hardly be counted on to produce evidence that reflected badly on colleagues who had convinced themselves of one person's guilt without looking at other possibilities. To clear the air, only an independent investigation would do. That was where I came in.

My first such case was handed to me by Mr Agostino himself.

The agency had been engaged to work on it. Maybe he thought I was ready for it, and maybe I could easily be spared for the job, while he and his partners got on with other, better projects. My low fee-schedule was something more affordable for the lawyers re-opening the case, who were both working pro bono.

It had a good outcome, and I became the investigator-of-choice for future cases. And I decided to go out on my own, as a specialist in such investigations. I left the agency with some regret, and with real gratitude for the training I'd received. There were no hard feelings. They wished me well. Quite possibly, too, they were glad to see me go: it meant they would not again be approached in a similar way, with the implication that they ought to reduce their fees because it was such a righteous cause.

Whatever the truth of that, we parted ways, and I set up shop in a small office mid-town. The investigations, at that point, paid only modestly. But they had to provide only a third of my income. The rest was made up of the fees paid me as an accountant and as a publisher of amateurish books. It was a somewhat precarious life. You could never be sure what the year would bring in. In a perfect world, there would be no miscarriages of justice to be corrected; every widow would know exactly how to pay her bills and file her income-tax return; and every hopeful author would win a Pulitzer Prize. Meanwhile, we all jog along, as best we can.

But meanwhile, I had an appointment for 10.00 o'clock on Tuesday morning – with a so-called Jane Smith who, for all I knew, might fit into any one of the three categories.

II

I was at my desk, pretending to be busy, when she arrived, promptly, at ten. She was young, in her mid-twenties, I guessed, a decade or so younger than I. She was good-looking, well dressed, poised. And she seemed just as self-possessed in person as she had sounded on the phone.

Cross off the elderly, helpless widow.

Also cross off the aspiring Margaret Atwood: she didn't fit the profile; there was nothing in her demeanour to suggest delusions of literary grandeur. Rather, her manner was completely forthright and straightforward. Unlike any of the neglected geniuses who occasionally sought me out, she hadn't walked in carrying a folder with her latest masterpiece in it – not even a large enough handbag: just a small, discreet purse.

So yes, cross off persona number one or persona number two.

Who, then, was she? And why was she here?

The answers weren't long in coming. I'd stood up when she arrived, and came around the desk. She came across the room, quite briskly, with a "Good morning, Mr Ellis," and shook hands, confidently but formally, as between equals.

"Nice to meet you," I said, pausing briefly, "Ms Smith. Do sit down."

She caught the pause. Smiled.

"Yes, it really is my name. Smith."

My error. Never leap to assumptions.

"I believe you know my aunt," she added. "Virginia Smith."

Indeed I did. A light began to dawn. But a confusing one. I'd known Virginia Smith for some years. She'd been intermediary in engaging me to serve as accountant for her widowed mother, Hortensia, who needed help managing her affairs. Fair enough. But why would her *niece* be needing me?

"Yes, I know Virginia," I said, "and Hortensia. You must be her granddaughter. So is there some way I can be helpful to you? I haven't seen Hortensia for several weeks. Is she alright? Is there anything wrong I need to try and put right?"

"Well, yes and no," she replied. "No, Grandma's fine; and so far as I know, all her affairs are in order – largely thanks to you, I dare say. But yes, there is something wrong that needs to be rectified, and maybe you'll be able to help do that. I hope so. Something seriously wrong. Let me explain."

She took a deep breath, as someone might who has to raise a subject at once difficult, perhaps embarrassing, certainly painful. Then she leaned forward across the desk, where I had resumed my seat.

"Does the name David Smith mean anything to you?" she asked.

That rang a bell, instantly. Until then, I'd made no connection. After all, the world is full of Smiths, most of them quite unremarkable. There'd been no reason to connect any of them with her, with nothing to go on but a surname. But put a first name in front of it, that's another matter. Not that David's an uncommon name. There must be thousands of David Smiths around. But say "David Smith" to someone involved in criminal law, like me, and we're pretty sure to know who we're talking about.

"Yes," I said, "I know of David Smith. Life sentence for murder, years ago. Relative of yours?"

"He's my father. My aunt's only brother. And he's no more guilty of murder than the chair I'm sitting on."

Of course not, I said to myself. Jail's full of cons who swear up and down they're innocent. Not that anyone believes them, except their loved ones – sometimes. Like this one, maybe. The loyal daughter.

But what I said out loud, that was something else.

"If you don't mind my saying so, Ms Smith ..."

"Oh, just call me Jane, why don't you? If we're going to work together we may as well drop the formalities. You're Mark, right?"

"Okay, Mark it is. Now I'm not quite sure what you meant when you mentioned us working together. We can sort that out in a moment. But what I was going to say, about your father, I'm sure it's natural for you – not necessarily accurate, but yes, natural – for you to back up his claims of innocence. Most daughters would, I guess. But I have to tell you, I remember the case quite well. And the evidence against him was pretty convincing. As I recall, it took the jury only a couple of hours to bring in a guilty verdict."

"Don't I know it? But that doesn't make the verdict correct. Mind you, I don't blame the jurors. There wasn't much else they could decide, the way the trial went. But that's not the point. The point is, the trial was all wrong. It was a miscarriage of justice."

"Jane, your feelings do you credit. But maybe you're knocking your head against a brick wall. I mean, facts are facts. The way they were presented in court, the jury was bound to convict. And correct me if I'm wrong, but defence counsel wasn't able to put a dent in them."

She sighed.

"No, he couldn't. And he said, afterward, there were no grounds for appeal. The witnesses had no axe to grind. The judge hadn't misdirected the jury. There were no procedural errors. He said there was nothing for it: I had to put up with it the way it was." Her voice hardened. "Except, I couldn't. The way it was, was wrong. Somebody else must have done it. They just never found the right man." She paused. "That's why I've come to you."

"Now? Ten years later? What are you hoping for?"

She sat back in her chair, and looked me straight in the eye, seriously.

"What I'm looking for, Mark, is the truth. And Justice. Remedial justice."

Obviously, her mind was set. There'd be no way to change how she felt or how her feelings ruled her intentions, even if those feelings were rooted in loyalty rather than logic. But there was something about her air of absolute conviction that made me pause before being immediately dismissive.

"Why me?" I asked. "Why come to me? And by the way, if you're thinking of trying to re-open the case after all these years, is that something you've dreamed up all by yourself? Or is your aunt with you on this? Or, for that matter your grandmother?"

"Oh yes, both of them are. But there's a bit of a difference, which may have to do with the lapse of time. You see, Aunt Virginia and Grandma, both of them, were devastated by what happened to Dad. Almost, for those two, it was worse than if he'd died. It cost Grandma her only son and Aunt Virginia a brother she very much loved. Of course, to begin with, they never thought he was guilty. Deep down, they still don't think so. But in the face of all that evidence, they started to feel qualms of doubt. They never say so right out, to other people. Perhaps not even to each other, for all I know. But there it is. They've had to accept how it is. They both go and visit him, of course – if only so he'll know they still believe him, still love him."

"And what about you, Jane? You too?"

"Of course. He was my Dad. I loved him. Still do. I was only a kid when it happened – a teenager, actually. Aunt V said it was important for me to keep up a relationship with him. So did Grandma. Aunt V used to take me along on visits; and then, when I grew up and had my own car, I started to go by myself. Quite often. And I've never doubted his innocence, whatever other people think."

"And what do those other two think, your aunt and your grandmother, about your attitude? Do they see it as just some sort of stubbornness?"

"Maybe, maybe for a while. But that's shifted a little, lately. For the longest time, they thought it'd be pointless to try and revisit what looked like an open and shut case, especially since Dad's lawyer had told them there wouldn't be a hope in hell of achieving anything."

"So what changed?"

"History changed. Too many cases of wrongful conviction came to light. Shocking ones. They got a lot of coverage in the media, and so did the two lawyers who fought to get things put right."

"Yes, I know about them. In fact, I've worked with them a couple of times."

"I know you have. So do Aunt V and Grandma. You may think Grandma is not too swift when it comes to money matters, but she's sharp as a tack about other things. Same goes for Aunt V. So when it dawned on them that those two lawyers had teamed up, successfully, to get guilty verdicts quashed that shouldn't ever have been returned in the first place, then some small glimmer of hope began to flicker inside them, that maybe Dad's case might he re-opened and his innocence proved. Even after all these years. Really, it wasn't such a preposterous hope. One man, wrongfully convicted, was freed after eighteen years for a murder he didn't commit. Name of John Swain."

She delivered herself of this in a sober tone, in which an habitual and unyielding hope was tempered with an air of learnt caution. I liked what I heard. She was so different from my other occasional visitors, many of them twice her age, who came armed with thick screeds of adolescent reflux. Some people never grow up. This one here, perhaps she'd had to grow up altogether too early, losing her Dad the way she had. Or not losing, him, as the case may be.

"Well," I said, "I can certainly imagine how that must have grabbed your attention, and your grandmother's, when Swain was freed – your Dad's, too, I guess. By the way, what about your mother? Where does she fit in?"

"She doesn't, I'm afraid. She died when I was six. Of Lou Gehrig's."

"Oh, I'm sorry," I said. "That must have been hard."

"Most of all on Dad. Kids get over things. But it was tough for him, missing her, raising me on his own. Mind you, Aunt V helped a lot, so did Grandma. We managed."

We managed; duly noted. Here perhaps was a clue to that youthful maturity, that whiff of engagement, of a readiness to take hold of life. And here, for sure, was the obvious source of a fixed devotion to the man who'd raised her, and of an unshakable belief in his innocence.

"So it must have been awful for you," I said, "when your whole world fell apart, the way it did. Good for you, that you never gave up on him. Now, here we are, ten years later, how did *you* react when Swain was exonerated last month?"

"Well, first of all, I wasn't even here. I was just finishing up a year in England, doing some post-grad, research."

What in? I wanted to ask, but didn't.

"Aunt V phoned me over there and told me about it, so of course I came home almost at once. My reaction? Mixed. Sure, you can't cling to hope for ten years, without something like that making you think maybe, after all, miracles could happen. But still, miracles aren't something you can count on. You learn that, over time. Either way, though, you don't just sit back and wait for life to happen. You grab onto it. Not just me, either. By the time I got back, Aunt V had already gone into action."

It was obvious I was all attention. She went right on.

"She made an appointment with one of those two lawyers in the Swain case, Irving Wolff. Hoping, I suppose, that he'd go to bat for Dad, the way he had for John Swain. No such luck. He happened to know Dad's case really well. He had studied the trial transcript right through from the start to finish – this was for technical reasons, nothing to do with guilt or innocence: he was doing a profile of the judge for a law magazine. Anyway, to our disappointment, he just reiterated what Dad's defence counsel had said afterwards: there seemed to be nothing wrong with the police testimony and there were no grounds for appeal in the conduct of the trial. In short, forget it."

"That must have been a blow to you all."

"It was. But he softened it. He went on to say, Mr Wolff, there was one other way to establish Dad's innocence. It was a long shot. But if we could prove that somebody else had committed the crime, then automatically Dad would be off the hook. 'Nice idea,' Aunt V said. 'But how on earth could we set about doing that? Surely the police wouldn't help, They'd got their conviction. Case closed.'

"I can imagine how my aunt must have felt. It was like being tossed a lifebelt, when you're drowning, only to be told it wasn't in working order. The police, clearly, couldn't be expected to come on side. Nor could he and his partner, Ross Burton: they were lawyers, not detectives. But, he added, there *was* someone he could recommend, who might be able to help: a private detective who'd done investigations for them in the past, name of Mark Ellis."

Putting it like that, she smiled across the desk. I nodded.

"So when Aunt V heard that, she said, 'Isn't that funny? Same name as my mother's accountant.' And Mr Wolff said, 'Same name, same guy. He does accounting work on the side.' Well, you can imagine I'm not superstitious. But I thought, if this chain of circumstances brings our family and Mark Ellis together from two entirely different directions, then maybe, just maybe, this is something that's meant to happen – for a reason. Which was exactly what Grandma felt, too. She speaks very highly of you. Says you're as shrewd as a shipload of Yankees – whatever that means: it's the kind of thing she comes up with from her days as a Wren in the war."

"Well," I said, "I've never heard that one. But she does have quite a way of putting things, I must say. She's a grand old lady, isn't she?"

"*That is for sure.*" Four emphatic monosyllables. "And Aunt V takes after her. A nice, clever, middle-aged woman with a good heart. But prudent, too. When I told her I was going to make an appointment with you, she said, 'Now, Jane, don't get your hopes up too high. He may not be interested; and even if he is, there may be nothing much he can do.'

"So of course I reassured her. 'Expectations,' I said, 'were far too often a pathway to disappointment. But we do have to try,' I said. 'At least try.' 'Absolutely,' she said, 'we have to.' 'But remember' she went on 'everything comes at a price. Mr Ellis is, after all, a professional; and if he does conduct an investigation, it could be quite costly. Grandma and I would pitch in; you know that. But before you jump in the deep end, it'd probably be a good idea to get an estimate. No different, really, from asking what it would cost to put new eavestroughs on the house'."

Good for Aunt V, my instincts said. She must be one of those people who know there's no such thing as a free lunch. Unlike others, who feel entitled to corner a doctor or a lawyer at a cocktail party and get a free consultation over a vodka and tonic. Me, I consider myself just as professional as any doctor or lawyer. Not that I charge fees quite that high.

But then, suddenly, I did something I'd never done before in my whole career, and quite possibly never will again. I was touched by her predicament, and there was something about the faith she had in her Dad that had an unassailable ring of truth to it. So I decided, right then and there on the spur of the moment, to take her on without a retainer and just see how an investigation might pan out.

"Oh really, Mark, you shouldn't do that. Really. I can't expect you to do this for free, just because it's a good cause. That'd be no different from expecting Aunt V to give an unpaid course in her specialty – which, incidentally, happens to be particle physics. Fair's fair. What goes for particle physics should go for any other professional work, like yours."

"Okay, let's not get into a hassle about this. Let me put it this way. If your Dad gets exonerated, the Feds will have to come up with a hefty compensation, and I'll submit an invoice for services rendered – at quite reasonable rates, I assure you: I can let you have a look at them any time."

Part of me hated saying that. I hate ambulance-chasing lawyers who suck people into suing for damages on condition they split the take fifty-fifty if successful. This was different. If David Smith really was innocent, he deserved his freedom and any millions that night come with it. I wasn't about to soak him for a cent more than I usually charged.

She had looked down, embarrassed, into her lap. When she looked up, I could see a tear had trickled down one cheek.

"Mark," she said, "you can't possibly know what this means to me."

"As a matter of fact, I can," I replied, pushing a kleenex box across the desk. "We've all had our losses, one way or another. Maybe, one day, I'll tell you about mine. All in good time. Meanwhile, we should lay some plans about how to go about this. First off, I'll need a week to get hold of the trial transcript and study it, and to put out a feeler or two about the original police investigation. So how about we meet next Tuesday, same time? Deal?"

She stood up. So did I, and came around the desk.

"Deal," she said, and once again, quite formally, shook my hand, as between colleagues. "Someday, I'll find a way to say a proper thank you."

"Well now, Jane," I said, "don't take this just as a favour to you personally. I'd like to do it for your Grandma, too: I really like her, and respect her. And from what I've seen of your Aunt V, I reckon I'll like her just as much. Most of all, though, look at it as something done not for you or your aunt or your grandmother, but for your Dad: if there's been a wrongful conviction, then, it's something needs correcting."

We were walking towards the door, which I now opened.

"By the way," I said, "you mentioned doing postgrad research. What's your field?"

"English Literature. I want to write a comparative study of John Donne and Robert Southwell."

"No kidding? That's amazing. I never did go on to do a Masters. But back then, if I'd opted for postgrad, I'd probably have tried to do something about Henry Vaughan. Kindred spirits, eh?"

And I wasn't sure, when I said that, whether I was referring to those three poets, or to her and me.

"See you next Tuesday," she said with a smile, put a friendly hand on my arm, and left.

III

You might think, if you met me, well, here's a fellow who pretty much lives for his work and not much else. In a way you'd be right. But it hadn't always been that way. Time was, I led a fairly balanced life, with three balls in the air, work and family and recreation.

Work came smoothly, as I've mentioned, starting out in my father's accounting firm, and then setting up on my own, with a bit extra on the side as a vanity publisher and private eye.

Family, too, was part of the picture early on. Married at twenty-four, happily, to a fellow-lover of good books and good music, and a fellow-hater of trash on commercial television. Anne was a program assistant for CBC Radio, in the classical music department; and between her salary and my freelance earnings we made enough to lease a downtown apartment, and to start saving for a house.

The house and our first baby, born when we were twenty-six, were central to our family plan. But we didn't just rush into real-estate: a two-bedroom apartment would be fine for a while. As it turned out, there were other things on our minds than house-hunting or mortgages. Our daughter, Louise, was diagnosed with infantile cancer when Anne was only halfway through her maternity leave. The next twelve months were agony for Louise and for each of us. She was an adorable baby, and we did everything we could for her, with wonderful doctors trying everything they knew. To no avail. Louise died a week before her second birthday.

I've known parents who pull together in grief after a loss like that. But then, sadly, there are also marriages that fall apart: losing a child can drive a couple apart, into realms of voiceless sorrow. I know, I know: we ought to have found a way to bridge that gap, but somehow we just couldn't. Anne went back to her job, and went to live with her parents for a while, before moving on elsewhere. I sublet the apartment – too many memories – and rented a smaller one in another part of town. The only way I could keep going was to immerse myself in work.

So yes, I was a workaholic if you want to put it that way. Still was, ten years later, when Jane Smith walked into my life.

***

The first thing to do was get hold of the trial transcript – quite easily done, for a fee – and study it. Wolff had said there was nothing in it that sounded fishy, and he was probably right. Certainly I didn't expect to find any trace of misconduct on the part of the judge or the prosecutor, or any jury shenanigans. And the police testimony about their investigation seemed straightforward enough – though print never conveys tone of voice or body language; so reading the transcript, I couldn't tell whether the police, at any point, were entirely comfortable with what they said. That was something worth looking into.

On the face of it, the trial-process was quite cut-and-dried. One or two of the witnesses were challenged, not at all effectively, by defence counsel. But the guilty verdict looked like a foregone conclusion, and it came promptly, as expected: guilty of murder; a life sentence followed.

So, nothing wrong with Irving Wolff 's opinion. The only realistic hope of freeing David Smith, if he *was* innocent, was not to contest the trial itself, but to prove someone else was the killer. That would mean I'd have to conduct a brand-new investigation on my own. Not easy to do, starting from scratch with nothing much to go on.

But I never assume that things are exactly the same as they seem to be. I'd read the transcript carefully and couldn't find fault with anything in it. Everything said at the trial, by the police, was credible and convincing. But I have a suspicious nature. It was all very well to accept what they said, at face value. But were there things that were *not* said?

In other words, were the police so taken with things they found out that pointed to David as the perpetrator, that they felt no need to pursue other leads? It's an easy trap for a policeman to fall into. Suspect Number One looks like a good bet for conviction. Why waste time on anyone else?

I'm not one to suggest that police always take the easy way out. But let's face it, they do suffer pressure from above, to get quick results. Nobody's really to blame, the budget's inadequate. It was something worth looking into, before I launched any more wide-ranging inquiry.

That's where my old pal, Al Agostino, came into the picture. We'd stayed friends ever since university, even though our paths had significantly diverged. We'd get together for a beer now and then, or throw a few hoops at the Y. There was a bit less of that, naturally, after I married – Al stayed single to begin with. But Anne got on with him very well, and never resented our having the odd boys' night out.

Anything like that came to an abrupt end, though, when Louise was born and was diagnosed, almost at once, with the cancer that killed her. We, Anne and I, had no time for anything other than fighting to save our baby. It consumed us, entirely. Anne was still at home, for the first while, on maternity leave, which she was then able to extend on compassionate grounds. As a freelance, I could set my own hours, at a minimum level; and I spent most of my time at home, either helping tend Louise or doing the shopping, much of the cooking, and a few household chores – not that our place met any high standards of elegance: we were totally preoccupied with illness and the fear of death. The only people we saw during those harrowing months were emergency doctors, pediatricians, oncologists, and nurses.

Then it was all over. We buried her, and sat stunned, no more able to reach each other than to rewrite the script. Time passed, without mercy. Anne left, taking her own stuff with her. I moved, and focused on my work. What else was there?

One day, a while later, there came a knock at my door. There was Al. He came right in, grabbed me in a big hug, and said, "Mark, I didn't know. Why didn't you tell me? What do you think friends are for?"

Good cop that he was, he'd tracked me down to where I was now living. And it was in that moment of kindness, his kindness, that I started to find my way back to human life.

Good cop that he was, Al had done well in the Force. They took him off the beat, and put him in Homicide as a Detective Constable. That made us colleagues, of a sort; so we had careers to talk about, as well as everything else.

Mind you, police detectives tend, sometimes, to be at loggerheads with private investigators. Often with good reason. For some of my confreres put their oar in and do more harm than good. And even if we don't, we operate with a freedom of method the cops lack: they're subject to a lot of restrictions we aren't hampered by; and that makes them a bit envious or even resentful. But nothing like that got in the way of the open friendship that Al and I enjoyed.

In fact, from time to time, strictly on the quiet, we used to give each other a helping hand, in a small way. Al would tip me off about a line of inquiry I could pursue, which he couldn't pursue himself, for various official reasons. Or, at other times, I'd happen on something in my own investigation which would help him, and would tip him off. More often it was that way round, me helping him. So I built up a line of credit with him, so to speak. Not that either of us looked at it that way.

However, when Jane Smith recruited me I needed to tap in on Al's savvy as an insider. Al had worked his way up to Detective Sergeant, always in Homicide; and I needed him to chat up a couple of old-timers and see if they remembered anything about that closed case which smelt a bit fishy.

"Of course," I said, "there's probably nothing. And even if there is, we can't expect your lot to act on it. Anyone sitting on a can of worms isn't likely to take the lid off it. But if there is anything, it would at least give us something to go on."

"*Us*, Mark? You in on this with Wolff and Burton?"

"Actually no. They looked at it, but said there was nothing in the trial they could act on. They recommended me for a kind of last-ditch crack at it – not at the trial itself, but at the original investigation. Maybe, and it's a pretty big maybe, maybe the actual perp had been someone else, someone who got overlooked."

"Sounds like a bit of a stretch to me. "

"Of course it is. But you never know."

"And this you're doing out of the goodness of your heart? Enter the knight in shining armour. Who's the damsel in distress?"

I shifted a little in my seat. You can't fool Al.

"His daughter," I said. "Jane Smith."

Al knew me well enough not to make anything of it. He'd seen me through the bad times after Louise had died and Anne had departed. He'd seen me start coming hack to my old self. But he wasn't about to touch on remaining raw spots by joshing me further about some presumptive romance.

"Alright," he said, "I'll see what I can do. Get back to you."

***

After he left, I did stop and think for a moment. Trouble is, I have a sharp visual memory. And there she was, in my mind's eye, well, let's face it, she was, well, beautiful. Come on, Mark, I said to myself: that's got nothing to do with the case at hand. But I did wonder. I hadn't seen a beautiful woman in ages. Not so I'd notice.

IV

Professionally, a good accountant double-checks everything. Especially a forensic accountant. I learnt this early on, from the forensic accountants in my Dad's firm. They would pore over a suspect's accounts, searching for the minute give-away details that unlocked the nasty little secrets.

Now, years later, that kind of scrutiny had become habitual in my work as a private eye. I had read the David Smith trial transcript twice, carefully, looking for any kind of error. No dice. But a third reading isn't likely to yield anything new. You've read all the sentences twice, and you get to know them so well that you know what's in them, and nothing leaps out at you.

It's rather like proofreading. That's one of the things I do in my role as a publisher of vanity hooks. As a publisher, I'm almost wholly a one-man operation. I do farm out the actual production of a physical book, putting the text between covers. But everything else I do myself: I choose the authors, edit their work, and run the business. So the proofreading falls to me, too.

It's a humdrum task, demanding a kind of exact but wearisome attention. Going through texts a third time for errata, is a skill that has nothing to do with the value of the text as literature – which may be fairly low, anyway, in the kind of stuff I edit. You have to hold boredom at bay and stay alert non-stop, like a grade-school teacher marking a spelling test for beginners.

The analogy, to my mind, is right on the mark. Two readings of the trial transcript were no guarantee that I'd spot anything now. Rather the contrary; the content was now so familiar that it was easy to skim over it in an almost taken-for-granted way, So I said, what the hell, try a different approach. Rewrite it, in digest form, by hand. The analytic act of reducing it to a précis requires actual thought, and the sheer physical act of putting the words down on paper, with a ballpoint, not a keyboard, is so much slower than reading that I then might, for the first time, notice a significance or two that had previously eluded me. So I set to and buckled down to it for a couple of days.

First, before reducing the transcript to a précis, I looked up the principal people involved. The judge was Willard T. Brodie, now retired: he was well-known as a stickler for due process, and had a reputation for fairness. The Crown was Alexandra Ziegler: mid-thirties, not at the time well-known, more so later. For the Defence, Dennis Baxter, Q. C.: long courtroom experience, but no firebrand. The Defendant, David Smith: resident of Toronto, aged forty-five, owner of a custom-furniture business, in partnership with the murder victim, Sven Bergman. Chief witness for the Crown, Inspector Leslie Levesque: veteran police detective, also now retired.

Then, here is what I came up with.

Last week of May 2005, Supreme Court of Ontario, Judge Brodie presiding. Prisoner David Smith brought in and charged with murder in first degree. Ziegler outlines case for Crown: discovery of victim's body; arrival of police and medical examiner; diagnosis of death by blow to head, obviously not accidental or self-inflicted; investigation leads to Smith as suspect with means, opportunity, and motive; sufficient evidence to prove guilt beyond, reasonable doubt. Baxter reserves Defence.

First witness, Ellen Bergman, widow of victim. Testifies that she had been away for the weekend in Montréal on the night of her husband's death. Knows of no reason why Smith would have killed Sven: there had been no personal quarrel she knew of, nor any business conflict. Asked if it was puzzling that her husband was at work in the small hours of the morning, answers it was not unusual for Smith to call him in for a late-night conference: if he had done so that night, she wouldn't have known, since she was out of town. Ziegler asks no further questions, but commiserates with her on her loss.

Baxter elects not to cross-examine.

Second witness, Lois Grinstead, identified as once-a-week book-keeper for Smith-Bergman company. Testifies she arrived at office 8.30 Monday morning March 20th 2004. Entered Bergman's office, found him dead on floor, bloody head-wound, phoned 911; was told to touch nothing and wait for police. Under questioning from Ziegler, describes firm's organization: Smith the furniture designer and maker, Bergman dealt with the customers; three sets of books, one for the whole firm and one each for the two partners. Was she aware of the firm's insurance policies? Yes, there was overall business insurance, but in addition a million-dollar life-insurance policy on each partner, to protect the firm from result of sudden death or incapacitation of either man: premiums on Smith's life paid up to date, beneficiary Bergman; ditto on Bergman's, beneficiary Smith.

Cross by Baxter. Where was Grinstead in hours preceding her arrival on scene? Answers, spent night in Ajax, with friends; grabbed a ride into city with husband of couple, who dropped her off at Smith-Bergman premises at 8.30. No further questions.

Two constables, P.C. Sanjay Gupta and P.C. Mary McDougall, describe responding to 911 call: arrived at 8.37; McDougall took Grinstead, very shaken, to police-cruiser, taking her statement; Gupta inspected scene, found bloodied hammer beside body; left everything undisturbed, pending arrival of medical examiner and superior officers. Inspected premises' workshop where hand-made furniture created, found a whole array of tools for carpentry and joinery, all of design similar to hammer, hanging on wall-hooks ; one hook empty where hammer might have been.

No cross from Baxter.

9.18 arrival of medical examiner, Dr Muriel Conacher, with Inspector Levesque and his partner. Conacher testifies death due to severe blow to head, probably by hammer; period of death estimated, and later confirmed, as between 2.00 and 4.00 a.m.

No cross from Baxter.

Levesque testifies he left murder-scene intact, pending arrival, of photographer; bags hammer for fingerprint analysis, goes to police-cruiser to have Grinstead repeat her story. Re-enters premises at 10, as Smith arrives for day's work. Testifies to Smith's reaction on confronting corpse: apparently horrified, but maybe a good actor.

Objection by Baxter; inspector no drama critic; suggesting Smith's horror was spurious, pure speculation. Objection sustained.

Levesque continues: Smith admits to owning carpentry tools and, on being shown hammer, admits it resembles one of his; asked for his whereabouts hours earlier, claims to have spent night at home, alone, no corroboration; also admits, when pressed, to being the listed beneficiary of life-insurance policy on Bergman. Smith arrested on suspicion of murder, taken into custody for further interrogation.

Ziegler now takes Levesque through police-station interview with Smith. Suspect goes over history of partnership, of twelve years' standing: pairing of talents, his being the woodwork and the creative design, Bergman's a gift for merchandising; harmonious working relationship, mutual respect, personal friendship. Insists on his innocence, but admits, wryly, that things look bad for him: demands lawyer; under advice says no more.

Levesque testifies further that Grinstead's alibi holds water. Only fingerprints on hammer are Smith's. No other suspects. Submitted case to Ziegler for prosecutions she agreed to prosecute.

Cross by Baxter. He challenges Levesque on two counts. Why assert no other suspects? Answer: Smith's guilt obvious; no need to look elsewhere; anyway, no one else had motive. Second question: if Levesque saw insurance policy as motive for premeditated murder, why would Smith not have provided himself with an alibi? Levesque, Baxter said, could not fall back on thinking Smith killed Bergman in a, sudden, unexplained quarrel – he couldn't have it both ways. Levesque answers: No, sir, just because he had a financial motive doesn't mean there couldn't have been a violent quarrel; the one doesn't exclude the other; so far as I'm concerned, the insurance is a clincher – like they say, "Who stood to gain?"

No further questions.

Ziegler sums up for the Crown. Runs over salient points of evidence. Reiterates that Smith had means (access to his own workplace), a weapon (his own hammer), opportunity (freedom to demand a late-night meeting with his partner, presumably for plausible business reasons), and motive (the insurance payoff). She urges Jurors to decide this all adds up to conclusive proof; and asks them to return a verdict of Guilty as Charged.

There is not much Baxter can do, speaking for the Defence. He questions Ziegler's assertion that guilt has been proved beyond reasonable doubt. He chides the police for not having pursued other lines of inquiry. And he focusses, briefly, on the issue of opportunity: there was, he says, no evidence, in writing or on the telephone or in a text message, that Smith had asked Bergman to meet him at the office late at night on the date of the killing. It was a small point, but it carried little weight in the face of all the evidence. He sat down, manifestly losing the case.

Judge Brodie's directions to the jury were a model of judicial propriety. He reminded the seven men and the five women empanelled, that they must consider only what had been presented in court. It was their duty to weigh the evidence and reach a dispassionate, objective verdict, nothing in what he said could be interpreted as urging either conviction or acquittal. They were to reflect soberly and carefully; and if they had any worries about matters of law or of fact, they should come back to him for guidance. Failing that, he hoped they would find a way to arrive at a unanimous verdict.

Court adjourns while the jurors file out to begin their deliberations. The wait is not a long one. After two hours, a Guilty verdict is returned, and. the judge sets a date for sentencing in the following month. Smith is hustled away in police custody.

***

On June 15th, David Smith is sentenced to life in prison, with no possibility of a parole hearing for twenty-five years; this is duly reported, in the next morning's *Globe and Mail* by their regular court reporter, Jonas Varga. He had covered the trial in May, and I looked up his report on it. There was nothing much there to add to the impressions I had of the trial, from reading the transcript – with one small exception. Varga found little drama in the proceedings. His portrayal of everyone there was restrained, almost flat. In only one exchange was there a touch of confrontational energy: that was when Baxter cross-examined Levesque and virtually scolded him for not pursuing other lines of inquiry. Levesque, according to Varga, reacted with a kind of pompous indignation, as though resenting the imputation that he, an Inspector with many years of experience, did not know how to conduct a proper investigation. The moment passed, and it had no discernible impact on the outcome. But I thought it at least worth a follow-up.

So I phoned. Varga and arranged to meet him for a coffee downtown.

"Well, I don't know if you'll get very far with this," he said when I explained what my interest was in the case.

"Maybe not," I said. "But I was struck by that one little moment in your report. What had been a quite sober-sided account of a rather pedestrian proceeding suddenly came to life with a touch of human friction. What kind of guy was Levesque anyway? Had you seen him in action in other cases?"

"Several times. He was an arrogant son of a bitch, was my impression. Especially where journalists were concerned. Dr Johnson called writers 'ink-stained wretches'. Levesque, I'm sure, had much more colourful language for us. Anyone who questioned the unassailable rightness of his views, or his methods, was an enemy. I was glad to see the end of him when he retired."

I thanked Varga for his time. Struck me as someone perceptive and honest – and maybe a useful contact, sometime in the future. He wished me luck on my quest, and I told him I'd stay in touch.

Next thing, obviously, was to contact Al, and ask him about Levesque.

V

Meanwhile, a week had gone by. Jane phoned me on the Monday, to check if tomorrow at 10 was still okay.

"Sure," I said. "But let's skip the office. There's a really neat little espresso bar two doors away called Mario's. Let's have a coffee there."

Al had put me onto Mario's years ago. It's a double-duty place: on one side, a coffee bar, with a counter and a few small tables, open early and closing in late afternoon; on the other side, a small trattoria, open for lunch and specializing in variations on home-made pasta – the quality was gourmet, the prices reasonable.

Jane and. I arrived, simultaneously, at exactly 10. I liked that. Maybe we had the same respect for punctuality. We ordered, she a latte and me an espresso, and grabbed a table.

"So where are we at?" she asked.

I liked that, too. Straight to the point: no need for empty small talk.

"'Well," I said, "I've gone over the trial three times, trying to find something to go on. And I have to say there's nothing much there that's encouraging. Wolff was right. As such things go, the trial was kosher – as a process, I mean. No possible grounds for appeal. But you've heard that already."

She nodded gravely. And stirred her latte.

"So not much hope there," I went on. "As Wolff said – and I believe him – there's no way to get the trial thrown out as legally flawed. Only remedy is to prove someone else was the killer, not your Dad. Starting from scratch, that won't be easy. However, there was one little moment in the trial that did snag my attention as being maybe significant. Only in a small way, when I was studying the transcript. But I read a bit more into it when I read the newspaper account of the proceedings in court."

I told her about how Baxter had implicitly rebuked Levesque for not pursuing other lines of inquiry, and how Levesque had reacted badly according to Varga.

"Yes, I remember that exchange well," Jane said.

"You do? You were actually there in the courtroom?"

"Oh yes. Nothing was going to stop me being there. He's my Dad."

23

That said simply, as though in this moment she was once again that forlorn, anxious teenager. It was very touching.

"But you were so young! How old? Fifteen?"

"That's right, fifteen. But I insisted on going. The school counsellor said I shouldn't. But Aunt V and Grandma both backed me up. Said I had the right to be there, even if it was painful. That's what I like about those two. They aren't bound by shibboleths. They recognize what's right. So yes, I was there. And I saw what kind of animal Levesque was. I hated him. Still do. But what's really stuck with me, over the years, is the big 'What if?' 'What if there were other possibilities that Levesque just couldn't be bothered with?'"

"Well, that's what I'm going to have to look into. Other possibilities. And for starters, I'll be talking to an old friend of mine, Al Agostino. He's a policeman, and he may once have known Levesque."

So I told her about my friendship with Al, ever since school. Told her he'd saved my life once, and I owed him. Not literally, in fact. Saving my life was a bit of an exaggeration. But he'd put me back or my feet when I'd been going through a really bad time – not that I went into that. Anyway, I said, we have the kind of friendship, Al and I, where you do things for each other. I've been able to help Al out a couple of times on his cases, where I have a greater freedom of movement, as an investigator, than a cop does. So he won't take it amiss if I press him for a bit of inside info, on the quiet, about Inspector Levesque. I'm going to have a beer with him tomorrow evening."

She smiled, obviously pleased.

Good, I thought: we're on the same track, together.

"By the way," I said, "there's something I need to ask you. When I was reading the trial-transcript, I noticed your Dad had said, when he was interrogated, that he was home alone, on the night Bergman was killed, but there was no one to corroborate that. How come? Where were you?"

"Me? I was in boarding-school. Just at home weekends. Used to go home Friday night, but back to school Sunday evening. Mind you, it hadn't always been quite that way. Mum died, as I said, when I was six, just starting primary school. We went to live with Aunt V to begin with, Dad and I both. Dad sold our house – too many sad memories, I guess. He went off to work every day, and I went off to school; and Aunt V had a housekeeper, so there was someone I would come home to after school, if Aunt V wasn't home yet."

(Oh, Louise!)

"So that's how it was, back then. Eventually Dad bought a new place, near his work, a two-bedroom condo, big enough for the two of us without our getting in each other's way – not that I ever found *him* in *my* way: we were very close. Anyway, I stayed with Aunt V for the time being, except for weekends. Then, when I was a bit older, Aunt V enrolled me in Holloway College, as a boarder, with her paying the fees. She insisted. 'It's the least I can do, 'she said. 'I'm a single woman with a good salary. May as well do something useful with the money'. So there I stayed, right through to university, and then through there, too. Aunt V's been my fairy godmother all my life. I owe her big. But the one thing I'll never get over is not being home with Dad that one crucial night. If only I'd been there, I'd have stood up for him and got him off."

"Jane," I said, in as soothing a tone as I could manage, "they'd have found a way around that. Who's to say your Dad couldn't have sneaked out quietly for a couple of hours while you slept?"

She stiffened, visibly; and I regretted having said *sneaked*.

"Don't get me wrong," I corrected myself. "I'm with you on this, all the way. But the rotten truth is, they'd have been all over you, if you'd testified he was home all night: 'What?' they'd say. 'You want us to believe that just this one night, this one night of all nights, you just happened to stay up all night, doing what with your Dad, playing Monopoly?' They'd have massacred you."

"I guess you're right," she said ruefully.

All this had taken time; and we now moved out of the coffee bar into the trattoria, in a kind of unspoken unison of intention, to have lunch together. After we'd ordered, Mario recommended a carafe of Frascati to go with our order: he's from the Frascati region, and it's a wine he never tires of proposing: I don't quarrel with his expertise.

"Now, Mark," Jane said, after taking a sip, "there's something I'd like to ask you. Last week, when I mentioned Southwell and Donne, you came back at me with Henry Vaughan. If I may say so, that's a fairly recondite thing to come out of a private eye. Or am I just thinking in stereotypes? Like not expecting Sam Spade to know the difference between a caesar salad and a caesura? I mean, anyone who's read a few books has heard of John Donne. But Robert Southwell? Or Henry Vaughan?"

"Touché. I guess most guys in my trade probably do stop short of reading *Paradise Lost* from cover to cover. But the fact is, back then in student days, I was less interested in playing cops and robbers than I was in coming to grips with the difference between real religious poetry and the kind of pious doggerel you find in hymn-books."

"Like hooray for Gerard Manley Hopkins but thumbs down on, say, Edgar Guest? I don't know, I've never read Guest, he's just an emblem of schmaltz. Did he ever write about God?"

"I don't know, either. But if he did, it must have been awfully mawkish."

"You're probably right. But tell me something. If you felt like that about some writers who aren't exactly best-sellers, how come you didn't at least go on to your Masters?"

"The usual reason: money. I paid my way through school, working in my father's business. Then, when I graduated, I had to get involved in something a bit more profitable than seventeenth-century metaphysics. No offence meant!" I added hastily. "If I'd had the guts, I'd maybe have stayed with English Literature rather than accounting or sleuthing, and never mind living on short rations. But I'd married young; we had a child, and needs must when the dollar drives."

Did I detect a flicker of disappointment in her? She looked down at my left hand, with its bare right-finger. Had been bare for years now.

I looked down at my plate, feeling awkward.

"Don't want to tell a sob-story," I said. "But that ended rather sadly. Our daughter died, just shy of two years old. Cancer. Metastasized. The marriage couldn't survive the loss. It ended. Long ago."

I looked up at her. If there's something hard to hear, when you're hurting, it's somebody else's pain on your behalf. She was looking at me with such sorrow in her eyes, it near unmanned me.

She reached across the table, put her hand on mine, and gave it a squeeze.

"Oh Mark," she said, "I'm so sorry."

Then she withdrew her hand, as though slightly embarrassed by the intimacy of it.

"Thanks, Jane," I said. "We can maybe talk about this another time. I don't mean to be a wet blanket." I dug into my fettuccine al pesto. "Let's go back to where we were. How are you coming along with Southwell and Donne? Is this towards a doctorate?"

"Yes: next year, I hope. But none of that's of any account compared with what's on our agenda over my Dad. I do hope your friend Al can help."

"Let's put it this way," I said. "If there's any way Al can help, he will. Count on it. Meanwhile, to use a phrase you laid on me last week, does the name R.S. Thomas mean anything to you?"

She lit up like a Christmas tree.

"You mean that marvellous poet and priest in Wales? I love him. So much better than the ever-celebrated Dylan. Wow! Good on you, Mark, as the Aussies say. You know something, half my professors haven't even heard of him. That's another thing we're going to have to put to rights."

On that note, we went on with our lunch, chatting amiably about books and people, exploring each other without, perhaps, noticing we were doing so. When the check came, I grabbed it.

"Let's split it," she said.

"No," I said, "this one's on me. It was my idea."

"Alright," she conceded. "But my turn next time. How about next Tuesday, here again?"

"Great," I said.

I paid the bill, and we left. She went to the nearest subway. I went back to the office.

And I must say, I hadn't felt so cheerful in ages.

VI

Al came to my place by subway. The last thing he needed, as a cop, was to be caught driving home with beer on his breath. I cracked open a couple of beers and asked him, "So, any luck digging up any dirt on Levesque?"

"Maybe, maybe not. Thing is, I have a colleague called Novak. Stan Novak. Detective Sergeant, like me. You won't have heard of him; he's never made much of a name for himself. But he's a good cop. Likes to do things right. Been at it a long time. Used to be junior partner with Levesque."

"So, were you able to get him talking about David Smith's case without making it obvious you were fishing for something?"

"As it turned out, that wasn't hard. We nattered away about this and that, cases that hadn't worked out, cases I thought might have worked out better if I'd followed a lead or two that I hadn't seen the point of. We just went back and forth along those lines. And then Stan came up with exactly what you were hoping for, like a memory that left a bad taste in his mouth.

"'I'll tell you, Al,' he said, 'there was one case left me kinda pissed off. Back in the days when I worked with Les Levesque. You know, that bastard had fixed ideas like nobody's business. He'd get it into his head that one particular suspect was the perp, for absolute sure. And nothing would budge him. He was going to get that guy, come hell or high water. Now, I'm not saying he planted evidence, or anything like that, he knew if he broke the rules there went his pension. But if he had a chance of getting a conviction with that one guy, he closed his mind to other possible perps. One case I remember, before your time, of course. Fellow called Smith. David Smith, Les had him lined up for murdering his business partner. Can't blame him: lots of stuff pointed that way; and he did get the conviction he was after. But early on, it could have been anyone, and I said so. Said maybe there were other guys we should be looking at, other ways it could have happened. I mean, what stuck in my craw was, it seemed to me there was a hole in Les's theory. Smith was a smart guy, but he had no alibi. Now, you know as well as I do, a smart killer always has an alibi. You may be able to poke holes in it, but at least he does have some sort of an alibi ready. But this Smith, who was protesting his innocence loud and clear, didn't have any kind of alibi at all. It didn't add up. Not to my mind. I suggested at least we should take a second look. But that Les, he just slapped me down. Said he could prove opportunity, means, and motive, so let's just fix it up and move on. I didn't feel good. about it. But what can you do? It was his call, I just had to let it go. But I was glad when he retired and I got to work with someone a bit less pig-headed.

"There you are, Mark. I don't know if that'll help. But at least it does give you a picture of what went on behind the scenes – for what it's worth."

"Thanks, Al," I said, and opened the next two bottles.

"How's the young lady in the case?" he asked.

"You know, Al, since you ask, I think this one might be someone quite special."

"I'll drink to that," he said.

VII

How to start out? From basics always. One basic question: "Who stood to gain?" It's a question which, if properly answered, then indicates, often enough, who the killer was, and which of the three commonest motives prompted the killing.

After all, in nearly all murders, what's involved is either sex or money or power.

There are endless variations, of course, on the sexual theme. Jealous husbands sometimes murder unfaithful wives or their wives' lovers. Unfaithful wives sometimes murder their husbands or have them murdered, in order to carry on with their lovers unimpeded. Or the whole thing vice versa. Then again, apart from such trite triangles, there are cases that plumb much murkier depths of erotic violence, more often in men than in women.

28

Money, or rather love of money, is so frequently a factor as to be almost a cliché. At the street level, things can go fatally wrong in a bank holdup, or when a store is held up for what's in the till. At a more sophisticated level, there are cases where people are killed for the payout of a life insurance policy.

Power's a more complicated motive. People kill, commercially or politically, to rise to the top of the ladder. But there are more subtle versions of power-lust than that; it's power not sex, for instance, that drives the killer-rapist. And religious fanatics, equally, can be driven to kill by a hatred of others unwilling to genuflect. These are sordid blood-baths.

What does make a really tangled web, for the investigator, is when a case is a mix of more than one such scenario. You have to keep an open mind, and just assume that everything will fit exactly into place in one familiar, but not necessarily conclusive, pattern.

In the David Smith case, for example, I had to start looking into it by paying attention *only* to the eight baldest facts, ignoring any interpretation of them that anyone else had dreamed up. Here is the list.

#1: Sven Bergman had been done to death with a hammer

#2: the hammer was beside the corpse

#3: the only fingerprints on the hammer were David Smith's

#4: there were no signs of break-in

#5: there were no eye-witnesses to the killing

#6: time of death was estimated at between 2.00 and 4.00 a.m.

#7: Smith's claim to be home at the time of the killing was uncorroborated

#8: listed beneficiary of million-dollar life-insurance policy on Bergman was Smith

Preliminary comments: –

a/ Cause and manner of death are beyond dispute

b/ Smith's fingerprints do not necessarily prove his guilt: theoretically someone else could be guilty who wore gloves, who wanted to frame Smith

c/ Whoever killed Bergman had a key to the premises

d/ Murders within a building are frequently not witnessed

e/ Time of death may be without significance

f/ Absence of corroboration for Smith's alibi is not in itself proof of guilt

g/ That Smith would benefit from Bergman's death is suspicious but not probative

Weighing all these considerations, I pondered how to move ahead. One obvious step was to find out what had happened to the Smith-Bergman business. Insurance on the business itself simply protected the building from fire etc, and protected the firm from fraud by rivals or customers. Ownership of the premises and its contents was vested jointly in Smith and Bergman or their heirs. Smith, as the convicted killer, was unable to benefit from the crime. But Ellen Bergman, the widow, who sold the building and its contents, divided the proceeds in two, keeping half and giving the other half to Smith's daughter Jane, in care of her aunt, Virginia Smith. As to the policy on Bergman's life, the insurance company refused to pay up, on the grounds that they were not liable because the listed beneficiary had caused the death: this decision was not disputed.

Most of these transactions were on the public record and easy to ascertain. Contacting Ellen Bergman was less easy, since she had remarried and moved away – but only to another part of town. I thought it generous of her to split the money with Jane: she probably could have gotten away with it if she'd kept it all for herself, but that certainly would have looked grasping. As it was, she looked as though she was doing alright anyway, and seemed comfortable in her new home.

Following that trail, I arranged to see Jane's aunt in her office at the university. I'd met Dr Smith, briefly, a couple of years earlier, when setting up arrangements to help with her mother's accounts. Apparently, the old lady spoke well of me, so Dr Smith was quite open with me about the money and, for that matter, about her brother and her niece as well.

Her office was pokey, maybe ten feet by eight. The usual desk with computer, printer, and telephone. A small window with a radiator beneath it – this was an old-fashioned building, pseudo-romanesque. Walls were lined with shelves full of books with rather forbidding titles. It was cramped quarters for a quite distinguished academic. But then, I suppose a lot of her work must be in a lab or a lecture-room. There was an extra chair beside the desk, presumably for a student having a tutorial. I sat in it. It carried me back fifteen years, when I used to sit next to the late, great Professor Liptrott, and sort out the rhythms of Hopkin's avant-garde prosody.

There was no small talk. Dr Smith came right to the point of our meeting.

"Mr Ellis," she said, "or may I call you Mark?"

"Of course."

"Mark, I'm so glad you've agreed to work with my niece. Jane's a fine young woman, and she deserves any help you can give her. How can I help *you*?"

"Well, as you can imagine, this isn't an easy case. I'm going to have to look every which way to sort it out. So far. I'm just in the early stages. But one thing I've done right away is look back into the closure of your brother's business. That must have been a heart break for you, going through all his stuff, with him sitting helpless in prison."

"It was. I was always very fond of David. Still am. I never doubted his innocence. And that wasn't just because he was my brother and I believed him. There was actually a perfectly sound, *logical* reason to believe him."

"Which was?"

"The hammer. As you probably know, David was the creative half of the firm, designing all that beautiful custom-made furniture and making it himself, in the workshop on the premises. He had a real reverence for wood. Not just as a raw material. For him, it was something almost sacred, and each piece of it had a personality all of its own. He didn't just make *use* of it: he worked *with* it. And if that was his attitude to timber, it was the same thing with his tools: he loved his craft, and they were his partners. He could no more have used that hammer of his for an act of violence, like murder, than a priest could use a chalice to administer poison."

It was an odd analogy. But not all scientists are unbelievers. Odd, and weak as an argument. But psychologically convincing.

"What happened to them? The tools, I mean."

"I've kept them. In storage. Except the hammer, of course. The police have that, wherever they stash such things. I saved all the rest, when everything else went up for sale. I knew David would want to have them back, if he ever gets out of where he is."

"So all the other stuff on the premises was sold off? I gather Mrs Bergman looked after that, mostly."

"That's right. It was the least I could do, to let her take over, after the loss she'd had. Especially since she'd lost Sven's income. It didn't bring in very much, the sale, but she seems to have managed, alright. And it was very kind of her, in the circumstances, to turn over half the money to Jane as a kind of education trust, until she was eighteen, and I administered it for her. There was enough to put her through school here, in residence at St Margaret's: and of course she's looked after that side of things herself, since she came of age. It doesn't go far, but she lives sparingly. All she wants out of life is to see her Dad free, and to focus on her work – in that order."

"Speaking of that," I said, "so far as I can make out, there was no extra money coming in from the insurance policy your brother had taken out on Bergman's life. He was the listed beneficiary, right?"

31

"Yes, he was. And I do reckon it made things look bad for him. But the only reason the policy was taken out was to protect the firm in the event of Bergman's death. There was an exactly similar policy for the same reason on David's life, to protect the firm in the event of *his* death."

"I know. But apparently the insurance company refused to pay up when Bergman was killed. You didn't dispute that decision? Even if the money couldn't go to David, maybe there was some way it could have gone to Jane."

"Not according to the legal advice I took. Not much of a chance, anyway. And I didn't feel right about getting into a protracted courtroom battle about it. My first priority wasn't money, it was Jane. She was pretty raw emotionally, as I'm sure you can imagine, after having to go through her Dad's arrest and conviction. Anything about the money would just have gone on rubbing salt in the wound. Besides, we weren't destitute. I earn a good salary, and I don't have expensive tastes. Helping Jane out was a pleasure. I love her dearly."

"Well, that's mutual. So far as I can see, she's pretty darn fond of you, too."

"That's nice to hear. Let's just say, we're good with each other. And we're both glad to have you on side. Is there anything else I can tell you that might be helpful?"

"I don't think so, not right now. But I'll certainly come back to you, if anything does come up."

I stood up. She did, too, and looked me straight in the eye.

"Mark," she said, ''look after this carefully. If you have to give her bad news, do it gently. Don't break her heart."

"I won't, Dr Smith, believe me."

I meant it – perhaps more than she realized.

"Oh, for heaven's sake," she exclaimed, "just call me Aunt V, Jane does."

I have, ever since.

VIII

The next step was more Mark Ellis, the accountant, than Mark Ellis, the freelance detective. I noticed when I visited Ellen Rowse (formerly Ellen Bergman) that she seemed to be fairly comfortable in her life. More so, perhaps, than she would have been ten years ago, in the aftermath of her first husband's death and the closing of the firm he'd been partner in. But I attributed this to a fortunate second marriage. She hadn't actually told me when she remarried, and I forgot to ask her. So I looked it up.

That sure alerted me. She'd married Jack Rowse only a few weeks after Sven was buried. Now, granted, people do sometimes fall in love right after a bereavement: it's a kind of compensatory jump sideways. Sometimes. But you can't spend long in the investigation trade without getting into a habit of suspiciousness. Maybe there'd been something going on between Ellen and Jack behind Sven's back, and they got hitched as soon as they were free to.

This would bear looking into.

It's no clean business digging into other people's private lives and trying, mainly through gossip, to see what dirt comes up. Far too often, in a murder investigation, nasty little scraps of unpleasantness surface, which are otherwise kept hidden. I didn't relish the prospect of prying such stuff out of the various individuals who might have something to say about a premarital affair of Ellen Bergman's with Jack Rowse – if indeed there had been such an affair. Going after it would mean a lot of dreary legwork.

Before embarking on that, though, I decided to pay a call on Lois Grinstead, book-keeper for the Smith-Bergman firm. When I phoned her and asked to see her about the case, I didn't know what to expect. Maybe she'd he willing to talk, maybe not. And if she was willing, maybe after ten years she'd have forgotten any significant details.

To my surprise, she was completely willing to meet and talk – almost, oddly, eager to. I made a mental note of that and arranged to have coffee with her the next day, in a café near her home.

She'd told me over the phone that she'd worked for Smith-Bergman for twelve years prior to the murder. So even if she'd started young, like right after maybe taking a book-keeping course at a community college, she'd now be middle-aged. I'd no idea what to expect. Perhaps a dowdy little woman who'd never married – book-keepers don't earn much, and she lived, apparently, alone. Now, mind you, I don't typecast book-keepers, or accountants. Everyone seems to think of them as colourless nonentities, with a good head for numbers but about as much personality as a vacuum bag. Quite wrong. I've met dozens of them around my Dad's firm, and they're just as varied as folks in any other line of work. So I didn't walk into her local Second Cup with any preconceived notion of what she might look like.

Even so, when she waved at me across the room (I'd told her I'd be wearing a blue beret; I usually do), I was a bit surprised. She had to be in her forties by now, but she could easily pass for thirty. No mouse she, scurrying through columns of figures while crouched over a calculator. She was tall, stylishly dressed with an open, welcoming face. No ring.

How come nobody snapped her up, I wondered?

Grabbing a coffee – she already had one – I sat down opposite her and said, "Thanks for seeing me."

"My pleasure," she said. "Actually, Mr Ellis, I mean it. When you phoned and said you wanted to look into the David Smith case, it was like that was something I'd been waiting for. That case had been bothering me ever since. What's your interest in it?"

I short-handed it for her. Told her how I'd been studying the trial, in case there had been a miscarriage of justice. How I'd been brought into it by Jane, the daughter, who was convinced her father was innocent.

"So was I," she commented. "Maybe not convinced, no. But I sure was uneasy. Innocent people shouldn't get railroaded."

"And; you think he was?"'

"Yes, I do. None of us are saints. We're all capable of something dicey now and then. You can't go over people's private records without seeing the odd little jiggery-pokery in someone's life. So, dicey, yes. At least, in lots of folks. But violent crime, no. Not that David Smith. He was a lovely man. I knew him. There wasn't a mean bone in his body."

Sadness looked at me across the table, even after ten years: sadness and, even after ten years, just a faint blush. So maybe that was why she was still single: a crush she'd never quite gotten over.

"A lovely man..."

She sighed, and I let her silence linger for a moment. Then I got us going again.

"I'm sorry, Ms Grinstead," I said, "but sometimes, you know, people do act out of character."

"That's true," she conceded. "But I had more to go on than just my feelings. There were things I knew that made me stop and think – fishy little suspicions that pointed away from David." (No sticking now to the formality of his surname.) "I mean, the evidence they brought against him was so damning, I had to admit the verdict was a kind of foregone conclusion. But afterwards I was still bothered by the things I knew. They preyed on my mind. Never stopped preying. That's why I was so relieved when you called me and said you were looking into the whole thing."

"Well, I'm trying to. What sort of things?"

"I'll tell you. I hope you can do more with it than the last person I shared it with. See, I didn't just let it fester inside me. I went back to one of the cops who'd worked the inquiry."

"Levesque? Inspector Levesque?"

"No, and I must say I didn't like that man. Struck me as a bit of a bully. No, a younger man – I seem to've forgotten his name."

"Stan Novak, the sergeant?"

"Yes, that's it. Good for you. So I told him, this Novak, what was on my mind. He listened, fairly enough. But he ended up saying there was nothing he could do about it. The police, he said, would never re-open a case like that, when they'd had such good evidence for a conviction – even if I did know a few things that made the results look a bit dubious.

"That's what he said. Dead end street. So I tried to put the whole thing behind me. But you know what? I haven't been able to."

Her discomfort was palpable.

"Then maybe you'd better try me instead," I said. "Tell me what you're referring to."

It came pouring out of her, like a dam had burst.

It all had to do with money – and records. She brought up the matter of the two life-insurance policies on the two partners, which I already knew about. But then she spoke of a third policy which I didn't know about. It was on Bergman's life, worth $200,000, taken out with a different company years earlier, when they were first married. Just the kind of insurance newly-weds do take out. Beneficiary Ellen Bergman. She, Grinstead, knew about it because she did Mrs Bergman's personal book-keeping, as well as the firm's. But here came the kicker: a month before the murder, Mrs Bergman paid much larger premiums and raised the value of the policy to a million dollars. Ordinarily, given the murder a few weeks later, that would have raised a red flag in any adjuster's mind. And there was no question of a payout while the investigation was going on or while the case was awaiting trial. But once David was found guilty, the insurance company wouldn't have a leg to stand on if they disputed the claim. So Mrs Bergman walked off with an extra million.

"I never really liked her," Grinstead said. "Sven used to go away a lot, to see out-of-town customers. And I did wonder, sometimes, if he was glad to get away. On the whole, he was a quite affable man. Typical salesman: glad-hander, hail-fellow-well-met; easy to get along with. But she struck me as a bit of a shrew. I don't know, it's not my place to make assumptions about other people's relationships – I've never been married, myself. So I'd never really thought about whether she might be having an affair. And even if she was, there's always two sides to a story. Did he go out of town, more than necessary, to get away from her? Or did she have an affair to get away from him, or because he wasn't home enough? Who could tell? Anyway, it wasn't something I'd given a lot of thought to.

"Until, that is, she married Mr Rowse right after being widowed. Well, maybe not right after. But shockingly soon. So I said to myself, Hey, Lois, let's just take a look back at last year's Visa Bills, and see if anything jumps out at you. H'm, it sure enough did. Every time Sven was out of town for a day or two, she booked into a motel. Not in town, or Kitchener or Windsor maybe. Oh no. Always someplace else. Usually somewhere back of beyond, where she wouldn't run into anyone she knew. And don't tell me she sat alone there playing solitaire. More like a regular piece on the side, if you ask me."

(Grinstead delivered herself of this slight coarseness with a touch of remembered animosity. Or was it envy?)

"Anyway" (she went on) "none of that proves anything. But it'd be interesting to know what that Mr Rowse's movements were on those dates. Because it made me think, what if there was more to it than straightforward screwing?" (Grinstead seemed to have given up on bourgeois decorum.) "Maybe she'd talked her lover into somehow getting rid of Sven so they could fuck themselves senseless. I've no idea how he could have managed it, how he could have fixed it to make it look like poor David had done it. But I do have a gut feeling that's what happened."

I left the Second Cup after thanking Grinstead and bidding her hang on to her records, with a mind pondering a whole web of possibilities. Maybe it hadn't been such a far-fetched idea for me to imagine someone other than David Smith as the killer, someone using David's hammer to implicate him and wearing gloves to leave no fingerprints on the haft. And if that someone was Jack Rowse, or even some one else that Ellen Bergman had talked into the job, there would be no problem about access to the premises. She would be sure to have had a key.

Moreover, if that was the way it came down, the whole problem of David Smith's alibi simply evaporated. He would have been safely and innocently at home in bed, while the real killer went to work.

There did remain, of course, the problem of why Sven Bergman would have been there in the small hours of the morning. But it wasn't much of a stretch to figure that Ellen would have found some plausible reason to get him there. That was a kink I'd have to work out.

But for the time being, Jack Rowse was someone who'd be worth looking into.

IX

Noon, the next Tuesday.

I had to admit to myself I'd really been looking forward to our next lunch. Jane and I arrived simultaneously – not a bad habit to be forming, I thought.

We approached with a big shared smile; and she gave me a big cheery hug. Apparently we were past the handshake stage.

Inside, Mario shepherded us, proprietariously but also avuncularly, to a corner table. This time he recommended spaghetti vongole, his Venetian specialty of pasta with clams and cherry tomatoes, which we went for happily. And, of course, frascati. We settled back to enjoy it.

"So, Mark," Jane said, "progress report?"

I started in to tell her about my session with Lois Grinstead. But I did warn her not to let her hopes soar too high all of a sudden. Sure, there were interesting possibilities in what Grinstead had told me. It had given me a direction to go in; but anything I found out wouldn't necessarily get us where we wanted to end up.

The food arrived, and we gave it the proper attention it deserved. That slowed us up; but by the time we left our plates clean, I'd recounted the whole of what I'd listened to in the Second Cup.

Jane put down her fork.

"Wow!" she said – a rather more slangy locution than would ever have passed the lips of John Donne. "So this Jack Rowse, how are you going to get on his trail?"

"Oh, most of that's just dull legwork. I won't bore you with the details. I'll have more to tell you after another week. Next Tuesday still okay?"

"Naturally," she said, as though the question had been unnecessary, as though it was automatic that I'd now be a regular part of her life. If that was so, the idea warmed me like a fine liqueur. Maybe 1.00 wasn't a good hour for that kind of thing: better after a dinner together. But that was no reason not to indulge in one of Mario's desserts. Following the provenance of the entree, he served us Venetian tiramisu with a bicchierino of marsala on the side. It was superb.

"By the way," I said as we tucked in, "I had a good sit-down on Friday with Aunt V. She's just as remarkable a woman as you told me she was. Your grandmother must be very proud of her. In turn, I could tell she was very proud of you, too. Obviously, a good female line. But tell me something about your Dad. I mean, he's naturally a central figure in your life. But fill me in a bit more than you have. All I know about him thus far, apart from the sad story of his ending up in prison, is that he's famous as a furniture designer and craftsman. Aunt V spoke quite warmly about him, not just as a well-loved brother, but as someone with, a kind of deep-down relationship with Wood."

I uttered the noun in a way that tried to sound like it had a capital letter, the way a Muslim would speak of Mecca. And when I had mentioned Aunt V – just so, not *your* Aunt V – I caught a tiny flicker of rightness in her eye, a kind of welcome-to-the-family look, almost a sense of coming home. But not to dwell on that: she was answering.

"That's it exactly," she said, "a reverence. I came to understand that as I got older. It was rather like the relationship I grew into with the Word."

Same kind of capitalizing.

"Of course," she went on, "there were things I didn't understand when I was only fifteen. Like most teenagers, I was chiefly interested in myself, in who I was, what I was doing. And Dad, when I was visiting him with Aunt V, was always asking about what was going on in my life. Gradually, though, my regard shifted away from myself towards him. Mainly because I loved him dearly, and because Aunt V told me so much about him. I don't know about you, Mark, but I guess one of the things about growing up is you start to see your parent as a person, not just as a role. So yes I came to know Dad for who he was in himself: a great artist in wood. He never speaks about how he misses it. But he must miss it acutely. I feel awful for him about that. It'd be like a music-lover going stone deaf."

"I can imagine."

"But here's the thing. He didn't just wallow in the pain of it. He found something else to do with his time. Time! God, how I hate that word, the way they use it in there: doing time. It's such a definition of emptiness, such a reminder of unfreedom. But that's what's so great about Dad: he found a way to be free within unfreedom – by teaching a kind of freedom to his fellow-prisoners, the freedom of the Word."

"Meaning?"

"He teaches literacy classes. Oh, to be sure, there's always a whole bunch of men in prison who're fixed in their own ignorance, and some of them in a sort of fixed malignity. But there are others, too, who somehow realize they don't have to stay landlocked in their own limitations: they could set out on the great sea of language. I mean, they weren't technically illiterate, in the strict sense. But learning to read and write properly, and to enjoy doing so, that opened them up to all kinds of ideas, gave them a basis for hope about their future on release.

"So you can appreciate how close that has made me feel to him. Here am I, in my safe liberty, spending my days with the likes of Donne and Southwell; and there is he, in dangerous prison – because prison *is* dangerous, you know – *doing time*, with street-smart cons learning an altogether different wisdom."

She drained the last of her marsala.

"Sorry to have carried on like that," she said. "But you did ask."

Point taken. If I'd been wanting, all along, to help *her*, I now, sure as hell, wanted to help him, too.

We finished up and got the bill. Mario was a bit taken aback when she paid it. That didn't fit in with his own cultural background. But he took it with good grace.

"Next time," he said, and he obviously knew there'd be a next time, "next time I make you a special peppardello con consiglio. Ciao, Marco. Ciao, signorina."

We went out, into the unimprisoning world, and shared a profound hug before turning away.

X

Another couple of beers with Al, another favour to ask.

I told him all about what Lois Grinstead had told me. He agreed it sounded pretty fishy, Jack Rowse's possible role in the matter. So I asked him if he could log into the relevant sources, to see if Rowse had any kind of record. He got back to me the very next day on the phone.

"Interesting," he said. "Only one conviction: for assault, but not with a weapon; served three months. However, because of that, his file was kept open. And the one other entry's sure to interest you. Twelve years ago, he was under suspicion in the death of his then wife. But no charge was laid, for lack of any evidence that would stand up in court. What do you think of that?"

What I thought of that was obvious: maybe Levesque pinned the Bergman murder on the wrong guy; maybe it was Rowse. Come to think of it, he had motive (an affair with Ellen), he had opportunity (her key to the premises). As to means, Smith's hammer was a handy weapon; and so long as he used gloves himself, the hammer would serve perfectly to incriminate Smith.

"That's what I think," I said. "And I'll tell you something else. Stan Novak may have been pissed off that Levesque wouldn't look at other possibilities. But if he'd known, back then, that Ellen was having an affair with Rowse, he'd have pushed Levesque a lot harder to dig deep, even if he *was* only junior partner at the time."

"Right. Definitely he would have."

"Any chance, d'you think, he might look at it again?"

"I don't know, Mark. Maybe yes, maybe no. It's tricky trying to get the Force to re-open a case that's closed – closed, I mean, with a successful conviction. People hate admitting they've been wrong. As of now, I reckon it's too early to make any kind of approach to Stan: not enough to go on. You'd have to give me more than you've got, before I could think of getting Stan involved. But here's what I *can* do, at my end. Let me see if we still have records of the inquiry into Rowse's first wife's death, when he was suspected of having killed her. Maybe that'll tie in somehow."

"Good. Thanks, Al," I said. And hung up.

It took him another couple of days.

While I waited, with nothing much to do, the thought came to me, as it often does, of how bloody stupid crooks can sometimes be. They get everything all planned out perfectly, or so they think; and then everything misfires because of one dumb thing they overlooked. Either that's just stupidity. Or else, it's a sense of invincibility, like Nixon not wiping his tapes – though I guess that was a form of stupidity, too.

Anyway, looking back on my conversation with Lois Grinstead, I was amazed at Ellen Bergman's stupidity. If she'd had her wits about her, she'd have found ways to cover her tracks over the million-dollar insurance, and over her love-trysts with Rowse. Leaving the paper trail lying about where her book-keeper could see it, that was simply moronic.

Some people just deserve to get caught.

Al got back to me again.

"Bingo!" he said. "You won't believe this, but there's an amazing parallel. Rowse's first wife died of a blow to the head, just like the one that killed Sven Bergman – almost exactly the same: I've seen the photographs. They never found the weapon. Only reason Rowse got off was there were no witnesses and he had an alibi. Said he was across town at the time, visiting a girl-friend. Yes, he had a girl-friend on the side, and that was why he was under suspicion, they'd have tried to break the alibi, but the girl-friend swore up and down he'd been with her, and they couldn't find anyone who'd seen him that night in his wife's neighbourhood. So they were stymied. Case is still open, technically. But nobody's moved on it for years. Maybe you'd like to look into it. I don't think there's anything I can get going at this end."

"Sure, Al. Besides, you've done enough already. I'll have a crack at it. What was her name?"

"Maureen Foss. Used to live at 112 Kingston Road. Telephone (416) 469-5493."

"Thanks, Al," I said again. And hung up.

112 Kingston Road no longer existed. It and numbers 110 and 114 had vanished, who knows when, and had been replaced, by a condo building and a visitors' parking-lot. Waste of time going there. But

people who move are often able to keep the same phone number. There was an M. Foss listed at the number Al had given me, at 325A Dundas Street East. A rather squalid neighbourhood. I tried the number around suppertime, when most people are home from work and haven't gone out if they're going to.

"Hello," a rather hoarse female voice answered. I could hear a TV in the background.

"Am I speaking with Ms Maureen Foss?" I asked.

"Yes, just a moment." She switched the TV off.

"Does the name Jack Rowse mean anything to you?"

"Jesus, that bastard?" Her voice was now raspy, and hostile. "Christ, I haven't heard that name in years. Who's calling?"

"My name's Mark Ellis," I said and added untruthfully, "I'm an investigator for an insurance firm, and his name's come up in one of my cases."

"You don't say. You mean you're investigating him?"

"Well, not exactly. It's complicated. I'm just looking for some information."

"Uh-huh. Well, I'll tell you this. If you want some dirt on that sonofabitch, you've come to the right place."

"Fair enough. D'you think we could arrange to meet and talk about this?"

"Maybe." She was being cautious now. "I don't know..."

"Oh, let me assure you," I said, "there's nothing here that could possibly involve you in any trouble." Which wasn't exactly true, either.

"Well," softening a bit, "how about you buy me a drink somewhere?"

"Sure," I said. "No time like the present. You doing anything this evening?"

"Not so as I know of." Then, almost roguishly, "Come by in an hour or so and pick me up."

"Be right there," I said. "See you."

She might have been attractive in her time, once. But she hadn't worn well: had the look of someone who's lived hard and looks fifty – before she's out of her thirties. Henna'd hair, a lot of make-up, and a figure that's gone puffy. She slid into the passenger seat, and directed me to what she called her home-away-from-home. On the way, she said, "Mind if I smoke in the car? They don't let you in bars anymore." Reluctantly, I said okay: no point in alienating a source. Before she lit up, I could smell the liquor on her.

Shorty's Place was about two steps short of being a dump. The lighting was garish, the canned music raucous. At the bar, a couple of brassy blondes were chatting up a couple of male customers. Everyone else was into serious drinking, at various stages. No one had started a fight, yet. Some of them obviously knew Foss, as a regular. Including the barkeep, who was probably Shorty in person, since he stood about six-four.

"Hi, Maureen," he called out. "The usual?"

"Just make it a double," she said. "This gentleman's buying."

I asked for a beer, and took the drinks to her at an empty table, where she'd already sat down and winked at an acquaintance nearby.

"Cheers," she said, hoisting her double rye and ginger enthusiastically. "So it's Mark, right? What gives with Jack Rowse?"

I leaned across the table, partly to cut through the din of the place, and partly to create, spuriously, a sense of intimacy that would loosen her tongue.

"Here's the story," I said. "Fifteen years ago, I gather you were in a relationship with Rowse. Probably a serious one. But from what you said on the phone this evening, it doesn't sound as though you care much about him now."

"Damn right I don't. That prick! He two-timed me."

"Still, you must have cared back then. After all, he left his wife for you. Some say he did her in. Could be he did. But they couldn't pin it on him. You said he was with you."

Her eyes narrowed. She looked at me coldly.

"Who told you that?"

"Nobody did. I just looked it up."

She swallowed that – along with a gulp of rye.

"Okay, so I did. So what? What's in it for you, mister?"

"Nothing, really. At least, not about that. Listen, he may be in a bit of bother about something else. All I want from you is a bit of background. If he *was* with you that night, fair enough. But if he wasn't, you don't need to be worried about saying so. Not after all these years."

"Not worried? Oh, sure! Look, Mr Ellis, whatever your name is, I wasn't born yesterday. If I go back on what I said, how'm I to know you aren't a cop? Maybe you'd nail me for watcha-may-call-it, accessory."

"Alright, I'll level with you. I'm not a cop, I'm a private detective."

I showed her my license. "All I'm trying to do is clear up something else Rowse got involved in, afterwards. Not in any way connected with you. Believe me."

She pondered it. Finished her drink. And said, "Go get me another, will you?"

I picked up her glass – my beer was still half full – and took it to the bar. But I kept an eye on her in the mirror. I was afraid she might run out on me. But she didn't.

When I got back to the table, she said, "Anything in it for me?"

"Depends," I said. I'd expected something like that, and had a hundred on me, in case. "Depends on what *you* come up with. Here's a little something for starters, anyway." I slid five twenties under my coaster. "There's probably more where that came from."

The words weren't out of my mouth before she had the twenties in her purse. Out of the corner of my eye I saw a guy at the next table noting the transaction. Likely, he put a wholly different interpretation on it.

"Deal," she said. "If there's a chance to do that bastard a bit of payback, I won't say no." She downed her drink, and grinned, slyly. "Not that the money doesn't help."

I stood up, leaving my beer unfinished.

"Let's go and do this in the car," I said, "where nobody'll hear anything you say. I'll bring you back for another round when we're done."

"See you, Maureen," Shorty called out as we left.

I guess he was used to her coming into the bar with a man for a couple of shots, and then leaving with him right away.

Strictly speaking, that was disingenuous of me, to suggest we talk in the car so as not to he overheard by others. The actual overhearing was going to be by a tape-recorder: I was wearing a wire.

We sat in the front seats. And sure enough, she lit up another of those bloody cigarettes.

"So, Maureen Foss," I began, "where were you living in the year 2000?"

It all came out non-stop, while she chain-smoked.

Kingston Road, number 112. A one-bedroom apartment. She'd moved there at the beginning of February. Met Jack Rowse at a party New Year's Eve. You know, a millennium party." We hit it off right away. I took him home with me. Not there; that came later. I had a studio in Cabbagetown, about the size of a broom-closet. You know how it is when you're starting out. I was only twenty, and you don't get big pay waiting table. Anyway, there we were, a bit plastered I have to say, but not so we couldn't function. In fact, I'd say we functioned pretty damn well, that night. Like there was no tomorrow.

"Course there *was* a tomorrow. New Year's. We went at it like rabbits all day. And the next night.

"First thing I knew, a month later he'd moved me into a bigger place. Didn't move in with me, not to begin with. He was married – getting a divorce, he said. Couldn't move out of the house yet: it would affect his separation agreement, something to do with ownership of the property, he said. But he used to come and see me a lot – sometimes overnight when he could tell his wife he had a job out of town. And we did eventually shack up after, you know, after his wife passed."

"So when was that?"

"Jeeze, I'm not likely to forget, seeing as how it was such a mess. June 20th 2000. Someone killed her, and the cops had Jack lined up for it. Couldn't prove it, though. No weapon, no witnesses, and he had an alibi. Said he'd been with me; and I backed him up. They sure grilled me about that. But I stuck to it, and there was nothing they could do about it. Far as I know, no one ever did get caught for doing it. Jack swore up and down he hadn't, and I did kinda believe him. Hell, what had I to lose? We were crazy about each other, and now he was free. What the hell?"

"You said you kind of believed him. *Had* he been with you when he said he was?"

"Not so's you'd say *all* night. I mean, we did start out together, like it was a fucking competition, who could come oftenest. But some time in the middle of the night, he snuck out for a while. Said he had to go to the bootlegger's for more rye. I nodded off. When I woke up, he was back in bed, and we went right back at it. No idea what time it was."

"I guess, then, you didn't really know, one way or the other."

"You could say that. Can't say I really cared that much. Told me his wife was a real bitch anyways. So whoever it was did her in did us a real favour. No more sneaking around. We just got on with our lives. I did wonder, sometimes, if we'd get married. But somehow I didn't feel like pushing it. Not right away. Shit, we were young and living it up. Who needs a ring?

"Leastways, that's how it was for a couple of years. Then things changed. He started disappearing on me. Always the same story: had to go out of town on a job. Well, I'd heard that kind of malarkey before. Sounded familiar? Sure, that's what he used to tell his wife. I'm not that dumb. So I figured something was going on. Like as not, another woman. No way to find out, and at first I didn1 know, only suspected. Then he just left me.

"Part of me, that broke my heart. I'd really thought he loved me. But I ended up feeling like crap about it. You know, just used, then thrown out like the garbage."

"So then what?"

"Well, the thing was, he had a fair bit of money, from selling his house. And he started spending it. On himself. Fancy suits and shoes. An expensive watch. Stuff like that. Not like he used to be, before. The Jack I used to know, it never made no mind to me. All we needed was a good bed and deaf neighbours. But once he started getting all gussied up, I had to figure something was wrong. Like he was trying to impress another woman. And what d'you know, when he did move out he shacked up with someone – let's put it this way – I was way out of her league. Ellen Bergman, that was her name. Quite the dame. Married to a businessman. Wore pearls and a mink coat – all that shit. Jack carried on with her for a year behind my back. And wouldn't you know it, her husband caught a blow to the head, just like Jack's wife had. First thought crossed my mind, I wondered if Jack had something to do with it. But I guess I was wrong. They got another guy for it. Anyways, Jack moved in with her, and that was that. I washed my hands of the whole thing afterwards. Don't care if I never clap eyes on the bastard ever again."

"But back a couple of years earlier, the night of the first murder, presumably you didn't mention to the cops how Jack had gone out to the bootlegger's, just covered up for him and said he'd spent the night with you. But if you did tell them now, they probably wouldn't hold it against you, so long as they got their man. How do you feel about that?"

"You know something, I don't really care that much, one way or the other. Jack'll get his comeuppance someday. He's the kind of guy takes one risk too many. I'll tell you one thing, though. I won't cry over his grave."

I took her back into Shorty's. This was a woman I'd do well to keep on the right side of. So I nursed a coke – after all, I would he driving – while she downed another three doubles. Then I took her home, now quite drunk but still conscious. When I pulled up outside her place, she turned, to me and said, with a hideous coquettishness, "wanna come up?"

"Not now, Maureen. Maybe another time. Night."

XI

Sitting down with Jane in Mario's next day was the ultimate contrast to how I'd spent the previous evening. I told her everything Maureen had said, summarizing it and leaving out the expletives.

"You don't have to censor it, Mark," she said. "I've heard many an oath in my time. But what sort of person is she? Do you think she's reliable?"

"Hard to tell. I'd say she's had a pretty hard life, maybe a little prostitution on the side. And if she ever got on the witness-stand for the Crown, a defence lawyer would probably try to carve her up like a trussed turkey. Mind you, she's feisty. I wouldn't put it past her to sit there in court and tell him to go fuck himself."

She chuckled. "About time. That kind of attorney needs getting slapped down. I've had it up to here, the way they treat women on the stand – or at least the men do: I can't recall a woman attorney doing that to another woman."

She sipped her frascati (of course), while waiting for the Mario version of rabbit. Then she said, "This Jack Rowse, do you think he could be a double murderer, simple as that?"

"Could be. But there'll be nothing simple about proving it."

The peppardello con consiglio arrived, with a flourish, and we dug into it with relish. It was delicious. Mario's food always is. Thank God he doesn't want to expand: no ambition to rule an empire; perfectly content with this little setup, where he can cook the way he likes for a few people who can appreciate it. He's a treasure. And those who do appreciate it don't insult the food by relegating it to second place, as though talking were more important. However, after a few minutes of gourmet silence, we laid down our forks and looked at each other with a simultaneous satisfied smile.

Then I said, "Jane, off topic, here's something I need to tell you about that I haven't mentioned up till now."

She looked slightly alarmed. Was I about to tell her my wife wanted to come back, despite the divorce? Or perhaps I was gay?

"It's about another job I do – not just the accounting or the investigations."

"Well, that's alright, I guess. So long as it isn't another woman."

The implications of that response weren't lost on me. Hooray, said a little voice inside my head. But out loud I said, "I'm a publisher."

"*What?*"

"Yes, really. Now, don't get me wrong. The Mark Ellis Press, to give it a fancy name, isn't about to publish a masterpiece by some as yet undiscovered genius. Rather the contrary. I run what you might call a vanity press. That is, for a fee, I print limited editions of books by unpublished, and probably unpublishable, amateurs – very limited editions: just for family and friends. You know the kind of thing: autobiographies by retired brigadier-generals; dreary memoirs by neurotics obsessed with the self. That kind of drivel. They just love seeing their words in print; and I guess it's a fairly harmless activity. Far as I'm concerned, it just helps pay the rent."

"Well, knock me down with a goose-quill pen. I'd never have guessed."

"I suppose. But the reason I'm telling you this – actually there are two reasons. First, I owe it to you: full disclosure, as they say. But also because of that poor woman I interviewed yesterday evening. When I think of the hard life she's led, I think to myself there's a story in her that's more a slice of reality than anything set down on the pages *I* print. Maybe no one will ever tell her story, and she sure couldn't write it herself. But there's something there that makes me recognize some uncomfortable truths that half the world has to live with... Sorry, I didn't mean to carry on about it."

"Maybe you should tell her story yourself."

"Me? Hell, no, I'm not a writer. Why would *I* try?"

"I can give you one good reason, for starters. One of the things I like about you, Mark, is you have a strong sense of justice. What you've just been saying about this Maureen Foss – was that her name? – belongs in the same order of kindness as the work you've been doing to free my Dad. And don't think I'm unaware of the rough side of life. Most of the guys in prison with Dad have done some pretty wrong things – a few even truly evil. But there's more to human beings than the sum of their offences. If I didn't believe that, I wouldn't want to write about Southwell. Because the awful thing about Topcliffe, the monster who tortured Southwell, is that even *he*, Topcliffe, actually meant well."

"How is that coming, by the way, your thesis?"

"Should be done later this year." She grinned. "Maybe you'd like to publish it."

"Not on your life! What, shovel you in with the narcissists? No, you deserve better than that. If it's as good as I expect it is, let the University Press publish it. Anyway, I'm thinking of getting out of the vanity business. There are more important things to do in life than pander to delusions of literary greatness. Better I should spend my time on cases like your Dad's; and I've always accounting to fall back on. There's a certain purity in numbers, you know."

Mario arrived with two espressos and poached pears in his own sauce, which, he said he'd learnt as an apprentice in San Sepolcro. He didn't linger. He could see we were more into each other than tales of the Old Country.

"What's next?" Jane asked. "Is there some way you can make use of what the Foss woman told you?"

"I hope so. Not me directly. Through my friend Al. I'll give him a copy of the tape I recorded of her, and he may be able to leverage it into official action. There's the cop I told you about in the Homicide Unit,

Stan Novak. You remember, he was the junior officer investigating your Dad. He's the one who thought Levesque was sort of precipitate in picking your Dad as the killer without looking at other possibles. Thought it a rush to judgment, and resented how Levesque wouldn't even give him the time of day on the subject; but in the end he had to figure Levesque must be right – too much convincing evidence. So when Al sounded him out, Al thought we didn't have enough arguments lined up for Stan to consider doing anything. In a way we still haven't: not to get your Dad's case re-opened."

Jane sighed. "Yes, I remember you telling me that."

"Never mind. Things have changed now. What Maureen Foss told me means the Force'll certainly take another look at Rowse over the murder of his first wife – the file is still open. And if they nail him for it, there'll be a ripple effect: enough of one, I'd say, for them to take a look at Rowse as a possible in the Bergman murder."

"You think so?"

"I wouldn't count on it, Jane. Most people don't like to admit they've been wrong, and that includes cops. After all, the Bergman murder's a closed case. But Stan Novak was never easy in his mind about it. Maybe now he'd have second thoughts about it – maybe he always has had. I'll have to leave that up to Al, to give Stan a bit of a push in that direction. He's a good guy – Al, I mean: I've never met Novak. Al won't just let the matter lie out of some misplaced belief that closed cases are sacred cows. He has too good a mind, and one of its virtues is doubt."

"So it's up to Al, eh?"

"That side of it, I think so. But me, I'm not just going to sit back and do nothing. Ellen Bergman, who's now Ellen Rowse, is worth my poking around about. You never know what might pop up."

Jane looked concerned.

"Oh Mark," she said, "do be careful. That Rowse sounds like he used to be a really dangerous character."

"Sure, I'll be careful," I promised her. "I always am. Besides now..." I hesitated, thought what the hell, and reached for her hand. "Now I have reason to be."

XII

Al and I trust each other. I had no qualms about turning over the Foss tape to him; to see what he could do with it; for I really did think the force would go easy on her if they could nail Rowse. As to how all that might impact Stan Novak, I simply couldn't predict: I just had to hope he was an open-minded guy. Sometimes you just have to throw a line in the water and hope it'll come up with a fat trout.

But I wasn't going to just sit back and wait for things to happen. I'd told Jane I thought Bergman's widow was worth my taking another look at. And I had reason for saying so – perhaps not a good reason, but at least a hunch. Because two things had crossed my mind. Number one, when I'd interviewed her, she didn't speak of Rowse, who wasn't present in person, as though he might be back any moment. And number two, in my experience, things tend to run in patterns: if insurance had been part of the picture ten years ago, maybe insurance might be relevant again. You never know till you look.

So I looked.

First thing, I went back to Lois Grinstead. With her, I expanded my inquiry, something I should have done in our previous conversation. I asked her to cast her mind back to when Ellen Bergman remarried, to Jack Rowse. Did she do the book-keeping for both of them, Rowse included?

Yes, she did.

And did she have any recollection of what their insurance situation was, the two of them? Maybe they set that up, as a couple, when they married. A lot of newlyweds did that; it was quite normal, especially if they were along in life – not so much, young people.

"That was a very interesting question," Grinstead said. "Sure, they took out life-insurance policies, each of them being beneficiaries of the other. A million dollars each. Quite a sizeable amount, of course. But if you like to live high, that's the only way to make certain your partner can go on enjoying the same life-style. Nothing odd about that. And yes, the premiums have been regularly paid, on time.

"But here's why your question is an interesting one," she went on. "The marriage broke up last year. No divorce, just a separation. But Ellen has kept up the payments on her insurance policy on Rowse, with herself as the beneficiary. Since the separation, I don't do Rowse's books. So I don't know if he's kept up the payments on the policy on her life, with himself as the beneficiary. But it wouldn't surprise me if he has."

She said this with a touch almost of accusation. Implicitly, she was perhaps hoping that Rowse could somehow be nailed for Bergman's murder. That would spring David Smith out of prison, the man she seemed to still have feelings for.

As for me, I could kick myself for being a bit sloppy. How come I hadn't cottoned on to the hook-up of Ellen and Rowse? Granted, he hadn't been around when I visited their house. That could have been for any number of reasons: he could simply have been out for ten minutes – whatever. Still, you're supposed to keep alert for all possible clues. Looking back, I realized that when I'd talked to Ellen Rowse, formerly Bergman, she hadn't spoken of Rowse with any discernible warmth.

Grinstead added, eyes narrowed with mistrust (of Rowse, not of me), that Rowse perhaps was a threat to Ellen's life, so long as he was her insurance beneficiary; which he would be if he kept up the payments. So, if I had any way to check on that, she could give me the file-number of the policy and the name of the insurer.

I thanked her, and she did so on the spot. She had come prepared. I forbore to tell her the reverse was also possible: if Ellen was keeping up the payments on the policy on Rowse, with herself as beneficiary, she in turn might constitute a threat to Rowse's life.

It reminded me of the old adage Mr Agostino had dinned into me, time and time again, when I started in on investigative work.

"Follow the money. Just follow the money."

I acted on it right away. No difficulty tapping in the relevant file. One of my Dad's forensic accountants had a pipeline into the insurance company. It took him a few days, but he did come up with an answer. Yes, the policy was still valid on Ellen Rowse, premiums were fully paid up, and Jack Rowse was the listed beneficiary.

In ordinary social behaviour, I always think it's discourteous when people drop in unannounced. What it says is, in effect, drop anything you're doing: it can't possibly matter, compared with having me walk in the door.

Conversely, in investigative work, the unannounced visit can sometimes pay dividends: you can catch people off guard, if they have some reason to be *on* guard.

So that was in my mind when I rang Ellen Rowse's doorbell.

When she answered the door, I reminded her who I was. Could I please have a few minutes of her time? I needed to talk to her about something that concerned, seriously concerned, her personal safety.

She let me in. We sat down in the living-room.

"Mrs Rowse," I began, "since we last met"

She interrupted me: "Just call me Ellen," she said. "My marriage to Jack Rowse doesn't exist anymore. 'Mrs Rowse' was alright last time you called. But things have gone badly sour in the last few days, and I'm thinking of going hack to my maiden name, which happens to be Wainwright. But 'Ellen' will be fine. What was it you wanted to tell me about?"

"Well, I have to risk sounding melodramatic, but this actually is a matter of life and death. Or it could be. I'm sorry, by the way, that your marriage went on the rocks. These situations can be extremely painful. And sometimes they have unforeseen consequences."

"That's true."

This was said cautiously.

"All too often," I went on, "separations or divorces get a bit messy over money matters. Now, I don't know what kind of arrangement you and Mr Rowse have for smoothing out such potential issues. That's really none of my business. But it does become my business when someone's life is at risk. That's anyone's business."

"So? How does that concern me?"

"It concerns you because Mr Rowse is the listed beneficiary of a life-insurance policy he holds on you, which would pay him a million bucks in the event of your sudden death. That's how it concerns you. And there's a very strong reason you should take that concern seriously. A while before you married him, Mr Rowse was under suspicion of having murdered his then wife. You must have known that about him."

As I was speaking, her attention never lapsed for a moment. History hung in the air between us, unspoken. Two suspicious deaths. And now, perhaps, a third being contemplated. As to the first, she could hardly pretend total ignorance.

"Yes, I knew that," she said. "But I never believed he killed her. Jack Rowse may have had his faults – and God knows I'm aware of them. But he isn't a killer. He doesn't have it in him."

"Easily said. But a lot of people have it in them, if pushed. Not just men, either. Women, too."

And as that commonplace passed through my mind, a variation occurred to me on the theme of Bergman's death. I'd figured on Rowse as the killer, with Smith as the fall guy. That had legs: Smith could be set up for it, but if suspicion fell on Ellen, she would be able, in advance, to create a watertight alibi for herself by being away, say in Montréal. However, if she thought the scheme of implicating Smith was really foolproof, she might have seen no need to arrange an alibi, or even to talk Rowse into doing the deed: she might have killed Bergman herself.

On second thoughts, though, that would have meant taking a stupid risk. Better she should have been out of town at the time of the murder, if she hoped to receive the big payoff from the insurance policy she'd taken out, clandestinely, on Bergman's life – as distinct from the policy on Bergman's life, with Smith as beneficiary, which had been taken out to protect the future of the business.

This was a tangled web that would somehow have to be sorted out. In the meantime, she had enough savvy to steer the conversation away from any explicit reference to Bergman's death: instead, she kept the focus on the ostensible reason for my visit.

"I don't get it," she said. "When Jack Rowse and I got married, we took out life-insurance policies on each other. That's something a lot of married couples do, I should think. You don't like to think of your spouse dying. But if you care for each other, you want to see they're looked after. But even if the marriage does go down the drain – which ours did – you don't have to end up killing each other. Besides, even if Jack did decide to bump me off, he wouldn't benefit from it, insurance-wise. Everybody knows you can't benefit from the proceeds of a crime."

Not everybody does, actually. Most people don't think about such things at all, unless they're planning to commit a crime and reap a windfall from it. But I held my tongue about that. Instead, I just stuck to the subject of his being a possible danger.

"It's not something to take lightly," I said. "You shouldn't just watch your back. You should think about perhaps applying to a magistrate for a restraining order against him. I might be able to help you arrange that. What's his current address?"

What I didn't tell her, of course, was that in the back of my mind I was considering the reverse possibility that Jack Rowse's life was in danger from *her*.

But when I asked for his address, I had not anticipated the violence of her response.

"74 The Bridle Path," she said, naming the ritziest neighbourhood in the city. Her tone was bitterly angry, its pitch vitriolic. "He's shacked up there with Sybil Grandsire de Boer."

I knew the name. Everyone does. She was the daughter of wealth and power in the person of Villem Grandsire de Boer, the billionaire magnate who'd made a fortune from South African diamond mines, amongst other enterprises; and she stood to inherit it all. But she was more than just an heiress. She'd inherited his drive and ability. He'd schooled her to follow in his footsteps; and in her mid-thirties she'd risen to CEO under his Presidency. On top of that, still single, she moved with ease in the upper-crust circles which, in our town, form the equivalent, money-based, of an aristocracy. She'd had a much talked-of affair with a federal cabinet minister (of Finance, needless to say), but had discarded him – no one was surprised: he was incredibly boring. After that, she could have had her pick of any man in the country. Given that, I was more than a little surprised that she picked Jack Rowse; and I said so.

"Oh, you have to hand it to him," she said. "He's always known how to rise in the world. Knows how to charm the birds off the trees. Worked with me, till I found out he'd screw anything on two legs, if it served his ambitions. Not bad for a janitor's son from the wrong side of the tracks. First he marries a kid from the stockyards, but dumps her for a waitress. Then he raises his sights and hooks up with middle-class me. And look where he is now: hobnobbing with the high and mighty, and living it up in the executive office she gave him in her headquarters. I hate him. I wish he was dead."

There wasn't much I could say to that – though I did store her last words in my memory, for future reference if useful. I extricated myself politely, and went home.

The following evening I decided to pay a call, unannounced, on the Bridle Path. Remembering what Jane had said, I got the .45 out of its safe, and put it loaded in the pocket of my raincoat. You never know what might happen in confronting a probable murderer. Not that I ever had.

My little old jalopy was certain, I thought, to be out of place in an environment of Rolls Royces and Ferraris, even if most of them were in their triple garages, not on display out in the driveway. Anyway, who would notice? It was dark already.

When I got there, surprise! The driveway wasn't empty. There were two police-cruisers in it. I parked on the road, at the end of the driveway, where I could see what was going on. One cruiser was empty. The other had two cops in it, just waiting, like me.

I didn't have long to wait. After a few minutes, the front door opened. Two cops came out, either side of a civilian, escorted him to the empty cruiser, and put him the back seat. It was Rowse. I recognize him from a photograph I'd procured.

The cruisers pulled out, and drove away.

Later, I got on the blower to Al, who fortunately was home. I told him I'd seen Rowse taken into custody. He told me Rowse was under arrest on suspicion of deliberate murder in the death of his previous wife; and the whole half-closed case was wide open again.

I thanked Al for getting into it so quickly. He said there was more going on than just that. He had put Stan Novak in the picture, and Novak was very interested in the possible implications for the subsequent murder of Sven Bergman. Maybe there had been a miscarriage of justice. Maybe the real perp was Rowse, and David Smith had somehow been set up as the fall guy. Novak couldn't quite figure out how Rowse might have contrived that. But it was definitely worth looking into.

Next evening, Al told me more. Under preliminary interrogation, Rowse had insisted he was innocent, but refused to answer questions until his lawyer arrived. When she did arrive – the formidable Claire Harris – she rather crisply told the police they didn't have enough to go on. There were no witnesses. No weapon had been found. His alibi had stood up in the original investigation.

"Maybe then, but not any longer," the interrogator had said – one Inspector Sharpless, whom I'd never run into. "Now," the Inspector said, "the witness has changed her statement about the alibi. She still says your client was with her that night, but that he went out at one point to get some more booze from a, bootlegger; couldn't say exactly when or for how long, because she was 'kinda out of it'. But that was enough to knock a big hole in the alibi."

"Not if the bootlegger corroborates it," Harris said. "Which I'm sure he'll be willing to."

"Think so?" from the Inspector.

"Don't answer that," Harris said.

But Rowse had looked glumly at his hands, and shaken his head. "Max is dead," he said.

That had been enough for the police to hold Rowse, pending further interrogation, and Harris picked up her briefcase and walked out, with a parting shot at Sharpless about proper procedure.

"Keep in touch, Mark," said Al. "This is getting interesting."

XIII

So I had plenty to tell Jane on our next lunch-date. She took it all in, with undivided attention, my own attention being equally given to the story itself and to her reactions – so much so, on both our parts, that we failed to give the meal its proper due: in fact, I can't now remember what we ordered; which is unfortunate, because I'm sure it was delicious. Mario didn't seem to mind, though. I'm sure he could see how deeply absorbed we were in each other. Romantic soul that he is, he probably ascribed that to young love; and he wouldn't have been wrong, at least in my case – I shouldn't speak for Jane. He would have been horrified if he could have overheard us; our discourse on bloodshed and guilt, to the exclusion of much else.

Most of the talking, to begin with, was done by me, with interpolations by Jane: questions and comments. When I was finally through bringing her up to date, with Rowse back in the cells, she leaned back in her chair.

"So, Mark," she asked, "how optimistic do you think we should be?"

"Hard to say. Naturally, there's reason for a limited kind of hope. At least this far: Rowse is quite likely to get nailed for killing his first wife. Where does that leave us? Here, I think we just have to wait and see. Just because he killed *her* doesn't mean he killed Bergman. It means he's capable of it. But proving he *did*, that's another matter."

Jane started to look a bit downcast. I tried to reassure her.

"My hope is," I said, "if he's convicted for the first murder, they might be able to put pressure on him to confess to the second one also. Especially if they, or we, do a bit more digging around and find a few things that point in some way to his possible guilt."

"I see." Rather flatly. Then, more spiritedly, "He sounds like a perfectly horrible man. Pity they can't nowadays put him through the old third degree to make him confess. But then," wistfully, "we don't live in Russia under Putin, do we?"

"No, we don't. And I don't think either of us would enjoy it, if we did. He seems to have taken a big step backwards to life under Stalin. Do you know what Stalin's favourite third degree was? Sleep deprivation. It usually breaks a man in about three days."

"I know, and there's nothing new about that. The Brits invented it, more than four centuries ago. I found that out when I first started researching Southwell. It was one of Topcliffe's favourite tortures. The others were straightforward physical pain: like stretching a prisoner on the rack, or hanging him by the wrists from a hook on the wall until his shoulders dislocated and then, *leaving him hanging there like that*. Stubborn ones, in that agony, still refused to talk, to betray other people. But no one could withstand sleep deprivation: the limit was two weeks."

A look of hero-worship and fury rose in her eyes.

"Except Southwell. He lasted forty-two days and still wouldn't speak. So they had to give up on him. His only response – and coming from him, it was the ultimate condemnation – his only response, in the end, was to turn to Topcliffe and say quietly 'Master Topcliffe, thou art a *bad man*'. I must say it gives me satisfaction to know that Topcliffe died stark mad."

"And that was when? When the torturing happened?"

"1595. So the Tower of London got a jump on the Lubianka Prison in Moscow by four hundred and twenty years."

She paused.

"But let's turn to a more cheerful subject. Here comes Mario with a surprise."

I looked up. Mario was advancing upon us, carrying a cake, which he proudly announced as "Poles di carota con mascarpone di calce, how you say, carrot cake with lime cheese." Stuck in the top was a lighted candle.

"Buon compleanno, Marco," he said. "Happy birthday!"

I stood up, and he gave me a hug and a kiss on both cheeks. Then, tactfully, he retreated.

I grabbed Jane and hauled her to her feet, and embraced her with all my heart – and she, manifestly me. That took a little while. Four Italians at the next table burst into applause. That would never have happened in an Anglo restaurant: ours is such an inhibited, tight-lipped culture.

Then we sat down.

"Blow out the candle," Jane said, "and make a wish."

I did that. Not out loud. But I think she knew what my wish was.

"How did you know?" I asked. For it was, in fact, my thirty-sixth birthday.

"I looked you up," she said, "You know, you're not the only researcher in the family."

XIV

I hadn't wanted Jane to get her hopes up too high. After all, her father was still, officially, a convicted murderer. And it would take a lot of investigation and a lot of luck to prove that someone else had committed the crime.

As it turned out, however, we were lucky. Almost right away, there was a fantastic turn of events that connected the two murders in a way nobody could have foreseen. It was the sort of maelstrom situation when an unsuspected twist complicates what had seemed plain: where former confederates turn on each other; where malice outweighs prudence.

And here I have to say how constantly I'm amazed at the way some people, planning the perfect crime with convoluted cunning, blunder into failure by simply allowing themselves to indulge a spur-of-the-moment emotion, instead of sticking coldly to their scheme as planned.

For that was what Ellen Wainwright, as she now called herself, allowed herself to do. Regardless of consequences, she walked into a police-station, demanded to see an officer connected with the Rowse investigation, and volunteered a statement incriminating him. Her motive, almost for sure, was spite. But that was beside the point. What counted was what she said.

Rowse, she said – and she signed a statement to that effect – Rowse had told her he had, in fact, killed his first wife. She had forgiven him, because he'd fed her a convincing line about what a bitch his wife had been.

(Incidentally, in the aftermath, I looked into this. I contacted family and friends of the dead woman, who had been so bad-mouthed by Rowse: they all spoke highly of her; none of them had a good word to say about him.)

Under further interrogation, Rowse broke down, and responded with retaliatory viciousness.

"She should talk!" he said of Ellen. "That's really the pot calling the kettle black. What makes you think she's so goddam pure?"

They knew enough not to interrupt.

"You remember that case ten years ago, when a fellow called Bergman, Sven Bergman, got himself killed? Well, he was her husband. And she was the one responsible. Knocked him on the head with a hammer, and fixed it so it would look like his partner did it."

"That's garbage," Ellen said, separately interviewed. "Rowse did it. Sure, he fixed it to make it look like the partner was responsible. But that just shows what an evil bastard he is. I've no idea what his motive was. Maybe killing had just become a habit with him."

Back and forth it went.

"Motive!" Rowse exclaimed, when told what Ellen had said. "Christ, if you're looking for a motive, take a look at her. She'd taken out a life-insurance policy on Bergman for a million bucks. And they had to cough up when Smith was convicted and she couldn't any longer be a suspect. That's how come she fixed it so Smith would have to take the rap."

"Nice idea!" Ellen countered, sarcastically. "But it won't wash. On the night in question, I was in Montréal, and I can prove it."

Facing an obviously certain murder conviction over the first killing, Rowse admitted his guilt over the second killing, too. It made no difference to him: he'd be going in for life anyway. But admitting it gave him the opening to get back at Ellen.

"She cooked the whole thing up in the first place," he said, "for the insurance money. Gave me her key to the premises. Told me where to find the hammer in the workshop. Told me to wear latex gloves, so as not to leave my prints on the hammer, or any place there like doorknobs – whatever. Okay, so she was away in Montréal. But she might just as good have done the job herself, when you get down to it.

"At least she did give me half the money," he added.

There was nothing Claire Harris could do for Rowse. He'd sunk his own boat. Ellen's, too, for that matter.

XV

I was not present, of course, at any of these conversations. They took place behind closed doors in police interview-rooms. But Al told me all about them. He also told me Rowse had been formally charged with Bergman's murder, and Ellen with conspiracy to commit that murder.

I shared this at once with Jane. She immediately contacted Irving Wolff. He, in turn, applied to the court to have David Smith released on bail, pending Rowse's and Ellen's trials. Ostensibly, his release was so that he could be retried for the murder of Bergman. But implicitly it was understood that Smith would be exonerated if Rowse was convicted. Wolff was sure of it; and his partner, Ross Burton, started laying plans for a suit against the police and the government, demanding compensation for ten years of wrongful imprisonment.

Meanwhile, on the day Jane's father was released from the penitentiary, a small group of people gathered there to greet him, and to congratulate him, as he emerged. Right there, at the exit, were his immediate family: his still sturdy mother (at eighty-nine), his sister (Aunt V), and Jane. I held back at a small distance, with the two lawyers (Al couldn't be there as he was on duty), so as to give family members first chance to welcome him back to the land of liberty. I was glad we did so. It was a moving thing to see them reunited. But then David, as I now thought of him, spotted Irving and Ross. He came over and gave them a big hug. The atmosphere was more than just cheerful: it was exuberant.

Then Jane came over, took me by the hand, led me over to David, and introduced me to him.

"Dad," she said, "this is Mark. I've told you what he's done for us these past few weeks. I don't know what we'd have done without him."

He shook my hand warmly.

"That's terrific," he said. "Jane's shared some of the things you've done. They mean a lot to me. They're important."

"Well," I said, a bit embarrassed, "it's an important case. Injustice needs correcting any time it happens."

"Somebody has to think so," David said. "I'm glad you do. But I hope this doesn't mean we're seeing the last of you, now this business is all cleared up and tidied away."

I certainly would have responded to that. But Jane beat me to it.

"Absolutely not, Dad," she said. "It doesn't mean anything like that at all. You'll have to get used to having Mark around. He's become very important to me."

That said, we all piled into waiting cars, and left for a pre-arranged lunch at Mario's, all by ourselves: he'd closed the place to other customers for the whole day.

The vintage Frascati sure hit the spot.

XVI

From his multimillion-dollar settlement, David insisted on buying Jane and me a house as a wedding present. So here we are now, in a two-storey abode, not far from the university. In the basement, next to the furnace-room and the laundry, are two rooms, formerly extra bedrooms, which we have converted into two dens. One is Jane's, and she has nearly completed "Robert Southwell and John Donne: two images of exaltation." The other den I use as an office for my work, but with a difference now. I still do the accounts for Hortensia (aka my grandmother-in-law) and a few other elderly widows who need some help. But I've given up the vanity press, as I said I was going to: it never did sit well with me; let others do service to such conceits. By way of more reliable income, I've gone back to work for my father's firm, not full-time but on a contract basis, as a forensic accountant; my sleuthing skills pay off well in that role; and there's a certain moral satisfaction to it. Innocent parties get hurt, sometimes badly, in the wake of fraud; justice demands the fraudsters be tracked down: and in some cases it's even possible to get the losses recouped.

As to the non-fiscal sleuthing, I still hang on to my license as an investigator; but I only make use of it now and then. No regular jobs as a private eye, up for hire in the sordid world of ordinary crimes, like larceny. Occasionally, though, I do still hook up with Irving and Ross, in their continuing campaign to exonerate and free the unjustly convicted.

Other things have changed for me, too. Where once was a somewhat directionless loner, scurrying in three different directions to make a life for himself on his own, there is now a happy family man with a settled career; and as I write this, Jane is pregnant.

No child can ever replace Louise. But this child, along with Jane, will be anchor for ever in a future solid as any man could dream of. Thanks to whatever gods there are.

SARGENT
an exhumation

for Anton Frisch
poet, ally

PROLOGUE

Who was Eleanor Sargent? And what was known of her life and personality? Not much, apparently. There was only one article about her, published almost fifty years ago; and it was sketchy, as dry as a gravestone. Mind you, its author, Ivor Prentice, didn't have much to go on. She'd done a pretty good disappearing act. How do you write about someone who leaves no personal trace, who seems to have existed only in what she wrote? And what she wrote was never about herself. Or so I thought.

This much I did know. Eleanor Sargent was born and raised in an obscure Lincolnshire village called Yarburgh in 1875. That basic information was recorded when she was admitted to hospital in Lincoln in 1913. Listed as next-of-kin were her father, the Rev'd Barnabas Sargent, and her mother, Martha. Neither parent's name was on record in the Visitors book; but visits were recorded, occasionally, by her brother, Geoffrey Sargent, and regularly by her sister, Dame Edith Sargent, OSG. The final item in Eleanor Sargent's case history was the date of her discharge from the hospital, in April 1920.

These bare facts, but not much more, were known to Prentice, who wrote his article following the publication of her last book in 1955. All her books until then, and that one, were published under her initials, ES; and she had made it known, through her publisher, that she wanted no personal publicity while she was still alive. That preference was readily respected: she wrote scholarly works, not sensational novels; so reporters were not hammering at her door, seeking interviews.

Prentice's posthumous article, in the *London Review*, was entitled "The Almost Anonymous Eleanor Sargent." He was moved to write it as an admiring reader of her seven books. They were all on classical subjects, Greek and Roman; and he himself, as a classicist, was intrigued by the self-effacing author, whose "Brief Lives" (she borrowed the title for her series, allusively, from John Aubrey) were launched upon the world to stand or fall on their own merits, regardless of who had written them.

Gaining access to some of the letters she had sent to her publisher, Prentice learnt only skimpy facts: that she had won a classics scholarship from the Louth grammar-school to the University of London; that after graduation she had taught Latin briefly at Stroud Ladies College; that she had suffered "ill health" for several years; and that she had ever since led a completely private life in a Cambridge flat, going out only to shop or do research in the University Library, and seeing no one other than her brother, on one of his trips south from Glasgow, where he was a ships' architect, and her sister, on one of her frequent visits from Saint

Athelwold's convent in Alvingham, where she was a Gregorian musicologist.

Beyond that, Prentice learnt nothing. ES had led a life of virtual solitude, and of a silence broken only by her books. Apparently, he said, there was nothing else to know, or at least to discover. And he was so impressed by her determination to hide, in a kind of anonymity, that he felt obliged to look no further – even if he had had the investigative resources to do so. Indeed, he simply acknowledged the value of her books, and he suggested that their few and specialized readers should continue to respect her wish, that the books alone, not their author, be of interest to them.

As to the books themselves, he confined himself to describing them and extolling their merits. Offered as partial portraits of seven classical authors, and none of them lengthy, they were an idiosyncratic mix of narrative prose, interspersed with passages of translation, and critical assessment; each of them ended with a poem inspired by the subject, written in free verse, the modality inherited from France and then well established in England by Eliot and Pound.

Prentice did not consider himself qualified to assess Sargent, or anyone else, as a poet, though he did admire Eliot and was rather condescending to the earlier and blustering talent of Whitman. However, as a classicist himself (MA Cantab 1920), he was fascinated by Sargent's Greco-Roman portrait gallery. As he noted, the portraits were only partial. There was no attempt to survey the whole of an author's oeuvre, but only a particular aspect of it or, in some cases, of one particular work.

Typical of this approach was Sargent's book about the poet Ovid and two of his major works: the *Amores* and the *Metamorphoses*.

The *Amores* was, essentially, a "how to" book, a manual for lecherous men eager to seduce equally libidinous women. It had offended the delicate sensibilities of nineteenth-century prudes in England. But such reactions were by now passé: Lytton Strachey had debunked the *Eminent Victorians* in 1918; and Sargent, writing a few years later, even though born in 1875, did not shy away from the realities of lust. She did, however, find an oddly similar puritanism in Rome, under Augustus, when Ovid was writing. The Emperor was, she observed, a blatant hypocrite: he paid lip-service to the ideals of the Pax Romana, but had no scruples about shedding blood in the pursuit of power; only when he won power did he become self-righteous and institute a regime of enforced obedience to moral orthodoxy. In such a climate, the poet best equipped to gain imperial favour was Virgil, whose *Aeneid* was a toady's homage to empire. Ovid's *Amores*, by contrast, did not merely cock a snook at the paraded rectitude of life among the privileged; it also reflected the actual libertinism of that life, even in the inner circles at court.

That was certainly enough to earn Ovid marked disapproval from on high, especially since the *Amores* proved to be very popular with the reading public. But with the *Metamorphoses* he went too far: he mocked the state religion. In fifteen satirical volumes, with sly irreverence, he retold the legends of the Olympian gods and goddesses, sparing no details of their sordid behaviour. Chief among them, of course, were Jupiter and Juno, partners in incest and baneful to human kind. Jupiter comes across as an obsessive sexual predator, who repeatedly disguised himself to commit rape. Juno is portrayed as a virago of jealousy, who vented her ire on his victims, transforming them into cruel absurdities, like a cow or a laurel-tree. And all this Ovid related, entertainingly, with sardonic wit.

Augustus was not amused. He banished Ovid from Rome to distant exile in Bithynia, on the Black Sea. There he languished for the rest of his days, grieving.

So touched was Sargent by this that in her *Ovid*, as Prentice read it, she gave great weight to what Housman had earlier called "the land of lost content." In him, Shropshire was just a metaphor, a stand-in for the heart's geography mapped in sorrow and, be it said, in lingering adolescent self-pity. In Ovid, Rome was a treasured reality, bitterly withheld. Sargent perhaps lay somewhere in between. If Prentice thought her being so clearly gripped by the subject reflected some pattern of similar loss in her own background, perhaps in rural Lincolnshire, he did not say so. Indeed, he had no information on which to base such a speculation.

In another book of Sargent's, *Euripides*, as reviewed by Prentice, there was no attempt to survey and weigh the whole canon of nineteen surviving plays. Instead, she chose one of his plays as springboard for her own text. *Iphigenia in Aulis* dramatizes the legend of Agamemnon's sacrifice of his daughter, Iphigenia, to win the blessing of the gods on his expedition against Troy. Euripides was no jingo-enthusiast for Greek imperialism. Elsewhere, in *The Trojan Women*, he had pulled no punches in portraying the tragic effect of war on women's lives – something that must have keenly affected any woman writing in the nineteen-twenties, as Sargent did, a few years after the first world war. In what she then wrote on the subject, according to Prentice, she argued strongly from a pacifist standpoint; but in his remarks on that, he saw no special significance in her having seen the start of the Trojan War as template for the outbreak of all other wars, or in her having singled out the killing of Iphigenia as ruthless presage of the carnages to come. What Prentice did not even hint at, nor could he in the absence of evidence, was the possibility that Sargent's response to Agamemnon's treatment of his daughter was somehow rooted in how her own father had treated *her*. This may never have occurred to him. He showed no sign of armchair psychologizing, of looking for Freudian phantoms under every bed.

He concluded his article by paying tribute to Sargent as a marginal but worthy classicist, little read any longer in an age that had little Latin and less Greek, and also perhaps as an unjustly neglected poet. He left it at that.

And so, for several decades, did history.

***

I came across Prentice's article, quite by accident, in 2010, when leafing through a back number of the *London Review*, specifically the issue of February 26th 1938, in search of a review by Douglas Cleverdon of David Jones's *In Parenthesis*, which had won the Hawthornden Prize back then. It is, in the opinion of many, by far the finest book to have emerged from the first world war, at least in the English language. And I was very struck when first reading it in 2005, because my own father had served amid similar carnage in the second world war. What he and other veterans went through inevitably affected their children and even, in some cases, their children's children. I was, if you will, a ripe candidate for what David Jones had to say.

Anyway, in unearthing Cleverdon's review, I turned the page and there was Prentice's article on Eleanor Sargent – whom I'd never previously heard of. Its presence there was, in a way, an apposite juxtaposition. For as I read it, I realized that here was reference to an author tangentially in tune with Jones. He had summoned up the ghosts of soldiers serving in battles long ago, even of Socrates in the Peloponnesian War. And Sargent, in her turn, had glimpsed, through Euripides, the killing-fields of even earlier armed conflict, in the war waged against Troy: the blood shed for no good reason; the collateral pain.

This was a mystery, and Prentice's article did nothing to enlighten me. I couldn't find out anything more about her in person. Trying to track him down, I found out he'd died long since. Nobody else could still be alive, after so long a time, who had known her. All I could do, apparently, was get hold of her books and read them.

That in itself wasn't easy. They were all by now out of print, and her publishing firm had disappeared from the scene years ago. I did a computer search for her in all the reputable second-hand bookstores. No dice. Last resort, of course, in such situations, is a chair in the reading-room of the British Library. Reputedly, they have everything. So there I went, and they came up trumps: all seven books.

One at a time, I read them all. Liked them. Respected them. And despite her silence about herself, her insisting on what Prentice had called her almost anonymity, I could read between the lines and get a feeling for the kind of person she was. Wanted to know more. But couldn't get to her.

Then on the morning of September 28th 2012, I was reading *The Times'* death notices after breakfast – a morbid habit of mine, daily – and the name Sargent caught my eye.

> Sargent, Edwin, peacefully on September 20th, in his hundred-and-third year, at his residence in the Alamein Veterans' Home. Military service 1939-46: front-line combat duty in France and North Africa included commando reconnaissance behind enemy lines; awarded MC, seconded to Bletchley 1944; promoted Lt Colonel 1945 and appointed to denazification duties in Germany; demobilized 1946.
>
> Pre-war career as Special Correspondent for *The Times* in Germany 1931-8. Re-appointed 1946 in London as foreign affairs commentator and editor. Retired 1982.
>
> Predeceased by his wife Kate (née Trevelyan), by his son Philip and his daughter-in-law Lauren (née Roberts), and survived by his granddaughter Emily Willoughby (née Sargent).

This was brief and to the point, consistent with the dignity of *The Times*, unlike the more elaborate and often gushing obituaries printed in the popular press. If this military man had been Eleanor Sargent's nephew, and the Christian name, temptingly, pointed that way, the brevity and lack of biographical detail were consistent, too, with the "anonymity" of his putative aunt; if Eleanor actually *had* been his aunt, I had to find out.

In hierarchical societies like England's, much depends on whom you know. The art of advancement, or even of survival, is pulling strings. Everyone has to have a network. Mine is fairly unimportant. As a Latin teacher in a snob school (Latin is defunct in the state schools), I'm not likely to make much of a mark in the world. Fortunately, though, I'm not infected with the ambition to do so. But I'm not above using a connection when someone owes me a favour.

One such someone had swum into my orbit in the person of Lady Millicent Armitage, the mother of one of my students, a fifteen-year-old handful called Jessica, who excelled at tennis and rock-guitar, but struggled to get any further in Latin than the present indicative of the verb *amare* – though in what she called "real life" she gave precocious indications of mastering its future tense in both the active and the passive form.

Jessica was scraping by, just, in other exams, but her Latin marks were abysmal. Any merciful academy would have allowed her to drop the subject. And certainly ours was a merciful school – some would say to the point of laxity. But Jessica's father, Sir Dennis, was not to be budged from his insistence that she "buckle down and man up and knock the bloody stuff sideways." He was a blustering man who had survived many disciplinary canings at public school, where he had been an all-round cricketer of some promise. But for all his blimpish traits, he did have a winning sense of self-deprecating humour. "If a chap like me," he bellowed, "can get the hang of that amo amas amat gobbledygook, *anyone* can. So," he said to his wife, "find someone extra to pump the stuff into her. She's not a fool, you know. A bit of hard work won't do her any harm."

So Lady Millicent hired me to coach Jessica in extra sessions on her own. And lo and behold, she wasn't a fool at all. She made terrific progress. In regular classes, not just mine, she had tended to slack off, and to make snotty, impertinent remarks. But none of that surfaced in her private sessions. It was as though she needed only individual attention to respond positively; and once that clicked, she got right on with the job. In effect, she started to take herself seriously and get results – in other subjects, too, I heard.

Lady Millicent was duly impressed, and grateful. "I don't know how you did it, Miss Jackson," she said, "but the improvement's absolutely amazing. My husband and I can't thank you enough. If there's anything we could do to show our appreciation, you be sure to let us know."

"As a matter of fact, Lady Millicent," I said, "there is one little thing Sir Dennis might consider..."

I trailed off, a bit embarrassed.

"Yes?"

Her husband, I knew, was Chairman of the Board of Directors of *The Times*.

"Well," I said, "I know Sir Dennis is a sort of power behind the throne at *The Times*. I need to find the address of the woman who submitted last month's death notice of Colonel Sargent – you may have seen it. He was something of a war hero. But the Obituaries department said that kind of information was strictly confidential. Do you think your husband might consider getting them to bend the rule just this once? I only need the address so as to contact her for some literary research. Apparently that woman's the only surviving relative of an obscure but rather important writer. Do you think he might?"

"Absolutely he might. Absolutely he will, if I have any say in the matter. You know, Miss Jackson, Sir Dennis isn't really the ogre some people think he is. Sure, he has a rather bluff manner that rubs some people the wrong way. But underneath that he has a genuinely kind heart. And there's a lot more to him than everyone realizes, including quite a good brain. Why else would you think he'd get involved with *The Times*? No, I'm sure he'll do what you suggest – and be glad to."

And he did. Promptly. On my computer:

edith willoughby, flat 4, 12 st peter's road, chiswick, tel 68432.
many thanks and best wishes. da

Equally promptly, I acted on his help.

Dear Mrs Willoughby,

It was with great interest and, of course, with appropriate sympathy, that I recently read, in *The Times*, the death notice of your late grandfather, Colonel Sargent. Please accept my sincere condolences.

The reason for this letter is academic – I am head of the classics department at Cotton's – but it is also, in a way, quite personal. I have come to admire the now little read author, Eleanor Sargent; to admire her as a writer and to like what I can sense of her as a woman. Not much seems to be known about her: she guarded her privacy fiercely. But she certainly deserves to be more fully known and understood than is the case.

It seems to me possible that she was your great-great-aunt – that is, your grandfather's aunt. If I am right, then you are probably her only living direct relative. If that is so, I would dearly love to come and see you, to ask if you have any family records of her life, or any recollection of family stories about her. It would be a real service to English literature if you could cast some light on the subject.

If it turns out that I'm wrong, and that you have no connection at all with Eleanor Sargent, the writer, then please forgive this intrusion into your life, especially at a time when you must still be grieving over the loss of your grandfather.

Yours sincerely,

The response was almost immediate.

She phoned and said Yes, she was Eleanor Sargent's great-great-niece, and would I please come round and see her, perhaps for tea next Saturday? She had a pile of stuff to show me, and lots to talk about. Maybe four o'clock?

I took a taxi, to be sure of finding my way to St Peter's Road, and arrived on time, at four. Flat 4 was on the second floor, up two flights of a large Victorian house, converted into apartments. Emily (we were instantly on a first-name basis) let me in, apologizing for her husband's absence: he was away on a business trip. She had tea ready; and after a few pleasantries, we got right down to brass tacks.

She looked to be about my age, mid-thirties, good looking, well dressed. I'd looked up her grandfather's pictures on my computer, both as a centenarian and as a much younger man. There was a clear family resemblance, though I couldn't guess if that would also be apparent in her now acknowledged great-great-aunt Eleanor – I'd never seen a picture of her, and didn't know if one even existed.

"That's Grandad," she said, pointing to a framed photograph on the mantelpiece. It was a variant of the older one I'd already seen online. "He was a great old guy, and I saw a lot of him. As you know, he lived to be a hundred and two, almost three. And life must seem a bit lonely when you get to that age. Especially in his case: he'd lost Grandma, 'way back in 1989, and then both my parents were killed by a drunk driver on New Year's Eve 1995 – that's their photograph next to his on the mantelpiece. In the end, he'd outlived all his friends and colleagues. I was the only family he had left. So I saw as much of him as I could. Not just out of a sense of duty: I was very fond of him. We didn't have a whole lot in common, given our age difference – I mean, for God's sake, he was born in 1909. But for all that, he was a very decent man; and I'd say, lovable."

"How long did he live on his own? *The Times* said he was in a retirement home."

"Yes, he was. But not till he was ninety-nine. And that's why I need to talk to someone like you. You see, I had to look after the move for him, when he finally gave up the house. Getting rid of almost everything, one way or another, except the few sticks he could fit into his retirement suite, and a few odds and ends he really cared about. That was, you could say, Step One. Then, after he died last month, I ended up having to clear away what was left."

"That's a hard thing to have to go through." I said, dreading having to face the same job when my own parents' time is up. "Especially if someone's affairs aren't completely in order."

"Well, luckily Grandad had everything tickety-boo, as he used to say. He even drafted his own death-notice for me, so I wouldn't have to bother filling in all the details – only the date. Trust a military man to respect good order and discipline. Not that he was a career soldier, mind you. Just fought in the war, and stayed on for a little afterwards. But what he'd learnt in the army, about doing everything just right, stayed with him in civilian life as well. And when it came time to bugger off, as he put it, he'd got everything tied up and ready for me in a neat little package. Literally a package. He'd put all his bank account and tax information in a single, explicit file. In a separate file were all the documents pertaining to his own pension and his state pension. In his so-called 'death' file was his will – he left everything to me – and a signed certificate forbidding medical efforts to prolong his life in the event of mental incapacitation; also a signed statement requesting immediate cremation and no religious funeral – he had never been a. churchgoer. He'd told me in person I was to do whatever I liked with his 'things.' Keep anything you fancy for yourself, he said, and anything else just donate it to a war veterans' home or any other charity you like to support."

It all sounded well thought through, even a bit cold-blooded. But that was only because it had to be efficient. Yet behind that efficiency was a clear mind and a sharp conscience. He was not about to leave a mess in his wake, for someone else to clear up, let alone his granddaughter who had cared about him in his old age.

I said so.

"Oh yes," she replied. "I never saw it as bloodless. To my mind, it was a sign of true affection, full stop."

Her eye wandered off to a corner of the room. On an old fashioned mahogany desk, perhaps his in the house he used to live in, was a sizeable plastic box, maybe fifteen inches by eight and some ten inches deep. She went over and brought it back to where we were sitting, put it down on the coffee-table, and opened.it.

"This is why I was so glad when you got in touch with me. It's full of stuff Grandad had kept forever. Said he hadn't the heart to throw it out, but couldn't think of what should rightly be done with it. Me neither: I can't. Maybe you can. You say my great-great-aunt Eleanor was kind of important as a writer. So this stuff here may have some value. You be the judge."

She pushed the box over to me. It was a treasure trove.

Inside were old photographs of Eleanor (at last!), of the Grandad's father, Geoffrey Sargent, and of his sister, Dame Edith Sargent, OSG, looking conventionally devout in her habit, but with the hint of a more than merely pious mind in her eye. Eleanor's face, as a young woman and then in middle age, was thin, her expression drawn and withdrawn, as though clamping down on some contained sliver of ice. It was at once the face of someone ambushed, and of a refugee. Exile, I thought: here was a woman who'd known serious loss, cast forth from the certitudes of trust; but one who yet plodded gamely on, through narrow passes of disquiet.

Also in the box, in higgledy-piggledy disorder, were letters to each other from all three of them, all mercifully dated. Also a year-by-year set of diaries kept by Dame Edith, plus a copy of a privately printed history of her Order. Also several diaries kept by her brother and by his son, the Grandad. Also typescripts of the seven books she wrote, with source footnotes interleafed that were not included in the published texts. Also handwritten drafts of the poems which concluded all of the books.

Emily wanted me to have the whole box: for study and evaluation. Naturally I was agog to have it. But first things first. I told her of course I'd be delighted to think about what should best be done. The materials, though, were all rightly hers, entrusted to her by her grandfather. The only proper approach would be for me to catalogue everything, to photocopy it all, to store the originals in a safety-deposit box, and then turn myself loose on the copies. Further, I added, we should work out terms of agreement, covering her ownership of the actual materials and my role as a researcher and literary adviser; and we should have the agreement formally notarized.

"I know," I said, "this all sounds like we're turning something human into something heartless, something aseptic. But we just need to get the formalities over and done with first. Then we can concentrate on sorting out what this all really means. Believe me, I'm not some pedant all wound up in red tape. Actually, I'm excited as all get out. Okay?"

"I guess you're right," she replied.

And poured me another cup.

ARCHIVE

Excerpt from "Domus: preliminary history of a Gilbertine house"; privately published, 1960.

September 20th 1953

It was with both sorrow and rejoicing that we this day laid to rest our beloved Prioress, Dame Edith: we sorrow in the loss of that great soul, so long enriching our lives; we rejoice for her that now her music has gone home, to join her voice to the eternal praise.

Edith Sargent came to us as a postulant in 1893, aged seventeen, and took her final vows three years later. Thus, at the time of her death, she had spent six decades in professed religious life. She will be remembered with affection and admiration by all who knew her, as long as any of us continue here. But in the longer term, her musical legacy will live on in this community, and perhaps in others, beyond any cession of the mortal flesh.

That legacy was well described publicly, beyond these walls, in 1936, in an article printed in the spring issue of the *Church Quarterly*. It seems appropriate, in the year of her death, to reprint it here, in fond recognition of what she achieved in her working life.

"The Anglo-Catholic renewal of the last century initiated, in many ways, a striking rejuvenation of faith and practice within the Anglican communion. Famously, or some would say notoriously, it re-introduced the mediaeval accoutrements of divine worship: the placing of candles on the altar, the use of incense, vestments in the seasonal colours. But these were only the surface aspects of revitalization. More profoundly, there was change of stance: in parishes, especially in urban ones, came commitment to a mission to the poor; and for the first time in four hundred years monastic life was reborn.

"In convents, male and female, whether active or contemplative, devout rites were resuscitated, and in them Gregorian music was sung once again. That made necessary an adaptation of the Latin chants to English texts; and sterling work was done, to answer that need, in new editions created at St Mary's Wantage and published by the Plainsong and Mediaeval Music Society.

"However, there was a problem with them, discerned and solved by a nun in Lincolnshire, where the Gilbertine Order had been refounded. Sister Edith Sargent is a musicologist who saw the technical flaws in the Wantage chant-books. The editors had contented themselves with a simple and somewhat pedantic approach. They imposed the English words on the notes, syllable by syllable, without regard for the intrinsic dynamics of English, which differ markedly from the dynamics of Latin. The result (to quote a glaring example) was to inflict on the second, weak

76

syllable of *blessed* a cadenza sometimes as long as ten notes: this had been acceptable originally on the last syllable of *benedictus*, which in good Latin pronunciation can bear that kind of weight; in English it is ridiculous.

"Sister Edith's answer is quite radical. In the first place, she regards such musical ornamentation as self-indulgent, as contrary to the fundamental nature of good plainsong. Chant at its best, she is convinced, was composed for the honour of God, not for the satisfaction of its composer or the delight of its singers; and that aim could be achieved only by knitting together note and word with proper respect for their mutual values and their true intention, but with no desire to create art for art's sake. To that end, she took as her motto, Simplify, Simplify.

"Without in any way bowdlerizing the ornate chants, or ignoring the essential purity of their melodic line, she pruned them of their excesses. At the same time she is scrupulous about the underlay, making sure that the natural rhythms of the music and the text match, are not at odds. The result is a set of chant-books used by her own community throughout the liturgical year.

"These labours took a long time. But the fruit of them has ripened only locally. Sister Edith's chants are sung in Alvingham alone. Their chanting, in her convent, may be said to constitute, as it were, an Alvingham Use. But there the matter ends. She has no wish, apparently, to engage in some kind of critical warfare with St Mary's Wantage. Moreover, as befits her calling, she seems content to work anonymously; none of her plainsong predecessors attached their names to their work. If the work was good, they implicitly said, it should be judged solely as made to the glory of God, not for the repute of anyone who wrote it down or uttered it. Sister Edith belongs in that fair company."

So much for what the *Church Quarterly* had to say.

Concentrating, as it did, on her musical exploits, the article drew no larger picture of Sister Edith's life and work. But there was much more to her than just music. Dame Edith, as we came to call her, led a very full life as an Anglo-Catholic religious. So it is only proper that this little History should take that into account.

Born in 1876 and raised in the flat, reclaimed land of the Lindsey Marsh, she was the second daughter, and third child, of an Anglo-Catholic priest, Father Barnabas Sargent, long-time Rector of St John the Baptist's parish church in the village of Yarburgh. The whole area, so far as it was Anglican, was strongly Anglo-Catholic, under the influence of Edward King, the rejuvenative Bishop of Lincoln. So young Edith grew up steeped in the culture of that faith: St John's is a superb fourteenth-century building; the mediaeval rites resumed there (the Mass and

Vespers, the Blessing of the Palms, the Stations of the Cross) fitted it like a glove. Small wonder, given such a formation, she felt a vocation to the cloister.

In late-Victorian England, staid and insular, such a calling must have seemed bizarre and somehow impertinent. Especially in a girl. Conventional thinking posited no proper future for a young female except as wife and mother or, failing that, as respectable but family-dependent spinster. Nunneries were for Papists, preferably across the Channel. And even to many Catholic-minded Anglicans, convents were thought of more as refuges for pious widows or reclusive mystics, than as fit destinations for teenage girls.

It is not known how far, if at all, Edith's vocation was fostered by her parents, for among us she seldom spoke of her father and mother. But we do know she was encouraged in it by her older sister, Eleanor. Top marks in the village school gained her further study at the nearby grammar-school in Louth; and there she excelled in Latin, History, and English. Musically gifted from an early age, she became a sterling member of the Louth choir, and showed a seemingly instinctive aptitude for Gregorian chant. By the time she was seventeen, nothing would do, for her, but the habit and the veil.

Nothing stood in her way, either legally or from family objection – though there is some suggestion that Father Barnabas acted a bit grumpy. But on October 15th, St Teresa's Day, she was received into our community, and entered into a religious life of uncommon devoutness, hard work, and imaginative fecundity. Her consecration as a novice was attended solely by her brother, Geoffrey Sargent, Esq. Her sister, Eleanor, was away, with apologies for her absence, having won a scholarship to read classics at University College, London. There is no record of her parents having been present. We draw no inferences from that: it may be that parish duties got in the way.

Letter to Sister Edith Sargent, OSG, from Eleanor Sargent, dated October 20th 1893 from University College, London

Dearest Edith,

I think you know how truly sorry I am not to have been with you on your Great Day. May God be with you on the road that lies ahead.

During the last twelvemonth, you have been very gracious in expressing to me a measure of gratitude for the support I've tried to give in defence of your religious aspiration. Your thanks are immeasurably meaningful to me. But that aside, you have also hinted at a strange doubt about what perhaps lay behind that supportiveness. Even you wondered, in puzzled fashion, if I might be wanting to send you away. Oh, Edith, nothing could be farther from the truth! To me, you are the dearest person in the whole world. If I had had my way, nothing would have pleased me more than to have you with me, sharing a happy home life. Sad to say, however, our home has not been the happy one it ought to have been. Geoffrey and I bore the brunt of that, as best we could; and we always tried to save you, as the youngest, from as much exposure to it as we could. That, though, was a burden on our minds and hearts.

Then, last spring, Geoffrey received offer of an appointment in Glasgow, in the profession of his choice; he will take it up in January next. At the same time, I was awarded the scholarship to London, for the term beginning two weeks ago. With Geoffrey departed, all too soon, that would have left you alone in Yarburgh, in unprotected misery. Oh Edith, dearest Edith, I could not bear the thought of that. I would have forgone the scholarship, to stay at your side. Abandoning you would have broken my heart.

However, perhaps God willed otherwise – and better. There had grown in you an absolute conviction that the one and only place you could completely belong in was a convent. Your heart was set on the novitiate, with the Gilbertines, and I believed the choice was genuinely right for you. Nobody could tell me otherwise. I've seen it growing in you, that calling, for years.

Papa was reluctant to let you go. But he could hardly forbid it, given the fact of his priesthood. I backed you up, and so did Geoffrey. And for once in her life, Mama spoke up, too. It is the only time I have ever seen Papa overruled. Not that he saw it as a defeat: that would have been a blow to his pride. So instead he pretended it had been his own idea in the first place.

As for me, dearest sister, I must confess your going did seem to be for the best, all around. Like Geoffrey in Glasgow, I will escape the narrow vale of tears in Yarburgh: the University will open a door for me onto a larger world, one I have dreamt of with a longing parallel to yours for the infinite world of Heaven. Greece and Rome beckon me like a lover, even if I do end up teaching Latin in some school. But even at that, Edith, at least I will have escaped.

So will you, though escape is surely the wrong word in your case. Yours is not a flight from, but a journey towards. It is not one I could ever join you in: my calling is elsewhere. But with all my heart, I wish you Godspeed on every step of the way. Blessings upon you!

I mean that from the very depths of my soul. Do not think me selfish or self-serving, sister mine, to be seizing the chance that has come my way, I would have let it go, if you had had to stay behind. As it is, all three of us will be free; and of the three freedoms, yours will no doubt be the finest.

If the rules of your novitiate permit, do write to me often.

Your loving sister,
Eleanor

February 14th entry in the 1896 diary of Sister Edith Sargent, OSG

St Gilbert's Day. High Mass at nine, our Chaplain as Celebrant. Afterwards, to Mother Superior's office. She assigns me a new duty. I'm to study chant interpretation. Why me, I ask. Well, child, she says, you're the only one here who can read chant notation when it gets elaborate: the rest of us do well enough with our simple psalms and hymns, by guess and by God you might say (she has quite a wit, our Mother), but our liturgy falls sadly short of where it should be; we need to raise it up to a higher level. She pushed a pile of books across the desk. The complete Wantage edition of all the music for the Mass and the Offices, year-round. Bids me pore over them in all our study hours, and write to Wantage for instruction, on how to explore the subtleties of all those dots and squiggles on the page, and then how to make them live out loud. So perhaps next May, on Founder's Day, we can give St Gilbert the Mass he deserves, *singing* his Introit and Gradual and so on, instead of just speaking them. I'm appointing you Assistant Precentrix, she went on – under obedience, of course. She paused, then added, You look rather pleased. Oh Mother, I exclaimed, this is extraordinary: I've been longing for something like this. Not for myself, of course, I added with seemly haste. Just because our Praise is so impoverished without our being able to serve in full... how shall I put it... the beauty of holiness. Thank you with all my heart. Don't thank me, child, she said, thank the Lord; and get on with the job. So I knelt to kiss her ring, and scurried off back to my cell with a huge armload of books. What a day!

Copy of contract signed between Eleanor Sargent and the Stroud School. Saxony le Wold, Lincs

This document will confirm an agreement made to engage Miss Eleanor Sargent, BA, as resident Latin teacher and teacher of Ancient History. Her duties are to commence at the start of the autumn term in this year of grace 1896, and subject to satisfaction will continue on a permanent basis. Miss Sargent is to be paid a stipend of ninety guineas per annum, paid quarterly, and will in addition receive full board and lodging on the premises. During school holidays she may continue to reside at the school, if she so wishes, but will at such times be responsible for her own board. Jointly signed this first day of August 1896, by Matilda Higgins, MA (Oxon), Headmistress, and Eleanor Sargent, BA (Lond)

Letter from Geoffrey Sargent to Eleanor Sargent, mailed from Glasgow and dated February 4th 1901

My dear Eleanor,

News from the North. As you know from previous letters, Master-builders Shipping has been very good to me. They've promoted me more than once, and assure me of a golden future. Well, now they've been good to me again! I expressed to them the desire to have a leave of absence, in order to serve Queen and Country in this dreadful war that has broken out in South Africa. Not only did they commend me for that and promise me my job back when I return, but also they arranged for me to have a commission as lieutenant in the Scots Greys. So in a fortnight I'll be on my way, all kitted out and ready for adventure.

I do wish, most earnestly, that there was time for me to come and visit you, and perhaps Edith too, to bid you farewell before I go. Alas, that will not be possible: I'm to report tomorrow at the regimental barracks in Edinburgh, for outfitting and two weeks of training. Then, with no embarkation leave, I take the night express to London and ship out from Tilbury Docks first thing in the morning.

So, for a while, I'll be far away, though not out of touch. I'll write whenever I can – fondly, for I think of you and Edith all the time, and always have since the three of us left home and went our separate ways.

Most people, I suppose, in such a dispersal, would look back on memories of home with a sort of wistful nostalgia. I can't say I do. Nor, I believe, do you. Edith, no, I can't speak for her. Somehow there seemed to be a kind of unimpaired innocence about her, despite all the Rectory's goings-on. As for you, I've always been glad you found your way to an independent life while still young enough to assert yourself.

Asserting ourselves never came easy, after all. Papa, to put it civilly, was never an easy man to live with. Spare the rod was not in his vocabulary, at least not where a boy was concerned. You girls, so far as I know, just had to put up with the harsh side of his tongue. Both of you, and Mama as well. And there, I must confess, if he had ever laid a hand on Mama, whatever people say about filial duty, I would have thrashed him within an inch of his life, once I was big enough to do so. As it was, he simply dominated her with a nasty line of contempt. We are well out of there.

Does it shock you that I am now so outspoken about all that? When we were growing up, we held our tongues – better, we thought, to create our own silent refuges: you in scholarship, Edith in her music, and I in that fleet of model ships I built, up in the attic. How shocked the parishioners would be, if only they had known!

But that's behind us now. Looking back, I reckon that I was the one who had it easiest. Going to the Louth boys' grammar-school as a boarder opened my eyes to a world less prone to sourness, with wider horizons. I used to feel sorry that the girls' school did not take boarders, so that the two of you could only be day pupils and were stuck at home, with a two-mile walk back and forth every day between Louth and Yarburgh. Added to that, I was always sorry, for your sake and Edith's, that our Mama was such a muted, fearful person. Girls should be able to turn to their mother for help and comfort whenever the need arises. The two of you could not. At least now, you're free of that deprival. You have a settled career which, by all accounts, you enjoy. And Edith, I gather, has found in her Abbess someone who truly deserves her title of Mother Superior. May we all flourish!

Meanwhile, dearest Eleanor, I must be off. I'm writing to Edith, too, to say goodbye. And I know that your thoughts and prayers will be with me wherever I go.

Lovingly,
Geoffrey (2nd Lieut!)

Letter from Sr Edith Sargent, OSG to Eleanor Sargent, August 7th 1901

My dearest Eleanor,

Last Sunday was the fifth anniversary of my final vows. It was a solemn moment in my profession. Almost like a seal on my heart, it ratified the original decision to dedicate my life, wholly, to God and this community. After Mass our Chaplain Father Andrew joined us for Recreation, which we had outdoors in the garth, because it was such a beautiful day. He brought with him one of those new-fangled box-cameras – you may have heard of them – and took a picture of Mother Superior and me sitting on one or our benches. I felt a bit embarrassed: we aren't supposed to set any store by appearances. But Mother said I shouldn't feel badly about it, seeing it was a special occasion; and anyway, she said, she also was in the picture herself, so "what was good for the goose was good for the gosling, too"; so that was alright. Rather a neat twist on an old saying, don't you think? Anyway, though, keeping it would somewhat smack of personal vanity; so I'll send it to you as a little keepsake.

 With much love,
  Your sister in Christ,
   Edith

Reply from Eleanor Sargent to Sr Edith Sargent, OSG, August 14th 1901

My dearest Edith,

 A heartfelt thank you for the photograph. It is beautiful, and I will always treasure it. When we are both old women, I'll look at it every day and say, "Hello, little sister mine, nothing has ever changed, we're still just as close as when we were young together long ago."

 That closeness, of course, stems from growing up with such mutual reliance on each other, and from our having such a likeness of spirit. To others, we may seem to be quite different, you in your cloister and I in my so much more pedestrian circumstance. But it's really only a superficial difference, isn't it? Underneath, we're very much the same. At least, I hope you won't think it frivolous of me to pair your vocation and my calling in the same breath. For I do think of my commitment to a life of poetry and study as similar, in its own way, to your pursuit of God.

 I've been thinking about that a lot, of late. There are you, in Alvingham, leading a life rooted in ancient usages – the veil, the horarium, the chant. But yet, at the same time, you modernize: in music, you take a Gregorian heritage and transform it into a message for today; and in your mission to the poor, you do not hide away in token charities, but go out actively, rather, into where the needs of an afflicted world must be met.

 Mine is a parallel case. Schooled in antiquity by no less a sage than Professor Housman (who is much finer a classicist than he is a poet), I may give the impression of being someone landlocked, so to speak, in a pedantic world of dead language and literature. But for me, ancient history for ever comes alive: its truths have resonance in our own inhabited time; and if I'm to be an historian, that conjunction must be the crux of my life. And if, too, I'm to become the poet I aspire to be, I cannot content myself with the automated recipes of Mr Yeats, with his wishy-washy moonings in iambic gossamer. No, that will never do. Rather, I must throw the whole raw ore of metre and rhyme, etcetera, into the crucible of actuality, and somehow mint a new coin of language that will speak a timely truth. This will not be easy. As yet, I am merely fumbling towards it. But that, dearest

sister, is the path I must journey on – as you journey on yours.
As always with love,
Eleanor

Extract from South African war diary of Geoffrey Sargent. September 15th 1901

For several days now, I have not had the heart to write a single word in these pages. Since I arrived here in the Transvaal, I have been too distressed, nay appalled, by what I found here: the misery, the hunger, the illnesses, the inconsolable sense of loss, whether of freedom or hope or human dignity – and all this inflicted, in equal measure, on men, women, and children.

In all the wars of history, while they are being waged, it has been necessary to detain captured soldiers in prisoner-of-war camps, lest they return to the fray. Clearly, in this South African war, the same need would apply: captured Boer soldiers would have to be detained, somewhere, rather than turned loose, especially since they have recently become so adept at guerrilla tactics. But we have gone much further than that, under Kitchener.

He has not been content merely to imprison Boer soldiers captured in battle. He has rounded up Boer civilians, from the farms and villages and small towns, and herded them into so-called "concentration camps," like this one here, where they languish half-starved, ill-housed, and lacking any medical attention. I am ashamed for us. This is no way to treat innocent people.

Innocent? Yes – or so it seems to me. What have the elderly, the women, the children done to deserve such abuse? Perhaps some blame can be attached to semi-governmental nationalists in the Boer territories: they felt threatened by British imperialists next door; and certainly it was they who launched the first offensive. But the retaliatory counterattacks by the British, however provoked, cannot be said to justify their brutality to civilians. Nor were the "concentration camps" the only atrocity of ours. Kitchener applied a scorched-earth strategy in the Transvaal and the Orange Free State, to bring the Boers to their knees: he destroyed their farms, despoiling the land and leaving it to rot; and expelled those living there holus-bolus. I am not proud to have served under him.

To begin with, of course, I knew and understood nothing of this. When I answered the call to arms, I was both ignorant and naive. The British Empire, I believed, was God's gift to humanity: if some of its subjects got uppity, like the Boers, they should be put in their place. I should have known better: I was living in Glasgow, where everyone knew what the English had done to the Scots – just as we had to the Welsh. But like most of us, I swept that history under the rug. And nothing opened my eyes when I took the field. It was so straightforward, so black and white: they were the enemy, we had right on our side. Even when I was wounded, my only thought was to get back in there alongside my men.

However, that was not to be. You don't get over three bullets in the leg and walk back into battle the next day. They shoved me on a train to Cape-Town and put me in hospital, for surgery and recuperation. It was time well spent: in a sense, I grew up – thanks to Jakob de Vries, my surgeon.

Jake, who is totally fluent in English, opened my eyes to the situation of the Boers. We used to play chess after supper and then yarn away through the evening. His chief interest was in world politics; and he had an extraordinarily balanced mind about it, especially on the subject of empire. Imperialism, he said, was the great scourge of history. Time and again, empire-builders had crushed other people under the heel of greed. For that was what it was all about: armies marched in and seized land that belonged to others, grabbed their goods, and quashed their rights. On the face of it, he insisted, glory was what impelled the conquerors: in fact it was rapacity – always: from Caesar to Barbarossa, from Cortez to Napoleon, they made a desert, as Tacitus put it, and they called it peace.

He shook me. I'd been raised with such a blind belief in what we English called the White Man's Mission. No one I knew ever questioned our right to colonize, or ever suggested our real intent was plunder. Yet once the cat is out of the bag, as the saying goes, there's no stuffing it back in. I was crestfallen, obviously. But we're all birds of the same feather, Jake said: you English and us Dutch, here in South Africa – not to mention Belgians, the French, the Germans, and the Italians elsewhere in Africa, or the Portuguese and the Spanish in South America. What we all have in common is a huge appetite for wealth purloined abroad. What is never mentioned is the cost to a native populace. You don't have to look any farther than Cape Town here, or Pretoria in the Transvaal, to see a subjugation of natives into serf-like roles, in the mines and on the land. That is a moral problem no one seems willing to address. Indeed, as rival overlords, we simply compete for access to the country's riches – hence the current war.

The remarkable thing about Jake de Vries was that he didn't take sides. There was I, his patient, sworn enemy of the Afrikaners, and he never tried to put our conversations on the level of antipathy. Rather, he kept his discourse (for I was mainly just the listener) on the higher level of objectivity. In effect, what he talked about all the time was Justice. So he had me rethinking everything I had previously valued. I'd volunteered, rather tritely, "to serve Queen and Country." But now I was in a quandary. What cause was I actually in service to? And how should I comport myself when my wounds were healed, when they called me back to the front line?

That was an awkward dilemma. My luck was that I was reassigned to a non-combat posting. I must confess it was a great relief, and one I'm not proud of, that I didn't have to take a stand, one way or the other. I said as much to Jake. And he said that wasn't exactly so: where I was being posted would, in fact, give me a chance to act on humane, unbigoted values. Nothing need stop me.

He was right, of course. They posted me here, to take over command of this concentration camp. There was no way I could reverse Kitchener's round-up of Boers, let alone his scorched-earth policy. But at least I could try to mitigate the suffering behind the grim barbed wire.

It won't be easy. The place had been run, since it was opened, by a platoon of guards under a sergeant-major, who was now recalled to combat duty. Under him, and reflecting his rather brutish attitude, they had turned a blind eye to the semi-starvation, to the foul living conditions, to the gravely inadequate shelter. That all had to be changed.

So, to begin with, I cooked the books. Citing a serious clerical error, I indented for extra food supplies, alleging there were almost twice as many prisoners as originally reported. Along with better rations, I indented for waterproof tents in large numbers, plus materials and instructions for decent latrines and showers. I demanded the posting of a medical orderly from the RAMC, and of a bilingual teacher who could offer optional classes in English for the prisoners, and compulsory classes in Afrikaans for the guards. In addition, I made it obligatory for the guards to treat the prisoners courteously, addressing the men as Mynheer and the women as Vrouw, and helping to organize games for the children.

To my gratification, the guards responded well. It was as though they were relieved to shed the overbearing mien they'd worn under the influence of Sgt-Major Angus McMurtry. With him gone, some of their natural Scottish good-heartedness came through, a sympathy with others

86

who had suffered expropriation like their forebears in the Highland Clearances. I'll not pretend that everything now was sweetness and light. How could it be? These people had lost their homes, their land, their farms. In all likelihood they were going to lose their sense of themselves as a nation. Their only hope, and mine is that this horrible war will end with some kind of reasonable settlement. That cannot come too soon.

Letter from Eleanor Sargent to Geoffrey Sargent, October 5th 1902

Beloved Brother,

What a joy it was to have you back again, sound in body and mind! All too brief a stay in Stroud. I wish you could have stayed longer. Perhaps you can come again at Christmas. Meanwhile I shall think of you in Glasgow, building ships once more, just as you did at home when we were children. I'm so glad they kept your job open for you. Indeed, that is only right in view of your war service, and that they should offer you, as they have, a significant promotion.

Geoffrey, it is very touching that you should have given me your war diary to read. We have such a bond, you and I. Reading it, I realized yet again how our thoughts and feelings run so clearly along parallel lines. And by the way, my dear, you write extremely well.

As you know, that's my ambition, too: to write well. In hope of that, I spend much of my time in the evenings doing preliminary research for my projected Lives – all of them portraits, as I've told you, of classical authors. But here's a strange coincidence: you mention Tacitus in your diary, with particular reference to his sardonic comment on Roman imperialism – this in connection with your friend de Vries's view of the British Empire, a view which, I may say, is as valid as it is uncommon. Anyway, your Tacitus reference just happens to chime with my own current reading; for Tacitus is to be the subject of my first Life, and I am enthralled by the muscularity of his mind and the pungency of his Latin. Interpolating passages of translation will be quite a challenge.

Of course, some may think this project dry as the dust that long since settled upon the ancient Greeks and Romans, I hope they are wrong. For what I most hope to offer readers is something independent of period, bridging the gulf of years. For the eternal verities, as they are some-times pompously called, are recognizably as true in the present day as in the mists of antiquity. To portray Tacitus, for example, is to portray a stunningly modern man, as modern as Mr Bernard Shaw or Mr Joseph

Conrad. If I can capture that timeless acuity in Gaius Cornelius Tacitus, I will place him irrevocably among the immortals whose special gift it has been, in any age, to scrutinize the contemporary world with an unflinching eye.

If anyone, Geoffrey, your friend de Vries would relish Tacitus, I think. For surely courage was Tacitus' mark: to live under Domitian, that most vicious Emperor, was dangerous for any liberal-minded citizen; but at the same time it was outstandingly brave, perhaps even foolhardy, to write about imperial power and policies as a critical historian, without toeing the official line. But then, maybe he only wrote secretly, and did not try to publish until after Domitian's death. If so, that could account for the fact that so much of his work was lost – though everything suggests that most of the losses came later.

There's a lesson to be learnt here, I suppose. Dr Johnson (I think it was he) said that only a fool writes not for money. It's a cynical remark. To be sure, it's true of hacks. But a real writer, I'm convinced, writes first and foremost out of an inner need to do so; and if his work sells, the money is merely a bonus. Who knows if anything of mine will ever find a publisher? I can only hope for that. But this project of mine, these Lives, is something I just have to work on regardless.

Meanwhile, a devoted sister wishes her beloved brother all joy and contentment in a world now again, thank goodness, at peace.

Eleanor

Excerpt from the 1903 diary of Sister Edith Sargent, OSG, dated August 15th. Feast of the Assumption

What a day! This morning, at Mass, we rejoiced in the Elevation of the BVM into the hierarchy of Heaven, and sang our hearts out on the Wantage version of the Introit (somewhat re-edited by me), proper to the occasion: "Great is the sight that hath appeared in Heaven: a woman clad in the sun, with the moon under her feet, and twelve stars in a crown upon her head." Then, after Mass, by today's post came news that Geoffrey's wife, Marion, has given birth to a baby boy. He is to be christened Edwin. This is great news; for I should not like to think that we three Sargents would leave no issue. Obviously I will not. Nor does Eleanor, at least as yet, show any sign of venturing upon marriage. As for Geoffrey I have always been happy for him in his marriage, and I do not doubt he will be a fine father to his son. Indeed, I pray so. For in all charity I cannot say that our own father was a model of paternal benevolence. Ours was by no means a happy home. Of course, it is not for me to stand in judgment on others. Rather, we have a duty to try and understand what moves someone else to be cruel. Papa, I think, never got over the sharp disappointment of his early manhood, when his own father died prematurely and bequeathed the family fortune not to Papa as the eldest son, but to his younger brother, Uncle Augustus. That embittered him. Money notoriously can corrupt. But deprival of money can be just as corruptive. It is not as though we lived in poverty. By one of those anomalies in Church finances, his annual stipend in our tiny parish was seven hundred pounds, more than enough to send Geoffrey to the Architectural Institute and Eleanor to London University, even without her scholarship, whereas the Rector of the next parish had to scrape by on two hundred. Yet Papa, despite being as well off as a parson can hope to be, did begrudge Uncle Augustus his wealth. It tainted his life – and ours in consequence. So I hope and pray that Geoffrey, in the goodness of his heart, will raise his son with kindness and affection (I am sure he will) and thus put our family line to rights.

Extract and enclosure from letter of Eleanor Sargent to Geoffrey Sargent May 4th 1910, copy to Sister Edith Sargent, OSG

Dear Geoffrey,

There is a young American poet, T.S. Eliot, whom you may have heard of, now living in England. He does not yet have a book out, but he has been publishing his poems in the literary magazines; and they are causing quite a stir, breaking new ground. Critics have remarked on him as an innovator with two arrows to his bow. In the first place, they say, he evinces a striking modernism in attitude and content – no more pastoral ditties: he is utterly post-romantic. Second, some of his technique is exploratory in a way that is both radical and immensely refreshing: there are poems of his written in free verse which is not verbally licentious, like the rhapsodies of his fellow-countryman, W. Whitman; rather, they are diamond-hard, with a precision of language that puts our contemporary poetasters to shame.

Apparently some of this comes from his having lived in Paris, where he was much impressed by the French poets' experiments in *vers libre*; and perhaps, too, he has been influenced by the extraordinary experiments of the French painters recently. Whatever the truth of that (and all artists, however revolutionary they may be, are subject to like-minded influences), the fact is that Mr Eliot is a new voice to be reckoned with. Like all innovative artists, he has evidently mastered traditional technique before breaking, away from it: some of his work is in conventional rhyme and metre – though there is nothing conventional in what he has to say. But I take that to be merely a phase, a nod to his heritage. More to the point, he has moved on towards a technical vocabulary that will blaze a trail into an open future, cutting away the dead wood of mindless dumty-dumty-dum.

It is a dangerous precedent, of course. For it gives *carte blanche* to anyone lacking his talent, to toss overboard all established craftsmanship and spew out vapid torrents of emotional mishmash. But that cannot be helped. In a time of transition, led by genius, there are always hangers-on, who hitch their wagons to a star but end up on the rubbish heap of posterity.

Anyway, I'm rambling on about all this here, because Mr Eliot's recently published poems have given me not only great pleasure as a reader, but also a sense of justification as a writer. In the past few years, before ever a word of his saw print, I have been struggling to forge an utterance, in free verse, quite like his. As you know, from a couple of things I've sent you, I want to append an honorific poem to each of my Lives (all as yet unpublished, of course). And I will do so in the belief that open-minded readers can appreciate a double treatment of my subjects: on the one hand a biography in prose, as objective as scruple can make it; and on the other hand, a poem reflecting on the subject personally, in an attempt to probe its meaning or at least to plumb its feeling. If I've succeeded is not for me to say. But I do congratulate myself (such is the vanity of scribes) on having been, in private, a predecessor of Mr Eliot's now public manner.

You be the judge. I enclose my latest attempt in this genre. A few lines about Ovid in his exile.

Fondly,
Eleanor

BITHYNIA

It's cold here, on this bleak promontory:
gulls wheel and cry on the alien air,
oblivious of hope or history, shrewd
about seafood; at shore's edge,
solitary and adroit, the fisherman casts his net;
leeward on a jagged crag,
a scarred heart grieves, precise and apt
in hurt hexameters.
                    Home is not here:
across other and unforgiving waters
beyond reach Rome calls and calls,

alma mater, irreplaceable; but no miraculous wing
can soar me far and wide to rightness
beside the Tiber.
                    Oh, but the seven hills there,
how they rebuke the stare of these grim
Bithynian cliffs! This is no place for a life's
finale, its time defined by endless kalends
of memory and regret: disconsolate and alone
in these rude latitudes, I hanker for a lost
civility.

Entry in the first peacetime diary of Geoffrey Sargent March 12th 1912

These days I'm much and often reminded of all those talks I had, years ago, with Jake de Vries. I wish I had not lost touch with him. He had a lot to say, back then, about the rival imperialisms that had changed the face of Africa – not to mention other continents, too. So, in the light of that, I'd love to hear what he'd think of the current state of the world. Germany seems intent on becoming a major power, under the Kaiser, and is building up its fleet to rival the strength of our own. Britain's only response has been to engage in a naval arms-race. W.S. Churchill, at the Admiralty, has launched the commissioning of new battleships, on a massive scale. And I cannot but see these developments as presage of an imminent war. It disturbs me deeply. On the other hand, though, as a shipbuilder, I must confess I am intrigued by the specialist skill that goes into creating these vessels. I just wish their intent was not so grossly lethal.

Yesterday I was much pre-occupied with battleships and their meaning. But the day before had had a more civilian cast. I was in Belfast, visiting the Harland and Wolff shipyard, where the *Titanic* is almost ready to be launched. Indirectly I was involved in its building: our firm here in Glasgow contributed the giant gantry over the slipway, designed by me, and I was invited to come over and tour the now completed vessel – this by courtesy of her chief designer, William Pirre, who is now Lord Pirre but who started out as a mere apprentice draughtsman.

I was shown around by the general manager, Alexander Carlisle. He evidently expected me to be impressed by all the workmanship that has gone into her; and indeed I was – but was not so dazzled as he might have hoped. To be sure, I made all the polite noises. Yet inwardly I had some serious misgivings. Allegedly, she is unsinkable, and much fuss has been made over that claim. But is there no end to human arrogance?

Have we learned nothing from history? We men of the sea are fools to think ourselves masters of all that Neptune, in his occasional rages, can inflict on our vessels. Pirre seems to think destiny cannot imperil the strength and beauty of his handiwork. I pray he is right. But if he is wrong, I dread the outcome. On a tour of the upper deck, I quietly counted and appraised the lifeboats. Roderick Chisholm designed them, and they look pretty serviceable. But there are only sixteen of them! There were supposed to be thirty-two, but only half that number have been installed; and even thirty-two would be far too few to accommodate the number of passengers this huge liner will carry. That is, or should be, a fundamental concern. However, of even more concern, to me, is what I found below. Pirre has been publicly proud, nay boastful, of the five "watertight" compartments that can be guaranteed, he says, to keep her afloat, in the unlikely event she's involved in a major collision. Well and good if the bulkheads hold. But I've put together too many a steel-plated vessel, in my time, to take on trust the impermeability of every bulkhead; if the seams buckle, blind faith won't keep her afloat. So I asked Mr Carlisle who had overseen their construction. Apparently not he: he had merely handed down the blueprints to a minion I'd never heard of. This does not bode well.

Letter from the Rev'd Barnabas Sargent to Eleanor Sargent, August 2nd 1913

My dear Eleanor,

You will, I am sure, be sorry to hear that Mama has been stricken with a palsy. It fell upon her some twenty days ago, with no warning of its onset. Dr Morton has been in regular attendance, but the prospects are not encouraging. Apparently there will be no need for her to be taken into care: she can continue at home, and will be able to manage the primary necessities of life. That is to say, she can clothe herself, bathe herself, and so on; and she does not need to be spoon-fed. Beyond that, however, she will no longer be capable of carrying out her duties as mistress of the household. She will be unable either to cook our meals or even to shop for the necessary foods.

As you may imagine, this creates a grievous predicament for me. Two of the parish women have come to my assistance, in provisioning me and offering their services in the kitchen. But this cannot go on. Another solution must be found. Obviously this means that I must turn to you.

Daughter, ever since you left home so many years ago, we have seen almost nothing of you. I never wanted you to go – you know that. But as a university man myself, I could hardly forbid you the scholastic opportunity that came your way. But I did assume that after your degree you would return to us, and would take your due place at your father's side, until it pleased God to furnish you with a husband.

As you will recall, none of that eventuated. You have preferred the role of a Modern Woman. That, I suppose, is your right. Notwithstanding, circumstance may sometimes impose obligations upon one that may not fully accord with what one might otherwise wish. That is now the case. In the new circumstance, I have no recourse but to insist you return home. It is, in a word, your daughterly duty; and it should outweigh any attachment you may have developed to the career you have been pursuing at Stroud – no doubt the school will have little trouble in finding a competent teacher to replace you.

I trust you will respond positively to this request, preferably by return post. You should know, by the way, that there is now an efficient omnibus service from Lincoln to Alford, that passes through Yarburgh on its way. The fare is quite reasonable.

Papa

Telegram from Geoffrey Sargent to Edith Sargent, August 4th 1913

ELEANOR GRAVELY ILL STOP AM ON MY WAY TO STROUD STOP MEET ME THERE IF YOU CAN STOP LETTER FOLLOWS STOP GEOFF

Letter from Geoffrey Sargent to Sister Edith Sargent. OSG, August 9th 1913

Dear Edith,

Finally all is taken care of – or at least as well as can be hoped for, given the straits we have been in. Here is where we now stand.

First you will be pleased to hear that Uncle Augustus has come up trumps. As you know there had long been a severance between him and Papa, mainly over finances. He had all the money that Papa felt should rightly have been his; and Papa, I now gather, vented a sour resentment upon him which should have been directed, if at all, upon the Grandfather we never knew. Anyway, whatever the truth of that matter, Uncle Augustus has certainly set all old scores aside. I will not say that he and Papa have made up (Papa remains his old bitter self), but he has come generously to the rescue of poor Mama and dearest Eleanor. As he can well afford to do, I might add; for he has no wife or children, and has never squandered his fortune.

Thanks, then, to Uncle Augustus, Mama is now in a nursing-home in South Cockerington, where she is being properly cared for. The nurses are kindly, and a doctor is on call. He will try to improve her condition, though he opines that her condition is probably intractable. If she deteriorates, he will do whatever is needed. My own opinion is a little more sanguine. As a layman, I of course cannot pronounce on her future medically. But in human terms, she does seem to me well reconciled to her present situation, despite the physical impairment. Indeed, in a strange way, she strikes me as happier than I have ever seen her. This I can only ascribe to her having no longer to put up with Papa. We both know, you and I, how he has always treated her. I won't go into that here, nor do I need to. But it does not make for pleasant memories.

As for Papa himself, he will remain at the Rectory, continuing as incumbent at St John's. Uncle Augustus has installed, and will pay for, a competent housekeeper. So he won't starve, or want for domestic support. Almost, I fancy, this will give him a contentment previously lacking: he can give his full attention to the liturgical pre-occupations he sets such store by; and the rest of his time he will not have to bother with family life, which was never his strong suit.

But what of Eleanor? There is no improvement, and perhaps never will be. Let me recapitulate here, carefully, what I told you, hastily, on the telephone. (By the way, it was no surprise to me that so up-to-date a school as Stroud possesses a telephone; but I had assumed, wrongly, that no such new-fangled machine would have been installed in a quasi-mediaeval convent.)

On August 4th, Eleanor failed to appear for luncheon. In the afternoon, someone looked in on her, and she was found lying on her couch, unresponsive. The first thought was that she might have had a stroke. So they immediately sent her by ambulance to the local hospital, and contacted me by telephone – I was listed in their personnel office as the next-of-kin to be notified in an emergency. I cabled you at once, and took the night express to London, then on to Stroud first thing in the morning.

The hospital was baffled. There was no discernible sign of stroke. For example, the pupils of her eyes reacted normally to light. There was no paralysis of the limbs, nor any contortion of the mouth, and her pulse was normal; so was her blood pressure. But she seemed totally withdrawn. No speech. No visible interest in her surroundings. Almost wholly unreactive to anything said to her. She would swallow food if fed and could, if bidden, walk to the lavatory and, with help, would use it. There was no sign of coma, but all she wanted to do was lie down, or sit down, in silence: she seemed to have lost any kind of volition.

They had no idea what to do with her.

At that point, I notified Papa. The hospital people were a bit shocked that he showed no interest in coming to see her, especially when they learnt he was a clergyman. But then, they didn't know Papa. Uncle Augustus, when I contacted him, was by no means so heartless. Of course he would visit Eleanor, he said, as soon as she was recovered enough to see people. But first things first. To begin with, we must move her to a hospital better equipped to deal with such a mysterious case. If you can arrange that, he said, never mind the expense: I'll look after the money side of it.

What a decent human being, I said to myself! After all those years of disconnection, and of ill-feeling at least on Papa's part, here is someone pitching in for his niece's sake, when most people would just turn a blind eye.

Fortunately, the head doctor at the hospital near Stroud, a quite young man for such a senior position, reckoned he knew of just the right place – in, of all cities, Lincoln! Eleanor's case, he said, presents an unusual combination of clearly physical and possible mental disorders; and it needs to be approached from both standpoints. As to the latter possibility, we can no longer rely on nineteenth-century theorems and practices, which were largely based on guesswork and superstition. Rather, we nowadays can consult a new discipline called clinical psychiatry, which has obtained good results in treating what are called psychosomatic illnesses. The County General Infirmary in Lincoln, he told me, is in the forefront of this ground-breaking therapy. Accordingly, believing the matter should be seen as medically urgent and scientifically important, he arranged for Eleanor's admission at the Infirmary, and organized her immediate transfer by long-distance ambulance.

I came with her, of course. Dr Gavin Wells, the psychiatrist here, has made a preliminary diagnosis of Eleanor's condition. Apparently, she is in what is called a catatonic trance. Cases are rare, and unfortunately stubborn. But in order to treat them, it's necessary to discover, if possible, what triggered the patient's collapse. That is going to be difficult, since Eleanor either cannot, or will not, communicate. So he has to rely, to a large extent, on what he can find out about her from people close to her. Her colleagues at Stroud may, in due course, be able to shed some light. But to begin with, he wants to talk to family members and explore her personal history. In other words, he wants to interview us about her, at thorough length – in effect, you and me: Papa would be about as forthcoming as a clam, and poor Mama is in no state, just now, to be questioned; it would be too upsetting for her.

Do you think your Abbess would give you permission to come here for a few days? As I said on the telephone last week, you should probably stay put until I could tell you more about what had happened to Eleanor and how she was; and then, no doubt, it would be alright for you to pay a visit. But a more extended stay might be tricky for you to arrange. You should look into this and let me know what the chances are. At my end, there won't be any difficulty: I can simply avail myself of some unused vacation-days, and then let them know, in Glasgow, how soon I'll be back in the office, at my own convenience.

This letter should reach you overnight. After a couple of days, I'll telephone you to find out whether your Abbess will give you permission to come to Lincoln for a few days. If she does, let me know what hotel or other arrangements you would like me to make that would accord with the precepts of your convent. I do hope that permission will be granted. It has been long, too long, since we have spent any time together. Our two commitments, yours to religious life in Alvingham and mine to a career in Glasgow, have kept us far apart. But our mutual bond, and Eleanor's, remains steadfast, and always will.

Much love,
Geoff

P.S. Further to the above, about Mama, Uncle Augustus has revised his plan for her. Although quite satisfied with the quality of care in the South Cockerington nursing-home, he has decided to switch her to a similar nursing-home in Lincoln only two streets away from the Infirmary – all this, incidentally, at his own expense: Papa, seemingly, is indifferent to her fate. That indifference, of course, is only the milder aspect of long-standing abuse of her. So far as I know, he never actually struck her, the way he did me. But the withering contempt he held her in was outrageous. She never spoke up to him – was probably afraid to. But once she was out of there, she may have confided in Uncle Augustus. If she did, that may have been in part why he decided to move her to Lincoln: South Cockerington is only half a league east of Yarburgh: too close for comfort, if Papa ever took it into his head to burst in upon her and re-assert his so-called conjugal rights. As it is, Mama will be safe enough in Lincoln, from the rough side of his tongue or anything worse he might have in mind. And with her here, she can have visits from you and me, any time we're in Lincoln to see Eleanor – also visits from Eleanor, too, if she is ever well again.

Reply from Sister Edith Sargent, OSG to Geoffrey Sargent, c/o the County General Infirmary, Lincoln, August 12th 1913

Dear Geoff,

Thank you so much for your long and helpful letter. We will discuss all these issues in person, when I arrive in Lincoln. For yes, Mother Superior has given me her blessing for the trip – much more readily than you perhaps imagined. I'll be coming to Lincoln on the l6th, immediately after the Feast of the Assumption; which is rather appropriate, given that some sort of exaltation of poor dear Eleanor in this world or, if you will, a re-vivification of her, is what we must surely pray for. But more of that when we sit down together next week.

Meanwhile, there is one point you raise, though, in your letter, which I should address right away. You very kindly offer to organize accommodation for me in Lincoln, of whatever sort I might care to indicate. Thank you, brother, but it won't be necessary. Our Order has a subsidiary Priory in Lincoln, called Sempringham House; it is manned, to use an inappropriate verb, by six Sisters. A seventh Sister, from the Mother House, is to join them. We will be journeying to Lincoln together – it is our custom to travel in pairs – and I will be staying in their quarters.

As you know, I'm sure, the Gilbertine Order was founded in Lincolnshire in the Middle Ages and had dozens of Houses in the county, Alvingham being one of them. Back then, until the Dissolution of the monasteries in 1537, ours was a purely contemplative way of life. It still has been, since the Anglo-Catholic revival of the Order fifty years ago. But in recent years, under the present Superior, it has widened its scope, to welcome postulants with a more activist calling, while still welcoming those called, as of old, to the contemplative path. In an odd way, I seem to have a foot in both camps: my involvement in Choir plants me firmly, and fruitfully, in liturgical soil; but as an Anglo-Catholic, I am also drawn to a more active role in the world, and it will be intriguing for me to see the Sisters' work in Sempringham House, with their mission to the poor. Not that I have any specialized skills myself, in that area. But there is more than one way in which a willing person can lend a hand. Reverend Mother understands that, and she has shrewd insights into how that might work for me.

Go to Lincoln, child, she told me, and in Christ's charity do there what you can for your afflicted kinswoman. But I would like you to stay there a little longer than is immediately necessary. There is work for you to do, which you can and should do there, which will greatly benefit our Order, the outer world, and your own spiritual welfare. She bade me take my chant-books with me, and undertake a major re-editing of the music for the Mass.

I won't bore you with a long account of the complex technical details involved – the parallel, if you will, is that anyone can admire the beauty and efficiency of the ships you design, without having to grasp the technology you put into them. What it amounts to, in my case, is that the essential purity of our Mass music has been overlaid with excessive ornamentation, to the point where it loses its original meaning and instead draws attention to itself as a kind of aesthetic indulgence. I am charged with the task of restoring its lost simplicity. If I succeed, not only will our own liturgies recover their primal health, but also the revised and modest chants will be singable by ordinary parish choirs throughout the English-speaking world. I shall aim to give them the clean, uncluttered line that has always distinguished the fine vessels you launch upon the world's oceans.

But why in Lincoln? you may ask me.

Well, the answer lies in personal kindness, on the part of Reverend Mother. Next year, Sister Cecilia, our Precentrix (that's how we title our choir-director), is going to move on to other duties, as Novice-Mistress; and I'm to take over the choir. Her work has been valuable. But she is perhaps a bit set in her ways. She would be very dismayed, if it was decided that the Mass music should be tossed aside overnight, which she has taught and loved for so many years. Reverend Mother feels that when I step in to fill Sister Cecilia's shoes, I should introduce the new chants slowly and tactfully, one by one. That will give everyone time to adjust, and no one's feelings will be hurt.

Forgive me for carrying on about this at such length. But it does occur to me, tangentially, that hurt feelings are very much the order of the day, in our family. After all, there was frequent sorrow in our house, much of it buried in silence; and now it has come home to roost, in Eleanor's extraordinary breakdown. I am glad to hear, from you, that Mama has found solace in living on her own, with Uncle Augustus's help, and that she seems happier than before. In the past, as an adolescent, I used to blame her for never standing up for herself, or for us, in the face of Papa's bullying. Later, though, I did realize that victims cannot be faulted for what is done to them. I suppose, too, it is not proper for us even to blame Papa. Who am I to stand in judgment on another? Nevertheless, I cannot but think he must have played some role in what has now happened to Eleanor. If there has been an inner damage to her soul, only now erupting, then surely its origin must be in things which have impacted her. Your Dr Wells is probably right to interview the two of us, hoping to discover what might lie at the root of her condition. What may emerge in these conversations, I cannot guess. Obviously, I pray they will shed some light, and will point to possible treatment. We must wait and see.

Meanwhile, dear Geoff, I am looking eagerly forward to seeing you again. Our lives have gone in quite different directions. But the bond is solid, and it always will be.

As ever, with deep affection,
Edith

Entry in first peacetime diary of Geoffrey Sargent, Wednesday 18 August 1913

Yesterday Edith and I had our first conversation with Dr Wells; there are more to come. Edith had arrived on Monday, and it was splendid to have her in the same room again, after all these years. She seems happy in her life, and in good spirits over all, except of course over the sad state that Eleanor is in. I had made a copy of the letter to her from Papa, which was found on Eleanor's desk, and I showed it to her. She agrees with me that it is a truly shocking document: so shocking that someone as sensitive as Eleanor might well faint on reading it. Faint, yes. But her total collapse into a kind of living death, that is a bewilderingly extreme reaction that boggles the mind. We showed the letter to Dr Wells; and he, too, considers it significant. More than that, he will not say, yet. But he intends, in the next few days, to probe more deeply into Eleanor's home life; and he assures us that he will furnish us, eventually, with a full report on her condition, complete with diagnosis and prognosis, so far as these can be established with reasonable certainty. In the light of Papa's letter, he did ask if he might be able to visit him, in Yarburgh, and interview him as well as us. I told him that he was welcome to try, but that the most likely response would be a blunt refusal – quite a rude one, if I am any prophet. Edith thought so, too. Dr Wells then asked us about our own relationship with Papa, given that all three of us, he understood, had left home in early adulthood and had not sustained a cordial link with Papa ever since. Speaking only for myself, I said, I had been glad to go, and had never looked back on my early years with anything like pleasure or gratitude. Edith, for her part, spoke feelingly about her monastic vocation. She had left home at seventeen, and the convent had given her a refuge from the Rectory's paternal regime of spite and humiliation. And this was at your father's hands? Dr Wells asked. Oh yes, Edith replied. Papa was always ready to stand up in the pulpit and orate on the theme of God and Country; but his pronouncements at home fell, I should say, rather short of the gracious. In fact, Edith said, where cruelty to children is concerned, he might have done well to remember what was said on the subject by the Founder of our faith: Whoso shall offend one of these little ones, it were better for him that a millstone were hanged about his neck, and that he were drowned in the depth of the sea. Dr Wells, whose background, I imagine, was not ecclesiastical, was momentarily startled by the vehemence of that dictum. But he recovered his dispassionate poise quickly, and asked, was it the same for both of you? Geoffrey, here, had it the worst, Edith said, with Papa's cane: six of the best at the drop of a hat, for no good reason. I just had to put up with being either scolded or demeaned; or, if I was lucky, ignored – just like Mama. And what about Eleanor? he asked. Who knows what went on there? I replied. Sometimes I thought she was his favourite. But always there seemed to be a hint of tension between them. Maybe that was because she didn't like to be singled out as special, when he was so hard on us two others. Maybe it embarrassed her, I said. You're probably right, there, Edith said: I remember more than once he said to me, why can't you be more like Eleanor? Imagine how that must have made her feel. Dr Wells nodded, and closed his notebook. Let's leave it at that for today, he said; and we bade him Good-day. It was all civil enough. But neither Edith nor I felt at all comfortable dragging up old miseries. To be sure, the two of us have gone on to better times. And for years we believed that Eleanor had, too. Yet somehow a latent catastrophe must have been germinating within, waiting to bear bitter fruit. It is very sad. Later in the day, of course, we looked in on Eleanor, in her room. God, I hope Wells can do something for her. She's like a breathing corpse, void of identity. Edith started to cry; and I had a hard time not doing so myself.

Letter to Geoffrey Sargent in Glasgow from Sister Edith Sargent. OSG, in Lincoln, December 20th 1913

Dear Geoff,

This brings you heartfelt Christmas greetings, to you in especial but also, of course, to Marion and little Edwin – no longer now so little, I realize. I hope you all have a grand holiday, with more to follow at the end of the month, Scots fashion, with the Hogmanay festivities peculiar to your northern clime.

As you know, I am still in Lincoln, and have been to see Eleanor almost every day. Dr Wells encourages me to do so. He sees no change in her, and offers small hope for recovery. But he insists that Eleanor's is not necessarily a hopeless case. Catatonia has no known cure: all we can do is keep the patient comfortable. But that does not rule out the possibility of spontaneous recovery; it has been known to happen. So keep up your visits. And don't just sit there in silence, holding her hand. Talk to her, even though she doesn't respond. Tests prove she isn't deaf. For all we know, your voice, a voice she knows and loves, may penetrate a realm of hidden consciousness we know nothing about. Who can tell? Half of what we *think* we know about the brain and the nervous system is more speculative than demonstrated, and the rest's a mystery. Thus Dr Wells.

So I do go in, as I said, almost every day. I tell her about the goings-on in the outside world. Talk about my work. Even sing her some of the chants I'm working on. It's heartbreaking, the total absence of reaction: she just lies there, or sits there, neutered – she who was so full of life, with such an active mind. All I can do is pray to make a connection. And if I may say so I'm pretty good at praying.

Tomorrow, I'll be going back to the Mother House for the Feast of the Nativity. So will all the Sisters from Sempringham House. But the staff at the Infirmary will still be on the job, will tend to Eleanor with all the fond care that is their special Grace. I shall wonder if Eleanor will miss my voice. It will be interesting to see if there's any reaction when she hears my voice again in the New Year, after my being away. We shall see.

I know I'm often in your thoughts – I cannot say in your prayers, for I know you're not a believer. Yes, you went through the motions at St John's when we were young. But that was tokenism. For you, religion meant only religion as practised by Papa, an empty ritual in church, but an hypocrisy at home; you spurned it. Unlike me. I went in the opposite direction: all too aware of that same dichotomy, I made up my mind to enter religion with my whole being, to become the person that Papa so signally was not. At a glance, that would seem to make us real opposites, you and me. Yet I have never been able to look at it that way. For all your unbelief, I see in you, Geoff, one of the most good-hearted people I've ever known: a loving husband and father, and a dear support to me in all my endeavours. So it is with a full heart that I greet you on the coming Day. I shall remember you, of course, at Mass, as I always do. But in addition I shall think of you up north, living a different ideal of your own, with a family centralized on love.

Blessings!

Edith

Entry in the first peacetime diary of Geoffrey Sargent, February 11th 1914

In this morning's post, a long letter from Edith. She begins, of course, with the latest news of Eleanor, which is in effect no news at all, for there is nothing to report: the poor girl remains as she has been now for months, unresponding. It is so sad. And it must be especially hard on Edith, confronting it almost every day, trying to console, hoping for a break-through, and failing. I am in awe of her, of her stubborn generosity. But then, that's Edith: she has a heart as big as a house. In her letter, she goes on to tell me about her work, her daily labours on Gregorian chant. That is a recondite subject for a rationalist like me. But still, in essence, we are very much alike, she and I, at least in what we do: she seeks simplicity and efficiency in her music, and purity of line; and so do I, in every vessel I design. But there is a new and wider aspect to her life, now, since she has settled, albeit temporarily, in Sempringham House. There, she now tells me, she has begun to participate in the activism of the priory. Apparently, the Lincoln Sisters are committedly engaged in a mission to Fallen Women – as prostitutes are so loftily referred to by the sterner class of moralists. Not so the Gilbertines. They don't preach at those women, or harp on sin. Rather, they look for creative solutions. Prostitutes, generally speaking, have a destructive background: they come from homes plagued by drunkenness, violence, and all kinds of sexual abuse, including incest; above all, they grow up with only the barest education and no skills at all for earning a living. What the Gilbertines do (and it's very forward-looking) is place the women in a Home where they can apprentice in a marketable trade. This takes money, of course; but funds have been raised from sufficient benefactors. The results have been most encouraging. Women who have had nothing to sell but their bodies, now find themselves earning a decent wage and growing into a stance of self-respect. Edith writes to me about this, with touching warmth. And as I read what she says, my mind goes back more than a dozen years, to Eleanor's grand break-out from time-encrusted convention when she bent her will to an independent future: to a literary career, however unremunerative, which she would underwrite by taking jobs as a teacher. I have always admired her for that, and so has Edith. That such a career should be arbitrarily struck down, as it has been, is a perverse twist of fate. If I were a praying man, I would be hammering on the door of Heaven, demanding help for

Eleanor. Well, I can leave that to Edith, I suppose. It's something she's good at.

Feast of St Adelwold, Patron Saint of our House of God. This has been a festal day for all of us – and for me in especial. Mass this morning was the inaugural occasion of our new Propers. When I came home from Lincoln after Easter, Reverend Mother duly installed Sister Cecilia as Novice-Mistress, and appointed me Precentrix in her place. I had made a start on re-editing and simplifying the Mass chants – and will continue to do so for the next many years, God willing. By Reverend Mother's directive, I had made ready the new version of the Gradual for St Adelwold's Day, had rehearsed the choir, and we sang it jubilantly, without any wrong notes. Even Sister Cecilia, who was thought by some to be a bit of a stick-in-the-mud, voiced a generous enthusiasm. So from now on, one by one, and with no fear of old-fashioned resistance, I will be able to introduce the new chants as I get them ready. They will, I hope, strike a responsive chord with the young women who come to us as postulants: they are, or many of them tend to be, children of a new and Modern Age, who like everything straightforward and clean; which is, of course, exactly what chant achieves when it is not burdened with a whole lot of fussy ornament. I shall enjoy this assignment immensely, and Reverend Mother is fully supportive of my commitment to it. She also has been very kind in allowing me, once a week, to catch the bus into Lincoln, to visit Eleanor. Thanks to that, I will be able to stand by her loyally, until her death, if need be, or until, God willing, she recovers.

Entry in the second wartime diary of Geoffrey Sargent, August 4th 1915

Exactly two years ago this day, Eleanor fell into her trance, from which she shows no sign of recovery. Exactly one year ago this day, the trance of peace was abruptly dispelled with the declaration of war. Blind optimists said it would be over by Christmas. They were wrong. And that was not their only error: they were blind, too, to what war was really all about. Propaganda bemused them. They saw the whole thing through the blinkers of jingoism: Huns are the vile enemies, we had right on our side. What they failed to recognize was that this whole catastrophe was the product of greed – on both sides! We want to have an Empire, and profit from it; and the Germans want to build one, and profit from it. We sugar-coat the process with fine-sounding words. We speak of the White Man's Burden, the Gift of Civilization, and all that rot. But behind the rhetoric we are moved by one common magnet: in a word, loot. Sadly, I've seen all this coming, having had my eyes opened in South Africa, by Kitchener's use of concentration camps. And now this same Kitchener stares at us from every postered wall with his baleful glare and his rallying-cry of "England Needs You", his finger pointed at every man of military age who has not yet joined up. I detest the man, and I will not engage in slaughter at his bidding. Nevertheless I cannot sit idle. If other men are going to the trenches, for whatever misguided reasons, I cannot ignore their fate. A duty calls me to their side. I will not kill, I cannot. Long since, I resigned my commission. But I will go to the Front, in a private's uniform, to serve as a stretcher-bearer. My dear Marion supports me in this, and it will be dreadful to part from her and our son. But that cannot compare with what our boys are going through over there in France. I shall go to the Recruiting Office tomorrow morning and enlist in the Medical Corps.

Draft of Gradual and Tract for Holy Innocents Day, with appended footnote

Praise the Lord, ye children: praise ye the name of the Lord. They shed the blood of the saints, round about Jerusalem, and there were none who should bury then. Avenge, oh Lord, the blood of thy saints, which is poured out upon the earth.
> This version of "Laudate Pueri," musically revised and Englished, was first chanted in St Adelwold's, Alvingham, on December 28th 1916, in honour of the innocent blood shed that year in the fields of France.

Entry in the second wartime diary of Pte G. Sargent. RAMC, 10th April 1917

Yesterday was a fearsome battle. Vimy Ridge is a hill previously defended, successfully, by the Germans against assaults by various Allied forces. The latest assault was made by the Canadian corps, to which my unit has been seconded. It was successful, if success can be measured by the storming of about half a mile of shell-shocked wasteland, at the cost of several hundred lives – on both sides. What is it all for? I ask myself. Certainly there is no glory in it of the sort trumpeted by the orators of King, and Country, of Kaiser and Fatherland. Only the men on the ground can see the futility of it. Not so the generals, or most of them anyway. Haig cannot, for sure. If any man is true heir to Kitchener, it is he: the carnage of his own troops troubles him not a whit, so long as he gains an inch of territory. And that carnage, on a massive scale, I have been witness to. We went over the top with the Canadians at dawn, after an artillery bombardment. Within a minute we were threading our way past corpses and picking up dozens of wounded. Carried them back, under fire; and went back for more. Left the dead for burial parties later. Then, when the engagement ended, transported the wounded from the first-aid stations to the makeshift hospitals in the rear. Those who were still alive, that is. Many had died of their wounds already. Many more will. And the padres will shovel them into eternity, with bland words about the resurrection and the life. "Oh death," they will intone, "where is thy sting? Where, grave, thy victory?" Well, I can tell them where death's victory is. Right here.

Letter to Pte G. Sargent, RAMC unit 73, British Expeditionary Force. October 12th 1917, from Edwin Sargent, aged eight

> *(The superscription is in an adult's hand, presumably a teacher's, the text itself in the boy's own hand; the document preserved, neatly folded, in the later pages of Geoffrey Sargent's second wartime diary)*

Dear Dad,
    Please come home safe.
    Lots of love,
    Teddy

Postcard from Pte G. Sargent, RAMC, to Mrs M. Sargent. November 12th 1918

Dearest, it's all over. The Regulars will take over in Germany. Our unit's to be demobbed, probably in Aldershot, as soon as a boat's available. From there a civvy train to Glasgow. Can't wait, I'll wire you when I know exact date. See if you can get Ted home from school for my return. Love you. Geoff

Lord, Lord, what shall I say? Is it our sins have brought this upon us? Oh, but we cannot doubt the wickedness of our kind, in the slaughters so lately wreaked on one another, out of pride, greed, and hatred. Let no man jib at his just deserts. For now, in less than a twelvemonth, a plague is come upon us, to match what the world endured for four-and-a-quarter years, striking down sinner and innocent alike, young and old, even the newly born. Is it that we have learnt no lesson at all? First, we unleashed the scourge of war, strewing the earth with corpses by the million, and leaving a million more for ever maimed. Then came the second scourge, this deadly influenza, as lethal as the weaponry of battle. It is a pandemic visited upon us, inasmuch as we, who remained home, allowed the consuls of wrath and malevolence to inflame our hearts. It has swept through the land, infecting rich and poor together. By the grace of God, this house has been untouched, perhaps through no special virtue of our own, but only thanks to the scant contact our cloistered life has with the outside world. At Marlborough it is otherwise: the school has been ravaged by the disease, my brother sends tidings of that; but fortunately young Edwin has not succumbed. In Lincoln, alas, the Priory has fallen prey: our beloved Sisters have gone out into the city, mercying the sick; and of their number, three now lie in secular town graves, along with a thousand others. May they all rest in peace!

Telegram from Geoffrey Sargent to Sister Edith Sargent. OSG, March 30th 1920

PAPA DIED OF FLU YESTERDAY STOP FUNERAL 3 APRIL 2.00 PM ST JOHN'S STOP WILL ATTEND AND BRING MAMA STOP HOPE YOU CAN COME STOP LOVE STOP GEOFF

Entry of the same date in the second peacetime diary of Geoffrey Sargent with marginal note "written on the train from Glasgow"

So the old man is dead at last. I cannot say his passing fills me with grief. Our time together, years ago, was harsh. Long since, I put all that behind me. There are better things to do in life than waste emotional energy on old resentments – his or mine. Before leaving, I phoned Uncle Augustus to let him know. He excused himself from attending: said it would be hypocritical in him to pretend to mourn. But he added that he thought I was right to take Mama along, or at least to offer her the chance of coming. It will be up to her. She may have unfinished business where Papa is concerned. I hope Edith can come. She perhaps may have unfinished business, too. But I know she'll feel bound to attend, so long as the Abbess permits it: her Christian conscience will bid her pray for the repose of his soul, a peace he seldom nourished in the souls of others – though I dare say that outward acerbity of his, lifelong, stemmed from an inner bitterness he was never able to shed. Whatever the truth, it is not for us to sit in judgment. And for all I know, his parishioners may take a generous view: after all, he did work hard at his job; and no one can deny he made a genuine contribution, if only locally, to the Anglo-Catholic revival in the county.   Chances are that St John's, during his incumbency, attained a higher level of ritual polish than it had ever aspired to in Papist times: back then, a mere dot on the diocesan horizon, it was probably served by a semi-literate cleric of minor rank and low performance. Papa raised it up, within its walls if not in the rectory. Those fancy ceremonies were unimportant to me, but they certainly nattered to him. And for Edith they laid the foundation of a true vocation, which did not stop at the church door, but opened her large and loving heart to others, to everyone. She, I know, will forgive him, and probably always has, whatever there has been in him that needs forgiving. If, though, among his sins, an unfeeling brutality to Eleanor caused her insensate state (and Dr Wells seems to think so), then that is something I, for one, will be quite unable either to condone or to forgive. With that in mind, I shall not be able to join the funeral in any easy state of mind. But for Edith's sake, and for Mama's if she cones, I shall do my best to put a good face on it.

Next entry in the second peacetime diary of Geoffrey Sargent, 4th April 1920

Yesterday afternoon we buried Papa. It made for such a day as I, for one, shall never forget. It began equably enough, with a visit to Eleanor in the Infirmary – uneventfully would be a better way of putting it: poor soul, there is no change in her condition. Edith was there, waiting for me. She agreed there was no point in taking Eleanor with us to the funeral, or even mentioning it: nothing seems to register with her. So we just said a goodbye to our unresponding sister, and went to pick up Mama. She seemed to be in remarkably good spirits – Edith, who sees her often, tells me she usually is nowadays. I had engaged a motor, with driver, and it took us only half an hour to get to Yarburgh, arriving at St John's well before two o'clock. We met the officiant, Father Healey from neighbouring Grimoldby. He uttered the consolatory clichés usual in the circumstances. But he went on to say that he was much privileged to conduct the obsequies for such a remarkable devotee of the Anglo-Catholic liturgical reforms; and he hoped we would feel he had done everything right. He took us into the chancel and showed us: there was Papa's coffin resting on a bier before the altar, headfirst – "Only a priest's body can lie head on to the altar" – and on it lay his biretta; around it were four tall candles in penitential purple. He, Father Healey, would be wearing a black cassock with a white surplice and a black stole; the choir would be enrobed in black cassocks, too, with white cottas, and would chant the Miserere to Gregorian Tone 1 and the Benedictus to Gregorian Tone 2 – "I understand, Sister Edith, you sang here as a young person and are familiar with such things." These pronouncements ended, he ushered us into the front pew, and retired to the vestry to robe, where choristers were now arriving, six strong. A few parishioners arrived, enough to almost fill the place – it is a very small church in a mere hamlet – and seated themselves. A verger lighted the candles and exited. A bell tolled solemnly and slowly for one minute, and then the service began. The choir processed up the centre aisle to the stalls, preceded by a crucifer and followed by a thurifer and the priest. Father Healey spoke the invitatory prayer, and the choir began chanting the Miserere. Nothing, apparently, had changed in St John's. Mama sat unruffled beside me. Edith next to her, must have been wholly at ease with such proceedings. As for me, I was carried back in time. The robes, the music, the whiffs of candlewax and musty old prayer-books, the smell of incense as Father Healey censed the coffin, it all echoed the boyhood I had put behind me and all the paraphernalia with it. Every bit of it, I'm sure, would ring true with people for whom such rites are only the outer surface of an inner and loving faith. But with Papa, beyond any question in my mind, it was only the surface that mattered: he was obsessed with liturgy, with gesture; inside there was an inhuman void. For Edith's sake, and Mama's, I of course kept all this to myself, and accompanied everyone else into the graveyard with the sober participatory mien of a regular churchgoer, which I am not. At graveside, Father Healey brought the proceedings to a close with the sprinkling of holy water, and with eloquent prescribed prayers committing the soul of the departed to the care of a God I no longer believed in. The verger had reappeared with a hefty helper, and the coffin was skillfully lowered into the grave. The verger then sidled over to Mama, as the widow, and unobtrusively gave her a handful of earth to let fall upon the coffin. Let it fall she did not. She flung it with main force, and cried out, "Goodbye, Barnabas, and good riddance! I hope you rot in Hell!". To say that others were taken aback is a massive understatement. Father Healey was at a total loss for what to say or do. His liturgical aides registered shock and disbelief. So did the laity. Edith was, quite literally, dumbfounded, though I had a sudden, immediate hunch of recognition in her, as if she knew, deep down, that Mama had long just been a bomb waiting to go off – but preferably not in public. Mama herself, her outburst over, seemed completely calm, as I hustled her away, with Edith's help, through the lichgate, to the waiting motor. We drove her back to Lincoln in silence, too stunned to say anything. But when she got out – she was up front beside the driver – she turned to us in the back seat and said, "Well, children, that was interesting, wasn't it?", and actually winked, and stalked off up her front path with more vigour in her step than I thought she had in her. We were both startled all over again. "I wonder, should I go after her?" Edith asked me. "No, I don't believe so, not right now," I replied. "We have to think this over, both of us. I don't know about you, but I need to ponder it, thoroughly." "Me, too," she put in. "Well then, listen," I said, "in that case let's talk tomorrow. I'm staying on in Lincoln for a couple more days, at the White Hart. Phone me, so we can talk it through." She nodded, and we finished the trip in silence. But I must say in a comfortable silence: we've always been at ease with each other, even though our lives have followed such different paths, and even though we so seldom have a chance to get together. Dear Edith!

Entry in the diary of Sister Edith Sargent. OSG, April 5th 1920

Dear Geoff! It is so easy for him to say "Phone me tomorrow and we'll talk." As if I didn't have commitments I can't scrap at the drop of a hat. But then, I suppose it wouldn't have occurred to him that the next day was Easter Sunday, a great day for our little Priory here in Lincoln. Reverend Mother has bade me stay on here for several days, to help the surviving Sisters put things back together in Sempringham House. After three flu deaths, it has been hard, with reduced numbers, to fulfill our twin responsibilities, to lead a life of prayer and to mend the wounds of the world outside. Nor does everything run smoothly, however hard we try. For example, plans had to be abandoned for a priest to come and say our Easter Mass: he fell off his horse the night before and broke his leg. So at the last minute, with Reverend Mother's blessing, we went to Mass in the Cathedral – not that they dare call it Mass: too many hidebound conservatives around, who look at Anglo-Catholicism as halfway down the slippery slope to Rome. Anyway, the Cathedral version took all morning – much pomp and circumstance. Later we would sing Vespers and Compline at home. But in between I'd promised the Matron at the Infirmary I'd come on over and look in on Eleanor. It was the least I could do, given it was Easter. I got there at half-past one. And to begin with it was the same old story as always on these visits. Eleanor sits or lies down in a kind of numb silence, seeming not to take in anything I say or to pay any attention to it. But I just chatter away regardless. Dr Wells encourages me to, in the hope that something may click. And I'd want to anyway: it'd be heartless to say nothing; that'd be like treating her as nothing more than a block of wood. Of course, it's hard sometimes to think of something to say. You run out of personal subjects. So instead I tend to prattle on about whatever's in the news. For instance, throughout the war years, I could talk about the latest bulletins from the Front. And after the Armistice, there was plenty to say about the Peace Treaty at Versailles. And on the Home Front, there's usually been something to say about postwar life in England. Last year, I was able to tell her about the posthumous publication of quite ground-breaking poems by a Jesuit poet, G. M. Hopkins: given her love of literature, I thought it might touch a hidden nerve in the recesses of her withdrawal. No such luck. But I've become used to her torpor, her absence. Today, I had no reason to think that anything might be different. "Eleanor," I said, "I'm afraid I have some family news for you, which we didn't really expect. A few days ago, last Tuesday in fact, we lost Papa in Yarburgh. He died." Eleanor sat bolt upright and looked straight at me. "Oh," she said, in a perfectly normal tone of voice, "what of?" I was astounded. All of a sudden, there she was, back in the land of the really living, looking at me with an unclouded eye, wholly *present*. I burst into tears. "Oh dear!" Eleanor said, "I didn't know he meant that much to you." Well, we got that sorted out. And for the next two hours we did catch-up. I had to tell her about the years she'd spent in complete withdrawal and so on. She took it all in with remarkable equanimity, while I was just bubbling over with happiness – and, of course, in the back of my mind, dreading the possibility of a relapse. Dr Wells was off duty, it being Easter. But when I relayed the news to him through the Assistant Matron, he dropped everything and hurried over. "Oh," said Eleanor, when he came in, "you're the Dr Wells ray sister's just been telling me about. Thank you for taking such good care of me. Any idea what caused it?" He frowned. "Essentially," he said, "yours is a baffling case. But my best guess is, it may have had something to do with a trauma connected to your father. Maybe now isn't the time to go into that. You may prefer to explore it at leisure, once you're used to the fact of recovery." "Oh no," Eleanor rejoined. "Feel free. I mean, was there anything *but* trauma where Papa was concerned?" Her tone was not in the least agitated: just sardonic. "You're a psychiatrist," she went on, "so presumably nothing shocks you. So let's not beat about the bush. I dare say you've run across other cases of similar trauma, even if they don't necessarily produce such extreme reactions. I'm referring, of course, to paternal incest." I winced, audibly. She turned towards me, away from the doctor, "Edith dear," she said, "I thought you knew or at least suspected. Didn't you wonder why I was so keen to encourage you into the convent? Oh, of course I respected your obviously genuine vocation. But it came so timely. Papa was starting to look at you the way he'd looked at me before, when he began coming into my bedroom. I was desperate to protect you. Then, once you were safely away, I made sure to put an end to it, even if that had to wait till after University and I could get a job. Are you alright with this, darling?" I gulped and nodded. "Oh Eleanor, dearest Eleanor," I said, "How can the word *alright* possibly apply? Just because you: saved me from *that*?" "Didn't you at least suspect?" she asked. I shook my head. But then a few things, in my memory, started to fall into place. Which I shouldn't ever have ignored. If only I hadn't, maybe I could have spoken up, and we could have done something. Then a point suddenly occurred to me, because of what happened at the funeral. "Did Mama know?" I asked. "Did she know and not intervene?" My tone, I knew, was sounding desperate, almost accusatory - though not of Eleanor. Her own tone was dry, eerily dispassionate. "Oh yes, she knew alright. Not that she ever said so, openly. Too afraid, I suppose, too beaten down by his bullying. For a long while I hated her, for not protecting me. But in the end, as time went by and I never needed to see him again, I realized that she was a victim, too: no one had ever protected her." She paused, then said, "Is she still alive, by the way?" I told her about the funeral. "H'm," she remarked, "good riddance! That's putting it mildly." We left it at that then. I was too exhausted to start plumbing the depths any further. Besides, I was nervous to broach the subject of Mama's palsy, her departure from the Rectory, and the browbeating letter Papa had sent Eleanor, which very possibly had precipitated her breakdown. All that will have to be carefully handled; and that, I hope, is where Dr Wells again can come in useful. For now, I must compose myself, and give myself over simply to joy at my dear sister's re-emergence on, of all days, the day of the Resurrection – indeed, the mercy of the Lord does work in mysterious ways, and for that there must be thanksgiving without end. That said, though, and more immediately, I must share the good news with Geoff. But should I tell him the dreadful root of

Eleanor's stunned withdrawal? Surely, if he had ever suspected, at the time, what was going on, he would have stuck up for her somehow, with his fists if necessary. But then perhaps, in his innocent male way, it never crossed his mind that her mood-swings as an adolescent were anything other than the vagaries of youth in the baffling opposite sex. Well, poor man, he is in for a nasty shock.

Entry in the second peacetime diary of Geoffrey Sargent, April 6th 1920

I am filled with anger, doubly so. At that evil man, whom I shall never again refer to as Papa – no father he! But most of all, I am angry at myself. How should I not have seen, and acted? Oh, to be sure, it is easy enough to tell myself there was nothing I could have done: that going to Mama would have been hopeless, so under his thumb was she; or that it would have been hopeless to try and expose his villainy to the world, for no one would have believed me. What? A man of the cloth doing *that*? I would have been shunned as a spiteful liar. But even so, I cannot excuse myself. Eleanor lost eight years of her life, and that is unconscionable. Well, I shall have to live with that. But what is more to the point, now, is that we must do all we can to ease her transition back to life, and to fill in all the gaps in her awareness of our utterly altered world. Incredibly, she missed the entire war! There is so much she will have to grasp. I don't know if she yet realizes the magnitude of it. I just hope that doesn't prove too daunting, doesn't plunge her back into rejection of reality. The estimable Dr Wells thinks not. He says that catatonic trance is an uncommon condition, usually irreversible and insusceptible to treatment, but that in the rare cases of spontaneous recovery the recovery is permanent and complete; so, to his mind, there need be no fear that Eleanor will relapse. In my lay opinion, and in Edith's, he is right about Eleanor's recovery being complete, at least in terms of attitude: she has instantly become her old self, shrewd, outspoken, inquisitive. She wanted, for instance, to know all about my progress as a marine architect, and all about Edith's re-editing of Gregorian chant. There is nothing self-absorbed about that. But oh dear, she does have a lot to catch up on. Meanwhile, she will stay on for the time being at the Infirmary, to make the necessary adjustments to her sense of time lost and time regained; and only then, without any urgency, we can figure out how best and most reasonably she can secure a place for herself in this so volatile a postwar world. I shall stay on here in Lincoln, to give her whatever brotherly reassurance I can; and I have written Marion and the firm, to say I will be back in Glasgow as soon as possible.

Letter from Augustus Sargent to Eleanor Sargent. May 15th 1920

My dear Niece,

    I am rejoiced to know, from your brother, that all is now well with you. That was a grave affliction befell you, and I send you my most sincere wishes for continuance in your recovery from it. Best wishes, in themselves are not enough. I feel very strongly that it is up to me to step in and offer some real help. Let me explain.

    As I'm sure you know, there was a long-standing breach between your father and me, which severed relations between us before ever you, or Geoffrey or Edith, were born. It all had to do with the family money. Your grandfather, for reasons known only to himself, cut your father out of his will and bequeathed all his fortune to me, which then came to me unexpectedly soon when your grandfather died in middle age. Your father deeply resented being supplanted by a younger son and, perhaps unjustly, he aimed his ire at me. Rather than perpetuate a rift, I offered to share the wealth with him. But a kind of stubborn pride would not let him accept the offer. "I am not going to go through the rest of my life," he said, "as a charity case." There was nothing I could do but turn away, sadly. As time went by, I did regret that you three young people, living in the straitened circumstances of a parsonage, were denied some of the advantages that more money would have provided. But making discreet inquiries, I comforted myself with the knowledge that all three of you had successfully found a good path to follow: Geoffrey with his ship-building, Edith with her vocation, and you with a down-to-earth determination to support yourself as a teacher while answering a literary calling.

    One should not speak ill of the dead, but I have to say that your father, in many ways, was not a very nice man. When your mother became unwell, he seemed quite uncaring – or rather, what he cared about, apparently, was the inconvenience to himself. I had never really gotten to know your mother, who married your father only after he and I parted our ways. But she was, after all, my sister-in-law; and if he was going to do nothing for her, the least I could do was step in, as tactfully as I could, and arrange for her proper care. I do not congratulate myself on this. Any decent man would do the same.

    All that was long ago. I am now an old man, and I cannot go to my grave with matters unresolved that ought to claim my attention. Every man has a duty to die with his affairs properly in order. So it has now devolved upon me to put things to rights that went so horribly wrong, years ago. Accordingly, I am making provision to share my rather abundant wealth in a way that honours family ties that I now acknowledge to have an importance outranking other considerations. In my will, I am leaving a sizeable bequest to Geoffrey, to be inherited by his son in the event of his death. I have discussed a similar bequest with Edith: she assures me she wants nothing for herself, but anyway would be prevented from accepting by her vow of poverty; so, with her agreement, I have ordered a. sizeable bequest to be made to her convent. Thus your brother and sister will be duly taken care of. That leaves you. I also intend to make some kind of similar provision. But given your current circumstances, I do not feel right about deferring the matter until my death. I intend to act at once.

Now, Eleanor, I do not want to hear from you any reprise of your father's stubborn pride; any reference to your being seen as a charity case. Think of it this way. Money does not have any intrinsic value in itself. All that matters is what one does with it. What I intend to do with it is to make it possible for you, now that you have recovered, to resume the independent life you used to lead, and to pursue the same goals as before, if you so wish. Unfortunately, it is vastly improbable that Stroud will have kept a teaching position available to you, after eight years, in the hope that you would become well enough to fill it. Nor would I want you to go looking for a similar situation elsewhere. Teaching Latin nouns and verbs to schoolchildren is a humdrum job at the best of times; and you only engaged in it as a pragmatic means of self-support while harnessing your talent as a writer. So I propose to eliminate the need for that kind of drudgery. As of tomorrow a competence will be yours, which should endure intact to the end of your natural life. Consider it, if you will, an investment in your future accomplishments as an author. How you decide to use the money (where you wish to live, and so on) will be entirely up to you. And you should feel no need at all to thank me. Fate dealt you a calamitous blow. Regard this contribution as one in the eye to fate – too often, in your classical world of antiquity, the gods felt free to torment us mortals at will. It's time someone took them down a peg or two. I fancy you're the right person to do just that.

Affectionately,
Uncle Augustus.

Letter from Augustus Sargent, 20th May 1920, to James Caldwell, Esq, at 27 Chancery Lane, London

Dear Jim,

Sometime in the next few days, I wish to come and see you on family business. There are two bequests I need to put in my will. And I need your help in setting up an annuity for one of my nieces.

Both matters are quite straightforward; but I want to have them properly sewn up stamped and sealed, the way you so expertly do such things.

As ever,
Gus

Entry in the diary of Sister Edith Sargent, OSG, July 20th 1920

This day a letter from Eleanor, to me in Alvingham, not Sempringham House, since I am returned here permanently. The Priory can get along alright without me now, and it is a joy to be back in Choir. In her letter Eleanor tells me she has leased a flat in Cambridge, using the money that Uncle Augustus has endowed her with. I am so glad for her. This means that she now can devote herself full time, with no need to bother about other and tiresome jobs, to realizing her dream of scholarly and literary work. It is her calling; and if anyone can understand the idea of vocation I can. Cambridge will be just the right place for her. It has a grand tradition of classical learning, and she will have access to one of the world's great libraries. Also, Cambridge is not far from here, a mere hour by train; so she can easily make her way to Lindsey any time she wants to visit Mama; and I hope she will consider an invitation to spend Christmas in our guest quarters.

Letter by Edwin Sargent to his parents, November 11th 1925, from Marlborough College, Wiltshire

Dear Mum and Dad,

You were asking about how everything's going with the German classes. It turns out to be quite super. Most of the chaps in modern languages chose French, having picked up a bit of it in prep school – probably thought they could coast through on what they already knew, though mind you their accents are terrible. In German there are only a few of us, which means we can really go at it with a vengeance. Not that that's really the right word for it, is it? I mean, surely it's a bit out of date to talk about vengeance nowadays, with seven years of peace under our belts. Anyway, the four of us get on well with the beak, Dr Krauss: he's a German who's lived in England forever; he was interned during the war as an enemy alien, but he doesn't seem to bear a grudge about it. We have to talk German in class, not just study it as a written language. Takes a bit of getting used to, the weird word order, with the verb always at the end of the sentence. But I must say, when he reads Goethe out loud, it makes a lot of sense.

Talking of poetry, there's a chap in our House called Louis MacNeice, who writes some. And it isn't at all what you might expect: none of the solemn stuff that our stone-age stalwarts sneer at as artsy-fartsy, but quite incisive satires of stick-in-the-mud traditions. He's founded a club called The Independents. They're a couple of years older than me, but they've taken me under their wing as a new member. Apparently, anyone must be independent-minded who refuses to join the sacrosanct Officers Training Corps, and who learns German into the bargain – oh horrors!

Actually, MacNeice is a classics man. He's won a first-rate scholarship to Balliol to read Greek and Latin and Ancient History. That might seem a bit odd in someone who cocks a snook at dusty academe. But he says No, you can make sense of modern life best if you look at it the way the Greeks did: they had a wise policy of building war memorials with wood; as such, they were perishable, so they didn't stick around as a fixed reminder of old quarrels.

I was reminded of that this morning, today being Armistice Day. Service in Chapel was full-out Kipling: it needed only a brass band, instead of the organ, for Pomp and Circumstance. Don't get me wrong. I'm ready as anyone to remember the fallen with proper respect. But let's face it, they weren't heroes, they were victims – of a war that didn't make sense, and of blind fools like Haig, the Butcher of the Somme, who squandered lives by the thousand, like so much cannon fodder, to wrest half an acre of mud from a bunch of fellow-men forced into it by equal butchers on the other side. Needless to say, this isn't something I've talked to Dr Krauss about. He might have mixed feelings on the subject. Perhaps, when I get to know him better, I'll figure out where he stands on such matters. As yet, I simply see him as someone with an interesting history, who's a dab hand at language and literature.

Meanwhile, like any standard Marlburian, I stand to attention when we sing the national anthem, and make all the right noises in Chapel, even though all that religious mumbo-jumbo is meaningless, at least to me. But I have to admit, some of the choir music is quite beautiful – not that one can say the same of the hymns; their texts are pure doggerel. You should hear MacNeice on that topic: sardonic as all get out.

We'll miss him in The Independents when he goes up to Balliol. I'm thinking about trying for a mod-lang scholarship to Cambridge instead. Dr Krauss says they have very good German profs; and apparently there are profs at Trinity who give tutorials in foreign politics, which I'd like to get in on if I can.

If I do end up at Cambridge, I wonder if I should go and see the mysterious Aunt Eleanor. She was ill for some years, I gather. But if she's herself again, she might welcome a visit. I know you've always been fond of her, Dad. What do you think?
Lots of love,
Ted

Entry in the second peacetime diary of Geoffrey Sargent, November 11th 1925

Eleven years ago today the bloody war ended, which I refuse to call the Great War; before it was over, millions had died, on both sides, in a conflict of competing empires that achieved nothing worthwhile. We British congratulated ourselves on having defeated an evil foe, but then we turned around and sowed the seeds of yet another Armageddon. All moral arguments aside, it is unbelievably short-sighted to have demanded monumental reparations from Germany. When Germany does get back on its feet, we will pay the price. Apparently, the passivity of defeat has now been replaced by a mix of sullen hatred and factional militancy. Kiel's shipyards, for example, are full of outraged workers, starving on worthless wages, and variously swayed by demagogues of the extreme right or left.

We, too, have had our own share of unrest in the Clydeside shipyards: anti-union bullying by the owners, long-standing worker-discontent over wages and job-security; but nothing to compare with the level of anarchy besetting Germany. I fear for the worst over there.

Here, I am not much affected, as an architect; I just design the vessels and have nothing to do with their construction. But I can't simply ignore the situation. On the whole, I reckon the workers are justified in the stands they take, while the company men are more concerned with profit than with fair play. History will decide. Meanwhile, it's enough for me to give a nod of private approval to the newly organized Labour Party: unlike the Tories and the Liberals, it had the guts – in the face of belligerent public opinion – to embrace a pacifist policy in the war. To some extent they were led to that by the late Keir Hardie, who had no illusions about the previous war in South Africa. Come to think of it, I learnt a thing or two there myself.

Letter from Eleanor Sargent to Geoffrey Sargent, May 26th 1926

Dear Geoff,

Your very welcome letter of May 24th arrived yesterday, and I hasten to reply. The news of Ted is thrilling. To have won a top scholarship to Trinity at only seventeen is amazing. You must be very proud of him. Please give him my hearty congratulations. I hope he will come and see me when he comes up.

During term, I'm sure he'll be busy with his studies and with the customary revels of undergraduate life, too busy to spend much time with a spinster aunt he hasn't met since early childhood. Perhaps he'd like to come to tea, occasionally, when he's nothing better to do, or even dinner – I've quite enjoyed learning to cook. But I certainly wouldn't want to inflict myself on him out of a mistaken sense of family duty.

Anyway, I do have a rather hermit-like existence here: occasional trips to the university library and for food-shopping, plus a few concerts, that just about sums up my social life; and I've no interest in breaching the depressingly male walls of academic exclusiveness. That may seem a bit odd to you, considering my ambitions are learned, of a sort. But to what end the grind of scholarship? Certainly not knowledge for its own sake. Rather, some kind of understanding.

You, if anyone, can appreciate how important that distinction is to someone like me, who slept through the whole war. As you can imagine, it's been hard to come to terms with the dire facts of that carnage, to make sense of it. People call it the Great War, with proudly capital letters, as though England's role in it was to defend civilization from barbarity. Stuff and nonsense! For all I can see of it (and here perhaps my total non-involvement, because of the coma, does give me a certain objectivity) the whole thing was just a recurrence of everything you objected to in the South African War: the pursuit of power and wealth disguised as patriotic duty.

It's still going on, that glossing over the facts, sometimes quite eloquently voiced. Just after the Armistice, Housman published an "Epitaph on an Army of Mercenaries." You may not have seen it, so here's what he wrote:

These in the day when heaven was falling,

> The hour when earth's foundations fled,
> Followed their mercenary calling
> And took their wages and are dead.
> Their shoulders held the sky suspended;
> They stood, and earth's foundations stay;
> What God abandoned, these defended,
> And saved the sum of things for pay.

Now that's all very well. As verse, it's beautifully crafted; and its sardonic tone redeems it from any charge of jingoism. But what in the end does it say? Who were the mercenaries? Is Housman referring, obliquely, to the Old Sweats, the shilling-a-day infantrymen who went to the Front in '14? And even if he implies they were simply doing what they were paid to do, is it not rather preposterous to attribute to them an heroic mission to save "the sum of things" from ruin?

Surely there is, here, a dichotomy: between words and meaning; between lines superbly crafted (they have all the terse gravity of epitaphs in the Greek Anthology) and the sentiments underlying them. Grudgingly, I have to concede that it's a literary masterpiece, while at the same time dismissing it as political rubbish. What do you think?

To me, it's unexpected. Housman, unquestionably, is the greatest Latinist in recent times, as I well know, having studied under him in my youth – and his "the sum of things" is a neat echo of the "summa rerun" in Lucretius. But who would ever have dreamt such a pair of hard-edged quatrains might come from the so much less than great rhymester who wrote "The Shropshire Lad"? I suppose those adolescent ditties about rustic lads and lasses were acceptable enough in 1896, when they first came out, even though they pale, limply, beside the mordant prose of his exact contemporary, Mr Bernard Shaw. But surely, in today's world, there are more important tasks for a poet than drivelling on about pastoral prettiness. Wilfred Owen thought so, whose newly published poems confront the sad reality of war with stubborn honesty. What a tragedy that he should fall to a sniper's bullet only seven days before it all ended! And he so much better a poet than the oft-lamented Rupert Brooke.

Owen got it right. With him, the chief task of the poet was to tell the truth. He did so, as he saw it and lived it. For that, he has my unqualified respect. But he was, unfortunately, still bogged down in the trapping of Pesie: substituting assonance for strict rhyme is hardly minting the coin of a new vocabulary; after all, the second task of a modern poet is to fit his language to the actuality of the modern world. I was already trying to do that years ago, before the war, when T.S. Eliot's first poems made their appearance; and now he has fulfilled their promise, superbly, in *The Waste Land*. It strengthens my resolve to go on with what I embarked on, too, before illness interrupted me.

Meanwhile, Housman lingers on. Whatever his limitations as a poet, he remains peerless as a classicist. He's very properly been given the chair in Cambridge; and he lives, a lifelong bachelor, in Hewell's Court across the road from Trinity, not far from me. If I ever met him in the street, I'm sure he wouldn't recognize me from the old days, when I sat at his feet, scholastically, in London. And certainly I wouldn't presume to approach him out of the blue: he has the reputation of being inordinately shy, and anyway a bit bristly with women. For that matter, I also prefer rather to keep to myself.

But don't tell that to young Ted. I'd love to see him when he comes up in the autumn.

Love to Marion, as always,
Eleanor

Letter from Edwin Sargent to Eleanor Sargent 19 September 1926

Dear Aunt Eleanor,

It was most kind of you, through Dad, to bid me welcome to Cambridge, where I will be reading German and Modern History, at Trinity. I shall look you up as soon as I come up, next month. It will be very pleasant to get to know you properly, for I was only three or four when you fell ill.

Yours sincerely,
Ted

Letter from Geoffrey Sargent to Sister Edith Sargent, OSG, August 4th 1929

Dear Edith,

Here we are, as I write this, on yet another anniversary of August '14, that outbreak of a war still seen by many, at least in Britain, as a showdown between Good and Evil. More properly, it is considered, by those capable of second thoughts, as a clash between competing Empires.

120

If it weren't so tragic, it would be laughable. The only hope I can cling to is that perhaps we'll prove capable of learning from history, rather than repeating it. If not, what will the world come to?

You, I know, in your Alvingham haven, do not dismiss such questions as of no import. You pray for it every day, and I'm sure there's nothing woolly-minded about your doing so. Clearly you keep up with what's going on in the world – with what, to your mind, needs praying for. So, in our different ways, we're both bothered about the same things.

Accordingly, I think you'll be interested to hear what Marion and I are planning for Ted in 1930 when he takes his degree. As you know, he's been reading both Modern History and German Language and Literature. He's actually become quite competent in German, having taken it his last two years at Marlborough. He's kept in touch with his teacher there, who encouraged him to try for a scholarship in the language – with great success. When he goes down, in May '30, he'll have to make up his mind what he wants to do for a career.

Obviously, he won't be following in my footsteps: designing ships never drew him the way it did me as a boy – you probably remember that whole fleet of model ships I built upstairs in the rectory attic. Rather, he seems keen on finding something to do with foreign affairs, preferably apropos Germany. Not an easy placement to find. He's aware of that. But he knows, too, even if he has to wait for something to turn up along those lines, he can always get by as a German teacher in some school or other that offers the language.

That's where his old teacher, Krauss, came in. He has a pretty good grasp of Ted's character and ambitions. So he has suggested to us, that perhaps Ted shouldn't fall back on teaching German in England, but should consider, instead, teaching English in Germany. If the idea appeals, he says he could easily arrange for Ted to be taken on as an English-teacher in one of the German gymnasiums – that apparently is what they call their academic high-schools, nothing to do with gymnastics.

Ted has leapt at the idea. So Krauss has started sounding out his contacts; feels confident he can come up with something useful in either Weimar or Berlin, starting in the autumn of '30.

Meanwhile, there'd be a few months to fill in. Marion and I would, of course, be happy to have him home for a while: Cambridge has long seemed almost as far away from Glasgow as Berlin would be. But Ted, ever the get-up-and-go young chap, says he'd really like to spend at least July and August in Germany first, in order to get properly acclimatized, so to speak, before settling in as a new teacher.

Seems like a reasonable approach. So I'm making an arrangement, through my firm here, for him to spend the summer in Kiel, as a sort of temporary dogsbody in the shipyards there. He's seen enough of the kind of work we do here, in the Clydeside shipyards, for him to be able to find his way around that kind of situation without making an ass of himself.

So there's his future (for the time being) in a nutshell. I'm sure you'll be delighted on his behalf. Next long vac I'll encourage him to come and see you in Alvingham. He's been seeing Eleanor from time to time in Cambridge, and gets on well with her. I'm sure he'd cotton on to you equally well: like many a specialist, he's comfortable with other specialists, even if their fields are completely different. Who knows? He may be able to run an errand or two for you when he's in Germany: I seem to remember your telling me once there are monasteries over there with a high reputation for their Gregorian chant. But that would be up to you.

Apologies for this lengthy letter. As Voltaire once said, I didn't have time to write a short one.

Marion sends her love, as do I.

Geoff

Letter from Edwin Sargent in Kiel to Eleanor Sargent in Cambridge, 24 June 1930

Dear Aunt,

As you know, I'll be teaching English this autumn at a school in Berlin. This was arranged for me by Krauss, my old German teacher at Marlborough. It promises to be an interesting experience. Certainly, it will widen my horizons. Hitherto they've been rather narrow: English culture is so insular; my tripos in Modern History made me embarrassingly aware of that.

Not everyone in England, of course, wears blinkers. Notably you don't. In our many Cambridge conversations, you were quite frank about living like a recluse. But even though you held yourself at arm's length from the bustle of public life on your doorstep, you did strike me as having a lively interest in the world of affairs. And I gather, from things you've told me and from some of the writings you've shown me, that a critique of our tines, as compared with those of the ancient world, is what above all else exercises your mind. So when I went down in May, I found it quite touching, as a young person setting out to make his way in the world, that you should bid me stay in touch and report, in some fashion, on what I found out there. I will, indeed, keep you posted.

In fact, doing so will be good practice for me, if I'm to make something of myself along lines I spoke of in your flat last April. Trinity, after all, has just been a stepping-stone. I'll do my best, as a teacher, in Berlin. But I'm not really cut out for the academic life. Political journalism is more my cup of tea, if I can get a foot in that door.

As it happens, something of the sort has been hinted at, quite unexpectedly. Not everyone in Cambridge leads a cloistered life immersed in abstractions. Some of the dons actually do get involved, on the side, in the rough and tumble of practicalities. One such, notably, is the Master of Trinity. He's been known to open doors for protégés into spots far removed from his own hallowed halls. Two years ago, for example, he was apparently approached, discreetly, by an old Trinity man wanting to recruit someone suitable for a rather mysterious government job in London – all rather hush-hush – and the chap they picked, a science-whizz at Queen's called Ken Fillmore, was very tight-lipped about the whole affair.

That kind of business, I suppose, is typical of what people call the Old Boy network. And now, seemingly, it may be my turn. The Master's been approached again, this time by a fellow-Etonian, hoping to recruit a would-be foreign representative for *The Times*, fluent in German, who could be trained to replace their current man in Berlin, when he retires.

The Master told me all this in confidence, of course. He singled me out on the recommendation of my tutor, Martin Fischer, who showed him a couple of papers of mine, including one on "The relationship of literature and political theory in pre-war Germany." It seems to have made a good impression; and the Master suggests I write a few reports this year, while I'm in Germany, describing cultural and politico-social life there, which he could pass on to *The Times* as a sample of the kind of work I might do if hired.

So that's what I'm going to do. And because I think some of these projected jottings of mine might be of interest to you, Aunt, I'll send you copies of them as I churn them out. Granted, Berlin in 1930 probably lacks the gravamen of Rome in Tacitus' day – at least by any intellectual measure. But in another regard, modern Germany can be deemed superior: Tacitus wrote, clandestinely, under the ferocious tyranny of Domitian; it's a different kettle of fish for writers in the Weimar Republic.

Strikes me that kind of difference is something pretty well up your street. Have you ever thought of Tacitus as someone for one of your projects?

With much affection,
Ted

Ever sensitive to calendar, Eleanor has sent me, as a present for the Feast of St Ignatius Loyola, a book of poems by Father Gerard Manley Hopkins, SJ. They are mostly, in a sense entirely, religious; and apparently they have caused quite a stir in literary circles, because they are strikingly, and it is said successfully, experimental. I have dipped into them right away, eagerly. They are indeed quite radical, technically; but their language is gnarled, their thought somewhat convoluted. His is a unique voice, and I can see how it must have startled the ear of anyone used to the indistinguishable flatulencies of our recent bards. I make no claim to be a literary expert, but even I can see the difference between run-of-the-mill rubbish and Father Hopkins. He is not an easy read, and I have trouble deciphering some of his meanings. But much of what he has to say must have great appeal to anyone who loves fresh and muscular words. And nearly all of what he has to say has extra appeal to me, as a religious: his spiritual journey was both beautiful and heroic. It is an extraordinary and deplorable fact that his work remained unpublished for more than thirty years after his death. In his honour, I shall say a special prayer for the repose of his soul tonight, this being the feastday of his Order's founder.

Letter from Augustus Sargent to Eleanor Sargent, August 1st 1930

My dear Niece,

Young Ted, my grand-nephew and your nephew wrote to me last May, to report happily on having passed his final exams with First Class honours. In his letter, he spoke very affectionately of the time he often spent with you during his undergraduate years. You are, I gather, a quite private and reserved person. But he seems to have hit it off with you remarkably well. Perhaps that has something to do with his fluent sideline in German poetry. Who knows? Or perhaps, however wary you may be of strangers, you have felt at home with him because he's so like his father. Anyway, be that as it may, you evidently have opened up to him not only about your feelings, but also about your work, even to the point of sharing some of it with him. He is deeply impressed by it, and says it *must* be published. He has hope it will be, but says he is at a loss for how to further its cause. As a Modern Historian, he has no contacts in the Classical world, which is not his field, but apparently you have flattly forbidden him to try and enlist help from Housman; that, you insist, would smack of sycophancy but something, he says, *must be done*. But how?

Well, Niece, I think I have the answer. If you have in you the same pride in your work as your brother does in his marine architecture, or Edith in her music, you will want your work to be judged solely on its merits, not just accepted because someone influential recommends it. But there is no harm in your being helpfully provided with an appropriate address to approach. It so happens that an old friend of mine, Horatio Baker, now deceased (I am ninety now and almost all my friends are dead), was founder and owner of the Parthenon Press, which publishes, amongst other things, books for readers with classical interests: not for scholar specialists, but for general readers with educated tastes. His son Wilfred took over from him twenty-three years ago. I've never met him; but if he's anything like his father, he'll be a very civilized man and an astute judge of good writing. So I would suggest you submit your work to him for his opinion. Make no mention of my name, in case he remembers that Sargent was his father's closest friend: if he accepts your work for publication, I know that you would not want to think that his acceptance was based, however indirectly, on the desire to do a favour to a former family connection.

Indeed, with that in mind, I would further suggest you contact him under an assumed surname. There is famous precedent for that: all three Brontë sisters published under pseudonymous male names; in their case, though, the motive was simply to avoid the usual condescension bestowed on female authors by reviewers – who were always men. It was a canny subterfuge on their part. With you, it would simply be a means of ensuring that a publisher's response would be completely disinterested. If you go ahead, I shall wish you luck, and will look forward to receiving a copy of the first edition. Meanwhile, I thank you for being so cordial to Ted.

Uncle Augustus

P.S. Parthenon's address is 11, The Strand, London Wl

First draft of Eleanor Sargent's poem and prefatory note appended to her Life of Thucydides

This poem is written in response to the atrocity perpetrated by Athens on the island of Milos in 416 BC. The island had been a willing member of the Delian League, which was founded and led by Athens to protect Greece from any further attack by Persia, after the defeat of the Persian army and navy at Marathon in 496 and at Salamis in 480. Over time, as the dominant member, Athens gradually converted the League into an Athenian Empire, consisting of Attica, the Aegean islands, and the Greek states on the west coast of Asia Minor. Milos was thus reduced to the status of a satellite. It had token autonomy, with its own governing council and its own fishing economy; but in any crisis, it was expected to do Athens' will obediently. When Athens launched the Peloponnesian War in 431 to attempt hegemony over the whole of mainland Greece, Milos refused its support, declaring neutrality. Athens was outraged, and invaded. Thucydides describes the episode in his History, recording the eloquent speech of the Miletians in defence of their neutrality, and the cynical reply of the Athenians, whose policy of realpolitik brooked no disobedience. Upon the refusal of the Miletians to come to heel, the Athenians slaughtered the entire adult male population, took the women and children into slavery, and sent colonists of their own to occupy the place. With the subsequent defeat of Athens in the Peloponnesian War, Milos sank into obscurity. The colonists, speaking Attic Greek, took over the fishing and imposed their own culture. Somehow, though, the local cult of Aphrodite reasserted itself: the conquered place, as has so often happened in history, absorbed the conquerors. A relic of that native cult was found in 1820 AD, when the famous Venus de Milo was unearthed in the rubble of an ancient temple. The statue is rightly regarded as a sculptural masterpiece; but almost like a reference to the tragic past, it has lost both arms.

APHRODITE

Goddess, regard this island now,
was yours once and again, before our age
of similar atrophy.
        Usurpers came,
with their shabby threats, iron intentions;
and the holy ground, inconsolable,
reeked with the stench of innocent blood
shed.
        To small avail, that foreign
yoke: somehow the old faith
inched up from under

         (between cracks in the rock-face of overrule)
stubborn, reincarnate
         (sure in the subsoil, where the roots are)
unbudged.
             Who then wrought in such obdurate stone
your fluid grace? No record survives. Perhaps
some doughty grandson, come back from bleak exile,
loyal to lost truths, making a resurrection.
                           Time,
in its temerity, buried your cult of kindness
under another ethos, alien, coercive, robed in the black
habit of privilege.
             Yet still on this island, instinct
with history, the peasant herds his goats on the rocky slopes,
autonomous, still set in the old ways; the tourist
snaps his condescending image and departs – unaware,
Goddess, of how your gentle, subversive presence,
here in this isolated pocket of generosity,
persists.

Letter from Edgar Simpson (Eleanor Sargent) to Wilfred Baker, Esq 15 August 1931

Dear Mr Baker,

It has been suggested to me that I should submit a text of mine to you, with a view to possible publication. It is entitled, simply, "Thucydides"; and as the title implies, it is a portrait of perhaps the greatest historian of the ancient world.

The importance of the subject needs no urging from me. Thucydides is widely and rightly revered. But you may well ask yourself why should yet another portrait be inflicted on the public. In my opinion, there is a need for one. Indeed, I would go so far as to suggest that there is need for a new one in almost every century – at least for those who cannot read him in the original Greek.

It is rather similar to the need for a new translation. Thucydides, after all, wrote in the vocabulary and style of his own time, contemporaneous as the day's weather. A translation should match that immediacy. Hobbes translated *The Peloponnesian War* in words that struck home to a seventeenth-century Londoner with the same impact as the Thucydidean words had had on an Athenian in the fifth century BC. But Hobbes's language today does not evoke fifth-century Greece: it evokes seventeenth century England.

If that principle is valid where translation is concerned, it holds good, too, for biography and commentary. Today's readers need to have a biography of Thucydides, and a commentary on him, that responds to him in a way that brings him alive in today's terms. That is what I have tried to do in the enclosed text.

I have not attempted a large and comprehensive Life – a mere profile, rather – nor do I make any claim to present an authoritative view of the man and his work, But I do believe that Thucydides has something to say in our day that can touch our minds and hearts with the same appeal as it had for readers in his own time. I have attempted to capture that in a prose portrait that includes passages of new translation; and I have appended a tributary poem that responds to him from the standpoint of a twentieth-century person.

If you find my "Thucydides" suitable for publication, I should also tell you that it is just one in a projected series of such texts about classical authors. I have a second one in draft about Ovid. And I have future plans for Caesar, Euripides, Tacitus, Aristophanes, Juvenal, and Aeschylus.

Yours faithfully,
Edgar Simpson

Letter from Wilfred Baker to Edgar Simpson, Esq, September 15th 1931

Dear Mr Simpson,

Thank you for submitting "Thucydides" to Parthenon, received four weeks since. I am pleased to inform you that it has made an excellent impression here. Our editorial staff think highly of it, and so do I.

Accordingly we propose to include it in our list of new books for issue next spring. Our business department will send you tomorrow a contract offer, which I hope you will find satisfactory.

If you do, please confirm your acceptance at your early convenience. When you do so, we shall be much obliged if you would kindly enclose with your letter a brief account of your literary career to date. This will furnish us with a basis for the customary publicity that attends our launching of a new author.

With kind regards,
Yours truly,
Wilfred Baker

Letter from Edgar Simpson to Wilfred Baker, Esq, September 19th 1930

Dear Mr Baker,

Your very gratifying letter of September 15th arrived the next day, a Saturday, and was promptly followed on Monday the 17th by the contract offer you had referred to. Needless to say, I am delighted by both communications. I am returning the signed contract to your business department by today's post.

As regards your request for facts about myself, I hope you will not take it amiss if I remain silent on the subject. It so happens that I have an extreme aversion to publicity, or to any incursions upon my closely guarded privacy. Indeed, so strongly do I feel about this, that I hope you will not credit the authorship of "Thucydides" to Edgar Simpson but will simply issue the book under my initials, ES.

Please regard this as a quirk in my personality, and not in any way as an abridgment of my gratitude to Parthenon, or to you yourself, for taking me on as an author.

Yours sincerely,
Edgar Simpson

Entry in the second peacetime diary of Geoffrey Sargent, 8 February 1931

Today a grand letter from Ted, all about his doings in Berlin. He is now on assignment for *The Times*. Other newspapers, of course, make a big fuss over their star reporters, to the point of turning them into celebrities important in themselves, almost more so than the events they report on: Ted's reports are unsigned; he is just "Our Special Correspondent." Being a modest chap, he doesn't feel he has any special qualifications for the job, at twenty-five and fresh out of Cambridge: says they only sent him there because no one else on the staff had fluent German. Well, privately, I beg to differ. He has an extraordinarily mature mind for one so young. Anyway, he tells me, if it's all the same to me, he'd like to write regularly to me about his impressions and opinions; says it's an interesting discipline to exclude his feelings from his oh-so-objective reports, but that doesn't mean he has no personal reactions to what he reports on; and he'd like to use me as a sort of sounding-board. I feel very flattered: not every father has an exchange like that with his son. Perhaps that's possible for us, him and me, because he was always asking me questions about the world, even when he was just a boy (a reporter in the making, I suppose), and I told him exactly what I thought, even if it ran counter to conventional thinking. So he grew up knowing the Great War was not great at all, and realising there were better songs to sing than national anthems. He was still really young when the Versailles Treaty plunged Germany into destitution and resentment. Now, years later, he has some hope of remedy: the poverty is appalling, and the well-to-do care little; but some of the politicians seem to mix idealism, encouragingly, with pragmatism. The Weimar Constitution, Ted says, in a model of enlightenment, not least in its enactment of universal suffrage. And politics aside, there has been amazing cultural renaissance, in literature, cinema, and art. Ted went last week to a new theatre-piece called *Die Dreigroschenoper* (*The Threepennny Opera*) which I would find especially interesting, if I hop over for a visit. It's loosely based on Gay's *The Beggars' Opera*, but has a contemporary tang all its own, jazzy in its music and street-smart in its language – a total contrast, he says, to the bourgeois clichés of Viennese operetta. Do come for a visit, he goes on: I'll translate for you. Maybe I will.

Letter from Augustus Sargent to Eleanor Sargent, March 2nd 1931

My dear Niece,

What a delight! Your "Thucydides" arrived last week, and I have devoured it. It is a triumph. Beautifully written, especially the poem at the end, and full of historical insight. I am very struck by the balance of your judgment. Thucydides, as you convincingly portray him, was a model of non-partisan objectivity; and you have followed most deftly in his footsteps,

I myself did not have a schooling in the classics, like yours. So "The Peloponnesian War" was an eye-opener to me. I had always thought of Athens as the birthplace of democracy, and never had any idea of how it slid into a corrupted brand of empire-building. But what an atrocity that massacre on Milos was! And how sad it is to know that human kind has repeated the crime over and over again – as recently as in our own time arid at our own hands. After all, has the British Empire been any different? I think not. But my club members would cut me dead if I said so out loud. Maybe we need another Thucydides to put us in our place.

By the way, I could not help noticing your extreme modesty in hiding your authorship under your initials alone. I think you should be very proud of what you have done, and I am very proud of you for having done it. But am I to suppose that you seek a kind of anonymity in this? If so, I must respect that, and not go bragging to my friends about my Niece's Brilliant Accomplishments. Anyway, just between you and me privately, accept my heartiest congratulations. And do let tie know of plans for your next book.

    Affectionately,

    Uncle Augustus

Entry in the diary of Sister Edith Sargent, OSG, September 5th 1931

Today was Mama's funeral in Lincoln. Reverend Mother gave me permission to attend. It was a rather sparse affair, almost no family, and two elderly and frail friends from the Home – at eighty-seven, she had outlived nearly all her contemporaries. That, I suppose, makes for a somewhat sad and lonely ending to one's life. And in some ways she had been a quite sad person for much of the time: life with Papa had never been easy for her. She never complained about that, in my hearing. But it was noticeable how she did pick up after Papa died, and I was glad for her. On my frequent permitted visits to her, we never talked about the dark years of her marriage. But not long ago, in the face of her impending death, she confided in me her feelings about the final rites. Convention might have suggested she be laid to rest beside her husband in the graveyard of St John's. She was absolutely adamant that this not be done. "I will not hear of it," she said. "I beg you, Edith, see that my wishes are respected." So I made this clear, confidentially, to the Matron of the Home, and everything has been done accordingly, here in Lincoln. The Chaplain read the liturgy with a very proper eloquence; and I must say that the Order for the Burial of the Dead is exactly and magnificently what every mortal needs and deserves in its passage out of this world. Geoffrey attended from Glasgow and, ever the gentleman, set aside his own agnostic view and behaved beautifully. It was wonderful to have him there – we're so seldom together now – and he has arranged for a headstone to be erected with her name and dates, with Requiescat in Pace inscribed, but with no mention of Papa on it – this at her stated request. He is a good son; and whatever his state of unbelief, I am happy that his life has turned out well, and that youthful miseries have not left an indelible mark. He and I were the only family present: young Ted is in Germany, and Eleanor declined to come. She sent me a note saying so. I think she still blames Mama for not having protected her from Papa. That seems to me rather unfair: nobody dared stand up to him. But who am I to judge? Meanwhile, in my prayers tonight after Compline, I shall make a special intercession for the repose of her soul. RIP, Mama.

Letter from Edwin Sargent to Geoffrey Sargent, January 31st 1933

Dear Dad,

Further news from Berlin. The Nazis have won the election throughout Germany, and Hitler has been named Chancellor. In effect, this makes him Dictator, though he does not assume the title. Instead, he just calls himself der Fuehrer (the Leader), and he seems to have a lot of support from the voters, though it is hard to say how much of that support is sincere, and how much of it is a reaction to the violence of his brown-shirted thugs who terrorize the landscape. I've written about this in my weekly reports, but I don't know how much impact they will have, if any, on the insular English mind: the Continent is too far removed from anyone's heed, from John o' Groats to Land's End, for people to think about Europeans at all except as Huns and Frogs and Wops, not to be taken seriously. A serious mind, like yours, will not be quite so indifferent. Hitler strikes me as being a very dangerous man, quite capable of forcing his country not only into a supine acceptance of his dictatorship, but also of leading it down a savage path into a war of post-1918 revenge. If that were to happen, I shudder to think of its effect upon you, as a pacifist: so often you have told me, convincingly, there is no such thing as a just war; and the last thing the world needs, right now, or ever, is another Caesar. So let's keep our fingers crossed.

Love to Mum,
Ted

Letter from Edgar Simpson (Eleanor Sargent) to Wilfred Baker, Esq, June 1st 1934

Dear Mr Baker,

Since the publication of my *Thucydides* in 1931, I have spent the intervening years beginning, expanding, abridging, and otherwise polishing two more texts in my series about classical authors. One, which I believe I have mentioned to you, is about Ovid; it is nearly finished to my satisfaction – so far as one can ever be really satisfied – and I will hope to send it to you in the not too distant future. Meanwhile, there is another one which actually is as ready to go to print as I can make it, about Julius Caesar. I enclose a copy of it, and hope you will find it worthy of publication. You will notice, I'm sure with relief, that the text, unlike the manuscript of *Thucydides*, is not handwritten, but has been typed: stodgy old Cambridge has now sufficiently joined the modern world that it boasts a typewriting agency which manages to decipher my untidy scrawl for a quite reasonable fee.

I am sorry that further writing has been so long delayed since you published *Thucydides*. You were very encouraging at the time, pressing me to submit more work. And I am grateful for that. I can only think, now, that since you so kindly took my work seriously from the very start you would also expect me to take it seriously myself, and not thrust it upon you prematurely. Anyway, now you have it: *Caesar* by E.S.

Whatever its merits or flaws, I think you may agree with me that publication of such a text, just now, is rather timely. Hitler's dictatorship in Germany, so far as I can gather, is sadly reminiscent of Caesar's. We can only hope he does not match the Gallic Wars with another assault upon adjacent France – or, for that matter, include England in his belligerence, as Caesar did in 55-4 BC. We have had enough invasions from Romans, Saxons, Danes, and Normans. A new one from Nazi Germany does not bear thinking of.

Yours sincerely,
Edgar Simpson

Entry in the second peacetime diary of Geoffrey Sargent, January 11th 1935

Is there no end to racialist intolerance? Hitler, Ted informs me, has taken a leaf out of Kitchener's book: he imprisons anyone who opposed his policies, especially Communists. But he does not stop short at political hostility: he has a fanatical hatred of Jews, and is herding them into his camps by the thousand. Some people may reckon this to be a malevolence peculiar to one man's nature. But I do not. I cannot ignore the history of anti-Semitic cruelty all over mediaeval Europe, including Germany. And I am ashamed to say it was not confined to the Continent. England was just as bad: there were slaughters and expulsions. That, sadly, strikes close to home: Lincoln was a hotbed of Gentile bigotry. Are we any better now than our forefathers were?

Entry in the diary of Sister Edith Sargent, OSG. November 17th 1935

Last week Eleanor sent me a copy of her new book, *Caesar*, which I have immediately read, with huge admiration. In it, she draws a fine line of distinction between his sparkling talent as a writer and his malign genius as a warrior, as a purloiner of other people's lands and freedoms.

What a paradox that is! And what a sad proof of our fallen nature! Eleanor, in her covering letter, points out that Caesar's death precluded any renewed attempt by him to incorporate Britain into what, in today's language, he would have called his "sphere of interest." That, of course, is a mere euphemism for "Empire." He was a stickler for appearances, willing to rule as a dictator, but refusing the title of King, which had been in bad odour ever since the monarchy had been overthrown, generations earlier, with the founding of the Republic. Others would not be so fastidious, would rule as Emperors, and Rome would never be a Republic again. Nor would Britain remain for long impervious to Roman arms. Eleanor reminds us not only that British subjugation, under Claudius and his successors, extended all the way up from the Channel to Hadrian's Wall, but also that it embraced, in doing so, land utterly familiar to us from childhood. Lincoln (Lindum in Latin) was a legionary barracks, and the whole of Lindsey was littered with signs of occupation and colonization – Market Rasen, for instance, was site of a Roman camp, and farmers thereabouts, to this day, have ploughed up shards of Roman pottery, even the occasional coin. She reminds me, too, because it would be of special interest to me, that the occupying force stationed in Lindum was the Tenth Legion, which had earlier served in Judaea and supplied the troops assigned to execution-duty on Calvary. They perhaps should bear the brunt of blame for what they did. But what is infamous is the aftermath of Caiaphas' exculpatory dictum, "His blood be on us, and on our children's children", which has been the excuse, over centuries, for retaliatory slaughter. I am ashamed that the Church, in tandem with the State, has adopted such a vicious attitude to the Jews: they were, after all, our older brothers in faith. You would never know it, if you looked at the history of Lincoln. It is all very well to celebrate the Feast of Great St Hugh, as we do each year on this his Day; he was a fine Christian and a superb Bishop. But what of Little St Hugh, the bogus boy-martyr? According to Chaucer, in the Prioress' Tale, he was murdered by Lincoln's Jews, who allegedly used the blood of Gentiles in their rituals. The poet, no doubt, was simply repeating a scurrilous legend that had no basis in fact. But it was no merely local slander: such malign inventions were widespread throughout England and the Continent; and genocidal massacres were pandemic. Moreover we are all party to them, if we make no public amends. Fitly, the General Confession requires contrition from us for having never intervened, for having "left undone those things which we ought to have done." Miserere nobis, Domine!

Letter from Edwin Sargent to Geoffrey Sargent, November 1st 1936

Dear Dad,

Hitler has now made his intentions clear, at least in my view. Siding with Franco in the Falangist revolution, he makes no bones about his challenge to the free world. Republican Spain's constitution is a model of democracy, but he and Mussolini will destroy it if they can, just as he destroyed, three years ago, the equally enlightened Weimar governance. I fear for the future of Europe.

Within Germany here, his anti-Semitism knows no bounds. He has deprived Jews of the vote, has barred them from the professions, has restricted their access to public transportation and recreational facilities, has purloined their savings, and has imprisoned many in the concentration-camps. Those not yet caged are trapped. Their plight is desperate. Only a few have enough money left to escape into exile – provided they can get away and can find a country willing to accept them. The rest can do nothing but numbly await whatever fate the regime has in store for them.

It is not the first time. The Jews have known captivity before, in Egypt and Babylon. And they have known exile before, when Vespasian suppressed their revolt and dispatched them into the Diaspora. But this time there is no way out: the German frontiers are closed; it takes cunning, courage, and heavy bribes to wangle an exit visa. All I can say to you, Dad, is reach out a hand, if you can; and I know you will, for it is in your nature to do so. A few German Jews have made their way, somehow, to Britain, but they are not too welcome there. So they are desperate to find asylum in some other country which will not deport them back to Germany. Two of them are friends of mine, Ernst Schillinger and Toni Meyer, both of them able-bodied and willing to tackle any kind of work. They snuck across the border into Holland last week, destination Harwich; and I have taken the liberty of giving them your address in Glasgow. If they turn up, perhaps you and Mum could take them in – they both speak pretty fair English – until something can be arranged for them. They both have relations in America, long time established there. So, with your connections in shipping, I wonder if you could book them passage in some vessel heading for New York. I don't know what they could afford, but if they're short, I could wire you enough to cover their fare. I've saved quite a bit over here, being paid in sterling with the Deutschmark being relatively weak. I know, it's only two unfortunates in a huge problem. But you've always said, Dad, the answer lies in one step at a time; and if there's anyone can be counted on to do the right thing it's always been you and Mum.

Love,

Ted

The coda of Caesar *(Parthenon Press 1937) is a poem and prefatory note, presumably written, in 1934 or earlier; original pen-and-ink draft of it, in Eleanor Sargent's hand, is attached by paperclip to her 1937 letter from W. Baker, in which he refers to* Caesar *previously published and to* Ovid *newly accepted for publication.*

When Julius Caesar, avid for conquest, set out to make himself master of Rome, and therefore, in his own mind, master of the world, he cared nothing for those he conquered, for their rights or rites. Not himself a religious man, he took it for granted that his own inherited formula of faith was the only true one: that other cultures, other creeds, should be blotted out, pushed aside like freedom. His sidestep into Britain, in 55-4 BC, was only a trivial incident in his Gallic War. But it opened a lock for Claudius to flood through, decades later, with his irruptive legions – among them the Tenth, posted to Lincoln, which they called Lindum. One of its men, older now, had been in Jerusalem, in Tiberius' time, had served on the execution squad that crucified Jesus of Nazareth. If he paid any attention to the condemned man's gibberings about the local god, that will have been nugatory: his own thoughts, so far as they were at all directed to heaven, were probably addressed to the goddess Fortuna, who would govern the roll of the dice as he and his mates gambled for the rather paltry loot available. Probably, as the years passed, he will have forgotten the whole episode entirely. Certainly it will never have occurred to him, as he served out his time in Lindum, that a new faith, based on that faraway incident, would supplant the religion of his forebears, or that the Roman Empire would ever fall.

That new religion, despite onslaughts from the uprisen tribes, would survive the Dark Ages intact, and would eventually flourish through an alliance of Church and State. Christendom, enjoying the fruits of secular power, dwindled into spiritual compromise. It persecuted the Jews, it mounted crusades against Islam, and it divided itself into many factions. Not all was bloodshed and corruption, of course: there were genuine saints, both clerical and lay, clean of heart and generous of mind. Moreover, whenever ecclesia grew stale and perfunctory, reformers came along to put things right. One such was Edward King, the nineteenth-century Bishop of Lincoln who, from the cathedral built on the site of a Roman barracks, led his diocese in the Anglo-Catholic revival. A long overdue reform, it went back to business, embracing a renewed purity of worship with an active mission to the poor.

In his multitudinous parishes, the clergy strove to maintain that balance. At least, those did who followed their bishop's lead. But some parsons, set in their Establishment ways, had no patience with such new-fangled notions; and others, imbued with a torrid evangelical fervour, were better suited to a Wesleyan chapel than a Gothic pulpit. Then there were also a few who focused only on the liturgy itself, to whom ritual was everything, the mark of a sterile faith. Such is the vanity of human kind, priests included.

The poem here appended has no loyalist attachment to any one form of belief or practice. Rather it strives towards a kind of independent response to history: to an acceptance that the world, whatever the vagaries of human behaviour, is a place sure at its roots, a grand compendium of earth and air, fire and water – above all, a fact.

LINDUM

Here on the wolds' peak, where the barracks were,
his bones rest, unremembered,
under mounds of rubble, grassed over
and built on; who once, far ago
on a similar height, served on a squad
for yet another seemingly inconsequential
triple execution – just another boring afternoon
of humdrum routine – and diced there
for the only item of decent loot,
a perhaps hand-woven coat
one of the three had worn.
                    In whose name,
afterwards, malevolence was preached
and slaughter wreaked: halfway down
this steep hill, the still called Jew's House
attests to it, a stone at the blind heart
of what purports to be love; and high above
where that old legionary lies, a huge minster
towers, monumentally stubborn but teetering now
on the edge of obsolescence.
                    Meanwhile below,
on the flat miles coastward, the same old psalms
ring in the same old rafters, but few attend:
some there are, yes, mean what they chant, truly;
yet in the perfunctory others, only emptiness obtains,
the mere tic of habit, a fumbling in the dark,

formulaic, reflex.
                        But earth abides
outside, dear as ever, creaturely, innocent
of good or evil. Time as usual
unfolds its weather, and everything connects;
wholeness is all; unison.
                        A bell rings,
matutinal: earlier, at first light,
rooks in the rectory elms have gone about
their offices; behind dunes, the woken land
flexes its limbs in the salt air;
and the sea beyond, adjacent,
pulses pulses pulses
geared to its own horarium,
primordial, indifferent to history
or us.

Letter from Wilfred Baker to Edgar Simpson (Eleanor Sargent) March 5th 1937

Dear Edgar,
  Forgive the familiarity of a Christian name, but I do feel that I have come to know you well through your writing, even though we have never met. Over the years I have respected your privacy and done nothing to intrude upon it. None the less I cannot help but draw conclusions, if only tentative ones, from clues you drop, inadvertently, in your pages.
  In your recent *Caesar*, for example, (which I aim to publish this summer) you address the post-Julian occupation of England; and you write feelingly about the posting of the Tenth Legion to Lincoln and about the Roman presence in the surrounding countryside. Who else but a Lincolnshire man, I ask myself, would so single out that one county for such particular notice? And now, in your newly arrived *Ovid* (which I will also be delighted to publish soon), you dedicate it "To the good memory of Augustus Sargent, 1840-1937, of Stamford, Lincs." A coincidence?
  Obviously, I should not make much of a small detail like that; but running through *Ovid* as a recurring undertone, there is a forlorn sense of exile, a wistfulness for paradise lost. You capture that brilliantly in your concluding poem, with its vision of Ovid exiled to Bithynia and longing for forbidden Rome. But no one, I reckon, could have written those lines without having, at some point, endured the pain of Absence, whether of

place or persons, and without perhaps also having experienced, as Ovid did, the rough impact of a tyrant's pleasure.

These are merely musings, of course. If they have any substance, and should you choose to confide in me anything about your own personal history, you may rest assured that whatever you might disclose would remain absolutely confidential. I'm well aware of your aversion to publicity of any kind; and I am still committed, as I always have been, to a policy of total silence. But then, on the other hand, you have every right to tell me, definitively, that such matters are none of my business

What you will be more interested in, I'm sure, is an editorial response to your text. My overall reaction to *Ovid*, as in the past to your previous books, is one of unstinted admiration. But you do ask, in your covering letter, how I react to your quite frank engagement with the Roman poet's obsession with sex. His *Amores*, as you rightly point out, is in effect a manual of seduction, an instruction-booklet on how to bed other men's wives. And you worry whether your treatment of that might drag Parthenon into disrepute by offending English readers, with their see-no-evil insistence on propriety. Have no fears on that score, my friend: Parthenon is not a timid firm, and anyway England is now much less prudish than it used to be. Possibly you're unaware of that, if your much-protected privacy has made you lead a rather secluded life. But let me assure you, life today is much more sexually explicit; writers can call a spade a spade, and nobody turns a hair.

However, leaving aside the relatively unimportant question of how Mrs Grundy might react to Ovid's peering into adulterous bedsheets, I suppose you will be curious about *my* reaction, as editor. Well, all I can say in that area, is that I'm struck by how balanced your approach is. Some modern writers indulge, almost orgiastically, in a fascination with coupling – James Joyce and D. H. Lawrence come to mind. Others, by contrast, are less convinced that the sexual act is the one ultimate good: either they ignore it altogether, like eunuchs; or else they submit it to some kind of moral scrutiny, not puritanically of course (they leave that to the puritans among us) but with approval of whatever is generous or empathetic, but with a dislike of whatever is selfish or unkind. What is remarkable about your approach, in *Ovid*, is your strict refusal to pass judgment. Somehow I would liken your attitude to that of a priest hearing confession: he does not condemn, for that is God's prerogative, his is only a ritual absolution, and nothing he hears can any longer shock him. You, seemingly, are not shocked by anything either: the evil men do, like their good deeds, is neutral in your impartial eyes. And if you dislike my sacerdotal comparison, I would liken you instead to Thomas

Hardy, who viewed whatever befalls us mortal creatures as just the working of a blind fate, neither malign nor kindly, but simply indifferent.

That said, I hope your mind will be at ease on the matter of what is acceptable in print. Your text is more than acceptable: it is a delight, and I am sending it to the printer this week.

As ever, yours sincerely,
Wilfred

Letter from Edwin Sargent to Geoffrey Sargent, July 1st 1938

Dear Dad,

I'm going to be coming home. It's been a long stint here in Germany, but now *The Times* is talking about recalling me. Briggs is due to retire next year, as senior political analyst, and they want me to replace him. It will be quite an adjustment, to work at a desk instead of out in the field. But a challenge, too: it means I shall have to cast my net a lot wider than the shuttered confines of the Third and threatening Reich. Hitler has been waging war upon his own people now for five years – not that many of them see it that way – but war beyond his borders is clearly his intent. He masks it with rhetoric, of course: says he is only seeking to defend the rights of German-speakers in adjacent lands. But already he has absorbed Austria; and now he's cocking an eye at Czechoslovakia and Poland. All this with a build-up of armed forces that our two governments, in Whitehall and the Elysée, are too pusillanimous to prohibit. When will this all end? I shudder to think. But at *The Times*, at least among the workaday journalists, there has been a tradition of facing facts on the international scene: marshalling them has been Briggs's job, and now apparently it's going to be mine. Fair enough. But I will have to counter a deplorable tendency, in some of my senior colleagues, to support what I have to call a policy of appeasement. Chamberlain is all too prone to truckle to Hitler; only Churchill seems to see the folly of that. We shall see. Meanwhile, stationed in London, I'll be not much closer to Glasgow than I have been in Berlin. First of all, though, I'll take a longish leave at home, and that's something I'll really look forward to.

Love to Mum,
Ted

Entry in the diary of Sister Edith Sargent. OSG, July 12th 1938

Just received, last week, a copy of Eleanor's *Ovid*. Have been reading it daily, since, in our Recreation Hour after Vespers. She apologizes, in her covering letter, for the frequent licentiousness of the subject-natter. Does she think I am so easily shocked? I must put her mind at rest on that. After all, it would be a poor thing with us, that we should pray over the state of a sinful world, if we did not have a proper grasp of what its sins actually are. I am, I must confess, a little amused at Eleanor's tenderness for my sensibilities. For she goes on to say that her next book, already in draft, is about Juvenal; and perhaps, she intimates, in contrast to Ovid's focus on debauchery, I will find Juvenal to be a salutary contrast, with his strict morality and what she calls his "savage indignation." Either way, she adds, what is really remarkable about both poets is that they write so beautifully, whether one agrees with them or not. Well, she's a better Latinist than I, so I'll take her word for it. She's probably right, given the obvious parallel in English: Kipling's imperialist attitudes are somewhat disgusting, but he does write like a virtuoso. And it's a strange thing, too, that such a jingoist could also write those utterly charming *Just So* stories for children. What a difference they would have made to our childhood in the Rectory, if we could have had those stories to fall back on, or Milne's adorable books about Winnie-the-Pooh! No point, though, in looking back with any savage indignation of our own: forgiveness is all.

Entry in the second peacetime diary of Geoffrey Sargent, August 12th 1938

It will be splendid to have Ted home with us next month. But over and above that, an enormous relief, considering how close to the wind he has sailed recently: the Gestapo would certainly clap him in irons if they knew what he's been up to. Fortunately he was able to send me his latest and final letter by the diplomatic mail, thanks to the British Consul in Hamburg. In it, he tells me all about what's going on in the concentration camp at Buchenwald. The prisoners there, almost all Jewish, are barbarously treated, half starved, bullied, and worked to death as slave-labourers. Ted hasn't seen this with his own eyes, of course: no outsider, least of all a foreign journalist, has access to the camps. But he has never been hoodwinked by the propaganda claims that they are run humanely according to the highest German ideals. No one believes that rubbish, of course, but everyone's afraid to say so, for fear of ending up also a prisoner. Still, Ted has his contacts: one such, a Lutheran minister, has a parishioner regularly entering Buchenwald as a truck-driver delivering supplies to the SS, who is appalled by what he sees there; he dares not speak up about it, except to confide in his pastor, who in turn has passed it all on to Ted. This, he tells me, he will bring with him in his head, memorized but not written down, when he leaves Germany. In London, despite his journalist's instinct to divulge, to expose malpractice, he will suppress what he knows, simply to protect the minister and the truck-driver from arrest and probable execution. *The Times*, then, will have to be content with his revelations about German rearmament: that much, anyway will give the lie to Hitler's pretence of peaceful intentions; it will be clear his aim is war, a war which, if victorious, would rob our world of any decency or truth. This will horrify me, if it comes. All these years I've been a pacifist, convinced that a just war is a contradiction in terms. But this war, so seemingly inevitable, may force me to change my thinking. It will not be a just war – there is no such thing. But if we are to eradicate what Hitler stands for, it will be a necessary war. Ted thinks so. When it breaks out, he says, he will feel it his duty to serve. I shall not, then, say him nay. Nor would it be my place to do so.

Letter from Eleanor Sargent to Edwin Sargent, October 3rd 1938

Dear Nephew,

It was with avid interest that I read, in yesterday's *Times*, the unsigned article about Mr Chamberlain, which was obviously by you. Leading such a reclusive life as I do in Cambridge, I am out of touch, directly, with the world's affairs. But that is not to say I disregard their importance. And I am much obliged to people like you, Ted, who can steer my thoughts in a sane direction, undistorted by political bravura or misguided hopes. The Prime Minister, you point out, has flown back from Munich waving a piece of paper like a chef brandishing a recipe, and mouthing empty words about peace in our time. It is all meaningless, you assert: Czechoslovakia has been dismembered, and that is utterly dishonorable, for we were treaty-bound to stand by her. And it is all, equally, too late: Hitler will next, it seems, have his way with Poland. What will we do then? Stand on the sidelines and say Sorry?

You may find it a bit surprising that a spinster aunt, like me, at an obscure address, should concern herself in this way about the larger world and I do thank you for helping me to see these matters clearly. But it isn't really all that surprising, in view of my current preoccupations. I'm writing a book about Juvenal, the Roman satirist. He lived and worked during the emperorship of Domitian, whose ferocity was remarkably like Hitler's. There was no way that he could confront the emperor's villainy: it would have cost him his life in very short order. But in attacking the vices and corruption of his time, he sent an implicit message that Rome was rotten from the top. For all I know, there may be prisoners in the concentration-camps who are paying the price for daring to criticize der Fuehrer, and we shall probably never hear of them again. But the Third Reich is not the only problem. Our beloved England is by no means free of its own brand of tyranny. Yet where is Juvenal when we need him today?

Ah well, there is nothing I can do myself, but stick to my last: to what I do best, and do my utmost to make it as good as I can – as you do also, with such clarity and good sense.

With much affection,
Aunt Eleanor

Letter from Edwin Sargent to Eleanor Sargent, September 30th 1939

Dear Aunt,
This will be just a quick note, in these hurried and harried days, to let you know how things are with me in London. The day after war was declared, I resigned my job and tried to figure out how best to serve. *The Times* solved that for me by pulling a few strings – something they're good at. The War Office has arranged a commission for me in one of the infantry regiments. There was some hesitation at first, when it came to light that I had refused, at Marlborough, to join the Officers Training Corps. But they took me on anyway, and are sending me on a crash course in military know-how; and I shall be joining the British Expeditionary Force next week in France. Hitler's threat to our world cannot go unrepelled.

It will mean a lot to me if we can stay in touch. I shall write to you as opportunity offers. How replies can reach a man on active service, I cannot predict. But the efficient way to write back is to address me by rank and number as follows: Lt E. Sargent, 22066875, BEF

If I were a praying man, I would pray now for your safety in Cambridge. Likewise for Aunt Edith in Alvingham, and for Mum and Dad in Glasgow. The actual praying I can leave to Aunt Edith, of course, But I shall be thinking daily of all four of you, with anxiety and love. No one in England can now rest secure: Hitler's practice of Total War puts civilian populations wholly at risk; he proved that with his infamous bombing of Guernica in the Spanish Civil War. Aunt Edith is just down the road from the RAF aerodrome in Manby; and it would be typical of the Luftwaffe to combine a raid on it with a gratuitous bombing of the convent. The intent, presumably, would be to strike a blow at British morale. What the Nazi mind does not comprehend, of course, is that any such atrocity would backfire: it would simply stiffen British resolve.

Dad and Mum, in their turn, would be strategically at risk, living beside the Clydeside shipyards, where the entire industry has been converted from the production of merchant vessels to the urgent build-up of our navy. Dad himself, as you doubtless know, retired from his firm last year, when that switchover was ordered. He would do so normally at sixty-five without having to make a moral issue out of it. But it was completely in character for him to quit, given his long-standing pacifism. However, as a profoundly honest man, he has had to admit to himself, with immense reluctance, that Hitler has to be stopped, that this world war, the second in his lifetime, is not the same as the first: that one, he has always said, was grossly unjustified; this one, as he puts it, is a *necessary* war.

I feel the same way. I have little stomach for combat. But we are all going to have to do the necessary thing. That does not mean *you* have to volunteer for some kind of war-work. Even in critical times, the cobbler should stick to his last; and yours is an intellectual contribution to be valued just as highly as that of the girls in the Land Army or the women in the munitions factories. When it is all over, we shall have had need of a sober mind weighing the human condition in the scales of history. That you have long done, in your books. If I survive, I shall want to come home and know you have carried on.

With deep affection,
Ted

Entry in the diary of Sister Edith Sargent, OSG, June 7th 1940

Every evening, after Vespers, we listen to the six o'clock news on the wireless. Contemplatives, in their calling, are not *in* the world. But if they are to pray for the world, they have to *know* the world. A suffering humanity needs our prayers, whether in peace or at war. So we, in our quiet house, must engage with what is so loudly going on. Three days ago, our men were safely evacuated from Dunkirk, thanks to a spur-of-the-moment flotilla of vessels, large and small, traversing the Channel with load after load of exhausted troops. People have started calling it a Miracle. I, for one, cannot use that term: it likens a human fact to an act of God. However, I do give thanks for it, as do all of us Sisters: better the men should be delivered, to renew the struggle, than that they should linger in some dreadful prisoner-of-war camp. Personally, of course, I am thankful that young Ted is safely back on our shores. I shall write to him, if I can. Perhaps Eleanor will know how to do so.

Letter from Sister Edith Sargent, OSG, to Eleanor Sargent, March 20th 1941

Dearest Eleanor,

What can I say that could possibly be of comfort? Our darling Geoff and his Kate both dead! Oh, to be sure, war is no respecter of persons Armies clash, and soldiers fall in battle. Navies fire their guns, and sailors die. The air force, on either side, drops bombs on targets geared to the war-effort, whether military or industrial. All of that, though lamentable, is to be expected. But the wanton assault upon civilian lives, that is another matter. Nothing can ever excuse the London Blitz. And now the attack on Glasgow has not stopped short at wreaking havoc on the navy shipyards: it has taken the lives of men, women, and children in all the city's neighbourhoods. That is unconscionable. God may forgive. But how shall we?

Eleanor dear, do you suppose this terrible news has reached Ted in North Africa? For all I know, there may be an official policy to keep such news from men at the Front, lest it dishearten them wholly. But I cannot bear the thought that he would set his heart on coming home later, only to learn his beloved parents were killed. Or, if there is no policy to keep him in ignorance, it is unbearable to think that he would learn of this by running across something so cold and stark as a casualty-list. Somehow, we must find a way to break the news to him, as gently as we can. I hate to burden you with this, but may I leave that sad task to you? I know you have managed to keep in touch with him, as I have not; so perhaps you know how to reach him. Forgive me for asking this. I would gladly do it myself, if I knew how. So do hand the task back to me, if it is too much for you, by sending me his address.

Now there are only the two of us left. It is some consolation that Uncle Augustus is gone before, for he had become very fond of us all. We, the remainder, must console each other. My heart goes out to you. My prayers and thoughts will be with you every hour of the day. And, of course, with poor Ted.

Love as always,
Edith

Letter from Edwin Sargent to Edith and Eleanor Sargent (both copies extant) April 3rd 1941

Dear Aunts Edith arid Eleanor,

I'm sure you must both have been in great distress, about whether I knew at all of Mum and Dad's death in the blitz on Glasgow; and if I did know, how such dreadful news reached me. At least I can put your minds at ease in one respect: it would have been agonizing to be aware of the Glasgow blitz but be left wondering whether Mum and Dad had survived or not; bad news may be tough, and this certainly is, but no news, in such a case, would have been torment.

For all its many rigidities, the Army does have a human side. If one of us falls in battle, it takes care to inform the next-of-kin promptly and with proper regret. Those bad news telegrams are much dreaded, but better they should be sent than that families should struggle with suddenly not getting any letters from their loved one at the Front. Letting them know is a sad duty, but a decent necessity. That is recognized, I think, by all concerned.

What is less well known is the reverse conduit. The commanding officer who sends those telegrams is sometimes, conversely, in receipt of bad news about next-of-kin which he must break to a serving soldier in his unit. This never used to happen, I suppose, in former wars, where only combatants were involved. But that has changed now. In the present war (Hitler's so-called Total War), civilians are targeted en masse. A civilian casualty-list is far from comprehensive. But when names on it correspond to names listed as a soldier's next of kin, then it falls to his commandant to break the news to him. Thus it befell that I was paraded to the Brigadier, who sat me down and told me about my parents. It must have been hard for him. He handled it very well.

Can't say I did. Maybe if I'd been faced with your standard commanding officer, all spit-and-polish and no-nonsense, I could have managed the expected stiff upper lip. But our man, Styles-Allison, isn't like that. He was in obvious distress at having to break the news, and I felt for him at once. That broke me and I crumpled. Actually, I cried like a child, and he let that pass as absolutely normal. Then he said, "Hell, Ted, this is absolutely the wrong way round. Our parents aren't supposed to be the casualties, we are. For you, three days' compassionate leave – that's an order. And let's see if we can find out if there's been any kind of funeral. D'you want me to arrange for a posting home?"

Well, of course, when I pulled myself together, I said No, sir, the best way I can honour them is to carry on doing what I'm here for. But I was glad of the three days off: it gave me time to move past the reflex anger, the hankering for revenge; time to start grieving. And now that I'm back on what approximates to an even keel, my first thought is of you two, and how you must be feeling.

You must be stricken, both of you. For I know how much Dad meant to you, your only brother. And you both had affectionate room in your hearts for Mum, whom he loved so much. There's nothing I can say to console you. But I also know that both of you, in your separate fashion, are capable of finding a way through this sorrow.

Aunt Edith, you have a religious faith which I happen not to share, but which I firmly respect; and it will sustain you, beyond doubt, in coming to terms with a loss that, to other eyes, would seem as meaningless as it is cruel. Dad and Mum always spoke warmly, and admiringly of you, even though they, like me, were unbelievers. Right now you must be praying for their souls. And I know they would not have it otherwise.

And you, Aunt Eleanor, whom I have come to know so well, despite a late start, one thing I'm sure of with you is that your shrewd understanding of the present, in the light of the past, will have given you a sane perspective on this latest wave of carnage, even as it hits so close to home. One cannot react to a family death with anything like detachment; but history can bestow a measure of stoicism.

I shall hope for a touch of that, myself. But as of now, my heart breaks for those two innocent people.

With much love to you both,

Ted

Entry in the diary of Sister Edith Sargent, OSG, April 11th 1941

Today being Good Friday has been all Remembrance from start to finish: notably with the three-hour Solemn Liturgy of the Passion in the afternoon; and then, at nightfall, with our annual rite of Tenebrae, its extinguishing of lights, its commemoration of the Death, its final antiphon of mourning "because the innocent Lord is slain", sung by us all in unison. And I listen, stricken, as Sister Winifred, our cantor, chants the Lesson from the *Book of Lamentations*.

> How doth the city sit solitary
> that was full of people.

Her gates are desolate:
>	the young and the old lie on the ground in the streets.
For the enemy hath magnified himself:
>	he hath sent down fire from above,
>	and great as the sea is her destruction.
For these things I weep,
>	mine eye runneth down like a river;
>	because the enemy hath prevailed.
Oh Lord, behold, my affliction!

Listening, I cannot but think of darling Geoff, and his beloved Marion, extinguished like wicks on the candelabrum so aptly called a hearse, and all those hundreds of others silenced with them in Glasgow three weeks ago. But let me not forget, either, the thousands upon thousands similarly doomed elsewhere, as much in Germany as here. Who ever knew that grief was so exhausting?

Letter from Eleanor Sargent to Sister Edith Sargent, OSG, April 18th 1941

Dearest Edith,

Bless you for Tuesday's last, arrived this morning. What a sweet soul you have! Only someone like you could transmute our grief into an Exultate over the Resurrection. You speak of Tenebrae, of the darkness at noon; but then, in the next breath, of Lux Mundi, the Light of the World, risen again upon your Easter morning. I envy you that.

Here in Cambridge, along the Backs, tulips are in riot, scarlet and golden, like proclamations of life renewed. It is, for me, a comfort in our sorrow. You, I know, have always been forgiving of my unbelief, so stark a contrast to your own strength of faith. And I am grateful, especially now, that you find common ground with me, you in your chanted Resurrexit, and I in my joy at Nature's re-emergence, year upon year, at winter's end.

Always, of course, there are parallels. The Blitz on Glasgow, tragically, has many a counterpart in other times and places. And almost every one, at root, is the work of malevolence in the seat of power. History, alas, is full of Hitlers, wreaking havoc around them out of their own sheer spite. I am much in mind of that, lately, because my latest book, now nearing completion, is about Juvenal and thus, by implication, is about the reign of terror he had to survive, under Domitian. He was lucky. Geoff and Kate, that lovely pair, were not. The world is empty for their loss. As best we can, you and I, we must soldier on. I send you my love.

Eleanor

Letter from Edwin Sargent to Eleanor Sargent from Cairo, 14 September 1941

Dear Aunt,

As an ironist, you will appreciate the paradox of this letter. Here am I, posted to a so-called theatre of war, settled cozily in one of the world's chief laps of peacetime luxury – Sheppard's no less. Army has taken over the place and, mind you, there's a fair bit of military hustle back here at HQ, not all of it heartening – but that's another story.

I'm not supposed to say anything about what's going on at the Front, when writing home. But there's no secret that things haven't been going well. In fact, the PM has sacked Wavell as C-in-C. Sent him off to Singapore, where he won't do any harm and can turn his mind to poetry, which was always more important to him than the prosody of combat.

His replacement is Bernard Montgomery, a breath of fresh air, already known to everyone as Monty. Apparently a quite original thinker in his field. I haven't actually met him. But chances are he'll get along just fine with our own immediate C.O., no less an eminence than Brigadier Sir Humphrey Stiles-Allison, DSO, who comes with all the pomp and circumstance of a baronetcy, distinguished, lineage, and a well-earned medal. If that led some of us to expect a cartoon figure out of Punch and Debrett, they would be wrong. Utterly. He's a true original, and a bit of an eccentric: lugs along a French horn in his kit and swears like a trooper when he hits a wrong note practising solo passages in the Mozart concerto. Says the horn is a bloody intractable instrument designed to teach humility, but he proposes to play it note-perfect atop the Brandenburg Gate and he gets all kinds of assiduity out of me by treating everyone of all ranks as fellowmen, not as cogs in a disciplinary machine.

He seems to have taken a bit of a shine to me, because of my years in Germany: reckons I must have clues to the workings of the German mind that escape us short-sighted compatriots of the doddering old Neville Chamberlain. Even Churchill is baffled by the Nazis, though he has a keen idea of how demented they are. Anyway Humpers, as he's called behind his back, apparently thinks I might be able to figure out Rommel's mind for us, and pass on any thoughts of mine to Monty, for whatever worth they might have.

How I'm supposed to go about this hasn't been made clear, but no doubt some makeshift plan will in due course emerge, new-hatched, from the Stiles-Allison brain. One thing can be counted on: whatever Humpers cooks up will be unorthodox,

Meanwhile, he's teamed me up, as a duo, with a rather ferocious Corporal Harry Fuad, an alumnus of commando school, who knows all the tricks of that lethal trade, including the noiseless killing of German sentries. One of his incidental qualifications is that he speaks fluent Arabic. Born Hari al-Fuad, he's the son of an English mother and a Lebanese businessman, raised bilingually; and he's much prized by Army for quick-wittedness and initiative. Humpers hasn't said anything much about how Harry's Arabic fits into whatever scheme he's formulating. But I dare say it has something to do with contacting the local population. People at home reading war reports from North Africa probably think of the place merely as a place where opposing armies fight it out. But what of the folk who actually live here? Surely they're a piece, maybe even a tactically important piece, in the jigsaw.

Dad used to speak about that, sometimes, from his days in the Boer War and from everything written about '14-'18. "Lest we forget" is a proper slogan for those who fell in the Somme and at Passchendaele, and so on. But surely also we are bidden to remember the civilians of French and Belgian villages and towns, on whose fields and streets those slaughters were conducted.

Either way, whatever Humpers' intentions for us may be, we make an odd couple. Harry and I, he with his ambiguous Arabic, me with my saturated German; he with his sanguinary skills, me with my reporter's nose for sniffing out the lie of the land. All will unfold. In due course I probably won't be allowed to say anything in a letter about what we're up to. But I will continue to send you word when I can, to let you know I'm still alright, for I know you worry about me.

Love,
Ted

P.S. Is there any evidence that Thucydides actually took part in the Peloponnesian War that he wrote so tellingly about?

Undated entry in the wartime diary of Edwin Sargent, evidently written before the Battle of Alamein on the eve of his mission with Fuad behind enemy lines.

Humpers has now lined me up, with Harry Fuad, for Special Ops behind Rommel's lines. He'll have the two of us dropped off by boat, after dark, just west of Benghazi, in Arab civvies.

"Of course, you do realize, Corporal," Humpers said to Fuad, "you're done for if they catch on. No way you'll be treated as POWs: you and Captain Sargent'll be shot as spies. No rescue from this end, I'm afraid. You okay with that?"

"Quite understood, sir," Fuad said.

"Tell you the truth," Humpers added, "I wish I could go with you. But they wouldn't let me. No point anyway, I don't speak German."

He turned to me.

"I know this is alright with you, Ted," he said. "But if worst comes to worst, I want you both to know I'll be making it my absolute first call of duty, after the war, to go and see your next of kin in person."

He harrumphed loudly, as though the conversation was edging close to the embarrassing.

"Dismissed, chaps," he said.

So Fuad and I both went to our respective quarters and wrote provisional farewell letters to our folks, to be held, for use if needed, in Humpers office. Fuad's was to his parents in Cardiff – he'd grown up partly there and partly in Lebanon, and that explained why his English was Welsh-flavoured, in contrast to my own somewhat Glaswegian. Dad and Mum being gone now, dammit, my farewells were, of course, to my two redoubtable aunts. It's not the same thing as saying goodbye to one's parents, which I had never had the chance to do. Even so, though, it was a rough experience trying to find the right words. I just hope they never have to be used.

(No such letter survives; probably destroyed when not needed)

Orders are, we are to infiltrate local communities and take soundings. Arabs in North Africa have mixed feelings about Europeans taking over their ancestral lands. They hated the Italian colonization of Libya, not to mention their treatment of Abyssinia; so they were pleased by our rout of Mussolini's troops. But they have no liking for the British influence in Egypt. Because of that, they somewhat welcome Rommel's driving us back across Libya into Egypt, seeing him as a liberator from foreign hegemony there. They don't seem to realize a German victory might merely mean, for them, a change of masters. So short-sightedly, they tend to collaborate with the Afrika Korps. Our job will be to probe the collaboration for info about Rommel's troop movements, and what they might reveal about his strategic and tactical plans.

Harry Fuad, with his fluent Arabic and Lebanese background will be a convincing character. He grew up hating the French overlordship in his father's birthplace, and he was delighted by our defeat of the Vichy troops there. Being a realist, though, he has his doubts about postwar independence: victors often divide the spoils, and local populations get the short end of the stick. But that'll be who knows when.

My role, unlike Harry's, is purely fictitious. I'm to pass as a trader of mixed race, partly Arab, with a pre-war connection to a family business operating, years ago, in the old German colonies in Cameroon and South-West Africa. Hence my knowledge of German – I've been practising how to speak it with an Arab accent. Rommel's supply lines will be seriously stretched; and the hope is that his lieutenants will reckon me to be, as a trader, a possibly useful source of supplies they need – and where they want them to go. They'd seize them by force, of course. But someone like me would know, purportedly, where such supplies might be found.

It's a loony idea, on the face of it. But if we can pull it off, we might be able to get back to Monty, via Humpers, with an inkling of what Rommel has in mind. A full frontal assault with his entire Korps? Or maybe a diversionary flank attack to draw the Eighth Army south and leave the centre clear for him to push through?

I'm keen to go. So is Harry. This job's right up his alley.

Letter from Eleanor Sargent to Sister Edith Sargent, OSG, May 17th 1942

Dearest Edith,

I'm writing this quickly and with rejoicing, to share with you good news about Ted, just received. He's alive and well, and safe(!), and his name has been put forward for the Military Cross. I get this in a personal letter from his commandant, no less a someone than Brigadier Sir Humphrey Stiles-Allison. Thereby hangs a tale. As follows.

You, in your cloistered life, are still very much part of a community, in no sense a loner. By contrast I, in the outer world, am barely part of a community at all, almost a solitary like the hermits in the desert, who were intent only on the one thing they did well, communing with God. I too commune, in my secular way, with the idea of Truth, as annunciated by history. It suffices me.

But I am not, and never have been, oblivious of the world around me – except, of course, during my years of illness. In the here and now, my charwoman's daughter Betty, as one example of a fellow-being, has come to see me from time to time, when she's home in Cambridge, to talk with me about her chances of getting more education when the war is over. She was part-way through grammar-school in 1940, thanks to her mother's insistence that she stay in school rather than take any available but menial job like her own. One has to respect that kind of working-class regard for "book-learning" in the face of disadvantage: it's common in Scotland and Wales, though sadly uncommon in England itself. Anyway, Betty, right now, is a Land Girl in Essex, helping offset the labour shortage on the farms. When all this hideous conflict is over, she wants to try for a scholarship here, at Girton or Newnham; and if she's successful, she could probably afford to go, because she could live at home and at least help out with the housework. So I've told her I could try and give her some tutoring when the time comes. The least I could do considering what a standby her mother has been to me.

It's quid pro quo. For it turns out that the big wheel in the Land Girl organization is Lady Alicia Stiles-Allison, wife of our nephew's commandant, the Brigadier. So I wheedled his address out of her and wrote to him last month, saying Ted's two aunts were very worried about him, not having heard from him for some time, and would he please put our minds at rest about him.

I rather dreaded his reply. But it was very prompt; and I enclose a copy of it with this letter. You will be as jubilant as I was to read it. And I won't waste any more time (not to mention nowadays valuable paper) getting this off to you.

Love,
Eleanor

Letter to Miss Eleanor Sargent from Brigadier-General Sir Humphrey Stiles-Allison from Cairo, May 2nd 1942

Dear Miss Sargent,

I am very pleased to reply with good news to your April letter, inquiring about the well-being of your nephew, Captain Edwin Sargent. He is in fine form and good health. In fact, he has been promoted Major; and I have recommended him for the Military Cross, in recognition of his recent audacious work behind enemy lines. I am not at liberty to tell you what his mission was and how he accomplished it. But I can tell you this much; what he pulled off in the desert, with just one man's help, made a vital contribution to General Montgomery's planning for the Battle of Alamein. We are very proud of him, and of his sidekick, a Corporal Fuad.

Not long since, I did have the sad duty of telling Ted about the death of his parents in the bombing of Clydeside. It was a hard blow for him to bear, for he was obviously very close to them. It must have been a hard blow for you and your sister, too. Please accept my belated condolences. Ted has done your family proud, since then, with his gallant exploits.

It will be no surprise to you to hear of Ted's reaction when I told him about the MC recommendation. Not being afraid to speak up when that's called for, he insisted that he'd decline the honour if Corporal Fuad wasn't also recommended, for the Military Medal – it's one of the quaint and somewhat undesirable anomalies of English class-distinction that the Cross is for Officers only, while Other Ranks qualify only for the Medal, like the snobbish separation of Gentlemen from Players at Lord's. Ted swore the Cross and the Medal were of equal value, earned in the same way; and what was done by a by a corporal was no whit less than what was done by a captain.

I was able to put his mind at rest by telling him I'd already recommended Fuad for the Medal. So that settled that matter; and I must say I agreed with Ted's view.

From Cairo, Ted will be reassigned to duty back in England, where he's being seconded to a top-secret post outside London, because of his expertise in German. It's so secret, in fact, that I haven't the faintest idea of what it is he'll be up to – let alone my not being allowed to tell you anything about it, even if I did know. But whatever it is, he wants me to tell you that he won't actually be in combat any more, which I'm sure will be a relief to you and your sister. Of course, he can tell you this in person when he does get back; and I wish you all joy in that reunion.

Then, when this is all over, I shall hope to have the pleasure, someday, of meeting you in person myself.

Until then, thank you for your concern,

Yours very sincerely,

Humphrey Stiles-Allison

Letter from Wilfred Baker to Edgar Simpson (Eleanor Sargent), February 7th 1943

Dear Edgar,

Your wonderful *Juvenal* arrived safely last week. As you mention in your letter, one of our wartime difficulties is a terrible shortage of paper – witness the minuscule size of our daily newspapers. Book publishers are all having to cut back on production, either printing quite small editions or, in several cases, deferring an author's work until the war is over. Somehow, though, I've been able to scrounge enough paper to plan on bringing out *Juvenal* in a few months.

It will be quite timely to do so. For as you rightly point out, there is an extraordinary similarity in the despotism of Domitian and that of Hitler. You make a very telling comparison. Like Hitler, Domitian exercised absolute power, imposed a reign of terror, and was supported by a sycophantic gang of vicious henchmen. What was a writer like Juvenal to do? Speak up and become a prisoner of conscience? Or tuck away his diatribes in the Ancient Roman equivalent of a desk drawer?

Well, literary chaps are not, as a rule, the stuff of heroes. Chances are, there's a writer, here and there in Germany, who's telling home truths about the Third Reich on paper, but stashes his manuscript away in prudent hiding. Juvenal hated Domitian, but dared not publish his hatred until after the emperor's death: instead, he contented himself with attacking the moral corruption all around him under Domitian without laying the blame for it directly at the emperor's door. It was, I suppose, a bearable compromise. The sad historical truth, of course, is that the sword is always mightier than the pen, until the sword is sheathed or turned into a ploughshare.

You make this very clear in your text. I shall be very proud to publish it.

Sincerely,

Wilfred

P.S. Have you had a chance to read *Darkness at Noon* by Arthur Koestler, just published by my friend Victor Gollancz? In case you haven't, I'm sending you a copy. It paints a forthright picture of despotism under Stalin – not a popular message in these days of cozying up to Uncle Joe. But time will tell. The cat will be out of the bag one day. Meanwhile, Koestler has had his say – uttered, of course, safely enough in his London exile.

Entry in the diary of Sister Edith Sargent, OSG, May 12th 1943

When will this terrible war end? We pray for it daily, here, in this House of God. But as yet to no avail. My epistolary friend, the Bishop of Chichester, tells me of a possible peace-overture suggested to him, via an intermediary in Sweden, by a Protestant pastor in Germany, called Dietrich Bonheoffer. He passed the initiative on to Churchill, but the response was a flat rejection: nothing less than an abject surrender by

Hitler would satisfy the PM. That won't happen, of course, Dr Bell informs me. Now, for his pains, poor Pastor Bonheoffer lies in a Gestapo prison cell, charged with treason. And his confrère, Pastor Martin Niemöller, also "treasonous", share the same fate, in a concentration camp. But where are all the other obligatory martyrs? Has the Roman Church under duress become a body of silence? Where has all the courage gone? Well, there has been no shortage of bravery elsewhere, witness Ted's Military Cross. He would be the last person to tell me how he earned it. But Eleanor somehow got hold of his citation and sent me a copy. Apparently, he went on sorties behind enemy lines in the Desert Campaign, and provided General Montgomery with vital information about Rommel's troop dispositions. We are very proud of him. Now he's back in Blighty, as they say, and the War Office has seconded him to a top-secret unit somewhere in the country outside London; he's not allowed to say where he is or what he's doing, of course, but he did let drop it has something to do with his fluency in German. I wonder what he would think, if he knew that our daily prayers, here, for all those in peril of death in battle, or on the home fronts, are said on behalf of *all* souls, Allied or German alike. Come to think of it, if he takes after dear Geoff, I'm sure he would approve.

Entry in the peacetime diary of Lt-Col Edwin Sargent, MC, September 15th 1945

It's all over now. Or is it? Certainly there has been Victory in Europe, and Japan has been atom-bombed into surrender. But what of the future? I've left Bletchley, along with everyone else. Yet all too soon, so far as I can tell, there may have to be another Bletchley, to eavesdrop on the Kremlin: Stalin has made his intentions pretty clear where Central and Eastern Europe are concerned. We shall see. Meanwhile, though, we have to deal with the problem of defeated Germany. I hope we won't make the same vindictive mistake we made last time. The last thing Europe needs is a Germany bent on reprisals of its own. Perhaps this time around, sanity will prevail, will see how vital it is to put the Germans back on their feet as partners in a peaceful Continent. First, of course, the guilty have to be brought to book. Not just the ringleaders, who are going to be tried in Nuremberg, but the small-fry, too, the guards and executioners in the camps, the gas-chamber operators. Even the rank-and-file members of the Nazi Party, with no blatant atrocities on their record will have to face the tribunals being planned to investigate them. Some will be punished, others cleared. It's called a Denazification

Process; and I'm being posted to the British Zone, to help set up the tribunals – I suppose because my German is still pretty good. That shouldn't take too long: I can assemble the right personnel, organize the materiel according to agreed-on principles, and then the War Office will let me go. After that, Nuremberg. *The Times* has been very kind: they've kept my job open for me, of course, as is only proper. But to begin with, before going back to a desk job in Fleet Street, I've asked for a temporary re-assignment, and they've agreed. So I'll be Special Correspondent again, covering the Nuremberg trial. After all those years of mine in the Third Reich in that role, this posting will bring the whole story, full circle, to a satisfactory end. At least, I hope there will be satisfaction. Now that the appalling truth of Auschwitz has been unmasked, it's going to be up to us, not to string those bastards up on the nearest lamp-post, but to have them undergo due process, rigorously, under international law. In other words, let us not besmirch the memory of a single victim by stooping to the barbarism of Hitler and his gang.
Letter from Edwin Sargent to Eleanor Sargent, March 1st 1946

Dear Aunt,

As you know, I became happily engaged last year to Kate Trevelyan, the splendid young code-breaker I met at Bletchley. We've decided to get married in London on May 8th, the anniversary of V-E Day. It seems apposite: marriage, after all, is supposed to be a haven, of peace and serenity; and that, surely, is what everyone, is looking for now that the war's over.

It won't be a big, splashy affair – who can afford such things nowadays? Cheerful, of course, with much to look forward to. But tinged with sadness, too: I'll miss Mum and Dad awfully, and Kate's in the same way as well – lost both parents in the London Blitz. So just the bride and groom, and two witnesses: Kate's asked two girl-friends from Bletchley, Bobby Osborne and Laura Greene; and Harry Fuad, my corporal in Libya, is going to stand up for me as best man. How apposite is that! He was my right-arm in all our desert capers. Probably I owe my life to him two or three times over.

We're getting hitched in the Kensington Registry Office. I know aunt Edith would have preferred we should do it in a church; but she knows I'm not a believer – nor is Kate – and I'm sure she would not want me to pretend otherwise: that would be hypocritical. As for you, Aunt Eleanor, we would both be truly honoured if you would like to join us. The ceremony is at 11.00, with a luncheon to follow at the Bletchley Club on Albemarle Street. I realize that you lead an almost hermit-like life in Cambridge; so if you prefer not to emerge, like a bear from hibernation,

neither of us will be the least bit offended. However, if you do decide to
come, it's a quite straightforward trip. The express train from Cambridge
to Liverpool Street station takes only an hour; and from there to
Kensington is only a short taxi ride. I could book you a room at
Durrants' Hotel, for the night before and the night after, and never mind
the expense: they're going to pay me a nice demob gratuity, and I can't
think of a nicer way to splurge some of it than by arranging a long
overdue get-together with you.

Now that I think of it, a little trip to London might give you a chance
to have lunch with your publisher. I have a strange feeling you've never
actually met him.

Affectionately,
Ted

P.S. Kate sends her greetings, and says she would very much enjoy
getting to know you, if you can come.

*Letter from Pfc Toni Meyer, U5 Army of Occupation, Munich, American
Zone to Mr Edwin Sargent, c/o* The Times, *Fleet Street. London EC1,
United Kingdom, January 10th 1946*

*(Pencilled note by Edwin Sargent attached to above: Meyer's letter
not forwarded to me in Nuremberg, lay unopened in my London in-
tray, awaiting attention; have phoned US Embassy to get addresses
for Toni and Ernst. 16/9/47)*

Dear Ted,

Here's a voice from the past, Toni Meyer, whom you befriended in
Berlin years ago, along with Ernst Schillinger. When we got out of
Germany you and your parents helped us to move on   to the States.
We'll never forget that. Really, you saved our lives. When my outfit
shipped over to Britain in later 1942, I made a point of spending my first
48-hour pass in Glasgow. I wanted to thank your folks for helping us out.
It was a rotten shock to learn they'd both been killed in an air-raid. They
were a great couple and you must miss them terribly. Please accept my
sympathy. I know what that kind of loss can feel like: all my relatives
were murdered in Auschwitz.

On a happier note, you should know that Ernst and I both did well in
the States. We're American citizens, proud of it and grateful. After Pearl
Harbour, we both wanted to join the armed forces, but Ernst didn't pass

the medical. Instead, he quit what he was doing, in car sales, and went to work in a factory building tanks. Me, I enlisted in the infantry, landed on Omaha Beach on D-day. Got through the Normandy campaign without a scratch. And when the war ended, they figured my German would be useful and posted me here as an interpreter.

It's been pretty weird for me, this experience. Believe me, when I enlisted, I couldn't wait to get my hands on a gun, to put paid to some of those sons-of-bitches who'd slaughtered my family. But you can't hang on to feelings like that when you find yourself killing another guy, dozens of times, just because he's wearing a different uniform. Hell, he's just an ordinary human being, just another draftee sent into a quarrel he never picked in the first place. In many cases no more than a kid. Breathes the same air; and when he's dead, smells the same as anyone else. In the end, most of my buddies felt the same way.

But nothing's that simple. Here in Germany, with the war over, things get complicated again. My unit was the one that liberated Bergen-Belsen. That was a scene of horror if ever there was one. It would still sicken me if I tried to describe it. And ninety per cent of the victims were Jews – could have been me, if I hadn't been lucky. So all my old feelings came back. We captured the camp guards. They'd run off like rats, but we rounded them up. And what I wanted to do was just shoot them on the spot. You can't do that, of course, not to an unarmed man. But a big part of me really wants to see them put down. Like vermin. Still feel like that, but something isn't right about it. And here in the American Zone, when I take part in interviews with former Nazi Party members, I have to somehow set such feelings aside and just let the facts speak for themselves. Like the man said, that ain't a whole barrel of fun.

Ted, I'm writing to you about this (and I'm sorry this has been such a long letter) because I want to sit down with you and have you help me sort myself out. A recent issue of *The Stars and Stripes* mentioned you were in Nuremberg reporting on the war-crimes trial. So I rounded up copies of your reports for *The Times* in London, and they're just great. You're faced with twenty-four of the worst villains in history, but what you write about them is a model of objectivity. I admire that; and. I wish I could be that objective.

I hope this letter reaches you. I'm sending it to *The Times* in London, with a request they forward it to you in Nuremberg. If they do; I'd like to come and see you in Nuremberg. First of all, of course, to say a long overdue thank you for 1936, and to offer you in person my condolences over the loss of your parents. But that said, I really need to come to terms with what went on and what we need to do about it. People are starting to call it the Holocaust, and I guess what's troubling me is the big question of how do we execute justice for the past, and how do we look out for the future. You probably have better answers to that than I've been able to figure out.

Cheers,
Toni

P.S. If you can get back to me, please let me have your permanent home address, so I can pass it on to Ernst. I know he would want to write to you and say thank you, too.

Entry in the diary of Dame Edith Sargent, OSG, June 28th 1952

This day has been a banner one: my seventy-fifth birthday, and a wonderful family picnic for me on our grounds, with Ted and his wife and their four-year-old, and with Eleanor come all this way from Cambridge – amazing, she never goes anywhere, except out to do her shopping. Sister Helena baked a huge cake, arid Mother Superior, who's ninety-two now and spry as anything, joined us for a few minutes to bless the occasion, but then left us to enjoy ourselves on this very rare family get-together. My real birthday, of course, is February 4th, St Gilbert's Day, which is the anniversary of my final vows in 1894, but that's more an occasion for the community than for relatives. Last year, they promoted me Prioress, so I am now Dame Edith. It sounds rather grand, but all it does is serve to remind me that "the last shall be first and the first shall be last." If I'm lucky, I'll be able to sneak in the door of Heaven behind all the others here, who are so much more worthy. And I'd better work on that while there's still time. Sister Amelia, who's our Infirmatrix and was a doctor before entering, says she's worried about my heart and wants me to see a specialist. I tell her not to bother about it. It's not in human hands to say when my time is up. Readiness is all.

Letter to Eleanor Sargent from the Most Reverend Catherine Lewis, OSG, June 23rd 1953

Dear Miss Sargent,

I am more sorry than I can say to be the bearer of bad news, especial by post and not in person. I would have called you, but I understand you have no telephone and are hard to reach.

Three days ago, our beloved Dame Edith had a severe heart-attack, and was not able to survive it. This will be a great grief to you, for I know that you and she were very close, despite living so far apart. I could witness that with my own eyes, when you visited us last year: it was very edifying to see such deep and enduring affection between (if I may say so) two old ladies who had spent their childhood together long ago. Please accept my profound condolences on your loss.

You will be glad to hear that I was able to contact your nephew, Edwin, and he was able to attend the funeral, which was this morning, after Requiem Mass. He is going on to be with you in Cambridge. I'm sure it will be a comfort to you to have him there.

Dame Edith will be sorely missed here. She made a tremendous contribution to our community life, and everyone loved her, young and old. She was very simple and pure, and we console ourselves with the knowledge that she has gone home to God's love like an arrow to its target. We will commemorate her with endless gratitude.

Should you care to visit again, to be at your sister's grave, please come any time you feel like it. There will always be a room for you in our guest-wing. We are setting aside for you all of her odds and ends (Dame Edith was extremely modest in such matters) and you would of course be free to choose from them anything you might like to have as a memento We have also gathered together in one bundle, so to speak, her diaries and her personal correspondence. All of that, I am sure, she would want you to have. So, in due course, perhaps you could let me know whether you would like to come and take possession of it, or if you would prefer we send it to you by parcel post.

Meanwhile, please know that my thoughts and prayers, and those of our entire community, are with you.

Yours in Christ,
Catherine Lewis, OSG, Abbess

Letter from Edgar Simpson (Eleanor Sargent) to Wilfred Baker, August 2nd 1955

Dear Wilfred,

Here, at long last, is *Aeschylus*. You've been waiting a long time for it; but I've been grappling with it, infuriatingly, ever since I first went at it years ago. Finally, I've got it in the kind of shape where I reckon my job is done – at least as done as I can make it. I hope you find it satisfactory. You've always been very good about my books, accepting them without demur. This one, by the way, will be my last one: I'm eighty, and think I've run out of steam.

When you read *Aeschylus*, you will see that it has a quite narrow focus. Far from being a conspectus of his whole oeuvre and what is known of his life, it deals only with one of his plays, the *Agamemnon*. It was timely enough for me to start on that text in 1945, when I first mentioned it to you; for the war had just ended, and that one play responded to the bloody aftermath of the Trojan War. I did not reckon, at the time, that I would become exclusively preoccupied with that theme, but so it was. Clytemnestra's axe-murder of Agamemnon, in revenge for his killing of their daughter, resonated, profoundly with me, because of parallels in my own life. I come from what would be called, in today's jargon, a severely dysfunctional family. I have struggled, lifelong, to come to terms with the resultant pain. I would not have you think that I've done nothing, ever, but lick my wounds. Indeed, I can honestly claim to have put the past in perspective, most of the time. Writing my books, in privacy, has been a salutary refuge; and I hope I have written them with the kind of objective detachment that every scholar should aspire to. Whether I can make a similar claim for *Aeschylus*, I am not so sure. You must be the judge.

That you will be a fair judge, I cannot for a moment doubt. Your discrimination as a publisher is flawless; and you have been so kind to me over my books that I have come to regard you as a friend, even though we have never met. Precisely because of that, I feel I must now, near the end of my life, make a clean breast of something I have deceived you in ever since the very first letter I sent you, with my first book.

The fact is, my dear Wilfred, "Edgar Simpson" does not exist, and never has existed. My real name is Eleanor Sargent – same initials. Once you have absorbed the surprise of that, you will perhaps think that I chose to write to you under a male pseudonym to preclude the kind of rejection many an authoress has had to suffer, just because she's a woman. Not so. If that had been the case, I would have let my books be issued simply under the pseudonymous male name, in full. Insisting, instead, on the mere initials, and refusing also to participate in any publicity, was a mark, rather, of my need for a kind of protected anonymity. I hope that kind of hiding away can be maintained, that you will continue to respect, as you always have, my cherished solitude. But I do owe it to you, after all you've done for me, to "come clean", as the saying goes. So here is the brief and sordid history of my early years.

My late father, the Rev'd Barnabas Sargent, war rector for many decades of a small parish in Lincolnshire, just outside the market-town of Louth. His faith, such as it was, took the form of an obsessive attention, in church, to Anglo-Catholic liturgy and rituals. But in the home there was no love lost on his family. He treated his wife, Martha, with dismissive contempt, and bullied his only son. Until puberty, my younger sister and I went about our lives like mice, in fear of his displeasure. But then, when I was fifteen, everything changed. He raped me, and continued to do so, intermittently, for the next three years, without getting caught – I must be physically barren, or I would have become pregnant. Throughout those years, I took refuge in study, and ended up winning a scholarship to London's University College. Around then, I noticed he was beginning to cast a lecherous eye on my sister, two years my junior. I would have forgone my scholarship to stay home and protect her, if necessary. But as it turned out, I didn't need to: she was highly gifted in Gregorian chant, felt a vocation to the cloister, and entered the Order of St Gilbert as a choir-nun. There, by the way, she remained for the rest of her life – she died last year – and was extremely happy. With her safely gone to the convent, I took up my scholarship and never went back home: between terms, I stayed on in London, supporting myself on odd jobs; and after my degree, I accepted a post in a girls' school, teaching Latin and Greek and Ancient History. My brother, too, left home and had a happy, useful, and productive career as a ship-architect in Glasgow. There, sadly, he was killed in an air-raid; and my only living relatives are his son, Edwin, the well-known journalist, his daughter-in-law and his granddaughter.

Experiences like mine, especially if undergone by women, leave scars, unavoidably. In early middle age, I had a major nervous breakdown, which incapacitated me for seven years. When I recovered from it, jobless and with out-of-date credentials, I would have been destitute, except that a rich uncle (also now deceased) came to my rescue with an annuity I have lived on ever since. It has enabled me to pursue my calling as an author, unembarrassed by money worries. And you have been my literary angel, so to speak, in making public my texts while preserving my solitude. There is no way I can ever thank you enough. What I *can* do, at this late date, is at least now be fully honest with you.

If *Aeschylus* seems worthy of publication, you will notice that I wish to dedicate it to Martha Sargent, whom I do not there identify as my mother. For many years, I resented her, feeling she should have protected me from the evil that befell me. In later years, I realized it was not her fault: she was too browbeaten by her husband, either to stand up to him in small matters or to intervene in matters of grave consequence. She could not possibly have taken an axe to him, as Clytemnestra did to Agamemnon over *her* daughter. But I had no right to sit in judgment on Mama. After she was widowed, she came more into her own, even bloomed a little in old age, and we became friends, of a sort, until her death – though I'm ashamed to admit I didn't see as much of her as I should have.

Old friend, you have been the rock of my writing life. Forgive me that I have made a career of keeping you in the dark.

Yours oh so sincerely,

Eleanor Sargent (no longer Edgar Simpson)

P.S. In the event of my death, I have instructed my nephew, Ted, to notify you. You should also know that I have given instructions, in my will, for all future royalties from my books to go to Parthenon, in my name, for monetary assistance to be given to any talented young writer whom you choose to encourage.

Entry in the peacetime diary of Edwin Sargent December 31st 1963

Here we are, on the last day of the year, and I sit facing the last page of this diary. I did keep a kind of professional journal for a while, just after the war. But I've never been much of a one for jotting down details of my own life – witness the virtually blank pages in most of this diary, or in any previous ones. I've always been more interested in other people's lives than in my own – that's probably why I'm a journalist. So here's my New Year resolution: not to bother with diaries any more. I'll close the cover on this one, and that'll be it. There's a certain timeliness to this, for in a way the past has been putting itself to bed this year, as it were. Grandpa died long ago (and as Granny said, "I hope he rots in Hell"), followed not long after by Granny (who had gone through Hell already, at his hands), and then by Great-Uncle Augustus some time afterwards (who was probably the best of all the Sargents, second only to Aunt Edith). Then Mum and Dad in the Glasgow Blitz (I miss them still, like it was only yesterday); and I treasure Dad's diaries, always will. And now Aunt Eleanor is gone, only last September. All her personal papers have been sent to me, as well as Aunt Edith's, too, which were evidently sent to Aunt Eleanor for safe keeping, when Aunt Edith died. I've gone through them all, and one day no doubt I'll figure out what to do about them. For now, though, I'll just shut them away, and get on with my own life and my own much happier family. One thing: I'll try, when the time comes, to be a better Grandad than that monster who was mine. Now that I've had a chance to go through all of Aunt Eleanor's papers, I'm deeply shocked by what I've read. Paternal incest, what a skeleton in the family closet! But over and above that, what a terrible thing for poor Aunt Eleanor to have endured when young! No wonder she vanished later into catatonic absence. I cannot think that Dad will have known, at the time – though he must have wondered what the trauma had been, which made her so ill, but which clearly had something to do with her father. Aunt Edith knew, though: that's clear from the two Aunts' letters. And what an amazing thing it was, that Aunt Eleanor should snap right out of it, as soon as she knew her father was dead. At least, she didn't have a relapse, so far as I can see from the documents. But I have to think her solitary, secluded life was some form of psychological withdrawal from a hurtful world. What saved her, I suppose, was her intellect; those fine books she wrote. All the same, though, the books themselves, in their content, were a kind of escape from lived pains into those of antiquity, into others' lives remote enough to be assayed with untroubled detachment. The one exception, perhaps, was her very last book, the *Aeschylus*; it turned on such a similarity between her own experience and that of Agamemnon's daughter, with its fatal consequence. Certainly she transcended that likeness: her text is in no way the kind of self-centred logorrhea that's better fitted to a therapist's office than spewed between the covers of a book. She was too good a writer for that, and I admired her for it. Yet even so, the feat must have been, at root, an act of exorcism. And that, likely enough, was why she felt impelled, in the end, to disclose her real identity, in quite explicit detail, to Wilfred Baker. Poor man, he must have felt seriously betrayed by all those years of evasion. Come to think of it, that explains why she didn't come to my wedding. I was a bit hurt by that at the time; for I had become fond of her, despite our actually having seen so little of each other. Now I realize, of course, she didn't want to risk coming to London, for fear I might somehow pressure her into meeting the publisher who knew nothing of who she was, let alone anything about her tragic past. Well, that's all over for her now. I cannot believe, as Aunt Edith certainly would have, that she's gone on into the peace of a consoling God. But at least I can take comfort from knowing she did manage with courage and integrity, to live out her time with hard-won peace of mind. Let the final word rest with her. As I read through all those dozens of pages, I found the summit of her achievement lay in the last of her poems, the one which she appended to the last and best of her books.

AULIS

Stalled in the harbour, fifty ships,
sails limp on the mast, useless;
the men rancid with boredom, picking
unnecessary quarrels, not enough brothels,
and the local wine tart as yesterday's dregs;
everyone impatient for Troy, the women there
for the taking, the golden plunder – but
where's the bloody wind?
                              Iron in his tent,
the general curses: this was not, look,
part of the calculations, this doldrum, this
indifference of heaven; he scans the dead water
eastward to where, out of armed reach,
the proud city awaits his halted fleet,
ripe for plucking, will sate his appetite,
if only the gods relent: considers, perhaps
the price is worth the paying.
                              Nothing stirs:
at the salt edge, even the gulls are listless;
in the olive trees, loaves curl in the scorched air,
gray with impotence; time stops,
still...
        Oh, it is not to be thought of, that
death! What will happen here, without hesitation
under the unblinking sun, is by any measure
unconscionable. Yet ineluctably the dice
fallen: there is no going back.
                              Prone
on the makeshift altar, the girl awaits
perforation, mute with grief for a father's
ill and heartless will. Sun glints on hard steel;
the blade descends.
                    This, in granite Argos,
will never be forgiven: the nursed hatred
coils in the gut, relentless, fixed, awaiting
opportunity; and one unpardonable death
will breed another, cold in the justicing

of an axe.

EPILOGUE

I report back. We sit once again over the teacups in Emily's Chiswick flat, and I tell her everything. "What do you think", I ask, when I'm done. "Should we leave it the way it's been, all these years? Or should we do something about it? It's your family, it's not up to me."

She sighs.

"I know," she says, "but what should we do anyway? I mean, maybe it's an extraordinary story, and someone should tell it, maybe turn it into a book. But then, on the other hand, what's to be gained by airing our dirty linen in public? There's enough bad stuff going on here and now, without digging up dirt that's more than a century old."

She had a point.

"But I'll tell you something," she added. "If we do decide to tell the whole story, because the truth, after all, *is* the truth, there's no need to be leery about shaming the family name. Granted, that bloody pedophile *was* my great-great-grandfather. But put that up against the rest of us. My great-grandfather was a highly respected ship's architect. One of his sisters, the nun, was a distinguished musicologist and a model of religious integrity. The other one was a capable historian and poet. My grandfather was a decorated war hero, and a first-rate journalist. My mother was the light of many people's lives, until she and Dad were killed by a drunk driver. Me, I don't even bear the family name, since my marriage; so in a sense, I'm the last of the line, the only living Sargent, and it shouldn't matter to me, one way or the other, if just one of my ancestors was a really rotten piece of work. In the end, it comes down to me, whether or not to sweep it under the rug."

"In a way," I replied, "you're probably right. But maybe not altogether. Consider this. Your great-great aunt, Eleanor Sargent, went to enormous pains to guard her privacy from intrusion – even to the point of publishing almost anonymously, whereas most writers, quite naturally want to take credit for their work. That disappearance of herself, so to speak, wasn't just a way of saying that only the books mattered, not the person who wrote them: it was more than that; it was a refusal, a quite sturdy refusal, to be seen as a victim. Of course, she *was* a victim, as witness her seven years of near coma. But she rose above it, and got on with her work, in an uninvaded solitude that mattered greatly to her. Her two siblings respected that. They may have wished that her books, just published under her initials, might have brought her the fame they felt she deserved. But they loved her, and they kept faith with her wishes. So did Baker, her publisher; even after her death, he never said a word."

Emily sighed again, this time not with puzzlement, but with a sort of relief.

"Put it that way," she said, "you're probably right. She opted for total obscurity, and who are we to say she was wrong? But it does seem a shame that the books themselves should be so obscure, too. Parthenon went broke long ago, and no one's likely to reprint them. I suppose classics scholars will always look them up and value them. But I have a feeling she was aiming for more of a readership than just academic specialists. From what you tell me, and from the extracts you've shown me, she seems to have seen History as an object-lesson, as a way to interpret the present in the light of the past. My Grandad took after her, there, in his own way: his Nuremberg articles were more than mere reportage on the recent crimes of twenty-four slaughterous racists; he saw them as more than just German or specifically Nazi villainy, he saw them as rooted in centuries of anti-Semitism world-wide, as pandemic in our culture. He was very like Eleanor in that regard, and he seems to have become very fond of her, even though they so seldom spent time together. He never broke her silence. So if *he* didn't – and I was very fond of *him* – then I suppose we should follow his lead, and honour her silence as well."

"You're right," I said, "I've come to feel that way, myself. But I didn't want to say so without first sounding you out about it. However, here's a small suggestion for a kind of republication that not only would do her a kind of posthumous justice, but would also be a great, belated boon to the general reading public, without in any way compromising her anonymity. Here's what I'd like to do. I'd like to excerpt all the poems she ended her books with and get them into print in a good literary magazine, while preserving her self-effacement, inviolate, under her initials – I'd write a short introduction to them, insisting on respect for her voluntary disappearance. That way, the poems would take their proper place in the canon of mid-twentieth-century poetry at its best. She deserved that. What do you think?"

"That," she answered, "is a really nice idea."

***

So that's what we're going to do.

170

AUTHOR'S FOOTNOTE

The text you have just read is a work of fiction: that is, the people in it are all invented people, and their lives are all imagined lives. However, as is usual in such stories, the setting is a real one, as regards both time and place: the period involved, from the late nineteenth century, to the present day, is riddled with history; and the actual location is drawn from life.

All of the world events referred to, such as the two world wars, are familiar to most people. But some readers may appreciate, here, a few words on the little known region in which the tale unfolds.

Lincolnshire is bounded on all sides by water: by the North Sea, by the rivers Humber and Trent, and by the Wash. To the south are the Fens, reclaimed land famous for pigs, potatoes, and tulips. Towering above them on hills called the Wolds, is Lincoln cathedral, one of the world's finest buildings. The coastal strip, the Lindsey Marsh (also reclaimed land) is a place of mixed farms. Throughout the county are multitudinous medieval churches, witness to a devout past − indeed, it was there that the great Pilgrimage of Grace almost unseated Henry VIII, when he suppressed the religious Orders.

Among the victims were the Gilbertine nuns, whose Order was founded in the twelfth century by St Gilbert of Sempringham. One of their houses was in the Marsh, in the village of Alvingham, where their church of St Athelwold still stands. I have taken the historical liberty of suggesting that the Gilbertine Order was refounded locally in the mid-nineteenth century during the Anglo-Catholic revival, an Anglican renaissance that flourished in the whole diocese.

I also took the liberty of inflicting on the nearby parish of Yarburgh a fictional incumbent, the Rev'd Barnabas Sargent, whose life was an unattractive mix of liturgical obsession and personal depravity. I would not want readers to think that I have intended, by so doing, to cast any slur upon the many priests who served the Marsh, at that time, so devotedly. The sad fact is, though, that one of the parishes there, in Somersby, did have a Rector of deplorable malignity.

The Rev'd George Tennyson, father of the famous poet, had no redeeming qualities other than a love of good literature. Eldest son of a rich man, he was soured by disappointment when a younger brother was preferred, over him, to inherit the family wealth. Taking to drink, he became a violent alcoholic, who beat his wife and bullied his children. Few of them survived emotionally intact; the poet suffered from lifelong melancholia; and of his siblings, one became a drug addict, a second

171

became alcoholic, a third ended up in a lunatic asylum, and none of the others were ever really happy.

Being by nature an optimist, I have imagined a much happier outcome for the three children of Barnabas Sargent. The son grows up to become a marine architect; and I have some sympathy with that profession, since my Newfoundland great-grandfather was a boat-builder. The elder of two daughters emerges from Lindsey to read classics at the University of London under A. E. Housman, as did my mother, and becomes a prolific historian and poet. The younger daughter follows an early vocation into religious life, and becomes joyfully involved in adapting Gregorian chant to English texts, as I often have myself. The only grandchild serves during the second world war, as did I just after the war, in the Bletchley code-breaking unit, and subsequently earns a living in the media, as did I.

Such small coincidences are merely marginal evidence of how a writer draws on his own experience to flesh out the invented world of his characters. In addressing the physical aspects of that world, I can claim to know the scene quite well, having spent some years there when my family moved to the Lindsey Marsh from British Columbia. Back home in Canada afterwards, and teaching classics at UBC, I had friends in the psychology department, where the graduate student lounge served the best coffee on campus; and one of them, a psychiatric nurse, told me about a fascinating case of his in Saskatoon.

A middle-aged patient there was institutionalized, for several years, suffering from a near-comatose condition called catatonic trance. Bidden to eat or dress herself or use the toilet, she would do so, with help. But otherwise she was totally unresponsive, answering no questions and not reacting to anything said to her or asked of her. This made her inaccessible to verbal therapy; and too little was known of her background to indicate what might have caused such acute withdrawal from the world. Her prognosis was dismal. Despite that, a younger sister continued to visit and talk to her, in the hope of somehow getting through to that silent mind.

Eventually, one day, that hope was rewarded. The visitor happened to mention, in a consolatory way, that their father had just died. The patient immediately sat up, looking fully alert, and said "Oh, what of?", in a perfectly normal voice. The sister was flabbergasted – and, of course, overjoyed – and the patient's recovery was instantaneously complete, as though an unbearable burden had been lifted from her shoulders. In convalescent conversations, it emerged that the father, when she was a teenager, had repeatedly raped her. She had escaped, as a young adult, but the after-effects, in her thirties, had precipitated a total nervous breakdown, plunging her into catatonia.

I purloined that story for use in my portrayal of the fictional Eleanor Sargent, and of the collapse that was a turning-point in her life. Accordingly, if people reading that account should think such a plot-twist rather far-fetched, let them rest assured it is solidly based on documented clinical fact.

Stranger things have happened.

J. R.
September 2015

FINAL LAP
a record

for Bruce Kidd
athlete, scholar, friend

I

It was all a matter of timing. In 1988 Andrew Coggin was sixty-four, and anticipating retirement. He could actually have retired earlier, on full pension. But he had chosen not to. For one thing, his job made full use of his mind; and he did not relish the prospect of a future without work, rattling around in an empty apartment – his wife had recently died. The other thing was, the partnership: he and Fred Sump had been on the job together for twenty-five years, and needed each other like Yin and Yang. Only now, at fifty-five, was Fred thinking of early retirement. "You know, Andrew," he had said, "I couldn't really work with anyone else, I mean, look around. Fatty Williams? Ernie Strabismus? God, no! Better I should pack it in. I'm okay now for the pension anyway. Besides, there's that job offer I told you about. May as well take it."

Coggin envied him. Fred, in his spare time, was one of the best track-coaches in Canada as a volunteer. The Canadian Track and Field Association had been after him to turn in his badge and come on side as a paid National distance adviser. It would be, in a way, every man's dream: to be paid for doing something he loved. Coggin had no such luck. In this case, what he loved in his spare time was the music of Bach. But nobody was going to pay him to listen to Bach full time. And anyway there was more to life than music, even the greatest music ever composed. There were problems in the world that needed solving. Murder, for example. He was head of the Toronto Homicide Squad, as Detective Inspector, and Fred was his long-time sergeant. They were opposites, well-matched, complementing each other's strengths and weaknesses.

Coggin, bone-thin and austere-looking, had the kind of analytic brain that thrived on puzzles: over breakfast, he would solve the *Globe and Mail's* cryptic crossword in under ten minutes; at the office, he was efficient at sorting out the tangled clues of a case and figuring out a possible solution. Offsetting that skill was a personal reserve, amounting almost to a crippling shyness, that left him short of insight into other people's psyches; he was not given to accurate hunches.

Sump, by contrast, stoutish and of genial aspect most of the time, was excellent with people. He had empathy in spades. It was a quality that made him a successful coach. And in talking to crime witnesses and suspects, he had an unerring feel for what made them tick. If they were evasive or confrontational, he knew exactly how to undermine their resistance with an overbearing approach quite out of kilter with his essentially kind nature. With other interviewees, he had an avuncular warmth, seemingly, that put them at ease and sometimes trapped them into inadvertent admissions which they would have been better off not to let slip. With both kinds of people, and with those in between, he had an intuitive sense of truth or deception. Sheer puzzle-solving he left to Coggin.

Their partnership had worked well for many years. In the Case of the Tell-Tale Tape, they had nailed a killer in the CBC, in part because of Coggin's astute sense of language. In the Case of the Precipitous Prior, they had solved a monastic killing, in part because of Sump's unprecedented collaboration with a woman constable, the first ever to join Homicide, who later entered the convent herself as a nun. In the Case of the Fake Firing-Squad, the real shooter had been trapped into confession by Coggin upon having to face possible death from his own weapon. And in the Case of the Martyred Minister, the two of them had helped finger the culprits in an assassination perpetrated many years earlier far away from home, in Prague.

That case, in particular, had to be solved under the gun of a fast-approaching deadline. Others, though, however urgent-seeming, all too often involved a thorough, even dreary, plodding away in routine inquiries. But even when a case bogged down, they did not lose hope: somehow time would be on their side; some clue, perhaps overlooked, would cast new light on the case. In the end, they had never closed a case unsolved. Patience was all. Always it would be merely a matter of time.

None the less, mid-morning on a mild April Sunday in Toronto, murder, which seldom conveniently happens on a nine-to-five weekday, interrupted the even flow of events with its nasty habit of bad timing.

Sergeant Sump was standing with his stopwatch at the start-line of a fifteen-mile road-race in High Park's annual Silver Relays, when his cellphone rang. Reluctantly, he answered it, for two five-man teams from his East End Track Club were about to tackle the hills, and his "A" team stood a good chance of breaking the course record. He was there to register their split times. But now HQ was telling him to get his arse downtown to an office on Grant Road, where a cleaner had found a body slumped at a desk with, said the constable now at the scene, a gunshot wound to the head. There was no way Fred could wait seventy minutes before responding. Irritated, he handed his stopwatch to the club trainer and left.

Simultaneously, Inspector Coggin was on his leisurely way to a Walter Hall performance of four Brandenburg Concertos, where he would feel no compunction about switching off his cellphone, for Bach surely outranked the chief of police, but had not yet done so. Equally irritated, he obeyed orders and turned south.

Time and Tide, he quoted to himself, wait for no man. Nor does homicide.

II

SUNDAY APRIL 26, 10.52 AM

Coggin had no trouble parking under the No Parking sign at 48 Grant Road. He pulled up right behind the police car that had responded, no doubt, to the original emergency call. One of its two constables was cutting off the sidewalk access to the front door with strips of yellow tape announcing it to be a crime scene. The second constable was sitting in the vehicle with a civilian, perhaps the cleaner who had discovered the body, awaiting his arrival. Fred arrived only seconds later, and parked immediately behind Coggin.

Grant Road, named after one of the city's nineteenth-century worthies, had little to recommend it nowadays. Only two blocks to the south, modernistic skyscrapers were pushing the sanctity of lucre towards a new idea of heaven, smugly proclaiming Toronto to be world-class. And a few blocks to the north, a midtown avenue of luxury boutiques rivalled, at least in its own mind, the ritzier purlieus of Manhattan. But Grant Road, in between, was a forgotten backwater of decayed real estate, of no commercial or architectural importance. Its buildings, mostly only two storeys high, were drab and grey. There was a down-at-heels tavern, a cut-rate tailor's, a boarded-up snooker hall, a hole-in-the-wall café of singularly unappetizing mien, and a pawnshop. Number 48 was a shabby low-rise office building. The ground floor, to left and right of the entrance, had For Lease signs in the two front windows, which appeared not to have been washed since who knows when. Four buzzers were on the door jamb, to buzz for admission. The bottom two, for the downstairs, were unlabelled. Above them, one read, hopefully, Guaranteed Investments. The other, which was their destination, read Ace Detective Agency. They did not need to use the buzzer: the door had been wedged open, pending their arrival or the arrival of the technical crew and the medical examiner, all of whom were expected.

They stepped into a narrow hallway, with two doors, to left and right giving access presumably to the unoccupied ground-floor offices. At the end of the corridor was a door, which the constable told them led to a basement furnace-room. Facing them, between dingy walls, was an uncarpeted staircase leading up to a pair of doors. Guaranteed Investments was locked with no audible sign of life within – today, after all, was Sunday, and citizens anxious about the future were more likely, perhaps, to be in the Church of the Second Coming than in this dubious

178

shrine of Mammon. The other door stood open, giving onto the premises of the Ace Detective Agency; and they went right in, stepping past a mop, a bucket, and other cleaning gear.

The main room (a washroom was at the back, plus a cubby-hole with a hot-plate) was sparsely furnished: a large, plain desk, with a swivel chair behind it and two uncomfortable chairs in front of it; on top of it a lamp, unlit, and an old-fashioned dial phone; beside it, an empty waste paper basket; in a corner, on a table, a computer and a printer; across from the window, a discouraged sofa underneath a framed and faded portrait of Sherlock Holmes; against one wall, a filing cabinet; the walls had once been white; in the ceiling was a naked light-bulb, also unlit; underfoot, a thin rug made no secret of its age. The whole effect was depressing: it reeked of failure.

On the desk was a standard but cheap blotting-pad, dating back to a time when people used ink and pens with nibs. If there were any residual ink stains from those days, they were not immediately discernible. For the blotting-paper, right now, had been absorbing blood from a bullet-hole in the forehead of the presumptive Mr Ace, who was still seated at the desk, and whose detecting days were now clearly done.

Coggin and Sump had both, over the years, seen enough murder victims to know that a life was over, without their having to wait for the medical examiner to tell then so. And since there was no gun present, this case was obviously not one of suicide. Or at least, both of them knew it was remotely possible that the man had shot himself and that someone else had removed the weapon, but the wound did not look as though it had been self-inflicted at point-blank range; and later examination found no powder traces on either hand.

The young constable, a P.C. Pierre Dubois who (such is Canada) spoke not a word of French and called himself Deboys, had come upstairs with them, and apologized that he couldn't tell them who the victim was.

"He's probably got ID in his wallet," he said to Coggin, "but I figured I shouldn't move the body till you got here. Sorry about that, sir."

"Quite right, son," Sump reassured him. "Nothing to make a big to-do about. Anyway, it so happens we actually know who he is. Was," he corrected himself.

"Yes," Coggin added. "The name's Oscar Pilch. You'll find his ID when we move him, along with his license, I dare say. He used to be on the Force, which is how we know him. But he didn't last, went private."

They had both rather disliked him, back then, and thought him untrustworthy, a bit too prone to shady maneouvres. But they forbore to mention that. Private sleuthing seldom sits well with policemen, especially when it rides roughshod over regulations that hamper their own investigations. And Pilch had never been a co-operative person, either before or since.

By the look of his office, though, he had not done well. Perhaps once he had managed alright with a steady supply of clients needing sordid help for a divorce. But that trade had long been in serious decline, thanks to changes in law and in social behaviour. It looked as though Pilch had ended up down on his luck; and neither of them could feel too sorry for him. Bu he was, now, a victim. And they would have to treat his case, professionally, with unbiassed detachment. So they left the room and went back downstairs with the constable.

"Who's your partner?" Sump asked.

"P.C. MacLeish, Sergeant. Menzies MacLeish."

Doubtless at his partner's insistence, he pronounced the first name correctly, to rhyme with dinghies. Coggin was pleased: he hated the speak-as-you-spell movement, which misled people into disfiguring the name Anthony with the same sound as in the first syllable of panther. Fortunately, he did not launch into a disquisition on the subject, which he often did on such subjects when Fred thought there were more important matters to address.

Instead, he asked: "The civilian in the car with him, is she the cleaner who called it in? It figures, I thought – that cleaning stuff upstairs is probably hers."

"Yes, sir. Should I bring it down for her?"

"Well, she will want it back, I guess. But that can wait. Let's see what she has to say."

Just then, two more vehicles arrived, disgorging the technical crew and the medical examiner. Coggin sent the doctor upstairs, but had a word first with the fingerprint technician and the photographer before sending them after him.

"You'll find a bucket and other stuff at the top of the stairs," he said. "Almost certainly belonging to the cleaner who found the body. See if you can get a good print of hers off any of it... And a print of hers on the door handle of the door itself. And maybe on the office phone if that's how she called it in. You'll be doing all the usual, of course. But I don't hold out too much hope there. It looks like a hit job; and anyone doing a hit wears gloves."

"OK, Inspector, we'll do what we can."

They moved in. He sent Dubois with them, and told him to ask the M.E. for an educated guess about the time of death.

Meanwhile, Sergeant Sump had gone over to the first of the police cars, spoken to MacLeish, and introduced himself to the woman in the passenger seat. He suggested she might be more comfortable in his own car, along with the Inspector, to tell them what she could. She was still visibly upset by what she had gone through; and he reckoned it might be an easier conversation for her with two older men in ordinary suits than with a young uniformed officer in a blatantly marked police vehicle. He was aware of how that might look to a lot of people: seeing her where she was right now, they would leap to the assumption that she must have done something wrong. It was not fair, he knew. But the opposite assumption was equally unfair: some people, seeing that, especially young people or aging hippies, would assume that the "pigs", yet again, were mistreating an innocent citizen. Either way she thanked him and went with him to his anonymous and unobtrusive sedan. He put her in the passenger seat up front, and got in beside her. Inspector Coggin climbed into one of the rear seats. None of them bothered with the seat belts: they weren't about to go anywhere.

Her name was Amy Buniak. She looked to be about thirty, with dark hair, a pleasant but not striking face, and a better figure, perhaps, than was visible in the rather drab work-clothes she was wearing.

"So," Sergeant Sump began gently (he had many voices: this situation called for the soothing one), "it was you, was it, who called 911?"

"Yes, it was me," she responded.

Inspector Coggin, behind her, chalked that one up for her. Here was someone who spoke real idiomatic English: whose parlance was not corrupted by the kind of semi-educated snobbery that thinks it correct, even obligatory, to say "between you and I." He made a mental note, but said nothing – only to learn, soon enough, that this young woman was in fact much better educated than appearances might suggest.

"And thank God for 911," she went on. "After all, it's not every day you come to tidy a place up, and find a corpse among the debris. Pretty scary. Especially if it's a corpse that looks to have been killed. In fact, I was scared shitless. If he had been killed, not just died, and that looked fairly obvious to me, I wanted out of there. Fast. First thought that comes into your mind is, maybe the killer's still around. Last thing he'd want is for someone to identify him."

She exhaled nervously, remembering how she had felt. And Sergeant Sump, too, made a mental note. Not everyone, in such a state of natural panic, would instantly think along such lines. Was she, perhaps, like him in his weaker moments, a reader of Ed McBain, that master of the police procedural? Making the same mental note, Inspector Coggin wondered if her remark had been a reflex echo of watching cop-shows on TV, which were, after all, only a cut above the other mindless inanities of pop-culture. But neither man made a point of the matter.

"Well, I can understand how you must have felt," Sergeant Sump said. "So I guess you got out of there quickly, but carefully. Then you phoned is that right?"

"Yes. First off, though, when I got out the front door, I looked around, partly afraid of anyone I might see, but also hoping there might be a bunch of other people I'd feel safe with. No one, though. Round here it's deadsville on a Sunday morning. Oh hell, I didn't mean it to come out like that: 'deadsville' is hardly the word for it, given what I'd just seen."

"So what then?" Inspector Coggin asked, forgoing the opportunity for a chat about appropriate choices of words. "I take it you hadn't called 911 on the phone in the office up there."

"Are you kidding? On the phone right there? With him sitting dead six inches away?"

Good, he thought. If there are any fingerprints on the phone other than Pilch's, they won't be hers.

"No, but I did remember I had my cellphone in my car. So I used it. Locked myself in, of course."

"By the way," Sergeant Sump asked, "where is your car?"

There had been no cars on Grant Road when he arrived, other than Inspector Coggin's and the first police-car.

"Oh, halfway down the block. There's a little alley a few doors along, with the far end blocked off. So I park there when I come Sundays. Never got a ticket yet."

That was a throw-away line; and the two men were unsure how to take it. Either it was the simple relief of a driver who's gotten away with it. Or did it smack, perhaps, of the average driver's resentment of curbside parking being unavailable?

"So anyway I called 911 from the car. Then I just sat there until I heard the cops arrive. Then I felt safe to go and join them."

Inspector Coggin went back to the moment of her encounter with the corpse.

"You were saying, a few moments ago," he said, "that when you went into the office, you were scared coming upon a dead man like that. That's a very natural reaction. But you seem to have been very sure he was, in fact, dead. What if he was just injured? Would you have tried to help?"

"Oh, come on, Inspector! You've seen him. Wouldn't you say it was obvious he was beyond help? Whoever he was. The fact is, it completely threw me. I even forgot my stuff up there. Could one of you guys help me get it? I really don't feel like going back up there by myself."

"On, don't worry about that," Sergeant Sump said. "We'll get it for you. But what did you mean just now when you said 'whoever he was'? Surely, if you could see well enough he was dead, you could see he was your employer?"

She bristled, clearly, at the imputation that she was somehow stupid or irresponsible.

"Actually," she retaliated, with a kind of defensive tartness, "I never had met what you call my employer. The owner of the building engaged me, part-time, just on Sundays. Wanted me to clean the two offices on the second floor every week, and said I could do the downstairs too, if he found new tenants. He gave me a whole set of keys, for the front entrance and all four offices, and started me in a couple of months ago, and paid me by cheque. I guess there were no complaints about my work. But I never did meet anyone in either office, it being always Sunday. Of course, I did get to know Mr Pilch's name, in the Agency office here; sometimes, when I came on a Sunday, there'd be some of his Friday mail lying on the floor that had been pushed through the mail slot at the front entrance. That's the extent of it, though. I never did meet him in person. I just figured it was probably him got killed. But I didn't have any way of knowing."

Inspector Coggin said, "Okay, but we'll need to know who the owner is, so we can look into this from all angles. I guess you can help with that – his name, the name of the firm, the address and so on. Some of that should be on your paycheque. But tell me a bit more about yourself? Here you are, a young person, and you sound like a well-educated one. What's with the cleaning job? A bit odd, isn't it?"

"Well, not really, if you think I'm going to make a career of it. Actually, I just take on these cleaning gigs to keep the wolf from the door. My real career is, I'm an actress."

Coggin warmed to her instantly. She hadn't said "I'm an actor." He hated the way political correctness was impoverishing English.

"There's never enough work in acting, for women – not unless you're happy doing nude scenes. So you take other odd jobs here and there, just to keep going. Cleaning's useful. Flexible. Doesn't get in the way of going to auditions, the way an office job would. Of course, when I'm a bit older, I'll get plenty of roles playing grumpy middle-aged women. But right now it's not a good time. I'm thirty-two and look it. All the young roles go to pretty little sylphs with perfect teeth, big boobs, and not much technique. Mind you, that's not so true of stage work, even if women's roles there are scarce as hen's teeth. But television: don't get me started on that pile of rubbish. I know, every once in a while something comes along on TV that might interest an adult mind. But not too damn often. I can count on the fingers of one hand the breaks I've had on TV or film that I could respect myself over.

"Sorry I went on like that," she added after a pause. "It's a bit of a sore point with me – and most actresses, at least in Canada."

Sergeant Sump wanted to stop the flow of this evidently pent-up frustration. But being the tactful man he was, he did so in a fairly disarming way.

"Well, miss," he said, "I certainly wish you well in plugging away at it. And I'll keep an eye out for you, if something worthwhile does pop up on TV. What did you say your name was again?"

He had, in fact, memorized it perfectly – neither of them had been taking notes: this was not an interrogation.

"Amy Buniak. But you can forget about that. Casting directors are seriously lacking in imagination. Stereotypes are what they trade in. Give them a Ukrainian surname and they automatically think in terms of some buxom, flaxen-haired peasant girl from the steppes. Makes me puke. So no, you won't see Buniak among the credits. Professionally, my name's Amy Barton."

"Duly noted," said Inspector Coggin, rather drily.

They walked her to where she was parked, sending Dubois to fetch her cleaning stuff. While they waited for him, they took out their notebooks for the first time, and wrote down the address on her driving license, and her phone number. Then, with her stuff safely stowed in the trunk, she drove away.

"What do you make of her, Fred?" Coggin asked, as she rounded the corner of Grant Road, past what used to be an obsolete bank but was now a second-hand clothing-store and a tattoo parlour.

"Hard to say, Andrew. She's certainly got her wits about her. And I didn't get the feeling she was telling any lies. But there may be more to her than meets the eye right off."

Coggin nodded. After all the years they had worked together their minds worked so much in tandem that some things could be left unspoken. Both of them knew that Amy Buniak-Barton was almost for sure the first person to have seen Pilch dead, except of course the killer: but also that it was equally possible she was the last person to have seen him alive.

They trudged back to number 48, to see what the M.E. had to say. And to have all of Pilch's files impounded, so they could find out what he'd been working on, and whether any of it might have a bearing on his death. It would be a mind-numbing job, like looking for a needle in a haystack. But it had to be done, along with a lot of routine inquiries. Experience told them, though, that something always pointed them in the right direction. It was only a matter of time.

III

MONDAY MAY 4, 10.15 AM

One of the things that came to light when they pored over Pilch's files was his connection to the Mahogany Emporium. This flourishing enterprise had been founded twenty years ago by an immigrant businessman from Central America, called Pablo Morales y Calderon. Born in Guatemala, he had fled across the border to Belize during the civil war; and then he had invested in a business that specialized in making mahogany furniture for export. Most of the product was of standard design and was sold to American chain-stores in kits for customers to assemble at home. But when he moved to Canada, he realised there was an untapped market in Toronto for luxury product in the growing ranks of the super-rich. He set up a department within the Belize factory to cater to them. It was run by a designer-cum-manager who used only the best timber, and who recruited native craftsmen with a talent for fine work. Back in Toronto he built a sizeable warehouse on the outskirts of the city, where land was comparatively cheap. This he filled with two lines of product: in large quantities the do-it-yourself kits for middle-class customers with upscale aspirations; and in small quantities the specialty pieces for deep-pocketed men who had a taste for beauty and good workmanship – or their wives did. To serve them, he had a small, high-end outlet midtown where they could come, by appointment only, to discuss possible custom-built purchases over a fine cognac.

Quickly a millionaire himself, Pablo Morales was at ease among men and women born to wealth; and with the nouveaux riches he helped them to feel equally at ease, to feel they really belonged among the elite, however humble their origins. His discreet brochures (he never stooped to the vulgarity of a mailing-list or, heaven forfend, a blog) were a blend of reassuring the secure that they had come to the right place, and encouraging the insecure to believe that they too could live as though to the manor born.

In catering to such people, Morales was simply a man of business seizing an opportunity. He was not, himself, a snob. He lived in a large but not ostentatious house in Forest Hill, with his wife Paula Morrison, who was Canadian-born. Their business income was beyond most

185

people's dreams, but they did not use it to support a self-indulgent life-style. That became abundantly clear when Ms Morrison, who had clung to her maiden name, won fifty million dollars in a lottery. It was absurd, she thought: other people need that kind of luck far more than we do; the least we can do is put it to good use.

So she and her husband started the PM Foundation, named after their shared initials; and they dispensed grants from it in aid of four causes they wanted to support. Matching grants would go to health care in Belize and Ontario. Grants to support the performing arts in Toronto were Pamela's especial purview. And Pablo supported amateur sports, notably track-and-field, both, nationally and locally.

This came to Coggin's and Sump's attention, when they leafed through a Pilch file labelled "Mahogany." In it were records of a business relationship with someone called Hedley Boyle, who was an administrator in the PM Foundation. A particular responsibility of his, it appeared, was to take care of Pablo Morales' current concern over drug use by elite runners in international and local track-meets. He contributed money to help the official watchdogs increase the frequency of their unannounced, out-of-competition testing. He also subsidized research into how offenders contrived to escape detection, and into how to close those loopholes. Morales was not satisfied, however, with the progress being made by officials or academics in their efforts to clean up the sport. To push those efforts a bit further, unofficially and confidentially, he had charged Boyle with the task of launching a private investigation into whatever parts of the drug trade were involved in supplying performance-boosters to athletes, coaches, or trainers.

Boyle's first step in that direction had been to entrust Pilch with the job. This was the first item in the file. It was followed by others, recording what was done and giving progress reports. But that first item had a scrawled footnote, reading See Boyle File.

Sump, of course, was enormously interested in all this. He asked Coggin if there was a Boyle file in the stuff they had sequestered. Coggin told him Yes there was, he'd read it, but had not thought it particularly significant: it was just one of the past divorce files, one of Pilch's several forays into the world of sexual sleaze and alimony dispute; it had not stood out, on first reading, as any way different from the others. Nor was it. But now, as they looked at it together in the light of the Mahogany file, they could see why Boyle might have picked Pilch for the assignment.

It had been a messy divorce, as were all of those worked on by Pilch. In this case, custody of a child was involved. Boyle's wife was severely addicted to drugs. There had been a trial separation agreement contingent on her entering a treatment program. When she emerged from it she stayed clean for about three weeks. But her addiction re-established itself full-blown, if anything worse than before. Boyle started divorce proceedings, and tried for full custody of their child, a thirteen-year-old boy, on the grounds that she was an unfit mother. To establish that in court, he needed supporting evidence. His rather low-life lawyer recommended he hire Pilch to come up with something: before setting up on his own, Pilch had been a police-officer on the narcotics squad, was familiar with the underworld of traffickers and addicts, and was known to be none too squeamish about the methods he used.

Using his contacts, Pilch cashed in a marker with Orville Marx, head rider of a biker gang involved in the local trade in drugs and prostitutes. Orville owed him a favour, from back in his policing days, when he, Pilch, had suppressed, for a consideration, some evidence that would have sent him to jail. Since then, Orville's brother, Wilbur, had ended up in jail on an unrelated trafficking charge, with Pilch now powerless to protect him. But Orville, still grateful to Pilch, had doubled the support he was giving Wilbur's wife, to persuade Wilbur to come into court, via subpoena, and to testify about all the drugs he had regularly sold to Boyle's wife, describing her as one of the most extreme addicts he had ever done business with.

It was enough to win the case and the custody suit. Not long afterwards, the ex-wife died of an overdose. The boy, now nearly nineteen, was currently away at university in Halifax, glad to get away from sad and scarring memories in Toronto. And Boyle had re-engaged Pilch for a second and non-marital assignment.

Its outline and intent were easy to read in the Mahogany file. Pilch, as instructed by Boyle, was to unearth any proofs he could of drugs being supplied to athletes in general and to elite runners in particular whether the pipeline of supply involved some or all of the relevant doctors, nurses, masseurs, dieticians, trainers, and coaches, not forgetting fellow-athletes either; what were the original sources of supply; and who paid for it all.

The whole subject was a bit distasteful to Coggin. In a long career on the Force, he had few illusions about human corruptibility. There was scarcely any field of endeavour untainted by malefaction. He had seen murder committed for revenge or gain, from thwarted lust or racist hatred, and even out of misplaced idealism. He had seen violent crime wrapped up in a tissue of lies, evasions, and flight. He had encountered it in unexpected places, a radio station, a monastery, an opera-house. But, not being a sports fan, he had always assumed, naively, that the playing of games was a more or less harmless pursuit. This case looked to be suggesting otherwise.

Sump had no such illusions. At heart he believed in the ideals of sport. He insisted on them with the runners he coached. But he could not blind himself to the uncomfortable facts. Drug use had long been rampant in cycling and weight-lifting. It was suspected in football and hockey. And in track-and-field it had been proved, sadly often, among shot-putters: and sprinters – notably among sprinters. Rumours had circulated, too, about distance-runners. Nor were these entirely baseless; for talented athletes from East Germany had been forced into drug-enhanced achievements by a secret but deliberate national policy – the list, from various sports, included several baritone women swimmers and one Olympic marathoner. East Germans apart, though, distance-running seemed to be clean. But that did not mean it escaped, or should escape, vigilant scrutiny. Sump had two runners in his club in East York, who were at the elite level, and consequently had to undergo frequent drug-tests. And a rival Toronto club, the Downsview Harriers, had had as a guest member the current holder of world records for the 5000 metres, the 10000 metres, and the half-marathon, Ross Lang. Wherever he was in the world, whether competing or training or even (rarely) taking time off, he was constantly peeing in a flask, to have urine analyzed in a lab.

IV

TUESDAY MAY 5, 7.45 AM

There were two men at his front door, when Ross Lang got back from his morning run – six miles of roadwork in North Toronto, culminating in lung-busting acceleration on the long hill up from the Bottom of Hogg's Hollow. He knew both men, from their frequent reappearance, unannounced, with their protocol and their flasks, labeled Sample A and Sample B.

He sighed, and let them in, to go through the usual routine. First, pee in each of the two flasks, while they watched. Then sign and date the two adhesive labels to be stuck on the flasks. Then let them out the door, and proceed to his shower and breakfast.

It was boring, but necessary. And actually he was glad of it. He had never taken a drug in his life, and all tests he passed would vouch for him as a clean competitor. What he really disliked about the situation was its accusatory implications. In a court of law, onus was on the prosecution to prove the defendant guilty. But at the bar of athletic justice, you had to prove your innocence, if your integrity was questioned. And all too often it was, indeed, questioned: a few times by rival runners who could not stand being convincingly beaten; more times by scandal-mongering journalists, who little cared whose reputation they tarnished with unfounded speculations.

Lang's reputation was stellar. This meant, in an envy-ridden world, it was suspect, for no better reason than that small-minded people like to see celebrities disgraced, and that the cynically-minded are ever ready to suppose that success must be somehow ill-gotten and anyway undeserved. The latter folk had an easy target in Lang.

He had been a gifted junior athlete in his late teens, but had then given up running to concentrate on university studies at Acadia in Nova Scotia. Upon graduation, he had come back to track, but had done so, as it were, from scratch. He put himself in the hands of a recently retired coach, Bill Northbrook, who had spotted his potential five years earlier, when he was still a high-schooler, and who now took him under his wing as an individual project, one on one. The results were spectacular, but very slow to come by.

The first several months, necessarily, had to be devoted, painstakingly, to trimming down an out-of-shape body, and getting it back into the kind of condition where it could handle an increasingly heavy workload. That involved a combination of weekly long runs, starting at ten miles and moving up to twenty, and of interval training – that is, as Sump would eventually explain to Coggin, typically a set of a dozen or more 400-metre runs at racing speed, with a one-minute rest in between.

To begin with, Northbrook got him a membership in the Downsview Harriers, a club that specialized in the distance events. They had late-afternoon interval workouts, Monday to Friday, on the track in Downsview Collegiate; and Lang joined them there. The standard pattern, there and world-wide, was for 400-metre repeats. But to prevent staleness, and to fine-tune the runners' sense of tempo, the pattern would often vary: sometimes the repeats would be flat-out 300-metre sprints, to speed up recovery from oxygen debt, and other times there would be repeats at 600 metres or 800; once in a while there would be repeat miles.

At first, Lang found it hard to keep up. On a bad day, at Northbrook's suggestion, he would lead the pack when the going got tough: if he led, it was his responsibility to maintain the targeted pace; and that hardened his will. By the time he was in his second year, Northbrook tightened the screw. Instead of running with the pack as it rounded the track repeatedly in sixty-eight seconds, Lang had to give it a four-second start; and on the last repeat, he had to wait ten seconds – this primed him to produce a good finishing kick at the end of a race.

Northbrook focused his attention exclusively on Lang. He and Lang were informal guests with the Harriers, and he did not want to seem to be interfering with the Downsview program. But on occasion, joining forces with the Downsview coach, he scheduled a session of his own invention, a fun but exhausting session, which he called the Shrinking Interval Workout. This consisted of sixteen repeats of 400 metres, each being followed by a short rest, but each rest being shorter than the previous one. For example, after the first lap, the rest would be seventy seconds; after the second lap it would be sixty-five seconds, then sixty-seconds after the third lap, and so on until there was only a five-second rest after the fourteenth lap; finally after the fifteenth lap, the rest had disappeared, and the participants had to run the sixteenth lap without any rest at all – that is, the last two laps added up to a continuous 800 metres. The tempo was only seventy seconds per lap, on the face of it an easier tempo than the sixty-eight-second tempo they were used to for 400-metre repeats. But that small mercy was offset by the increasing rigour of the exercise: the whole point of the workout was to simulate the deepening fatigue of a hard-fought distance-race.

Theoretically, completing the workout was an attainable goal. In practice, though, none of Northbrook's runners had ever reached it. After thirteen laps, many had fallen by the wayside. At the end of the fourteenth lap, the survivors had nothing left in them to tackle 800 metres after only a five-second rest. However, in the third year of his comeback, Lang succeeded, and actually ran the last 800 metres faster than tempo.

That was when Northbrook decided he was ready for serious international competition.

He had a remote counterpart in Nicola Porpora, the famous eighteenth-century teacher of virtuoso singers. His pupils spent years learning the intricate craft of bel canto, by exacting exercises in voice production and florid roulades, before he allowed them to practice singing actual arias. But when he did at last launch them on their careers, two of them, Caffarelli and Farinelli, became the superstars of their time. History does not relate how they responded to their teacher's keeping them under wraps until he felt they were ready: human nature being what it is, and singers being what they are, his pupils probably did tackle a few arias in private, out of their teacher's earshot; but still they must have needed a lot of patience in the preparatory years, must have had a lot of faith in their teacher's good judgment; for singers love to sing, and real performance is their lifeblood.

Similarly, runners love to race. They are not, like many singers, greedy of applause or dependent on it. Rather, they give of themselves as to a vocation, with the same single-minded focus as painters to their art or as mystics to their prayers. For runners, racing is the raison d'être: training, however rich its rewards, is simply the means to an end. All runners know this, and so do all good coaches. Northbrook, accordingly, knew that he could not too long postpone Lang's entry into the field of competition. He had faith in Lang's talent, just as Lang had faith in him. But neither of them could quite have expected what happened when Lang, unheralded at twenty-five years old, was entered in the ten-kilometre run at the 1983 Canadian Championships. Northbrook expected him to do well, as did the runners he had been training with. Yet none of them was prepared for the time he clocked. Leaving everyone else in his wake, he set a new world record, beating the old record by a staggering twenty-eight seconds – this in a sport where record improvements in sprinting are measured in hundredths of a second and in distance-running by at most, usually, a couple of seconds. For once, when sports-writers speak of someone "shattering" a record, the hyperbole was apt.

Fred Sump had been in the stands that day. He could hardly believe his stopwatch.

V

TUESDAY MAY 5, 10.00 AM

Sump was not alone in finding the Mahogany file of absorbing interest. He would have been interested anyway, since Morales was well known as a generous donor to track-and-field, and as a patron devoted, like him, to the ideals of drug-free competition. But Morales' very possible connection, through the PM Foundation, to the crime they were investigating, made the file highly relevant to the case.

Coggin, for his part, was equally intrigued, for a quite different reason. For him, the musical highlight of the year, locally, was the annual Bach Festival, directed every year by Gottfried Krauss, the eminent Bach specialist from Cologne. And it was largely financed, he knew, by the PM Foundation, thanks to Pamela Morrison. Whether there was any connection, tangentially or directly, with Pablo Morales' parallel investment in sport was not clear from the Mahogany file. Nothing suggested that any such connection did exist. On the face of it, it seemed unlikely. But the possibility could not be summarily dismissed. It was an odd coincidence that both beneficiaries had the same benefactor. Maybe it was no more than that: just a coincidence. But Coggin and Sump had long since learnt, with chagrin, to mistrust coincidences – as in the Case of the Heinous Homonym, where they followed a false trail after the name Simon was inaccurately heard on the phone as Hyman. Anyway, coincidence aside, they always had reason to think of money, or the lack of money, as often figuring in the background of a crime. In either branch of the PM Foundation there was a lot of money. Maybe there was nothing shady about it. But there had certainly been plenty about Oscar Pilch that was shady.

Since Pilch was unavailable for an interview, thanks to a bullet in the head, perhaps they should start with the man who had hired him. If, in fact, the man who had hired him had also killed him.

Hedley Boyle's inner sanctum, unsurprisingly, had a solid mahogany desk, comfortable chairs, and an admirable absence of clutter. In an outer office, a single secretary-receptionist was sandwiched between two tall filing cabinets, dedicated, Coggin and Sump surmised, to the Arts and to Sport respectively. She had a quite standard computer and printer. There was a sofa for visitors with a coffee table in front of it; on it a couple of magazines, *Performing Arts* and *Canadian Sports*. It was clearly a lean operation – a model, Coggin thought, of how a grant-giving organization ought to be run, with minimal sums spent on infrastructure and the bulk of the money going to good causes.

Their appointment was for 10.00. They were on time, and were quickly welcomed by Boyle in person. They already knew a bit about him, having looked him up: that he was forty-three, divorced from an addict wife now deceased; that he had one son, currently away at Acadia; that he had worked his way through university for a degree in commerce; that he had been hired as a young man on the bottom rung of the Mahogany Emporium's business office; that he had worked his way up in the enterprise; and that he had been picked out personally, by Morales and Morrison, to run the business office of the PM Foundation when it was founded.

All this they knew from his easily accessed c.v. and from Pilch's files. But such data are dry and lifeless when scrolled up on a computer screen or read in a file. They were eager to meet the man in the flesh, to put a face on the facts. The face, as it turned out, was hard to read, at first glance. It wore an expression of professional goodwill, such as is assumed by salesmen. But conversely it might be perfectly sincere, might not be pasted on at all. Sergeant Sump, who was better at reading faces and body language than Inspector Coggin, had seen the outstretched hand, the cordial tone, and the ready smile in many men who had something to hide. But he had also seen it in other people who had suffered pain and who then took refuge behind a mask of bonhomie. He remembered Boyle's sad marriage: nobody, he knew, could emerge unscathed from living with a drug-addict. So, as he shook the man's hand, he looked beyond the affable manner to the eyes. They were not at one with the smile. There was nothing necessarily sinister in that. But they had a veiled quality, a guardedness.

Inspector Coggin introduced his colleague, and they both sat down, declining the offer of coffee. If there was any tension in the air, he ascribed it to the uneasiness triggered in even the innocent when they are descended upon by the police. To relax any such tension, he began the conversation on a transparently friendly note.

"Mr Boyle," he said, "you won't know this, but it so happens I've particular reasons to be grateful to the PM Foundation. I'm a great Bach lover, and I go to the Festival concerts every year. So it's nice to be able to come here to the Foundation and say thank you."

"Inspector," Boyle replied, "you shouldn't really be thanking me, you know. I'm just the office-boy. It's Ms Morrison signs the cheques; and it's her idea in the first place. And not just for the Bach Festival either. She does a lot else, too. Some of it really original. I mean, who else nowadays would put up money to revive the operas of Haydn? Or the plays of Machiavelli?"

Sergeant Sump intervened. All too often, in his experience, interviews got bogged down in his superior's tendency to ramble on down musical or linguistic paths. They were the only kind of small talk he could manage, but they seldom bore investigative fruit.

"Well, sir," he said, "I'm sure that's all very admirable. But what we really wanted to ask was about the other side of your Foundation: the side that has to do with Mr Morales's concerns about drug use in sport."

"Yes?" This cautiously.

"You see, we know you hired Oscar Pilch to look into that and see if he could come up with anything useful. And if he did, we can't ask him because, as you know, he was murdered last week – it was in all the papers. So anything you can tell us in that connection might help. Presumably he kept in touch with you."

"Actually, the way I left it with him, he was to pass on to me any findings that seemed significant. But so far nothing much, really."

"Okay," Inspector Coggin put in. "But how come you picked him for the job? I mean, him, not some other snoop?"

He used the word deliberately. It was mildly derisive, flavoured with the policeman's built-in contempt for private eyes. But there was nothing spontaneous about choosing *snoop*: it put the matter on a shabby level that Boyle, with his air of composure, might find uncomfortable.

"Oh, no special reason. He was recommended to me by a friend."

"I see," Inspector Coggin said, "would that be the friend who recommended him to you, when you needed evidence for your custody suit?"

It was, in Shakespeare's words, a very palpable hit.

Boyle swallowed. Rather lamely he said, "Oh, so you know about that."

"Yes. It's our business to know things. Mind you, in a way, Pilch wasn't a bad choice. He certainly had plenty of connections with the drug world—rather dubious connections, I should say—for him to get on the trail of banned substances in the track world. That, I gather, was what Mr Morales was after. To your knowledge, did he want you to have Pilch look beyond Canada? Sergeant Sump here is a bit of an expert in the field. And I gather from him it's a world-wide scourge, this doping by athletes. I doubt, though, if Pilch had the resources to go global."

"No, probably not. But all I got him started on was the local scene."

"And when did you last see Pilch?" Sergeant Sump asked.

"Some time in February, I think. If you want an exact date, I can try to figure it out – it should be in my daytimer."

"Well, let that go for the moment. But not going back that far, perhaps you can tell us where you were a few days ago, on the evening of Saturday the twenty-fifth of last month."

The request was couched in language that was, on the surface, completely neutral. But implicitly it smacked of interrogation. An indignant response, at some level, was to be expected from any innocent party who had had nothing to do with the crime. But a guilty party, with half a brain in his head, would certainly simulate indignation. Sergeant Sump knew this, and he was mainly interested in gauging the personality the other side of the desk. But his request was also a trick question. Newspaper and television reports of the murder simply mentioned it as a Sunday morning occurrence. It was reasonable therefore to expect that the killer, whoever he or she was, would make sure to have a foolproof Sunday morning alibi. What the police had not told the media was that the time of death had been estimated as on the Saturday evening, somewhere between eight o' clock and eleven.

Boyle expostulated, with vigour. "You mean the night before the murder? You know something? I find that really offensive. Does this mean you're treating me as a suspect?"

"Not at all, sir," Sergeant Sump replied soothingly. "We just have to ask everyone the same question, so as not to treat them as suspects, if they were somewhere else. No offence meant."

Only half mollified, Boyle said, "That's easily said. The trouble is though, I was home by myself, watching 'Saturday Night at the Movies', and I can't prove it. I live alone, you know. Afterwards, I went to bed. Didn't get up till seven-thirty. Then had breakfast round the corner at Starbucks – I can show you the receipt. After that, I went to church at Rosedale United. There were probably forty or fifty people there who could vouch for me."

It was slickly said, almost assertively. Both policemen knew that the church service was irrelevant, even though Boyle perhaps did not. They duly noted that Boyle had provided an alibi for what any possible suspect might think was the crucial tine; but that he had no alibi for the time which was, indeed, crucial – not that there was any significance to that if he was, in fact, innocent.

"Thank you, sir," Sergeant Sump said, adding truthfully, "I don't think we need bother the congregation. Actually, we've probably asked you all we need to for now. Right, Inspector?"

Inspector Coggin nodded.

"But if anything else does occur to us, I hope we can contact you again – or you contact us, if anything comes to your mind about Pilch. You have our number, I think."

They rose to go. Then Inspector Coggin paused, halfway to the door.

"Just one thing," he said. "A couple of minutes ago, you were saying that the scope of Pilch's investigation, at least for the time being, was local. Does that mean he was just focusing on athletes in Canada? Here, I'd better defer to my sergeant. He knows far more about such things, than I do."

"I think what the Inspector's driving at, sir," Sergeant Sump put in, "is what kind of guidelines did Pilch have for pursuing his investigation. Everyone knows that Canada's done a pretty good job of catching druggy sprinters. They're all being tested regularly, according to the international protocol; and so far they've come up clean. In other words, the official watchdogs seem to be right on the ball. If the sprinters were coming up dirty, there'd have to be a lot of digging to find out where the drugs were coming from. Then maybe someone like Pilch would be the right guy to put his oar in. But seeing as how our sprinters are apparently clean, maybe there's nothing going on that needs investigating. Maybe hiring Pilch was a waste of money.

"Of course, though," he went on, "sprinters aren't the whole story. Distance-runners are another matter entirely. They don't pump themselves full of crude steroids, like the hundred-metre freaks – easily detectable. Sheer unnatural speed isn't what they're after. What they want is extra endurance. And sad to say, there are a couple of ways to enhance stamina that we don't yet know how to detect. If any of that's going on in Canada we just don't know. So was that the kind of thing Pilch was supposed to concentrate on? That is, if you can't nail the distance-runner yet by testing, perhaps you can nail the coach or the trainer or the trafficker who's involved."

"Exactly," Boyle responded, "That's it. The whole area of distance-running is where things get murky. You take someone like Ross Long, and rumours are bound to start up: his records are so way ahead of what looks to be humanly possible, that a lot of people have a hard time believing they're kosher. Anything's possible given the right chemical technique, just so long as you can keep one step ahead of the bloodhounds. You were asking what kind or guidelines Pilch had. Well, they were quite precise. He was asked to ferret about in the drug world, and. see if he could come up with anything that looked like a black-market in stamina-aids for distance-runners in Canada. And because we currently have only one Canadian distance-runner who's top of the line internationally, that means Pilch had to focus on Russ Lang."

VI

TUESDAY MAY 5, 10.55 AM

The PM Foundation's suite, a quite modest one by the bloated standards of corporate real estate, was in an office tower at the corner of Bay and Wellesley Streets. Emerging in bright sunshine, Coggin and Sump walked north up Bay to the parking lot where they had left their vehicle, right behind the Pontifical Institute of Mediaeval Studies. To their great surprise, they ran into a former colleague whom they had not seen for some time, who was leaving the institute to go to the same parking lot: the erstwhile Constable Nancy Pringle, who was now Sister Nancy Pringle, of the Order of St Gilbert.

Both men were extremely pleased to see her. Coggin had a very gratifying memory of her: at a time when the Metropolitan Police locally, like the Mounties nationally, had yet to embrace the idea of equal opportunity for women on the Force, he had been personally responsible for rescuing her from stultifying routine duties, and having her assigned to his team in the Homicide Department. He was able to contrive this, despite the foot-dragging of the bureaucrats, because it was self-evident that a woman was needed on the team, since the murder they were investigating had taken place in a convent, Tathwell Abbey, in North

196

Toronto. She had been of invaluable help, and he had been sad when she left the Force not long afterwards.

Sump had been equally appreciative of her talents as a policewoman, but he was not really surprised when she quit to become a nun, in that very convent. Raised Roman Catholic, though no longer an observant one, he had sensed how much their work on the Tathwell case had precipitated in her a profound crisis of faith. He had wished her well, and had kept in occasional touch ever since.

Now here they were, together, through a chance encounter on a midtown street. Coggin and Sump in lightweight suits for the warmth of the day; Sister Nancy in the sedate black of her Order.

Their delight was mutual. Coggin shook her hand warmly. Nancy (she told them to drop the Sister) gave Sump a big hug. To her, he had long since become just Fred. With Andrew Coggin she had not felt quite so first-name easy – partly out of a residual respect for him as her former superior officer, and partly because she had always been aware of his personal reserve.

None of them was about to make light of such a welcome but unexpected opportunity for a proper catch-up. So they sat down on a park bench, just south of St Basil's church, and chatted just as cordially as if they were resuming a conversation left off only yesterday.

They told her they were still on the same old job, though contemplating retirement. And they asked her about how things were for her in the convent, and what she was currently doing – Sump, better informed on such things than Coggin, did not think of a nun's life as a mere combination of household chores and pious exercises. He knew that women in religious life, and men also, had many ways of fulfilling their vocation. To be sure, the discipline of prayer was central to their life, but their communal work covered a multitude of activities, according to their individual talents: scholarship, music, medicine, nursing, teaching; whatever would be of gratitude to God and of service to the world.

"Am I happy? Oh yes," she said, "completely. After I finished my novitiate and took my final vows, they put me to work on a project that's right up my alley: to research and write a History of the Order."

"That sounds like a pretty big job," Coggin said. He had reason to think so. For while investigating the murder at the Abbey, he had picked up a few scraps of its history: the Order, he knew, had been founded in England, in the twelfth century, by St Gilbert of Sempringham, in Lincolnshire; it had escaped to France, when all the English monasteries were suppressed in the sixteenth century; and in the nineteenth it had resettled in Ontario.

"Big enough, I guess," she replied. "It'll probably keep me busy for a good long time. Fortunately, though, the primary sources have all survived. When we decamped to France in 1537 we were able to take all our records with us. These were added to over the years, variously in English, Latin, and French. And the whole lot came with us when we crossed the Atlantic. The Latin doesn't give me any trouble, of course. You may remember I did an MA in mediaeval monasticism before I joined the Force; and that came in useful a couple of times when we worked together at Tathwell."

"Indeed I do remember," Sump said. "It stopped a couple of people in their tracks. They probably thought we were all just dumb cops who never read anything more demanding than the Police Regulations. Well, they were wrong, weren't they? But I'm surprised you folks haven't written a history of your Order before. Maybe they were just waiting for someone to come along with the right qualifications."

"Nice of you to say that, Fred. But you shouldn't think of me as a kind of specialist lucking into the right assignment. Sure, I have some of the right background. But I still need help. Seventeenth-century French is tricky for anyone who isn't fully bilingual. And I have to say my Middle English is more than a bit rusty, that's what I was doing in the Pontifical Institute: getting some help."

"Any trouble about that?" Coggin asked. "If I recall correctly, the Gilbertines are a strictly contemplative Order, devoted to prayer and study, not allowed out into the world. Yet here you are, roaming the streets, so to speak, in the evil metropolis. I thought that was forbidden."

"Used to be, Mr Coggin, used to be. But quite a lot's changed in the last few years. Not long after you solved our homicide, you and Fred, we elected a new Abbot, from the men's side of our community. You may remember him: Dom Antony. A very sound choice. He's not a stick-in-the-mud about out-of-date rules. Nothing's wrong, in his mind, about my popping out for valid research reasons. But all the same, he never does lose sight of what we're supposed to be about. Which is, if you'll excuse a technical word, Grace."

Sump had heard the word often enough, in his Roman Catholic boyhood. But back then, before he quit church-going, the word smacked, he thought, more of pietism than of real devoutness. Even if he was wrong about that, it still seemed to him to belong in the rarefied air of incense and arcane sermons. He brought the conversation back down to earth. Literally. To the soil.

"I'll tell you one thing I remember about our time in your Abbey. What was the name of the Sister who had charge of the Infirmary?"

"Sister Agatha."

"Oh yes. As I remember, she was a colossus – not far off three hundred pounds, I'd say. And. from what you told me, she had a kind of steam-roll personality, too. You had a bit of a run-in with her, right?"

"You could say that. But we forgot about all that after I entered" she interrupted herself, conscious of having used a piece of religious jargon – "after I joined the Order, and we got to know each other. She was quite glad to pick my brains as an academic, because of her hobby. Her medical hobby. She had all the usual RN expertise about drugs and diet and bandages and so on. But she was also fascinated by the way her predecessors, centuries ago, grew a whole heap of plants for use in herbal medicine. Some traditions die hard. We Gilbertines carried right on, growing a herb garden and other stuff, without ever dismissing it as old hat when modern medicine evolved. We took cuttings with us when we were exiled to France, and grew our own garden there. Same again when we came here. Generation after generation, the garden survived, tended year after year by a long succession of Sisters, including Sister Agatha – who, I'm sorry to say, died last year. She would have loved to see the text I'm currently working on. It's a fourteenth-century document, in Middle English, which was tucked away among some old Latin materials of no special interest, and had lain there unnoticed until I started sorting everything out for this history project. From internal evidence, I've been able to date it to 1397. It's an account of all the herbs and other plants they grew for medical purposes, and of how they used them, and what they were good for, and so on."

"You know something?" Coggin said. "It's quite remarkable, isn't it, how things come round in the end. They get tossed overboard as rubbish, then they come back into fashion. Herbal medicine, I gather, has become quite the thing in some quarters. And not just among the weirdos, either who believe in reincarnation or aroma-therapy. There are quite sober people who take it seriously. So maybe you Gilbertines have been onto something all along. And this text, you say, is in Middle English, not in Latin?"

"Yes, in the East Midland dialect, the Gilbertines being mostly Lincolnshire people. That makes it a bit different from Chaucer, who wrote in the Southern dialect. But anyone who can read Chaucer could decipher it fairly easily."

Coggin doubted if he could. Chaucer had crossed his path in university but he had had to rely on a modernized version.

Sump was out of his depth. He kept up to date in his reading, with all developments in his trade. In his spare time, he occasionally indulged a paradoxical taste for the fictions of Agatha Christie – paradoxical because her pages were filled with cardboard stock characters; whereas his own insights into human behaviour were both astute and empathetic. As to things mediaeval, his mind encompassed nothing at all beyond a distant memory of boyhood exposure, in snippets, to tales of King Arthur. But even if he lacked the background to appreciate the calibre of Nancy's scholarly endeavours, he could still discern, and rejoice in, his ex-colleague's happiness in the life she was leading and the work she was doing.

"Mind you," Nancy went on, "there are a few local peculiarities, of vocabulary and pronunciation. Some of the words are so peculiar to the area that they haven't found their way into Stratmann's Dictionary of Middle English. Take *markerie*, for instance. It's listed as one of the plants in the original Tathwell garden, and I haven't the faintest idea what it is. There are lots of other plants listed, with ordinary names that have survived in common use, like burdock and comfrey and fennel. But markerie isn't in any of the botany books I've been able to get hold of."

"That's the trouble with words in the mother tongue," Coggin commented. "Either they go out of fashion and disappear, or they change their meaning. When I was a boy, you could go to a party and speak of having a gay time. Not anymore. Maybe you'd know what markerie is if your Infirmarian had written in Latin. Most plants have a Latin name."

"Yes, but she couldn't. She was writing for her work-force, not the nuns who were the bosses. Indoors, these were lay sisters doing the household chores; and they had a very shaky grasp of Latin, if any. And for outdoor work, in the gardens and the fields, they hired manual labourers, who had no Latin at all. But those men must have grown up, like everyone in country places, knowing all the plants by name and being familiar with their use in folk-medicine. Over the years, the Infirmarians became quite expert. And they brought their know-how with them, along with their cuttings, from Lincolnshire to France to Ontario. We still use them, in our garden here."

"You know, Nancy," Sump said, "that's really interesting – I mean, to me as a track coach. Male athletes used to be just meat-and-potatoes men. A lot of hockey players still are. But we're much more scientific nowadays about nutrition. And good old-fashioned herbal medicine has made quite a comeback, especially with women athletes – they seem to be more open-minded than men. I'm all for it. What everyone's looking for is how to build a better body, without turning to drugs. And if common or garden plants can do the trick, so much the better."

"Funny you should say that, Fred," she responded, "about building the better body. In that fourteenth-century text I've been rambling on about most of what the Infirmarian says has to do with illness or injury, not with health, with plants that have curative properties or can mend a wound. She describes what they're good for and how to use them. But there's one plant, she praises as a kind of effective body-builder. Not along the lines of Mr Universe – that's just freaky. No, as a kind of dietary supplement that builds up a labourer's capacity to endure long hours of hard toil. It's that markerie I was mentioning, and it was a staple for the Tathwell field-workers. According to her they outdid the productivity of other farms, and she rather proudly compares the Tathwell revenues with what was earned elsewhere. I don't know. Maybe markerie is extinct, like the secret of mediaeval stained glass. But I bet a lot of your athletes would like to get their hands on it if they could, Fred. Winning Nature's way, so to speak, not in a laboratory."

That's a thought, the two policemen reflected. Maybe somebody has got his hands on it.

VII

1987-8 WINTER
During the past winter, as every year, there had been no long-distance races in the northern hemisphere. After the last of the fall marathons and cross-country championships, runners could do their speedwork on short indoor tracks. But long road-runs had to be done outdoors, in sometimes bitter weather, unless you could afford to train in Florida or other warmish places.

This conferred a modest advantage on distance-runners from New Zealand or Australia. Their international racing season, from April to September, was in Europe and North America, which was where all the action was. But if they stayed home in the Antipodes from October to March, they could train in peak conditions there and still retain a racing sharpness by entering local meets.

One Australian runner who had been doing this for years was Tom Kippax. Consistently in the world's top ten, he had never held a world record. But he was a canny tactician, much feared by his fellow competitors at 1500 metres, 3000 and 5000; and he still won a lot of races. Of late, he concentrated on the 3000 and the 5000, being now thirty-five years old and probably, many thought, near the end of his career. It was that reputation, as an incipient has-been, that brought him an invitation to run in Toronto on May 22nd. The invitation was from Pablo Morales who, along with secondary sponsors, was financing the event. It was to be at the rare distance of two miles; and it was to be an attempt to break the existing world record of just under eight minutes. The star attraction would be Ross Lang, whose records were all at longer distance. To push him to the target, and quite possibly to beat him in the attempt, Morales and his advisers had assembled a top-rank field of eight other runners from Europe and Africa and Asia, with Kippax, the Australian, to serve as rabbit – that is, to lead the pack through the first mile at potential world-record pace and then, presumably to drop out. It was a slightly demeaning role for him to play, but the pay was good; and anyway there were other races coming up, in which he could be an authentic contender in his own right. Either way, he would be ready.

So would Lang. There had been nothing secret about his workouts or his races in the winter months. He had amassed hundreds of miles of road work, partly in Toronto despite the weather and partly in Florida, all done alone. The sheer quantity of it led people to think that perhaps, at twenty-eight, he was contemplating a move up to the marathon, a move often made by 10k runners at that age. To be sure, he kept up doing speed-work on indoor tracks; but that was what a would-be marathoner would do in winter, anyway. Nor was the speculation about his marathon intentions undercut by the occasional indoor races he entered: these were at 800 metres, run against specialists, and he usually finished no better than third or fourth; people thought he just did it for fun, as a light-hearted break from the grind of chalking up a hundred miles a week on the road.

People, for such is life, do tend to believe what they want to believe. Rivals, constantly outrun by Lang at 5k and 10k on the track, would be relieved if he gave up those distances in favour of the marathon. And his fans, who were many, especially in Canada, would have been delighted if, like the great Zátopek of 1952, he could be the supreme champion at all three distances.

What nobody realised, except Bill Northbrook, was that Lang had everyone fooled. He was not contemplating a switch to the marathon; and his 800-metre races were deadly serious. It was not that he intended to win them, or even try to. But moving along with the pack of middle-distance specialists, he conditioned himself to set his inner clock for a 1.50 pace at that distance. This pace he then transferred to his winter workouts, run solo on an indoor track and unobserved by anyone except Northbrook, who timed them. These workouts consisted of four such 800s at the same pace with only a half-minute rest in between, adding up to a total of 3200 metres, Just about two miles. The theory behind that pattern was that on race day he would be able to put those four 800s back to back at a slightly slower pace (1.56) for a two-mile record at 7.46.

That, in effect, would mean running two sub-four-minute miles non-stop at 3.52 each. At even pace, with no sprint finish, that would compute to eight successive laps at 53 seconds each. That then was the arithmetical blueprint. But he and Northbrook modified it, for sound tactical reasons. Runners prefer to start out a bit conservatively, to have something left for a finishing kick. With that in mind, they hoped to go through the first mile in exactly four minutes, at sixty seconds per lap. If Lang could then do a long, relentless acceleration (like Viren in the '76 Olympics), running the next three laps at fifty-nine, fifty-eight, and fifty-seven seconds respectively, a final lap at fifty-two would, bring the winner in at 7.46. They had every hope, and good reason to believe, it would be Lang first across the finish-line.

The plan was cleverly devised to outrun, and outwit, most of his rivals.

In the field there would be milers who sometimes tackled longer distances but who, when doing so, counted on a slower tempo, to keep plenty in reserve for their usual finishing kick over the last 300 metres. They might even think things would pan out that way for them when the field went through the first mile in what was, for them, a quite manageable speed. But Lang's acceleration through the fifth, sixth, and seventh laps would erode the finishing kick they liked to count on in the final lap.

Also in the field would be 5k specialists, to whom the shorter distance of two miles would, present no problem. But they would probably get into trouble with an opening tempo faster than they were used to.

Theoretically, the one competitor who posed a significant danger was Moses M'bongo from Kenya, the world-record holder at 3k, a distance that Lang had never bothered with. M'bongo had set the record a year ago, in Oslo, and everyone had still been with him at 2600 metres, run at a speed that was not overwhelming; but then he had clinched the matter with an astonishing last lap in forty-nine seconds. Clearly, he would have to be watched if he was still around after seven laps.

Much would depend on the rabbit. Kippax was reliable. He could grind out laps like clockwork, with all the accuracy of a Swiss watch. He was known to be in good shape, and had agreed in an e-mail today to lead everyone through the first mile in exactly four minutes. He could be counted on.

After that, everyone would be on his own.

VIII

WEDNESDAY MORNING, MAY 6

Coggin and Sump had already spent a lot of time laboriously going through Pilch's records, not just those in the Boyle file and the Mahogany file. Nearly all of them were the stock-in-trade of private investigation, divided about equally between sordid marital conflicts and sordid financial disputes. None of the latter seemed to have any-bearing on the homicide. And of the former, only the Boyle case of years ago might have an indirect bearing. So they went over it again.

What they were looking for now, in their office, was documentation of the evidence Pilch had been able to come up with, in the custody suit of drug abuse by Boyle's wife, now deceased. More particularly, they were interested in knowing how she had obtained her drugs, and how Pilch had traced her getting them. They reckoned it was possible that Pilch, back then, had made some useful contacts with dealers, and that he had revisited those contacts now in his search for hypothetical trafficking in performance-enhancing drugs for athletes.

The documentation was there alright. In the Boyle file, it was sparse. Pilch had found what was needed for Boyle, years ago, to win his suit. But there was hardly any detail, by name or address, about the traffickers contacted: just a few cryptic handwritten notes. In the Mahogany file, though, there was more. A few individuals were referred to without phone numbers or addresses; and there were copies of reports e-mailed to Boyle. The first few of them merely claimed that some progress was being made, without anything definitive to go on. According to Pilch, his principal contact, Louie (no surname), thought he might be able to come up with a useful lead – obviously for suitable reward.

This would be a friend, of Louie's, who had wide connections in the trafficking network. Most of these people were traders in heroin or cocaine or both, raking in money hand over clenched fist; and they would probably regard the illicit doping of athletes as very small beer. But even at that disdained level, information was always valuable: money can change hands, and then open mouths.

Leafing through the preliminary material, the two men both had reservations. If Pilch was onto something, he had not given any particulars. Now he was dead, and it might be tricky to do a follow-up with this Louie. They could contact Narcotics, but a first name alone wasn't much to go on.

"If Louie even exists," Coggin said.

"Yeah, right," Sump concurred. "After all, Pilch was a rather dubious character, when he was on the Force. Probably no better on civvy street."

"And even if Louie does exist, there's nothing to say Pilch wasn't just stringing Boyle along. Feeding him bits and bobs of bullshit, to keep the weekly cheque coming in for a while, but not really doing anything much, or even anything at all, to earn it. By the way, Andrew, how much was it?"

Coggin had organized a couple of constables to search Pilch's apartment in a shabby low-rise on Maitland Street. They had found nothing of any apparent significance. But they did find his bank statements, from the branch bank around the corner, and his account number. One of the constables, bidden by Coggin, had gone to the bank and obtained a printout or all Pilch's recent transactions.

"Three hundred a week," Coggin replied. "Just the kind of figure someone like Pilch would ask for. Anything less, and it would look as though he wasn't taking the job seriously. Anything more, and he'd have Boyle on his back every week, demanding results. At three hundred, he could hope to string Boyle along almost indefinitely."

"Hold on a second," Sump said, who had turned up the last of Pilch's e-mails to Boyle. "Maybe he wasn't stringing him along at all. Look at this. It's dated April 9th. And he says, 'big news, too risky to send e-way. suggest you see me privately. suggest 10 saturday morning. ep.' Maybe Louie had come up trumps."

"Maybe so, Fred. Even a sleaze-bag can do something honest once in a while. Look at this for a connection. He sends that message on April the 9th. Three days later, if Boyle acts on it, they meet in Pilch's office, on Saturday the 12th. Five days later, on the 17th, Pilch's bank account shows a cash deposit of ten grand. Nine days later, on Sunday the 26th, he's found dead in his office. So maybe he needed a good lump sum, to pay off some informants. And maybe someone in the drug trade had a score to settle over that transaction, and needed to close someone else's mouth. Pilch's."

"Yes, and maybe that someone else did it, with Pilch's own gun. We know he had a license. But there wasn't one in his office. And our lads didn't find one in his apartment, either. What do you think?"

Ever cautious, ever wary of leaping to conclusions, Coggin said, "One step at a time, Fred. First thing we do, we check if that ten grand did come from the PM Foundation. If it didn't, let's not get carried away. It may have something to do with Pilch's death. But that might be only because of whatever else Pilch was working on, not because of what he was being paid to do by the Foundation. Let's pay them a visit."

IX

WEDNESDAY MAY 6, 2.00 PM

After they parked, in the same lot as before, they walked south on Bay Street to the corner of Wellesley, where the foundation's office was. In the foyer, they had to wait for one of the elevators to come down. When it did, several passengers emerged. One of them, not in her work-clothes but smartly dressed, was Amy Buniak. All three of them were surprised.

"Well, Ms Buniak," Sump said, "how are you doing? Last time we met, you'd just had a rather harrowing experience. Not easy to get over. Hope you've been okay."

"You're right, Sergeant. You don't get over something like that as though it was just your everyday trivium."

Coggin registered that singular noun with respect. He lived, despairingly, in a world, where people, even professional writers, forgot that the word media was plural; here was someone who could assume, accurately and with apparent ease, that the singular of trivia was trivium.

"Any better luck with the acting?" Sump asked.

"Maybe. You never know. Actually that's why I was here. There's a Foundation upstairs that gives grants sometimes to plays, and I was hoping to see the grants officer about a project. But he wasn't in."

"That wouldn't by any chance be Hedley Boyle, would it?" Coggin asked.

"Yes, it would, actually." She did not expand on that. "But how about you? How's your investigation going?"

"Oh, it's coming along," he replied, non-committally. "We'll let you know if we catch whoever it was. And don't forget to contact us, if anything comes to mind that could be relevant. Sometimes when you're under stress, as you certainly were, you forget about little details, and only remember them later."

"Sure, I'll do that," she said; and turned to go.

"And best of luck with your application," Sump called out as she left.

***

They took the elevator to the fifth floor. They had not made an appointment. On purpose. With someone like Boyle, who might or might not be involved in questionable activities, the element of surprise can be useful, catching people off guard. Had he been in, they would have begun an exploratory conversation, to see where it might lead them, depending on the flavour of his responses to questions. Sump was particularly good at such conversations. He had a great knack for putting his finger on the pulse of a person's feelings. He would begin smoothly

206

enough, even affably. But sometimes he would interject a sudden, jolting question that would throw the person off balance.

Boyle was not in, however. And they were glad of that. For it meant using plan B instead, with Coggin leading off, and pulling rank with Boyle's assistant: he had noted her deferential demeanour on their first visit; and he calculated, unfairly but accurately, that she might be easily cowed in the face of official authority – even though he had no warrant up his sleeve.

Gladys Maybee looked to be in her early forties. She was slightly overweight, as many people are in sedentary jobs. If she was married, she wore no wedding ring, or any other jewelry for that matter. She had wispy hair, that had not been improved by a salon. She wore rimless glasses.

Sump felt sorry for her. It looked like a dead-end job she was in, unexciting and tedious. He hoped she was good at it, and reasonably well paid. As to that, he doubted it: the clerks at Headquarters didn't earn much; but at least they had a union to rely on, and a pension. This poor woman, like many a secretary in a small office, had only a desultory future ahead, and probably a straitened old age. He hoped she had a happy home life. But she did not exude content.

Coggin wasted no time on such reflections. After reminding her of who they were, and of their rank, he came straight to the point.

"Ms Maybee," he said, "as you know, we're investigating the murder of one of your clients, Oscar Pilch. We have to question anyone who has had a connection with him, including Mr Boyle. Now don't get me wrong. That only means we're trying to cross people off the list of possible suspects. It's just a routine check. If Mr Boyle were here today," – he was one of the few men or women, nowadays, who knew when to use a subjunctive and when not to – "there are some questions we'd be asking him; and we will another time. Meanwhile, there are a couple of things we'd like to ask you."

She stiffened, nervously.

"Just minor matters," he reassured her. "Now, am I right in thinking that when you employ a freelance like Pilch, you mail him his cheques according to what his contract is. I don't mean you sign them – presumably Mr Boyle does. But presumably you send them out and keep a record of them."

"Yes, I do. But I don't know if I ought to be showing you that stuff. It's pretty confidential, you know."

This with a valiant little attempt to stand up for her rights. Sump thought, good for her. But he knew it wouldn't get her anywhere.

"I think I should remind you," Coggin. said, "that this is a murder investigation. We expect citizens to co-operate. Now, either you show us the file right now. Or if you don't, Sergeant Sump will go and get a warrant, and I'll wait here till he comes back with one. Of course, if that's how it has to be, you do realize you might be charged with impeding a police investigation."

She sighed, and shrugged. And turned towards one of the filing-cabinets. Opening a drawer, she pulled out a file and handed it over.

"There you are," she said, with a touch of asperity in her voice. "But I'd like to go on record that I don't like your attitude."

Sump was pleased by this. Perhaps there was more to the woman than he had thought at first. As to Coggin, he did not read his overbearing approach as an instance of police brutality: it was simply a tactic, used to get results. In fact, his partner was essentially a courteous man.

"Thank you," Coggin said. "Now, why don't you just get on with whatever you were doing, and we'll go through the file and check that it tallies with the information we've already got?"

They went over to the sofa underneath the window, and sat down with the file in front of them.

"Actually," Ms Maybee said, "if you're going to sit and go through that file, I'll take a few minutes for a coffee on the ground floor. Don't bother answering the phone. I'll put it on answering."

She did so, and left the room.

They could not believe their luck. She had left the filing-cabinet untended. Perhaps she felt she had done all she could. She had registered her protest. If they wanted to pry into other matters, there wasn't any way she could stop them, not in the face of a threatened warrant.

Sump went to the door, peered cautiously out, and saw her press the elevator button at the far end of the corridor.

"Okay, Andrew, go to it," he said. "I'll keep an eye open for her."

Leaving the file open on the coffee-table, Coggin quickly leafed through its contents. He found weekly records of regular payment of $300 made to Pilch. They corresponded tidily with the deposits made in Pilch's bank account. There was no record of a payment made to him of $10,000 on April 17th. Nor did he expect there to be, at least not in this file: the deposit had been made in cash.

He got up and went over to the filing-cabinet, saying to Sump across the room, "I'm going to look and see if there's a file called Discretionary Payments, or Special Funds, or anything like that."

He rifled through all the drawers, with no success. Similarly with the second cabinet. Hoping there was still time, he went through into the inner office, and took a quick look through Boyle's desk drawers. None of them contained a file like what he'd been looking for in the outer office. But what he did find was a file containing stubs of his salary cheques and related materials, including the details of his chequing and savings accounts in the branch bank on the ground floor of this very building.

"Here she comes, Andrew," Sump called out, audibly but quietly. Both of them were seated on the sofa, innocent as mice when she walked in.

They stood up, and handed her back the file.

"Here you are, Ms Maybee," Coggin said. "I don't think we'll need to bother you any further, and we won't need to xerox any of these materials. Thank you for your co-operation. Anything else you want to say, Sergeant, before we leave?"

"Just one thing, sir," Sump said – he and Coggin were always formal with each other when talking to civilians. "I understand the other half of this Foundation gives grants to projects in the performing arts. Is that right?"

"Yes." Guardedly.

Perhaps she was wondering if this not-so-objectionable officer was going to ask for a grant application form, to support a concert-series by a male-voice choir of stalwart but not very sophisticated policemen.

"I understand," he said, "one of your current applicants is an actor called Amy Buniak, professional name Amy Barton. She has a quite indirect connection with Oscar Pilch, but more to the point with Mr Boyle. We want to know more about her. So we'd appreciate it if you could run off a xerox for us of her grant application."

"Oh, what the hell," she said, rather more spiritedly. "You've already talked me into showing you one confidential file. I guess another one won't make any difference now."

She opened the second cabinet, pulled out a file and switched on her xerox machine.

X

THURSDAY MAY 7, 1.30 PM

Amy Buniak was worried, and sleepless. She had been quite open with the police about what she was doing in the Grant Road building, under contract to clean the offices on the second floor every Sunday morning. She had told the truth. But not the whole truth. In fact, if only by omission, she had lied to the police. She had left the impression, quite credibly, that on discovering the body she had simply panicked, and had got away from the scene as quickly as she could, hoping that the killer

209

was not still around, good and ready to shoot her, too, as a witness who might identify him.

This was plausible enough, on the face of it; and the police swallowed it whole, so far as she could tell. But it was by no means a full or exact account of what had happened that Sunday morning.

She had not said anything about the gun. And that might turn out to be a dangerous mistake. It might have been better for her to have been completely open about the gun right away, and just hope for the best; after all, she was innocent.

Or at least she was innocent of the murder. But how would it look if she had to admit having pried through Pilch's desk drawers the week before. In the course of doing so, she had found his revolver and picked it up to look at it, comparing it to the fake weapons she had occasionally worked with as stage-props. From that handling, it was bound to be covered in her fingerprints. And now, a week later, she had panicked. She opened the desk-drawer, and it was still there. Rather gingerly, she picked it up, and wondered for a moment what to do with it. Occasional crime stories she had read spoke of adroit criminals wiping their prints off a weapon they'd used. But she had no idea how to set about doing that effectively. Cleaning it would look bad for her if they found the gun with traces of her fingerprints still on it that had been incompletely wiped away. Then it also occurred to her that it might not be a bad thing to have the gun with her as she left. Even though she had little idea how to use a firearm, it might afford her a moment of protection if the killer was still around. She didn't take time to think this through logically. She simply slipped the gun into the large pocket of her wind breaker and left. Going down the stairs without incident, and along the street to her car, she stashed the windbreaker in the trunk. Then she had called 911.

Now, this day, she had run into the two detectives again, the rather austere Inspector, whose reserved manner hid what might be an astute brain, and the more outgoing Sergeant, whose bonhomie might very well be a front; meeting them seemingly by accident. Why were they there, she wondered? Were they onto her as part of their investigation? Had they had her followed?

"Oh come on, Amy," she said to herself. 'That's just paranoid."

It had seemed like a purely chance encounter. But there was no getting away from the fact that all three of them were connected to the one crime and the only previous time they had met was at the crime-scene. Co-incidence?

Probably, she thought, without significance.

But then she remembered that three weeks ago, the only piece of mail lying on the floor, having been pushed through the mail-slot perhaps on the Friday afternoon, addressed to Oscar Pilch, Ace Agency, and marked Personal but unstamped, had been from the PM Foundation, with Boyle's name scrawled on the back of the envelope.

It had caught her attention, because it was to the PM Foundation that she had recently applied for a grant, to help fund production of a play she was writing. And after she sent in her grant application, Boyle had sent her a formal note acknowledging receipt of it.

But how on earth was he connected with death at the Ace Detective Agency? If at all?

Oh dear, she had thought, this is altogether too complicated! Am I getting involved in something way beyond my depth?

Be that as it may, though, she had decided on impulse to pop in at the Foundation, ostensibly to make a simple enquiry about her grant application, but really to size up this Boyle person, if he was in.

He had not been. But emerging from the elevator on the ground floor, she had run into those two confounded policemen. They had been cordial enough, even solicitous.

She had been a bit taken aback when the Inspector named Boyle as the probable reason for her presence there. But she covered it well. They exchanged pleasantries, and she turned to leave, just the two of them entering the elevator. After she left, she turned around and went back to see what floor the elevator stopped at. Sure enough, it was the fifth floor.

That gave her pause to think. And the Sergeant's last words were still in her ear, guileless enough perhaps, but nothing was necessarily what it seemed to be in these murky waters.

"Don't forget to contact us," he had said, "if anything comes to mind that could be relevant."

And now she remembered one detail which she had genuinely forgotten. When she had arrived to clean Pilch's office on the fateful Sunday morning, his office door had not been locked.

It was just the kind of thing that could be important. Ordinarily she would have mentioned it. But should she now? Would they see her doing so as suspicious, as a way of deflecting attention from herself? Or might it be better to bring it up as just the kind of memory lapse that the Sergeant had alluded to as quite commonplace? Certainly she could do so with a convincing air of veracity: after all, she was a trained actress and anyway it would be true, a genuine memory lapse. But truth, she had always known, was sometimes ambiguous, was occasionally treacherous ground to stand on.

Amy Buniak was worried.

THURSDAY MAY 12, 9.00 AM

Sister Nancy Pringle, OSG, was lucky. She had written a letter to the North Toronto Botanical Garden, explaining who she was and how the Gilbertines had a long background in herbal medicine, with a Lincolnshire origin in England and with a subsequent refoundation in Toronto. She asked if there was someone on staff who could answer a couple of related botanical questions for her.

She received a quick and courteous reply from a certain Geoff Willoughby, who identified himself as the resident Master Gardener, and who said he would be fascinated to have a conversation with her, not least because he had been born in Lincolnshire before coming to Canada as a young adult. He suggested an early appointment some day at 9.00 a.m., if that would be convenient. That way, he said, if need be, they could phone long distance to his elderly father in England, where the local time would be five hours ahead of Toronto time, in order to consult with him about any obscure details.

She duly arrived at the suggested time on an agreed date; and they walked around the Gardens together, especially the herbaceous section, as a beginning.

He was a pleasant-looking middle-aged man, with an outdoor face and workaday hands: clearly a man of the soil, but an expert one, proud of his profession. His voice had become halfway Canadian, but still bore traces of his East Anglian origin.

"So tell me, Sister," he asked her, "how much is known about the way your predecessors used herbal medicine in the Middle Ages? And how much of that sort of thing has survived into the present day?"

"Quite a lot," she replied. "We have nearly all their records, and fortunately the botanical stuff is in English, not Latin. The plants are listed, with their common-or-garden names, plus the uses they put them to medically. And more than that, when they had to leave England, first for France and then for Canada, they were able to take plants with them, for re-cultivation abroad. Their second move was over a century ago; so I guess, back then, there weren't the same strict regulations as now, forbidding the importation of plants."

"Are you telling me, Sister, that you have a herbaceous part of the garden in your convent that is, so to speak, a replica of the one in mediaeval Lincolnshire?"

"Yes, you could put it that way. The layout may not be the same – we couldn't be sure about that. But the plants are, so to speak, direct descendants of their ancestors."

"And do you still use them for herbal medicine?"

"To some extent, yes. But not at the cost of ignoring modern medicine, of course. A recent Infirmarian of ours was a fully qualified doctor."

As they strolled around, he pointed out to her the various plants in the beds, using both their vernacular names and their Latin ones, fluently.

"It's part of my training," he explained, "and my Dad's before me, and his father's before him. I don't know if you're aware of this, but there's a great tradition of gardening in Lincolnshire, all the way back to the eighteenth century. The top botanist, back then, was Joseph Banks

"He was a Lincolnshire man, and he introduced plants into England from all over the world. And I only mention him because, as a young man, he gave a lot of time to studying the Physic Garden in London, where plants were grown to cater to the needs of apothecaries for extracts to use in herbal medicine."

Their stroll at an end, he ushered her into his office.

"Do sit down," he said, "and tell me how I can help."

"It's quite straightforward," she replied. "At least, it may be. I'm writing a history of our religious Order, and I've run into a stumbling-block in the old records of herbal medicine. Latin wouldn't be a problem for me, whenever they used it. And a lot of what they wrote in fourteenth-century Middle English is fairly easy to figure out, too. But one of the plants they listed has a name I can't find in the mediaeval dictionaries: markerie."

She spelled it out.

"So I wonder if you've ever heard of it. And I'm thinking perhaps you have, what with you having a Lincolnshire background and my source being from those parts."

"Markerie? Yes, I have. But my Dad's the real expert. So he's the best chap to ask, I reckon. Going on ninety, but smart as a whip. I phoned him yesterday and asked him to be home this morning – that is, this afternoon by British time – as we might need to call. Would you like me to ring him?"

She had noted, in passing, his unconscious mixture of Canadianisms and unextinguished English idioms. But that was a small matter.

"Yes, please," she said. "That would be very good of you."

"There's just one thing, though. Lincolnshire, as you probably know, has long been a bastion of Methodism – it's where John Wesley was born and raised. So I don't know if Dad would be immediately at ease in talking to an RC nun. Would it be alright if I simply introduce you as Nancy Pringle?"

She was struck by his sensitivity: the courtesy to her, and the concern for his father's feelings – even if the latter reflected some kind of Protestant hostility that matched the reverse hostility, or at least condescension, voiced by some Catholics.

"Absolutely that would be alright. In fact, why don't you forget about the whole Sister thing, and just call me Nancy yourself, too?"

He smiled at her gratefully, picked up the phone, and dialed a number he obviously knew by heart.

When he got through, he said, "Hello, Dad, it's Geoff again. I told you I might be calling about something. There's a young woman in my office called Nancy Pringle, who has a plant question she can't find the answer to. Funnily enough, it's a Lincolnshire plant she'd like to identify. So I'd like to put her on the line right now. Okay?"

Obviously it was okay and he handed her the phone.

"George Willoughby here," said a voice at the other end. Elderly but still robust. Warm. And unaffectedly rich in the vowels of his shire.

"Hello, Mr Willoughby," she said. "I'm working on a bit of plant history that's local to your part of the world. Have you ever heard of a village called Tathwell? It's near Louth, just where the Lindsey Marsh rises up into the wolds."

These, however slender, were her preliminary credentials. Not many Torontonians would have had the faintest idea what the Wolds were.

"Tathwell? Oh, ay, I been there a few times. Grew up nearby, in Legbourne. What about it?"

"Well, back in the fourteenth century, they had a garden there, full of plants cultivated for use in herbal medicine. I don't suppose there's anything like that still there. But there are some old documents I'm working on, that describe the place pretty well. And they name some of the plants by their old country names. Plants like borage and comfrey and so on, that I've been able to figure out even if the spelling of the names has changed a bit over the years. But there's one I can't identify. Have you ever heard of a plant thereabouts called markerie?"

"Markerie? Course I have. Mind you, it's rare. And nobody'd know what it was if they weren't familiar with North Lindsey dialect. When I were a boy, all the village people still spoke the way their grandparents did. That's gone out of use nowadays, I'm sorry to say. But back then, farm folk still used all the old names for things, and pronounced them the old way. For instance, they used to call a wagon a rully, pronouncing it to rhyme with fully."

She half hoped he would go on in this vein: someone had recently sent her a copy of the recording Tennyson made, in old age, of two of the poems he wrote in the dialect of North Lindsey where he had grown up.

But Mr Willoughby, Senior, turned back to where he had left off.

"Markerie? The way you say it is middling close to how the old people used to speak of it, when I were a boy. Like I said, it's rare. I hardly ever saw it anywhere back then. I used to do some junior gardening jobs when I were fifteen. And I do mind seeing a patch of it in the back garden of Grimoldby Rectory, round behind the blackcurrant bushes. But nobody took no note of it then, or since, far as I know. But what you really want to know, I reckon, is what markerie is, what its real name is."

"Yes. Please tell me."

"Well, a kind of wild spinach is what it is. And markerie isn't far off its proper name: mercury. Different spelling, different sound, in the old way of talk. A dialect word."

She felt chagrined. "I should have been able to figure that out for myself," she said. "Spelling variations aren't a closed book to me, ordinarily."

"Maybe so. But even if you had thought it was mercury with a different sound and spelling, you still wouldn't have known what it was. My guess it hasn't gone into the text books as mercury. And if you looked it up under spinach, you're not likely to find any mention of wild spinach. It's virtually disappeared from the landscape. And anyway the two species are quite different."

"How? I mean, what way are they different?"

"In taste, but also in their effect, and their reputation. I've eaten both. Now regular spinach, there's nothing wrong with it: if you steam it and serve it with butter, it's quite tasty; nourishing, too, like any green vegetable. But a lot of kids, when they get past the baby-food stage, take a right dislike to spinach: it's the old story, they don't like having to eat things with an unfamiliar taste, and somehow they fix on one food as a pet loathing; quite often it's spinach, and they grow up swearing they'll never touch the ruddy stuff again – it doesn't help either, if they're told to eat up 'because it's good for you'."

"I know what you mean. I have a younger brother just like that. He used to throw a tantrum if Mother put spinach on his plate. She didn't persist. Some battles you simply can't win. Anyway, is it different with markerie – mercury, that is?"

"Sort of. But there isn't that much to go on, seeing it's rare, and kids most places haven't been exposed to it. But you ask Geoff. He had not much liking for regular spinach. But when my wife served up markerie he gobbled it right up. It tastes quite different: it's just great."

She was pleased by his unaffected manner. He had the voice of an educated man, skilled in his trade; but one who was unashamed of his origin. He had not, unlike the Thatcher woman, manufactured a snob accent to make his way in a class-ridden world. He was content to remain who he was. He spoke of markerie without bothering to modernize it as mercury. And when he said it was great, he quite unconsciously slipped into the old village version of the word, familiar to her from the Tennyson recording, with two vowels as greät.

"Mind you," he went on, "it's a funny thing. The old folk always used to say that eating markerie made a man real strong – like some sort of magic recipe. Probably just an old wives' tale. Yet somehow, when markerie more or less disappeared, the same old idea just got attached to regular spinach. No reason for that. You can eat a ton of spinach everyday, it won't turn you into a superman. But some people do cling to some weird ideas. That must be why the Popeye cartoons used to be so popular, about Popeye the Sailorman who had huge muscles on his forearms, because he ate a lot of spinach."

She had a vague memory of seeing a Popeye strip in the comics years ago, as a child. But an interesting other connection leapt instantly to her mind.

"Mr Willoughby," she said, "I think this may interest you. The mediaeval document I told you about, lists the various plants in the herb garden, including mercurie, and how they were used in herbal medicine. What it says about mercury kind of corroborates what you were saying about its effect. Maybe that wasn't an old wives' tale, after all. Labourers on the farm owned by the herbalists, allegedly, could work harder and longer hours than labourers on rival farms, to great profit. And the reason given was that they were fed a lot of markerie."

"I'll be damned! I'll have to give that a good old think."

"Me too. I mean, I've known what the document says for quite some time. But it didn't make a whole lot of sense till you told me what markerie was."

"Well, it makes a whole lot of sense to me, too. Maybe I've been doing myself a fair bit of good with my markerie patch, without really knowing quite why. I always just liked the stuff."

"Maybe you have. Your son tells me you're going on ninety and spry as a kangaroo. Anyway, I mustn't keep you on the phone. Except, of course, to say thank you for your time and help. Would you like me to put Geoff back on the line?"

"Oh, I don't think that'll be necessary. I had a good long yarn with him yesterday. And thank you, too, Miss Pringle. It's been a pleasure talking to you – and quite illuminating. So I'll say goodbye now. And thanks again."

"Bye-bye," she said. And hung up. And turned to the son.

216

"Thank you for that. It was incredibly helpful. And I must say your father sounds like a wonderful old guy."

She told him, succinctly, what had passed between them, since only one end of the phone call had been audible to him.

"So that's what markerie is, seemingly," she concluded. "And that's why the mediaeval nuns set such store by it. What's really striking about that, though, is how it survived – indeed, that it survived at all. Of course, it did survive here and there, locally, in Lincolnshire. But as your father said, people lost interest in mercury over time, especially after the nuns were exiled from England. Patches of it continued to grow almost spontaneously, in out-of-the-way places. But it wasn't actively cultivated – except by the nuns wherever they went, first to France and then here in Canada."

"And by Dad. It was kind of a pet hobby with him."

"As you must have known. He said he brought you up on it."

"That's for sure. And very tasty it was, too. Any time I take a trip home, he ladles it onto my plate right away. I do kind of miss it. But I've never run across any of it over here. Now, though, you tell me you have a patch of it in your garden at the Abbey. Dad would be fascinated by that."

"I'm sure he would be. You, too. Does he ever come over here to visit you? Or is it always you going to visit him?"

"Used to be. But since Mum died – he looked after her for a long time – since then, things are a lot different for him. I'd like to see him take the trip. Might perk him up a bit. Mind you, ordinarily that'd be a pretty dumb thing to say. He needs perking up about as much as a firecracker. Most people see him as eighty-nine going on forty. But he has been a bit slowed up since Mum died."

"Well, I hope you can talk him into it. I'd be delighted to show him around. Meanwhile, why don't you come one day yourself, and take a look for yourself?"

"I'd love to. But," diffidently, "are visitors allowed?"

"Not as a rule, no. Except for access to the Abbey church. But I'm sure an exception would be made for you or your Dad, considering how important markerie was in the history of our Order. So: you have my number. Give me a call, and we'll fix something up."

On that friendly note, they were done for now; and he walked her to the exit.

XII

217

Fred Sump had been ten years old in 1952, when he first became interested in sport. Until then, he had given games the kind of diverse seasonal attention common in most energetic Canadian boys: pond hockey in winter, baseball in summer and fall. That all changed overnight, when CBC Television broadcast Hockey Night in Canada every Saturday from September to April. It riveted him, and millions of other boys. Back then there were only six teams in the NHL, so the deep supply of native talent was funnelled through a narrow conduit into a small pool. The result was a climate of excellence not matched in later years, when the league, greedy for more ticket sales, expanded to twenty-six teams, thus spreading the talent thin over a ludicrously wider geography – involving such unlikely spots as Arizona and Florida, not known for their icy winters.

Old-timers shook their heads, mournfully, and referred to the six-team era as a Golden Age. They were not entirely justified. There was something to be said on the other side. Improvements in equipment and training took raw talent to a higher level of skill than before. However, such improvements were offset by a general descent into intentional violence. Strong-arm players were hired to launch on-ice attacks on star opponents, to prevent them from scoring, and the league was notoriously lax in ruling against such barbarity. Granted, there had always been loss of temper and exchange of blows, inevitable in a fast-moving contact-sport. But they had been mere ripples on the surface of a game played more for the love of it than for any fortune a player might earn from it.

It was not that star players would not have liked to be paid more. As it was formerly, the owners paid them a pittance, for the usual reason of greed. It took years for the players to unionize, and only then could they command big salaries, to the point where their own affluence seemed to match the owners'.

But that lay in the future. When ten-year-olds watched stars like Jean Béliveau, Gordie Howe, Maurice Richard, and Gump Worsley, they were watching men caught up in a vocation, not acolytes of Mammon. Any priest could tell the difference, and some of them did. Fred had gone to Catholic school, and was early taught to set himself higher standards in life than the shameless pursuit of money.

By the time he was twelve, it had sunk in on him that fair play should be just as important in sports as in the rest of life. Corruption too often was when money crept in through the back door. It was not a belief that he ever lost as an adult. Raised by loving parents, he had a kindly nature, and he tended to think well of people until he had reason to think otherwise. But experience had taught him, as a policeman, that a lot of crime had its roots in money: in the love of it, in a society rotten with cupidity; or in the lack of it, in a society indifferent to the poor.

Meanwhile, when he was twelve, in 1954, the great switch occurred in his spring allegiance, transferring it from hockey to an arena unsullied by violence or greed, to track-and-field – more specifically to middle-distance and long-distance running. The school he went to, St Philip Neri, had a strong tradition of success in high-school track, with a string of victories in the Ontario Secondary Schools championships; and young Fred aspired to make the team.

That kind of ambition is quite common in young males seeking to find an identity for themselves, and finding a door to it often in competitive sport. It makes serious demands on them to achieve particular goals by relentless hard work; and it rewards them with goals achieved, and with the bonding that is such a powerful ingredient in team-spirit.

At St Philip Neri the track-coach, a Father Joseph Carducci (Father Joe to his athletes), was an inspiration. The secret of his success lay in two strengths. He kept himself fully up-to-date on the latest advances in technical know-how, both physical and tactical. And he framed all he spoke of in the context of the sport's history, at its best. He appealed to the boys' sense of national pride in the two gold medals of Percy Williams in the 1928 Olympics. And going beyond mere nationalism, he talked about Paavo Nurmi, the unbeatable Finn who dominated distance-running in the same period. Of more recent vintage were the 1952 exploits of Emil Zátopek, the Czech who gold-medalled, unprecedentedly, in all three Olympic distance-races, the 5k, the 10k, and the marathon. Even more recently, in 1954, the world had been agog over the efforts of milers to break the four-minute barrier, culminating in the triumph of that consummate amateur, Roger Bannister of England, who broke the tape in 3.59.4 on May 6th.

Later that year, the British Empire Games (afterwards renamed the Commonwealth Games) were scheduled for Vancouver, and their centre-piece was to be the mile, in which Bannister would have to confront John Landy of Australia, who had recently lowered the world record to 3.58. The press had dubbed it the Miracle Mile, which Father Joe had scoffed at: there was nothing miraculous, he said, about running that fast; it was the simple result or hard training, courage, and technical savvy. All of that was borne out in the event, with two great runners putting on a magnificent display of tenacious speed, with Bannister, in the last hundred yards, outkicking Landy, who had grittily led all the way.

The Neri boys, of course, watched the whole thing on television. And amid all the fanfare, Father Joe pointed out to them that the third-place runner, Rich Ferguson, five seconds back at 4.04, had broken the Canadian record. He also pointed out to them with some asperity, the same afternoon, that Jim Peters' spectacular collapse from dehydration, just before reaching the finishing line of the marathon, was due to appalling mismanagement by the Games organizers. The boys never forgot that double lesson: that high accomplishment lay in their own hands; but that other factors, beyond their control, could trip them up.

Fred Sump did make the team, in 1960, as a diligent but not world-beating half-miler. Then, after graduation, he hung up his spikes and went to Police College. Law enforcement made him feel useful. He knew that the so-called justice-system often fell short of its professed ideals: there were judges with their own excessive agendas, either punitive or permissive; there were expert psychiatrists, called for the crown or the defence, who contradicted each other on the basis of opposing doctrines; there were lawyers for whom the adversarial system was more an arena for egotistical point-scoring than it was a forum for establishing truth; and there were, unfortunately, a few crooked cops, who planted or suppressed evidence to serve their own ends. Like life in general, it was not a level playing-field.

The same was true in track. Even as a teenager, following the Olympics, Fred was uncomfortably aware that the level playing-field was a chimera. There were simon-pure amateurs in the West who struggled to fit arduous workouts around the demands of an often exacting job, with no government support. But in the Communist East there were ostensible amateurs, who could train full-time while holding down a token job in the government service. Even the great Zátopek, who was unquestionably a dedicated athlete known for his idealistic sportsmanship, had that advantage over his Western rivals.

(It should not be forgotten, though, that he also consistently defeated Eastern rivals who enjoyed the same advantages as he.)

In that financial discrepancy, there lay wounded the spirit of fair play. Its impact, however, was diluted when the principles of strict amateurism were abandoned, allowing professional athletes to compete in the Olympic Games. There had been, in the West, an under-the-counter system of payments to athletes, especially in Europe, where track-meets drew large crowds and meet-directors could well afford the cost of such illicit arithmetic. Then it came about that overt professionalism replaced hypocritical amateurism. In a sense, this was all for the best: talented runners in impoverished countries, especially in Africa, could at last earn a respectable living from doing what they loved to do. In some more prosperous countries, like Australia, governments set up well-funded development programs for promising runners.

But therein lay the seeds of almost unavoidable corruption. The rewards were so great in prize-money, prestige, and sponsorship contracts, that some runners began turning to performance-enhancing drugs to reap the benefits. This was particularly rife among sprinters: there the available drugs had more relevance, since they increased explosive power, but seemingly did little for sheer stamina. The severity of the problem, which had always been prevalent in weight-lifting and cycling, became increasingly apparent as more and more sprinters failed their drug-tests and were (somewhat) penalized.

Fred Sump, who had turned from half-miling to coaching, once he found the time as a fully qualified Constable, was able to combine his shift-work with his workouts in a constant juggling of time. When the shift-work got in the way, he simply handed the assistant coach a detailed workout program (such as perhaps a repetition of 16x400 metres at 68 seconds with a 75-second interval), with a request that he receive a report afterwards on how it had gone.

That way, with constant adjustments depending on progress and weather conditions, he helped his runners, divided into an A group and a B group, fulfill their potential.

As in sport, so at work, cream rises to the top. A few years on the beat, he showed his stuff early, passed his Sergeants' exam, and was appointed to the Homicide squad, under Inspector Coggin, in 1970. Now, eighteen years later, he was still in the same job, with the same superior and this month he was faced with a case that unexpectedly bore upon his athletic avocation.

The PM Foundation, apparently, had commissioned an investigation into drug use by athletes; and that, in turn, had led directly or indirectly to a murder. All murders, by their very nature, were perturbing. But in this case the murder was especially so. It raised the horrid spectre of chemical cheating by distance athletes enhancing their stamina by either of the two procedures that were, as yet, undetectable in lab-tests: the injection of human-growth hormone, or so-called blood-doping – this was the lay term for systematically withdrawing an athlete's red blood cells, well in advance of a race, and then re-injecting them the day before it. Sump was sure that none of his own athletes were at fault: they could hardly get away with it without his knowing. But at the same time he was worried for the good of his sport. If either practice was secretly widespread, the whole exercise would be tragically futile. Down the drain would go any pretence that honesty and honour, as a program for life, were worth a scrap of effort. The only remaining hope would be for the development of new and foolproof tests,

Coggin, for his own and different reasons, felt the same way. He had long admired the PM Foundation for its substantial contribution to the support of serious music. It had been a salutary correction to the cultural degradation of pop music which, at its best, seduced listeners with its polished skills, but never rose above a dreary level of banality.

Somehow, he and Sump would have to crack a case singularly short of helpful pointers. The next step, they agreed, would be to try and break it open in an interview with Lester Boyle. They made an appointment to see him tomorrow.

XIII

1958-1977, TORONTO

Ross Lang was the son of oddly matched but deeply bonded parents. His father, Samuel Lang, was a non-observant Jew; he was also that comparative rarity, a successful businessman with a strong social conscience. His wife, born Margery Ross, was a practising Roman Catholic but one with strong reservations about the Church's stance vis-a-vis society: to her, the refusal to ordain women was offensive; the ban on contraception was a major cause of overpopulation and poverty; and the demeaning of Jews was unconscionable. When she married outside her faith she promised, at priestly insistence, to raise any resulting children within it; but she did so equivocally, with her fingers, so to speak, crossed behind her back. Some would have said, and did say, that such a position was dishonest, that she was trying to have her cake and eat it. In her own mind, she was simply accepting the best of what the Church had on offer, and discarding the rest. Loyal to its ancient forms of liturgy, with its magnificent tradition of ceremonies rich in compelling rhetoric and stirring music, she attended Mass every Sunday; and because she lived in a time when most parishes had declining standards of language, spoken or sung, she chose Tathwell Abbey as her place of worship, the one remaining place where the old standards of excellence were maintained, unimpaired.

During the first two years of their marriage, Sam and Marge remained childless: by choice. It was not a choice condoned by the two sets of would-be grandparents. But they stuck to doing things their own way; and while they waited, Marge stayed on at work, as a publisher's reader of manuscripts and proof-reader of those that were accepted. It was not well paid; but it did give her a valid sense of being her own person, and it involved her in stemming the influx of rubbish which the mother tongue was starting to drown in.

Only when they decided to start a family did she plan on staying home, at least for a while. Ross, bearing her family name, was born in 1960. She stayed home to mother him, with some enlightened help from Sam; and then, when Ross was enrolled in kindergarten, she returned to her job at the publisher's, where she had been valued and was welcomed back.

During her five years of domestic captivity, as some feminists would have described her life at the time, she found motherhood a truly absorbing and rewarding role. It was, to a degree, draining. But once Ross began to sleep through the night, she had enough energy and opportunity to pursue her long-standing passion for gardening. It was a passion clearly linked to a related passion for health-food. She had been converted, as a young woman, to the gospel of the dietary counter-culture. It sneered, quite rightly, at sugar. But in some quarters it ran right off the rails into extremist fads that equated carbs with Sin, and that preached secular sermons about Coca-Cola as the Devil's Brew.

Marge was too sensible to be taken in by fanatics. But she gave prudent study to the shortcomings of conventional menus, and she avoided foods that were seductively tasty but nutritionally without value. Vegetables and fruit were her mainstay, along with whole grains and yogurt. These staples she supplemented with appropriate health-foods. But she did not purchase the entire alphabet of synthetic vitamin pills that were proclaimed by advertisements as conferring virtual immortality on the consumer. Rather, she set about cultivating the herbs and other plants in her garden, and in her greenhouse, that would provide real nutrition in a natural way.

One Sunday when Ross was two, she fell into conversation after Mass with the Guestmistress, a Sister Alice Newstead, who also served as Infirmarian.

"Nice to see you again, Mrs Lang," she said. "You're pretty regular, aren't you? Is there something particular about the Abbey that draws you here, instead of your local parish?"

"Simple good taste, as it happens. I don't mean I'm claiming to have good taste myself. That would be arrogant. I just love the way your community handles the liturgy. It's so beautiful: words and music to nourish the soul. I always think a Mass, or any other act of worship, should offer God only what is best. That you do, brilliantly, here. I can't say the same for the parish churches."

"Well, I'm sure they do the best they can, with limited resources. By the way, I've no idea what happens on the men's side of the building. Does your husband attend, too?"

"No, actually he doesn't. He's Jewish."

There was a momentary stiffening in the nun. Marge noticed it, but did not pounce on it. There would be other areas where loyalty to Sam could more usefully send her into confrontation with both guns blazing. She let it go. All she said was, "Actually, his being Jewish has been very helpful to me. He's not really active in religion, but he is heir to a kosher tradition that has a good deal to say about a balanced diet. And that fits in remarkably well with my own ideas about healthy eating. I'm what you might call a bit of a health nut. I even grow my own herbal border, for the extracts I can cook up for my husband and son."

Sister Alice felt remorse for her knee-jerk moment of reflex racism, and was grateful that this nice young woman had not, apparently, taken offence.

"You know, Mrs Lang, I find that really interesting. It's not something the Abbey makes a big song-and-dance about, but we've been in the health-food business for seven centuries, ages before it became fashionable in the last few years. We've always had a herb garden, and we still use it for herbal medicine and for helping prepare good nourishing meals in our kitchen. Listen, if you don't need to rush home right away, would you like to come back in, and I'll show you our garden?"

"I'd love to, thank you so much. And everything'll be fine at home. My husband's taking our son to visit his parents."

***

And thus it came about that Marge had an enthralling hour in the Abbey garden.

And thus it came about that Marge went home with an armful of cuttings for her own garden and greenhouse.

And thus it came about that her garden and greenhouse, from then on, boasted a thriving patch of markerie, which Sister Alice instructed her to serve steamed, or raw as salad, and to put up as an extract in small sealed jars, in her freezer.

And thus it came about that Ross Lang grew up taking markerie for granted as a normal part of his intake, the way other boys count on hot chocolate in winter and ice cream in summer.

Other boys' mothers sent them off to school with a packed lunch full of calories but short on nourishment: a baloney sandwich on white, a slice of cake, a chocolate bar, and a can of Seven-Up.

Marge packed him a mixed bag of fruit and nuts, peanut butter on rye, some breast of free-range chicken, and a jar of markerie juice.

This by itself would have been enough to mark him out as different, as someone not to be sought out for friendship. But that handicap was offset by his athleticism: he was multi-talented at basketball in winter, cross-country in the fall, and soccer in the spring; and he was sought as a team-member, at various age-levels, in all three seasons. This made him quite popular – popular enough to counter his unfailingly high marks which would otherwise have hung the label of Nerd upon him.

Primary school and high school, for him, were both in the public system, not the Catholic one. When she married, Marge had said she would raise any child she had as a Catholic. But she had always had reservations about keeping her word with absolute exactitude. From the start, she had encouraged Ross to believe in the Catholic God, and she had answered quite openly the inevitable questions that all children ask on the subject. She took him to church occasionally whenever he showed interest in going. But she was also quite open with him about Sam's being a Jew. He came, she explained, from a long tradition of benevolent ethics, just as deserving of respect as any equivalent in the Catholic tradition or, for that matter, the Protestant one. Sam strongly approved of her ecumenical attitude, and she persuaded him to take Ross to synagogue a couple of times, to give the boy a proper glimpse of a wider world than the somewhat narrow one she had been raised in.

Sam himself was non-observant, but as a father he had all the virtue of his background. He adored his son, and treated him always with kindness though without spoiling him. The two of them became very close.

It was, therefore, a terrible blow to Ross and, of course, to Marge as well, when Sam died suddenly of a heart attack in 1975. Fifteen is a rotten age for a boy to lose his father, especially a father so dearly loved and respected. In his grief, he withdrew into himself. Not to the point of ignoring his mother's equal grief. But he began to isolate himself at school. Marge worried about him. His moods vacillated between acute sorrow and understandable anger. She knew that these were common reactions to the loss of a loved one. She had the same reactions herself. But still she worried. After all, he was still a kid, her little boy; and she didn't want his life, at a critical age, to founder.

His salvation, mercifully soon, was the Armour Heights Collegiate track team. Even in primary school, of all his sports running had been where he had really shone. Now, at Armour Heights, he dropped everything else (except his studies) and focused exclusively on his running. To begin with, he put his grieving heart into it, and raced to every success with an inner voice saying "This is for you, Dad." But gradually as his heart began to mend, his passion for running became something valid in its own right. It was self-fulfilling, a way to become who he truly was and wanted to be.

He was lucky in his coach. Bill Northbrook was notably expert in training distance-runners, just as expert as Father Joe at St Philip Neri. His team always ran second to the Neri boys, lacking the same depth of talent. But he had just the right kind of personality, outgoing and empathetic, that Ross needed after Sam died. He knew exactly how running could help Ross at this point in his life. And he did what he could to help him without being intrusive. As time went by, he became a sort of father-figure and role-model. No one could ever replace Sam. He could always look to Marge for affection and support. But it was from Bill that he received encouragement and ratification in laying the foundation of an authentic career.

Talent, unequivocally, carves its own path. Ross's special talent was his endurance. He lacked the devastating speed of a Miruts Yifter, who was known to finish an already fast 10k with a 200-metre kick in twenty-two seconds. That might perhaps come later, with maturity and specialized workouts. But already, as a high-schooler, he had the stamina to run his rivals into the ground with a relentless tempo they could not keep up with.

Long gone were the days when pundits asserted that juniors could not expect to run world-class times in distance-races: they were just too young. That myth had been exploded years ago by Bruce Kidd, who broke Canadian records not only for the mile, but also for the 5k and the 10k before he was twenty.

Ross Lang never came quite that close to exceptional times while he was still a teenager. But he did come promisingly close. And he placed tantalizingly close to winning in open, adult races in international competition. The big meets could wait. He had a whole future ahead of him.

"Your Dad would have been proud or you," Marge said to him, more than once.

So did Bill Northbrook

XIV

1940-1947 CANADA, GERMANY, CANADA

Already before he joined the Police Force, Andrew Coggin had experience at interviewing suspects. As a teenager, thanks to exceptional marks in school, he had gone to university at seventeen, in 1940, spending two years there before volunteering for the armed services. As a student, he majored in German language and literature. It was an odd choice of subject, given the then pervasive climate of prejudice against all things German. But he picked it because he was outraged by the injustices visited upon his neighbours' family, who were German Lutherans. He wanted to show a kind of solidarity with them.

In 1942, the recruiting officer who interviewed him, a Captain Roger Wilson, turned out to be not a bloodshed-and-bullshit trumpeter, but a perceptive interlocutor with a keen eye for who might best help the war effort, and in what capacity.

"Look here, Coggin," he said, "I see you have two years of German under your belt. Any special reason? Got some German in your family background?"

"Actually no, sir. No special reason. Except, I guess, we have neighbours who are second-generation German-Canadians; and I don't like the way they're treated. I hate the Nazis as much as anyone. But that doesn't mean I have to hate every single German – let alone here in Canada."

"Fair enough. That doesn't make you pro-German, or anti-German for that matter. Seems to me you're somewhere in between. Now listen: you're obviously an intelligent young man, and you can probably be more useful to us than just another volunteer good for sticking bayonets into other people. So what do you say to this? I'd like to recommend you for a branch in the army that needs people like you. They'd polish up your German and send you on special training courses for behind-the-lines work. Mainly they're looking for men and women fluent in French, to drop them into Occupied France. But a good German-speaker'll be useful, too. This war can't go on for ever. And when the Nazis are done for, we'll have to go into Germany and help clean up the mess – plus help catch the war criminals and bring them to justice. That's what's important: justice. We don't want a fanatic hungry for blind revenge. We'll want somebody reasonable, who can weigh things up objectively. So if you figure that'll be right for you, you should go home right now, and wait till I hear back from HQ. Okay?"

"Thank you, sir. Any idea how long that might take?"

"Hard to say. Depends whose desk it lands on. But guys in the Intelligence units are probably a bit swifter than some of the dimwits in the regimental officers' clubs. Forget I said that, though."

Acceptance came through in three weeks. During that time, embarrassingly, he had been ordered to keep his mouth shut about what he might be doing. Only then did he get a face-saving uniform, some travel money, and a train ticket to Ottawa. There he was more rigorously interviewed, and was then packed off to a top-secret training camp where he was taught the mechanics of short-wave radio transmission, the use of code and of lightweight explosives, and the various lethal and silent methods of self-defence. As he acquired those skills, he also underwent immersion in German culture, both political and social, that was the formative influence on what might loosely be called the national character.

This last left him with a very mixed bag of impressions. On the one hand he was repelled by a climate of authoritarianism, by an appetite for violence, and by a long history of hate-filled anti-Semitism. On the other hand he revered Goethe and Einstein, and he fell in love, lifelong, with the music of Bach.

The war, of course, did not end as quickly as Captain Wilson had hoped. It dragged on, in Europe, for three more years, until May 8th 1945. Thereupon, it fell to the victorious Allies to enter Germany and take charge of a country divided into four zones, American, British, French, and Soviet. Canadian forces operated in the British zone. Coggin, now a corporal, had never been deployed as a behind-the-lines agent. But he was now seconded to a unit charged with interviewing rounded-up Germans who were suspected of having, at worst, committed war-crimes or, perhaps less criminally, of having been members of the Nazi Party – these latter had to undergo intensive questioning as part of what was called the Denazification Process.

This took a while to organize, at least until August, when the war ended in Asia. At that point, Canadian soldiers began to return home. Coggin could probably have returned, too. But he felt an obligation, somehow, to stay on for a while. To his mind, the war had been fought for the idea of justice, and he was not about to betray men and women who had died for that cause, so long as the need remained for replanting the tree of justice in soil where it had been so viciously felled. He stayed on until early 1947. Then he came home.

After demobilization, he forgot about going back to his university. The Department of German Studies there had little to teach him which he did not already know. Instead, using assistance he was entitled to from the Department of Veterans Affairs, he enrolled in Police College. With him, it was going to be Justice again, of a somewhat different stripe. It would become both his livelihood and, at root, his way of life.

XV

FRIDAY MAY 15, 10.00 AM

Gladys Maybee picked up her phone and buzzed her boss. "The Police are here, Mr Boyle," she said. "Inspector Coggin and Sergeant Sump."

She put the phone down. "He says to go right in."

They went to the inner door past her, and Boyle opened it in a gesture of welcome, with the same ready smile on his face as before. Coggin again thought it neutral and probably meaningless. Sump, seeing it again, thought it glib.

"Come in, Officers," Boyle said, "and take a seat." He took his own seat behind the desk, across from them. "Want can I do for you this time?"

Sump found that immediately interesting. The man must have known they were here about the Pilch murder. Why else? Yet here he was, reacting to their arrival casually and politely, as though it had no connection to him or to anything that might cause him concern.

"Well, for starters, Mr Boyle," Coggin said, "we'd like to talk to you about your contract with Oscar Pilch. Or, to be more precise, your Foundation's contract with him."

"Yes?" Guardedly.

"According to our reading of his files, you've been paying him a retainer of three hundred dollars a week, to investigate the possible use of performance-enhancing drugs by Canadian athletes. Is that right?"

"Yes."

"And so far as we can tell, he reported back to you regularly, but had discouragingly little to say that was of any moment. Until recently, that is. But since the last report he sent you, he e-mailed you, on April 9th, to say that he had important news, and he suggested that you come to see him in his office quite soon, to discuss it. Did you do so? Go and see him, I mean."

There was an uncomfortable moment of silence. The kind of pause in which a quick-witted man would have to choose between two responses; either to deny any such visit, which could be dangerous, if the police had evidence to the contrary; or to admit the visit had occurred, which might carry other and unknown risks. He opted for the second course, as more prudent.

"Yes, I did go and see him. On April the 11th or 12th, I think. About five-thirty, if I recall correctly. Does the time matter?"

"Not particularly," Coggin replied. "But we would be interested to know what transpired at that meeting – what the important news was that Pilch wanted to share with you, and so on. If it was some kind of breakthrough in his inquiries about drugs in sport, Sergeant Sump here would be especially interested. In his spare time, he's a track coach. So obviously the whole matter of drugs in sport is of great concern to him."

"I don't know if I'm comfortable answering that question," Boyle said. "It has a lot to do with other people's privacy."

"I dare say it has. But obviously we can't ask Pilch, now he's dead."

"Would that matter have anything to do, sir," Sump interjected, "with the ten thousand dollars you paid Pilch, in cash, out of your own account?"

Cornered, but quick on his feet, Boyle said, "Well, if you know about that, you probably also know that I had a previous business relationship with Oscar Pilch, nothing to do with this Foundation. A strictly private thing regarding my divorce. And like many divorce cases, this one involved my signing a non-disclosure agreement."

It was a neat evasion, if that was what it was. Neither policeman was willing to take it at face value. But there was no point in challenging it right away. That could wait until they looked into the divorce court records.

"Okay. But we may get back to you on that," Sump said. "Chances are your non-disclosure agreement's no longer binding, since your ex-wife's now dead."

"Maybe so. But I'd really prefer that you not go poking around in all that ancient misery. I've been raising our son ever since the divorce, and there's stuff in there would really hurt his feelings if it got dragged out in the open. He was only a little guy when we split and I've always tried to have him honour his mother's memory."

"Very creditable of you, sir. Whatever there is in the file, we'd do our best for your boy, to keep it confidential."

"Thanks. I'd appreciate that." Boyle paused. "Was there anything else you wanted to talk about?"

"Yes," Coggin said, "but it probably doesn't have anything much to do with Oscar Pilch."

"Yes?" Again the guarded tone.

"It's just this. I gather your Foundation here operates in two different areas, and you are the manager in both of them. Both of them are, I guess, philanthropic. On one side, thanks to Pablo Morales, you spend money on amateur sport, especially track-and-field – and that includes spending money on Oscar Pilch over the drugs problem. On the other side, thanks to Mrs Morales – Paula Morrison, that is – you dispense grants to projects in the performing arts, particularly in music and theatre. Is that right?"

"Yes, it is. So?"

"It's my understanding you recently received a grant-application from an actress called Amy Buniak, stage-name Amy Barton. Does that ring a bell?"

"I'm not sure. We get literally hundreds of applications every grant-year. It's hard to remember them all."

"Then let me refresh your memory. This particular application was for start-up money to develop a play about two famous women – or should I say notorious? Clytemnestra in Ancient Greece, and Charlotte Corday in Revolutionary France. And what did they have in common? They both assassinated a powerful public figure, in each case catching the victim in his bath. Needless to say, in my line of work, I'd find that oddly interesting. But that's beside the point. Now that I've reminded you about it, do you recall receiving Ms Buniak's application?"

"Yes, kind of. We get so many..."

"I'm sure you do. But what I want to ask you is, how do you review the applications? Do you throw out the rubbishy ones with a polite rejection slip? And with the better ones, do you interview the applicant in person, before deciding whether or not to pass it on to Mrs Morales? If so, did you at some point interview Ms Buniak?"

"Not that I recall, no."

"But we do know that she did drop in to see you, just recently. Apparently you were out just then. Did she come back another time? Did you get to meet with her?"

"No, I didn't. And I told my assistant, if she did come back without an appointment, to just tell her, we'd be the ones to call her in, if we wanted any kind or exploratory conversation. I don't know if that ever happened. You could ask Gladys. But no, I never did actually meet her in person. I don't like it when applicants get pushy. Everyone has to wait their turn."

"Fair enough. I guess that covers everything for today. If we need to see you again, we'll give you a call. Thanks for your time."

He and Sump stood up, and moved to the door.

Before opening it, Sump said, "By the way, sir, just one more thing. Does the name Louie Larose mean anything to you?"

He had remembered the surname from an earlier case: Larose had been a hit-man, unconvicted, brought in from Montréal, who had stayed in Toronto when things got too hot for him in Québec.

"Larose? Can't say it does, no."

"Okay. Thanks anyway."

And they left.

"Nice try there, Fred," Coggin said, as they waited for the elevator. "What do you think?"

"I'm not sure. Maybe he was lying, about Larose, but the rest of it: evasive. Perhaps we should look into what gives with him and the Mahogany Emporium. That ten thousand bucks smells fishy to me."

"Me too," Coggin said, as the elevator arrived.

XVI

TORONTO, WOLFVILLE, TORONTO, 1975-88

When Ross Lang's father died in 1975, his insurance policy paid up handsomely. Other assets of his, in addition, left Marge comfortably enough off for her to continue working or not, as she chose. Sam had also settled a trust on Ross, to take care of his education. By the time he graduated from high school, his mother was sufficiently come to terms with her bereavement for him to feel free, with her blessing, to leave home for Nova Scotia, where Acadia had special courses in Canadian Studies to enroll in.

Some of his friends, especially his running friends, were quite surprised by this. They had more or less assumed that he would stay in Toronto, to enroll in U of T, where there was a very enlightened Phys Ed program, run by Bruce Kidd. They were surprised that Ross did not; and were even more surprised when he announced that he was giving up running until he got his degree – you can't do anything, he said, by half-measures: either you run full-time, or you study full-time; but you can't do both.

He was a good son. He kept in touch with his mother, with a long weekly phone call. But he enjoyed his time away, making new friends and working hard at his classes, though not obsessively. Like many a student he now and then pulled an all-nighter. But he soon gave up doing that: he no longer had the same level of energy he could always count on back when he was still running. He just attributed that to his no longer being razor-fit. And he kept promising himself to get properly fit again as soon as he was finished at Acadia.

When he did graduate, in 1981, he came home to Toronto right away, and was glad to be back. He had always come home for the holidays, of course. But he was pleased, now, to be home permanently – as was his mother, to have him back.

One of the first things he did was to go on a couple of road-runs. That was an eye-opener. He could hardly believe how unfit he had become. But the stopwatch does not lie. He had to believe its daunting truths. Sometimes, as Viren had once declared, it is necessary to enter the wilderness. In Ross's case, that meant a two-year desert journey of hard-going relentless mileage, and measured improvement: all of which culminated in his startling breakthrough with his 10k record in 1983. He followed it with records at 5k and the one-hour run.

From then on, unbeaten in season after season, he was a marked man. Rival runners threw everything they could, at him, tactically. They set an ambitious pace, sometimes, hoping to shake him off, but he outlasted them. Other times, he dictated things with abrupt changes of pace that destroyed their rhythm. Occasionally, speed-merchants relied on a trusty finishing kick, but he outkicked them. Always, he studied the opposition to weigh their strengths and vulnerabilities. Nothing they tried seemed to work.

He was also a marked man scientifically. Sceptics abounded, who muttered about performance-enhancing drugs. The World Anti-Doping Agency tested him often with unannounced visits, but he passed all tests; and continued to win.

Strictly speaking, he did not remain unbeaten. In the winter season of 1987-8 be was consistently outrun in the 800-metre races he entered indoors. But that had been a mere training exercise. As a distance runner his primacy was unflawed. And now, in the late spring of 1988, he was, in his own mind and in Bill Northbrook's, ready for the upcoming two-mile challenge.

XVII

MONDAY MAY 16, 10.26 AM
Grant application to the PM Foundation, dated March 24th 1988.
Covering letter.
Dear Foundation,
I enclose an application-form with all the required information filled in. As you will see, the request is for $5000 of development money to conduct research and write the first draft of an historical drama, entitled "Two Women", intended for production variously on stage, radio and television. You will find my c.v. on page 2 of the form. As requested I also enclose a synopsis of the proposed text.
Yours sincerely,
Amy Barton.

"Two Women": synopsis.

This two-act drama has the form of an Imaginary Conversation, in an after-life, in which two female assassins are interviewed by an impartial male interlocutor. He will perform the same function in both acts. In the two acts, the female lead is played by the same actress. What the two women have in common is that they both, historically, killed a man in his bath, one with an axe, the other with a knife. The dialogue, in each case, explores the motives and the possible justification.

Act One features Clytemnestra, Queen of Argos in Ancient Greece at the time of the Trojan War. Her husband, King Agamemnon, was commander-in-chief of the Greek army; but before his expeditionary force could set out, his fleet was stuck in port for lack of favourable winds. To appease the wind-gods, he sacrificed his daughter, Iphigenia, in a ritual slaughter. To Clytemnestra, this was an unforgivable crime. He was away at Troy for ten years. During this time, he took a concubine. His wife, with his infidelity added to his crime, felt free to take a lover. And when Agamemnon came home, having sacked Troy, and went weary and naked to take a bath, she followed him in there, with an axe, and hacked him to death.

Act Two features Charlotte Corday, who also killed a man of national importance in his bath: Jean-Paul Marat, one of the chief figures in the French Revolution. He, as a radical writer and politician, played a lead role in the libertarian but bloody revolt that overthrew the monarchy and guillotined many nobles. France, at the time, was a deeply divided country. The exploited poor demanded a Republic and the downfall of the aristocracy. The aristocrats wanted only a return to the privileged status quo. In between there were traditionalists who acknowledged the need for reform, but believed that the best future lay in a reformed system of monarchy. One of their number was Corday, who came to believe that the extremist Republicans could only be stopped in their violent tracks by an answering violence. Gaining access to Marat's suite, she found him in his bath and stabbed him to death. Like many assassinations from that of Caesar in 44 BC to that of Archduke Ferdinand in 1914 AD, with momentous consequences in both cases, it had its roots in firmly, if wrongly, held political principle.

Without belabouring historical analogies, "Two Women" is a timely project in a world where public power and private passion combine, sadly often, to deadly effect.

***

234

She had written that synopsis weeks ago, quite some time before Pilch's death. In a life hitherto devoted to versions of reality as depicted by playwrights, she had more than one precedent to go on, when it came to dealing with a slaughterous woman – notably in Shakespeare's chilling psychological portrayal of Lady Macbeth. She proposed to follow in his footsteps with her study of Clytemnestra and Corday, not intending to portray either woman as a one-dimensional and evil murderess, but rather as a fully rounded character with complex motives.

If she succeeded, it would be true theatre, not mere melodrama. But it would still be an artefact. Real-life murder was something else again. That was something she had never encountered, fortunately. Now she had not only met it face-to-face, so to speak, in its gory actuality: but she had also been indirectly implicated in it. She knew she was innocent. But she knew, too, that appearances might go against her; might put her on a suspect list. It stood in her favour that she was the one who reported the crime, which would be consistent, on the face of it, with her innocence. But it did stand against her that she had opportunity and means, if no discernible motive.

The opportunity, self-evidently, was her cleaning job on a Sunday morning in an empty office-building on an empty street. And as to means (that is, a weapon), she had what was perhaps the fatal gun.

What to do with it? She was far from sure. Then there was the other matter of the unlocked door. If she now, belatedly, told the police about that, would they accept it as a genuine lapse of memory on her part? Or would they figure she was up to something? A clever killer might well masquerade as a simply forgetful innocent party. Either way it was tricky.

At least about the door, if not the gun, she reckoned truth was the best option.

So she placed a call to Sargeant Sump.

XVIII

MONDAY MAY 16, 3.02 PM

Toronto prided itself on being a safe, clean city. It was, when compared with Detroit or Mexico City. But increasingly, in the nineteen-seventies and -eighties, drug addiction and trafficking rendered it crime-ridden, with rival gangs fighting each other, violently, for control of the action. The two main gangs were well known to the Narcotics squad, which was powerless to remedy the situation, being under-manned and under-funded. Individual assassinations could not be anticipated; nor could spontaneous gun-battles. The police did the best they could. But their occasional small successes were due to the courage of officers assigned to the highly dangerous task of infiltrating one or other of the gangs as plausible recruits.

The qualifications to do so were both devious and precise. There was a branch-plant of the Mafia, called the Syndicate: to get in at ground level, it was essential to be fluent in the argot of mob-Italian. To become one of the East End Boys, it was essential not only to spout anti-white hostility, but also to be black. The difference between the two gangs was that the Syndicate was basically interested only in money however ill-gotten, whereas the Boys were only interested in violence for its own sake. The similarity was that both groups were heavily armed and utterly ruthless in turf warfare.

Narcotics and Homicide seldom needed to work together. Many run-of-the-mill murders, especially domestic ones, had little or no connection to drug problems. But with those that were drug-connected, investigations were usually carried out by Narcotics; and when it came to arresting an "armed and dangerous" offender, holed up in some fort-like hideaway, the job was not usually assigned to Homicide, but to the Emergency Task Force.

None the less, the two units, Narcotics and Homicide, prided themselves on co-operation rather than rivalry. So when Coggin, as head of Homicide, asked his opposite number in Narcotics for help, the response was civil and help was forthcoming.

Inspector Edward Ainslie called back after only a couple of days.

"Andrew," he said, "you asked if we have anything currently about that Louie Laporte. Was he a local kingpin in the drug trade or anything? A kingpin? No, more of a muscle-man for the Syndicate. *Was*, not *is*, because he's dead. We know about him because he was only a small cog in a bigger machine we're trying to get a handle on. Anyway, we thought we might pick him up on a couple of charges, and see if we could drag anything out of him in a plea bargain. So we went round to his place. Trouble was, the damn fool pulled a gun on one of our guys, young Watson, and he had to shoot him in self-defence. So Watson's partner had to call in for help, and Watson had to surrender his gun and his badge while it was officially looked into. Should be an open-and-shut case, with no reprimand. He stuck to the rules, and Louie was a known gangster, with a rap-sheet long on violence. Not that anyone'll mourn Louie much. But it did mean we got nothing out of him. Which is really too bad. We were hoping to make a bit of progress. We've been a bit bogged down."

"Something big? Oh, silly question. It's always something big, with drugs."

"Sure. The usual. Regular loads of the stuff coming in – and so far we haven't been able to figure out how it gets here. We've picked up a rumour that says look into somewhere in Central America but not Colombia. Colombia's already covered. Oddly enough, Belize has been mentioned. But we don't have anything much to go on."

"Too bad. Still, while we're on the phone, let me ask you something else. We have a case over here of a killing that's indirectly connected with drugs, but in a way you'd probably consider fairly unimportant compared with the problems you guys have to deal with."

"Yes?"

"Somehow it seems to be connected with an attempt to track down how some athletes are getting their hands on performance-enhancing drugs. That must be pretty small beer to you. The only reason I mention it is, you said Belize might be somehow involved. And in our case over here, Belize definitely *is* involved – though I should add, its involvement may be completely innocent. But maybe we ought to keep in touch about that. Might be useful to you, might be useful to us."

"Sure. Will do."

"By the way, Ted, one other little thing. Louie's piece. I assume your guys took it off him."

"Natch. Unregistered, of course. But we sent it over to Ballistics anyway, to fire it and run its markings through the computer file, to see if they match up with any other solved or unsolved cases, Canada-wide. Well, you know those fellows in Ballistics: you ask for something tomorrow, and it's next month if you're lucky. I should have kept after 'em. I'll give 'em a nudge right away. And if there *is* a match, you'll be on the same list as everyone else, whatever it is they come up with. By the way, that Belize connection you mentioned: anything there, you think, that maybe we should look into at our end?"

"Who knows? All we can say yet is that there's a Belize guy, here in Toronto, who's been putting a fair swack of money into trying to track down the villains in sport-doping. Name of Morales. Pablo Morales. Runs a high-end business in imported mahogany furniture. Seems like a good guy, by all accounts. Ring any bells at your end? I mean, any import business in legitimate trade could be currently bringing in illegal goods on the side. Either organized by him, or without his knowledge by an employee."

"H'm, interesting. As I said, Belize was only some vague rumour. One of our sources said something along the lines of 'Oh, you guys, you never think outside the box! It's always either Colombia or Mexico.

What about Peru? Or Belize?' May be nothing in that. But it might be worth looking into. This guy Morales, what's the name of his outfit?"

"The Mahogany Emporium. It's up in the north end. On Steeles."

"Okay, Andrew. I'll let you know if I stumble on anything."

"Thanks, Ted. Bye for now."

"Bye."

***

Coggin retailed the entire conversation to Sump.

"What do you think, Fred?"

"Well, I must say, all along I've felt there was something fishy about our Mr Boyle. Much more him than Morales. But that's really only a hunch. But it's interesting what you just said to Ainslie, about perhaps it had nothing to do with Morales himself, and perhaps someone inside Mahogany was organizing a nice little sideline for himself in smuggling."

"Yes, that's what I've been thinking, too. For a couple of reasons. First, we've looked into Boyle's background. He joined Mahogany as a young man, and rose through the ranks; and on the way up, he seems to have gotten to know the inside workings of the company, and earned Morales' trust; and then eventually was rewarded with a better job, managing the Foundation. So we should look into who he knew on the way up, who in particular he cultivated. Go-getters always know how to seize the main chance without making enemies.

"Second thing, there's that little matter of a ten grand payoff to Pilch. How does a middle-rank office-manager come up with money like that, out of his own pocket, not out of the Foundation's funds? If he was in on a smuggling caper, he could probably afford it. But how does Pilch fit into the picture?"

"Good question. Here's what I figure. We know Pilch was poking around in the drug world – he was paid to by the Foundation. Maybe in the course of doing so, he stumbled across proof of what Boyle was up to on the side, as a smuggler. That would put him in a perfect position to blackmail Boyle, with a threat of exposing him. So Boyle makes a preliminary payment just to keep him quiet. But like anyone in a predicament like that, he knows all too well that blackmailers always come back for more. The only way to make the problem go away, permanently, is to shut Pilch's mouth, with a bullet."

"Sounds good, Fred – in theory. Trouble is, it leaves a lot of question marks. Even with Ted Ainslie's help, there's no guarantee we can find out if Mahogany was somehow involved in drug-smuggling, whether organized by Boyle or cashed in on by him – and we can't leave Morales out of the picture, either. And if there has been smuggling going on, who organized it at the far end? Boyle or Morales or a third party? If we can sort that out, we'll be on our way to establishing motive. That leaves opportunity and means. Opportunity isn't much of a problem: Boyle has no alibi for the estimated time of death – the evening before it was called in on the Sunday morning. As to..."

"Just a moment, Andrew," Sump interrupted. "That doesn't work. If Boyle is the killer, surely he'd have come up with an alibi for the Saturday evening?"

"Not necessarily. That might be simple carelessness. We had given the media the impression we were treating the murder as a Sunday morning event, even though we knew the Saturday evening was the probable time of death. So Boyle made sure he had a Sunday alibi. It didn't occur to him, perhaps, he should cover his Saturday, because the media didn't point that way – nor did we. It should have occurred to him, of course. But you and I both know how often even a really smart villain drops the ball. Remember Hoskin?"

"Sure," said Sump, ruefully.

Hoskin, several years ago, had been the master-mind of an ingenious scheme to murder his wife's lover, which had misfired through a stupid mistake on his part. Every Saturday night, regular as clockwork, the lover finished his graveyard shift in a local factory at 6.00 AM, got in his car at 6.05, and drove home, always alone. Hoskin planned to kill him by planting a time-bomb in the car after the shift began, timed to explode at 6.07 – allowing himself a two-minute margin, to be on the safe side. Everything was prepared down to the finest detail, including an iron-clad alibi for himself from midnight to twelve noon. He scheduled this for a weekend in March, to coincide sadistically, with his wife's birthday. And it all went wrong because that was the weekend when all the clocks were put forward an hour for Daylight Saving Time; so the bomb went off an hour early, and no one was hurt.

No murder thus had taken place. However, the Homicide unit was involved already, because of an unrelated killing in February, which Hoskin had participated in (but with less dexterity of planning), and which Coggin and Sump managed to solve in May. But when the exploded time-bomb was traced back to Hoskin's partner, they felt chagrined over not having caught on to his March scheme while tracking down his February activities. Chagrined and thankful that the attempted murder in March had resulted in no loss of life.

"So," Coggin resumed, "if Boyle is our man, let's hope he's another Hoskin and trips over his own feet. Opportunity isn't a problem. All he'd have to do would be to set up a Saturday night appointment to meet Pilch in his office, and Pilch would leave the front door open and let him in upstairs. As to means, obviously a gun was used. No gun's been found: that's run-of-the-mill in such cases; only a fool leaves the gun behind. Mind you, it is a bit odd that Pilch's own gun has disappeared. But if it never shows up, we'll just have to let that go as a loose end of string that we couldn't tie off."

"Happens often enough," Sump said. "I agree, opportunity's pretty clear, and the means is obvious, even if the gun, for now, is missing, whether Pilch's gun or some other gun. This leaves us with motivation. And I stick with what I was just saying: if Boyle did kill Pilch, it was because Pilch was blackmailing him. And the only way to ferret something out about that is to do some digging, somehow, at Mahogany."

"Agreed. But let's not forget another angle. Maybe we can also find out if Boyle's taken any trips to Belize – or, for that matter, if Pablo Morales has. Maybe we could worm something out of that woman at the Foundation office – what's her name, Gladys something or other."

"Oddly enough, Maybee. Gladys Maybee. Yes, a job like hers often involves looking after travel arrangements. And even if either one of those two had an undercover reason for going to Belize, a trip like that would strike her as being quite above-board, seeing that's where the goods are being imported from."

"That's right. We can look into that ourselves. We'll need help tackling Mahogany. I've been thinking about that. Let me run a couple of ideas past you."

XIX

TUESDAY MAY 17, MORNING AND AFTERNOON

It was a time of change.

Internationally, the Soviet Empire was starting to show the cracks that suggested its impending dissolution. Communist bosses in the satellites could see the writing on the wall, and were making desperate last-minute concessions in the hope of staving off their ouster. Their own slogan, "History will not forgive," was coming back to haunt them.

Nations in the West, long burdened with the cost of the arms-race, began to think of how their economies might recover if the Cold War ended. Optimists spoke of Freedom, in self-congratulatory tones. And only the wary hinted at a possible future, not of idealistic reforms, but of bloated consumerism.

Contemplative monks and nuns, focused on things of the spirit rather than of the wallet, prayed for the well-being of a world they had chosen not to be part of. But within their own parameters, they had their own issues of change, either embracing it or resisting it.

That had always been so. Sister Nancy Pringle, OSG, writing the History of her Order, was well aware of that. The Gilbertines had a good record of fidelity to their founding ideals. And that had been due in part, perhaps, to a stubborn need to survive with their identity intact while living through periods of seismic change. In the sixteenth century, all monasteries in England were suppressed, and the Gilbertines fled to France, settling beside a like-minded Order. In the eighteenth century, when the French Revolution imposed a similar suppression there, they returned to a now more tolerant England. Renewed local hostility to all things Papist, however, forced them to resettle yet again, in Canada, in the mid-nineteenth century. There, in conventual isolation as Tathwell Abbey, and living unto themselves (or, more accurately, unto God), they were hardly affected at all by the massive changes occurring in the secular world outside. But in the second half of the twentieth century, they were directly affected by radical changes within the Roman Catholic Church itself.

At the time, Nancy Pringle, not yet a nun, would have referred to herself as a lapsed Catholic. She had not lost her basic beliefs, but she was unenthusiastic about what she saw as arrogance and rigidity in the institutional Church. The reforms ushered in by the Second Vatican Council opened her mind and heart to the possibility of making her peace with the Church. That, however, would be a slow process. Meanwhile she had other agendas. First there was a degree to be completed, in Mediaeval Studies. That was followed by a doomed love-affair with a would-be defector from Russia, who was snatched by the KGB and put on a plane to Moscow – she never saw him again. Justice denied kindled in her a passion for real justice; and because two justice-minded Montréal cops had done their best, sadly in vain, to thwart the KGB, she stepped away from academia and joined the Toronto police force. Recruited in due course to the Homicide squad, she worked with Inspector Coggin and Sergeant Sump on a murder case that involved Tathwell Abbey. Her exposure there to a life of faith lived as it ought to be, devoutly and humbly, turned a key in the locked door of her soul and she became a Gilbertine.

The timing was perfect for someone like her. A new Superior was instituting significant changes. The tradition was scrapped which kept the nuns and the monks adamantly apart: they could now worship as a unified body. Gregorian chant was still used, in English now: but in addition a mixed choir was formed, to sing polyphonic music, some of it in Latin, requiring both female and male voices. Monastic habit was optional; it was still the attire of choice among the elderly, but the younger members tended to prefer the simple dresses and suits now on offer. The old rule of enclosure had been relaxed, so that scholarly members could pursue research downtown. And from outside, new and progressive ideas filtered in: the Gilbertines were not an activist Order, vowed to help mend the sores of a wounded world; but in their contemplative otherness they yet welcomed the just ethos of Liberation Theology.

So, on this warm mid-May morning, Sister Nancy files into her stall for Mass. All is done as it has been done, liturgically, for many centuries, but with this difference that the Mass text throughout is in English and the Gregorian chants have been reworked from their former elaborateness into a new and cogent simplicity. In a breakaway from paternalistic formula, the Last Gospel is read by the Prioress, not by the Celebrant, concluding, as it does daily, with "The Word was made flesh and dwelt among us, and we beheld his glory, the glory as of the only begotten of the Father, full of grace and truth."

The words die on the incensed air – and are at once repeated in the immortal Latin, as the two sides of the choir, north and south, combine into a single polyphonic body with music by Palestrina.

"Verbum caro factum est, et habitavit in nobis; et vidimus gloriam ejus, gloriam quasi Unigeniti a Patre, plenum gratiae et veritatis."

Mass now done, they all file out of Choir, to go about the business of their day. For Sister Nancy, that means grabbing a coffee and settling in at her computer to get on with the History. She switches on and, somewhat to her surprise, finds she has an e-mail from Sergeant Sump. He has kept in touch since she left the Force, usually just a Christmas card and a note of greetings on St Gilbert's day. But this is different.

> hi, sister nancy. hope all's well with you. sorry to butt in, but perhaps you could give me a hand over one small detail in our current investigation. in your former life you were a very good cop. give me a call if you don't mind being one again for a couple of minutes. but if that's too intrusive never mind. take care. fred

***

For Ross Lang, the business of his day follows an almost monastic routine of dedicated work. He has risen at seven, after eight hours of sleep. He does a one-hour road-run, that culminates with a 600-metre sprint up the hill from Hoggs Hollow and is followed by a warm-down jog to his house. Then shower and breakfast. After that, a couple of hours at his computer, updating his training-log, paying household bills, doing his laundry; writing a shopping-list and going out to the stores, preparing his lunch and eating it. After lunch, duly needing to use his mind while resting his body, he does some of his mother's proof-reading which frees her to focus on the more specialized editorial side of her work. Then a short nap, before heading out to the track for an exacting interval-workout with Bill Northbrook. Around the time Vespers is finishing in Tathwell, he is soaking tired leg-muscles in a long hot bath. By then, Marge is home, cooking their supper, which they eat together. Evenings vary: sometimes Marge goes out to see friends, or Ross does, or friends come over; often they just stay home, chat, play a rubber of cribbage, watch the news on television, and go to bed early.

Marge had been a widow for a long time now. Grief had consumed her for a while. But it did not cripple her: raising Ross was more important to her than succumbing to sorrow. When she went back to work, it was not because she needed to but because the job gave her something to get on with.

As a professional athlete, Ross was envied by people who did not have the talents, or the opportunity, to be paid for doing something they wanted to do. Lucky Ross, they thought, as they toiled on in some humdrum job: that's a pretty cushy job, running around in a stadium for such big bucks.

What they did not realize was that running, for Ross, was not a job: it was a vocation.

***

Amy Buniak, in her vocation to theatre, had a keen sense of life's inequities. In a just world, she thought, there would not be such a gulf separating the poor from the rich. She had no quarrel with the middle class, or even with the modestly well off: it was the super-wealthy who sickened her. To make ends meet, in difficult times that never seemed to get any easier, her mother worked as a teller in a local bank. The job was wickedly underpaid, and it had no security or benefits or pension. Meanwhile the bankers themselves, in the top ranks, worked no harder but had seven-figure salaries plus enormous stock-options. Amy, seldom at a loss for the right adjective, called the discrepancy obscene.

She did not fancy herself as having all the answers. She knew far more about theatre and literature than about economics – though she was well aware that serious plays could not rely on the box-office alone, that they needed support from public or private funds or both. Theatre, she knew, was only one pauper with its hand out. But in a North America deformed by unbridled capitalism, she did wish that the available cake might be shared a bit more equitably. Why, she asked herself (and received no comforting answer), should the arts receive such grudging fiscal crumbs when large slices of tax-cuts, for example, were offered to businesses of dubious social value? There ought to be, somewhere, a better balance. Where was the famous Canadian compromise?

These questions were much in her mind as she awaited word on her application for a grant from the PM foundation. Her immigrant father, who had a doctorate in philosophy from the university of Kiev, was used to disappointment in Canada, but he tried to keep her hopes alive, while earnestly hoping himself that she not receive a slap in the face. What had intrigued him about her project, from the start, was its exploration of two kinds of assassination. In the private realm, he could fully understand, in Clytemnestra, the hatred of a parent wreaking vengeance on a man who had murdered her own daughter. And in the public realm, he could relate to Corday, who murdered Marat: his own grandparents, if there had been opportunity, would gladly have murdered Stalin.

Amy herself was not interested, with either woman, in taking sides. There were moral questions to be examined and weighed, but a good drama does not pass judgment: that is up to the audience – the jury, if you will. Her father respected that in her, as did her mother, too. And whatever the outcome, he knew the project was in good hands if it ever got off the ground: she would play both roles, and she was a very fine actress.

For her, however, it was deeply ironic that she, as the project's would-be author and performer, at this point in its development, should have been involved in a homicide investigation, not only as a prime witness, but also perhaps even as a suspect. Her innocence, she knew, was a fact. But her own two blunders had left that fact open to doubt.

Ancestrally, Amy's attitude to policemen was coloured by tales handed down of KGB behaviour in Ukraine. There, anyone had been condemned as guilty who could not prove his innocence; and such proof had been almost impossible in a system where ostensible defence attorneys were tools of the state. Born and raised in Canada, she knew things were different here; Inspector Coggin and Sergeant Sump had struck her as sympathetic and probably fair-minded – especially Sump. But she still had built-in misgivings where any cop was concerned. So it was a real leap of faith, on her part, to have phoned the Sergeant and told him (better late than never) about the not-locked door.

It is, therefore, with some trepidation now that she switches on her computer and reads the one e-mail received.

please contact me asap. f. sump, sgt

XX

WEDNESDAY MAY 18, DAYTIME

9.15 a phone rings and is answered.

"Good morning. PM Foundation. Gladys Maybee speaking. How may I help you?"

"Yes, Ms Maybee, it's Inspector Coggin here. Will Mr Boyle be available this afternoon, if we came by to see him?"

"Let me just look at his calendar – he's not in yet." A pause. "Yes, he's free at two o'clock. Would, you. like me to tell him what it's about?"

"Oh, just a couple of routine questions. By the way, while you're on the line, I have a routine question for you, too. If Mr Boyle or Mr Morales needs to travel on business, do you look after the arrangements for them? The tickets and hotel reservations and so on?"

"Well, only for Mr Boyle, not for Mr Morales. And I've only had to do that once since I've worked here. Last year. It wasn't really business it was a holiday; but I was glad to do it for him. What with it not being business, he didn't charge it to the Foundation: paid for it himself."

"Right. Last year, you said?"

"Yes, last spring. I can put you on hold and look it up for you, if you like."

"No, don't bother. You can give me the details later, when we come in. By the way, just out of curiosity, where was it he went for his holiday?"

"That's the funny thing. It was Belize. I said it wasn't a business trip, and it wasn't. But he'd heard so much about Belize, while working at Mahogany, and everyone said it was a great place for a vacation, so that's why he chose it. And of course Mr Morales helped him with a couple of connections, and tips on where to go, and so on. He said he'd had a great time when he came home."

"I'm sure he did. Well, thank you, Ms Maybee. We'll see you later."

"Bye-bye, Inspector."

***

11.00 a phone rings and is answered.

"Homicide. Sump here."

"Oh, Fred, it's Nancy. I got your e-mail. How are you?"

"Just fine, thanks. And you?"

"Couldn't be better. What can I do to help?"

"I'm not sure if you can. But anyhow, here's the thing. You remember when we met downtown a few days ago, we got talking about this and that; and. you were telling us about that old document you'd found about herbal medicine centuries back. And there was one plant you mentioned – what was it called, markerie?"

"That's right."

"And you said it supposedly did a lot of good for the stamina of the Abbey's field hands. And then you went on to say all that herbal stuff came over to Canada with you people when you immigrated. So maybe that markerie plant is right here in Toronto, in your back garden. How about that?"

"Yes, it is. We do have a markerie bed. And what's more, it just so happens I've looked into it a bit further: talked on the phone to a master-gardener in England, who knows a lot about markerie. It's a species of wild spinach, occasionally found in Lincolnshire. Over time, people ignored it and forgot about it, when regular spinach was introduced as a marketable crop. But this old fellow in England was fascinated to hear we had some here. He may be coming over some time to visit his son; and I'll make sure he gets to take a look at our markerie bed."

"Good for you, Nancy! Obviously you haven't lost your touch: always were good at tracking things down. Now here's what I wanted to consult you about. Inspector Coggin and I are on a case right now that's a bit complicated – well, aren't they all? But anyway, this one has a drug connection that's particularly interesting to me personally. The victim was working on an unofficial inquiry into the use of performance-enhancing drugs in sport. Things like all those steroids and human growth hormones and so on. Chances are, he got a bit too close to the pot of gold, and paid for it. We don't know about that yet. But I did start to wonder, when you told us about markerie, if maybe someone in sport, maybe in track, had found out about markerie and figured this was the answer to everyone's prayers: it would enhance a runner's performance just as well as the banned substances, but it would be legit because it's a natural plant. That got me thinking, what if someone got access to it who was interested in that kind of possibility."

"Fred, do you believe in co-incidences?"

"I hate to admit it, but yes. Sometimes. Why?"

"Listen to this. There's a lady comes to Mass in our visitors' narthex quite often. Has done for years. Well, a while back she got to chatting with our Guestmistress, Sister Alice Newstead, and it turned out they're both keen gardeners. So Sister Alice showed her round our herb-garden, and she had all the usual herbs in her own garden, but she'd never heard of markerie, or seen any. So Sister Alice gave her a bundle of cuttings to take home with her, to see if they'd take root in her own beds. So far as I know, that worked. So arguably our garden at the Abbey isn't the only place where markerie is grown nowadays. We eat it from time to time ourselves, cooked or in salads. I can't say if it has any magic properties that enhance our performance as religious. But who knows what it would do for us if we still did field-work and ate it all the time? Anyway, when you lump everything together, it does add up to a pretty fair bunch of co-incidences. First, I run across markerie in a mediaeval document, and then I trace its journey from England to France; and eventually here. Then I try my luck in the Botanical Gardens, to see if anyone there knows anything about markerie, and it turns out the guy there has a father in England who knows all about markerie. After that, no sooner have I stashed all that in my notes, than Sister Alice happens to mention to me how she had given markerie cuttings to some woman she met. From there, it isn't much of a stretch to wonder if markerie's being peddled to some would-be Olympic superstar."

"And this markerie, you say, is some kind of wild spinach?"

"Apparently."

"Good Lord! You know, that reminds me of the old Popeye comic, the one about the spinach-eating sailor with the enormous arm-muscles. Do you think, behind that notion there might be a trace-memory of peasant forefathers beefed up on markerie and famed for their feats of strength."

"Oh, I don't know about that, Fred. I always thought it was just a case of mothers latching on to Popeye as a way of persuading kids to eat their greens. Which is perhaps why a lot of kids grow up saying they hate spinach. Not that there's anything magical about ordinary spinach, of course. Oh, and by the way, old Mr Willoughby – he's the master-gardener I phoned in England – said that markerie is a Lincolnshire dialect variation on its real name, which is mercury. That gave me a chuckle, because Mercury's the name of the Roman demigod of speed, and not long ago the Ford company ran an ad for its Mercury model that boasted its miles-per-gallon value for long-distance driving. Somehow, everything in this whole business seems to be coming full circle, all fitting together. At least, that's how it looks to me at my end. So if it helps to clear up a thing or two at your end, I'll feel I've done my good deed for the day."

"Sounds to me like it'll probably help a lot. I'm sure the Inspector'll think so, too. If it does, we'll know who to thank. Though I doubt if your Superior'll be especially pleased to know one of the Sisters has been moonlighting as a supernumerary cop. Meanwhile. I mustn't keep you, but there is one more thing I could ask you, not right now, but when you do have a spare moment. D'you think you could find out from Sister Alice the name of the lady she gave the markerie cuttings to?"

"Sure, no problem. I'll e-mail it to you."

"Thanks. I owe you."

"No problem. Bye, Fred."

"Take care, Nancy."

***

2.00 an intercom buzzes.

"Inspector Coggin and Sergeant Sump to see you, sir."

"Sure. Let 'em in."

After the usual courtesies, Hedley Boyle says, "and what can I do for you today, gentlemen?"

Sergeant Sump's tactic, quite often, was to put an interviewee at ease with an affable demeanour, and then unexpectedly spring a jolting question.

Inspector Coggin, by contrast, preferred not to beat about the bush useful results came, sometimes, from putting an interviewee immediately on the defensive – politely, but with a certain coldness.

"I will not conceal from you, sir," he said, "that you are a suspect in the murder of Oscar Pilch. Now, before you start blustering indignation about that, let me briefly outline why. Any case against you has to satisfy three basic requirements: you have to have had opportunity, means, and motive.

"Opportunity? That's easily answered. By your own admission, you had a business relationship with Pilch that involved you in meeting with him, in his office, after hours, at his request; and clearly you could arrange for that to happen again, at your request, any time you chose. None of that counts against you, if Pilch died on the morning of April 26th: you have a watertight alibi for then. But that wasn't when Pilch died. He died the preceding evening. And you have no alibi for then.

"So much for opportunity. As to means, all we can say is that guns are easily come by, sad to say, and you could easily get hold of one without our being able to trace it. Certainly, if you did, you'd have got rid of it afterwards, so there wouldn't be much point in our getting a warrant to search your home for it. Granted, not every middle-class respectable businessman would know how to acquire a black-market weapon. But interestingly enough, Pilch's own handgun is missing. We can't discount the possibility that you took it from him, and used it. Let's leave that on one side for now, and move on to motive.

"Why would you want to kill Pilch? On the face of it, you had no reason to. He was simply an employee, hired to look into drugs in sport and chosen because of his previously known contacts in the world of drug trafficking. He reported back to you regularly, and you regularly paid him a small agreed fee, out of Foundation funds. Nothing wrong with that. But then, all of a sudden, the picture changes. Pilch is paid ten thousand dollars by you, out of your own bank account. To my way of thinking, there's only one explanation for that. Pilch, in the course of his investigation, had discovered something you'd been doing, that would cost you your career and reputation, and would put you behind bars; and he decided to blackmail you. Nothing else fits. So you made the first payment, to keep him quiet right away. But you realized there was only one way to keep aim quiet permanently: to kill him. We may not know what gun you used, or how you acquired it. But any jury would agree you had a compelling motive.

"That's the case against you. What do you have to say?"

At moments like this, the two policemen had seen various reactions in men trapped in such a spider's web of circumstantial evidence. The guilty sometimes remonstrated disputatiously, sometimes clammed up, sometimes turned verbally abusive, sometimes even smugly boasted they could beat the rap. The innocent (for it sometimes happened, evidence notwithstanding, that innocent people were accused) evinced all shades of fear, from stunned dread to horrified panic. In this case, what they had not encountered before in a man thus trapped was what now occurred,

Hedley Boyle burst into tears.

All they could make out, between the sobs, was a kind of desperate appeal that they not get his son mixed up in it.

Finally the outburst was over, and Boyle sat up and blew his nose.

"Your son?" Sump asked gently, "what has your son got to do with it?"

"Oh, everything." Boyle said, "Tommy's everything to me. Always has been. And he's always looked up to me. I can't bear to think what this'd do to him."

"I take it, then, you don't mean he's some way involved in the mess you've got yourself into. You just don't want his image of you to be damaged."

More nose-blowing.

"Well, sir, that's just the trouble when someone goes wrong. Other people get hurt."

Boyle took a deep breath. Then he said, "I don't suppose it's any good my telling you Pilch was already dead when I went to see him that evening."

Both policemen shook their heads.

"The truth is," Boyle went on, "I did go over to have it out with him. Yes, you were right: he was blackmailing me. And I couldn't get him to stop. I was at the point of trying to figure out how to kill him and get away with it. But that conversation with him never took place. He was a real shit, deserved to die. But somebody else beat me to it. Not that I expect you to believe me," he finished up forlornly.

Inspector Coggin, for one, was not prone to going on wild goose chases at a suspect's request. He withheld comment. Sergeant Sump, on the other hand, remembered with chagrin their mortification in the case of the Executed Executive, when painstakingly compiled evidence had convincingly pointed to an ambitious subordinate as his Chairman's ingenious killer, only for it to transpire that the victim had been killed by someone else over a totally unsuspected adultery that had nothing to do with business. So he, Sump, was always willing to give suspects, momentarily, the benefit of the doubt: their versions of events might be implausible; but every now and then they did contain a grain of truth.

"Mr Boyle," he said, "let's get off the subject of who killed Pilch for a moment."

Boyle seemed to relax, silently. But only, as it turned out, briefly.

"I'd like to ask you," he went on, "about your trip to Belize last spring. I gather you paid for it yourself, as a private vacation, and it had nothing to do with business. Okay, fair enough. A lot of people, in your position, would have cooked up a plausible reason for giving it a business twist and putting in for travel expenses. But maybe that would look a bit fishy, seeing you now work for the PM Foundation, not for the Mahogany Emporium the way you used to. All well and good, so it was a private vacation. But then I ask myself, why Belize? True, if you wanted a holiday in Central America, Belize is an English-speaking country. True, too, Mr Morales could probably give you lots of tips on how to have a good time there. But, but, but, I still ask; why Belize, and not some other less out-of-the-way place that's really known as a hot spot for tourists?"

"Oh, for heaven's sake!" Boyle exclaimed, recovering a bit of aplomb after the dents made in his poise, "You think I'd choose the vulgarity of Vegas or the jaded rites of spring in Florida? Give me a break. Belize is a perfect getaway. Great beaches, perfect climate, interesting food. Peace and quiet."

"Okay, I'm sure that's all very enjoyable, sir. But I can't help thinking it'd also be pretty convenient for you, if you were up to something crooked. And you must have been, either there or elsewhere, if Pilch had found out what it was and was blackmailing you. Now, this is only speculation, of course, but I put it to you that a possible scenario is a drug-smuggling caper. You figure out a way to hide a package of drugs in one of the furniture shipments; and when that particular shipment arrives in Toronto, you go to the warehouse after hours (I'm sure you still have a key to the place, from when you worked there) and simply retrieve the package. Risky? Yes, it'd be risky. But not half as risky as butting in on organized crime as an amateur. What were you thinking? You could outsmart the pros? I mean, you'd have to organize one of the craftsmen in the factory to stash a package in one of the shipments – perhaps not too hard to do in a poverty-stricken country. And before you even do that, you have to organize a reliable supply of the stuff. Granted, there's plenty of it up for grabs in Central America. But horning in on the drug cartels, that's an appalling risk to take. Chances are, you slipped up somewhere doing so, and that's what Pilch somehow latched onto. Who knows? Something along those lines'll probably surface when we dig really deep."

"I think," Boyle said, "we probably shouldn't take this conversation any further without my consulting a lawyer."

"That, of course, is entirely up to you," Inspector Coggin said. "But I should point out to you that you're not at the moment under arrest. The Sergeant and I work in the Homicide squad, and have been assigned to this case because of Pilch's death. But the case has a wider range than that. The Narcotics squad is also involved. They would look at any picayune bit of smuggling you may have tried your hand at, and they'd probably think it pretty small beer. But it might just so happen that you're privy to overlooked facts, that would help them break through to a really big drug-bust – one involving major figures, not just small-fry like you. Naturally I promise you nothing. You could be under arrest any time I choose. But as a larger case develops, if you co-operate, there might be some kind of mitigation in it for you. In the meantime, don't go anywhere. I'll have to ask for your passport, of course. Is it here, or do you keep it at home?"

"No, it's right here," Boyle replied, opening a desk drawer. He fished it out and handed it over, wryly.

"We'll be in touch," Inspector Coggin said, rising. And they left.

3.45 a phone rings and is answered.

"Homicide. Coggin here."

"Andrew, it's Ted Ainslie. I've got some interesting news for you. Ballistics has come up with a match for Louie Larose's handgun, A match, that is, for a slug fired from it. This is one of those times when everything works the way it should and doesn't get lost in the shuffle. The gun and the bullet both landed in the same lab, and the clerk there had a kind of slack day with nothing much to do, so he tagged them together for comparison testing. The bullet was the one that killed your fellow, what's his name, Pilch; and it turns out it was fired from Louie's gun. Well, you know these guys: they never let go of their own weapons. So it looks like you've got your perp and your victim lined up like ducks in a row. Plus, the perp is dead, too; so you can probably close your case."

"Yes, I guess we can."

This was said a bit ruefully; for Coggin had pretty much figured Boyle as the killer. But Boyle was still on his mind.

"Listen, Ted," he said. "While you're on the line, there's something I should share with you. Fred and I've been working on the Pilch case and one aspect of it seems to touch on drug-trafficking, not just on homicide. One of our suspects may have been involved in smuggling narcotics from Central America to Toronto in shipments of mahogany furniture. If so, there might be some useful leads there for you to look at. So perhaps I should fill you in on that. How about I pop in and do that, if you're not tied up?"

"Sure: come right on over."

"Okay. See you."

"Bye."

***

4.15 a phone rings and goes onto its answering machine.

Hi, you're reached Amy Buniak or Amy Barton. Please leave a message after the beep.

Beep.

"Ms Buniak, this is Sergeant Sump. Inspector Coggin and I both want you to know you're completely off the hook, if you were afraid we thought you had anything to do with Mr Pilch's death. We now know who killed him. Just for the record, we want to thank you for co-operating with us the way you did. Oh, and one more thing. In the course of our inquiries, we had occasion to read your application to the PM Foundation. Very interesting project, especially to us homicide detectives. So I hope you get your grant. If you do, let us know, and we'll come and see it. All the best. Fred Sump."

***

4.45

    e-mail from sr nancy pringle, osg, to f. sump
    fyi name of woman with markerie cuttings is mrs margery lang
    np

XXI

THURSDAY MAY 19

To non-Canadians, and even to some Canadians themselves, it is a matter of some wonder and no little amusement that every year, in late May, there should be a public holiday in honour of Queen Victoria's birthday. She had presided over an Empire steeped in bourgeois respectability, but Canada was no longer the bastion of imperial uniformity that she had taken for granted. Its provinces were filled with Africans, Asians, and Europeans to whom the British crown meant nothing. And a genuflecting to the Buckingham Palace of generations ago was an absurd anachronism. The tradition lingered on, however, because Canadians love any excuse for a day off, and no one had bothered to give this particular public holiday a new name.

The official date of the holiday is May 24th, but that is only observed if it falls on a Monday. If it does not, it is transferred to the preceding Monday. So this year, 1988, it will be May 23rd. That fits very neatly into Pablo Morales' idea of staging a Dream Two Mile as the feature event in an otherwise low-key track-meet in Toronto. The timing is perfect. Spring is far enough along for runners to have returned to top shape. But the year's Olympics, in late September and early October, are far enough in the future for one eight-minute race to be no significant disruption in anyone's preparation for the big showdown in Seoul. Accordingly, he has had no trouble, with expert advice, in securing a commitment to participate from the nine top international runners who, with Ross Lang, would constitute the ideal field.

The great attraction, for them, is the opportunity to try and knock Ross Lang off his perch. Any athlete who rules the world consistently, in

253

his event or events, is fair game for everyone. Nurmi, in the nineteen-twenties left the track undefeated, despite valiant attempts to outrun him. The same was almost true of Zátopek in the late nineteen-forties and early-fifties. So now, in Toronto, the would-be pretenders to the distance throne will assemble, all expenses paid plus a good appearance fee, to try their luck.

They are a motley crew. Kippax, Australian champion, the designated rabbit. Moses M'bongo of Kenya, world, record holder at 3k; Zbigniew Milosa, of Poland, Juko Salanen, of Finland, and Otto Keller, of West Germany, respectively winners of the 1500, the 5k, and the 10k in the European Championships (no invitation has been sent to East Germany, because of that country's notoriety as a hive of chemical cheats); and four national champions at 5k and 10k, Haile Donegel, of Ethiopia, Mori Kanabata, of Japan, Ian Mackenzie of Great Britain, and Sidi al-Hafid, of Morocco. All nine men have raced against Lang in international meets. Whether at 5k or 10k or half-marathon, none have ever beaten him or even come within five seconds of his world records. Every one of them believes his time will come – perhaps this weekend.

***

Easing up. That puts the finishing touch on the dour months of preparatory workouts. The last three days before a major race are a gift to be savoured. Yesterday, instead of a tough road-run before breakfast, Ross went for a heartening walk in the early morning sunshine; and in the late afternoon, he ran a dozen single laps at race-tempo with ample rest between them, to tune in, as usual, to his legs' built-in muscle-memory of that tempo, but to do so without making any inroads on his built-up stamina. Tomorrow, the same again. Saturday and Sunday, he will go for a light jog along a nature-trail, feeling a one-ness with the world, and readying his heart and mind for the proving-ground on Monday, for the test of who he really is.

Meanwhile his mother has put her latest editorial assignment (critiquing Mayor Heath's preface to the *Collected Poems* of Jack Sheriff) on hold, and tends to his meals. Marge has always been her own person, but in the last few years she has taken the time, as well, to become quite expert in the dietary needs of an elite athlete. This has been of great help to her son, and of real benefit to her, too. His own calorie requirements are far higher than hers, of course. But she thrives on the same regime, simply in much smaller portions. One constant, among all the judiciously balanced carbs and fats and proteins and liquids, is the inclusion of markerie from her garden. She has figured out several ways of using it: steamed, or mixed in a salad, or whizzed in a food-processor as a drink. She takes its presence in their lives for granted as a fixed habit, and seldom gives it a second thought. But if asked, she would probably refer to it as the Tathwell Ingredient.

It will be several days before Fred Sump gets around to talking to her about it.

XXII

FRIDAY MAY 20, 2.00 PM

Inspector Ainslie, fully briefed by Inspector Coggin and Sergeant Sump, has made an appointment to see Gerald Wolstencraft, manager of the Mahogany Emporium. On the telephone, having identified himself as head of the Narcotics squad, he hastened to reassure Wolstencraft that no one at Mahogany was under suspicion of any wrongdoing: there were just some background questions he wanted to ask that might help with another investigation.

The advantage, if one were needed, lay with him, of course. For while Wolstencraft could have no idea, in advance, of what might crop up, he (Ainslie) had read Wolstencraft's website and at least knew what kind of person to expect. He had also read the profile of him that was circulated within Mahogany upon his appointment to his present job.

Wolstencraft, he understands, is an English immigrant, aged fifty, with a strong background in the furniture trade. He came from a long line of skilled carpenters and joiners, he had taken courses in business management, and before coming to Canada he had been assistant manager in a London firm that was quite like Mahogany in catering to two clienteles, the elite and the bourgeois – in an age of political correctness, the profile refrained from putting it quite like that, but Ainslie could read between the lines. Moneyed families in Toronto, he knew, set much store on luxury and on the appearance of luxury; they aped the manners and habits of the British Establishment; and they were doubtless flattered by having an experienced Englishman like Wolstencraft treat them as a transatlantic version of the lords and ladies he had rubbed shoulders with, albeit as an employee.

"Mr Wolstencraft" he begins, "you must be wondering why a narcotics detective should want to see you. It's very simple, really. Drugs, as you know, are a major social problem. And many drugs, as I'm sure you also know, are not home-grown, they're smuggled in."

"I dare say. But what has that to do with Mahogany?"

"Maybe nothing at all. But the fact is, if we're ever going to clamp down properly on drug trafficking, we have to stop the stuff coming in. We can't stop it at source, not while the governments in Latin America turn a blind eye to the cartels. But we can try to stop it at our own border. Mainly by intercepting it."

"I'm sure that's all very desirable. But where exactly is this leading?"

"Well, to put it crudely, maybe it's leading to your own doorstep. Or then, maybe not. Here's the thing. Any company that regularly imports goods from Central America, like yours, has to be looked at. Has to be presumed innocent, you might say. And certainly we can't scrutinize every shipment year round: that would require a sizeable army of investigators. But every now and then we do a random check on shipments. Just as a matter of routine."

"Are you telling me you've been vetting our shipments behind our back. That's disgraceful."

"What would be disgraceful, sir, is not to do so, given the scale of the problem. However, I'm happy to tell you none of your import shipments have given us any reason to suspect the Mahogany Emporium of being involved in anything illicit."

"Thanks very much." This with dry sarcasm.

"At least, that's true of your regular shipments. But you do also, once in a while, bring in shipments of special orders, I believe: custom made pieces. Right?"

"Yes. Occasionally."

"Right. And I'm sure those shipments are just as innocent as all the others. But there has been one shipment, a little while back, that might be different. It didn't actually come to our attention in the course of our regular duties: it's actually a spinoff from a murder investigation in one of our other departments. I don't need to bore you with all the details of that. Let's just say it goes back to before you joined Mahogany. So you're not personally involved in any way. Or I should say you weren't here when the special order was placed. But I gather these custom-made orders can take quite a long time to fill, depending on how complicated the design is and how large the order is. Anyway, this particular order was placed before your time, but delivery wasn't expected until later last year or perhaps early this year. Maybe you could look that up in your records."

"I'm sure I could. But what makes this particular shipment different from any others?"

"Quite possibly nothing at all. But we do have evidence that it might have been used as a container for smuggling drugs in. And if it was, if they were cleverly hidden, the crate may have simply slipped through the net at customs – as I said, we haven't the staff to double-check everything. So, if that's what happened, the crate may have arrived in your warehouse unopened and uninspected, with whatever illicit drugs it contained, if any, undetected. So what I want you to check in your records is this: the name and address of the customer; who discussed the specifics of the order with the customer, its content and design and so on; when the crate arrived in your warehouse; when it was unpacked and assembled; and when it was delivered to the customer."

"Alright, I can do all of that and get it off to you right away. But while you were talking, I've remembered who the customer was, he's such an unusual character. Name of Hertling. Strictly speaking, Graf Nikolaus von Hertling. Scion of an ancient German family of landowners. Born rich, and made it uber-rich as a top man in Big Pharma. Has offices in Munich and London as well as Toronto. Living here, he just likes to be known, without frills, as plain Nick Hertling. But in private, it's a different story. Not so plain. He bought a double lot on Massey Road, amongst the other billionaires, and built a mansion on it. That's where we delivered the furniture eventually, after it came in from Belize. And it's an amazing place: a colossal monument to bad taste, German style; gothic grandeur with all the armorial fittings. The one exception, touchingly, is the master bedroom. There his wife apparently had found the heavy Teutonic decor altogether too depressing. So she had insisted on gutting it and refurnishing it and redecorating it more to her own taste. Mind you, there was nothing very modern or daring about that. In a way, her hand was almost as heavy as his, but at least it was more in tune with Torontonian money-culture. She spent a lot on expensive drapes and high-end wallpaper and deluxe carpeting. But all that was carefully chosen, in colour and style, to harmonize with the mahogany furniture. That's where we came in. It was all to be custom-made from top-quality mahogany. Two elegant chairs. A dresser. Bedside table. And the centre-piece, a magnificent four-poster bed, king-size. No expense spared. I wasn't involved, myself, in the original discussions: the choice of materials, the design, and so on; that was before my time. But it was still being talked about when I joined the Emporium; and it fell to me to make the delivery in due course. That's how come I got to see inside the place. It really is a monstrosity – except for the master-bedroom: it at least is in passably good taste."

"Okay, now let me get this straight. The deal was negotiated by your predecessor, but you were here when the shipment arrived. And then you were the one looking after the actual delivery. Right?"

"Right. But we couldn't deliver it right away, because the Hertlings were away in Europe. But they were eager to have it delivered as soon as they got back."

"And that was when, approximately?"

"Several weeks ago now. I'll look it up for you."

"And after it arrived in the warehouse, did it just sit there until the Hertlings got back? Or did you open the crate and check it out, in case there were any parts missing, or any damage in transit?"

"Of course we did. We couldn't just let it sit there. Even if everything was all present and correct, we'd unpack it anyway and put it in a temperature-controlled, humidity-controlled storeroom. Fine wood is very sensitive to climate-change, you know, however well-seasoned it is."

"Sure. Now this next question is very important. During the time it was in the storeroom, who would have had access to it, sir?"

"Anyone on the staff here, I suppose. That is, during working hours. Most days we lock up around six."

"And how about overnight? We've no reason to suspect that someone on your staff has been up to anything shady. But suppose an outsider got hold of a key somehow, what kind of security system do you have?"

"Interesting you should ask that. One of the first things I did, after I took this job, was a complete revamp of the security. There's been a bit of a crime-wave in this area, so I proposed to the board we beef up security, and they agreed. We put bars on all the ground-floor windows. We installed heavy-duty steel doors. And we replaced all the conventional locks with an electronic access system: entry by code only and you have to know the code to get in – it's foolproof."

"Sounds good. In your opinion then, sir, the consignment could not have been tampered with between the time of its arrival and the time of its delivery to the home of Mr and Mrs Hertling?"

"I really do think that's so."

"Well, I hope you're right. You probably are. Anyway, thank you for your time. You've been very helpful. Here's my card: it's got my fax number on it and my office phone number. I look forward to getting the little details you said you'd fax me. They probably aren't necessary, more routine than significant. But we do like to cover all bases. And please get in touch if anything occurs to you that might have a bearing on our inquiries."

"I will."

And with the usual courtesies, the interview ends.

XXIII

SATURDAY MAY 21, NOON

The Toronto Police Force, over the years, has earned a good reputation for efficiency and probity. As with any institution, nothing is perfect. There have been corrupted cops, sometimes, and cops guilty of planting evidence or suppressing evidence; but these cases have been rare. There have also been units led by old-timers who are slow to embrace new ideas or who just put in their time perfunctorily until they qualify for full pension; but these men, too, are rare (there are no women unit-heads) and they vanish through attrition. Occasionally units, with a strong sense of territorial entitlement, have failed to co-operate with each other as well as they should; but on the whole the Force has been free of inter-departmental friction.

It is in that spirit of flexibility that Ainslie and Coggin have teamed up, informally, over their somehow connected cases of smuggling and murder. At Coggin's request, Ainslie has looked into the possible involvement of the Mahogany Emporium. He has learnt the details of a possibly suspect shipment being delivered to the Hertling mansion. And now, briefing Coggin on that, he has asked Coggin to take the next step: pushing sixty, he knows a lot about Coggin's history, about how Coggin as a young man was fluent in German and had actually been assigned, once, to the task of interrogating dubious Germans. Coggin has protested that his German is now quite rusty; but he sees the point and has said okay.

Chances were, Hertling would be fluent in English: he was, after all a high-ranking international businessman. But even if they didn't need to talk in German, Coggin could still bring to the conversation a practised ear for the nuances of German character. And taking Sump along, as always, would be valuable, especially if Mrs Hertling was present, as she probably would be, since the furniture shipment was, so to speak, her baby; he, Sump, had a great knack for reading human character, of whatever background.

Today is Saturday. Nobody answers the phone at the Hertling number, but an up-to-date answering machine says that everybody will be away for the holiday weekend. So Coggin leaves a message identifying himself, and asking Hertling to call him back, requesting a few moments of his time on a routine inquiry. There the matter must rest until he hears back.

Now, with time on his hands, he turns his mind away from the world's depravities which so much occupy it in his professional life.

Instead, he proposes to re-engage with higher things, as so excellently celebrated in the works of Bach. For this weekend is not only a quaint national holiday, honouring a defunct English monarch of obsolete importance. It is also, for those who care about such things, a weekend of great spiritual value: tomorrow is the Feast of Pentecost; and that was celebrated by Bach, superbly, in his Whitsuntide cantatas, *Erschallet ihr Lieder* and *Erwünschtes Freudenlicht*. Coggin pulls a recording of them from his vast Bach collection, and readies himself for an hour of Germany at its best – such a contrast with Germany of years ago, when he was assigned to examine the sinister architects of its ruin.

Before he can put the disc on his machine, however, his eye falls to a cryptic crossword that Fred lent him the other day. It was featured in Fred's copy of *World Athletics*, and was given to Coggin as a trifle to add to his regular sources of puzzles. He had solved it quite quickly but put it aside unfinished: only the clue to number 17 across had given him momentary difficulty. He glanced at it again briefly, but decided not to give it any heed right now. Bach was a lot more important than crosswords. And certainly, he was not about to trivialize good music by giving it anything less than his full attention.

CRYPTIC CROSSWORD #5: "VARIOUS SPORTS"

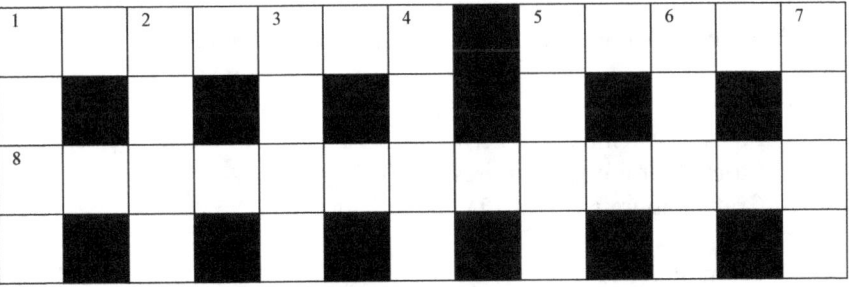

ACROSS

1/ Brokenly A. Peters runs again on TV (7)
5/ Goes round in rider's head, initially: "To trot or not?" (5)
8/ What the clay pigeons suffer (8,5)
9/ Records broken at the end of races (5)
10/ What the final relay runner is on (4,3)
11/ Going up, the ring is born of loveless origins (6)
12/ Endlessly discuss a 2-kilogram implement (6)
15/ Artwork at sea goes quickly (7)
17/ Atop old-style bedposts, unlike in athletes' village (5)
19/ Starless sport until London Olympics (7,6)
20/ Betting levels (5)
21/ Greek swimmer reformed, but burdened again (7)

DOWN

1/ Put stopwatch back to zero for start a race (5)
2/ Strict chair umpire requires this (6,7)
3/ Craftsman trains anew (7)
4/ Not married in curtailed athletic vest (6)
5/ Circumference of the squared circle (5)
6/ Both a great racehorse and a Russian groom (6,7)

7/ Pro offered a contract again (7)
11/ It is ludicrous when iris loses her head over four characters in The Bible (7)
13/ Formerly used by pros on signing (7)
14/ Williams: the diver, not the sprinter (6)
16/ Flo-Jo had long ones (5)
18/ She sees two Poles embracing the American team (5)

In fact, he hated that kind of disrespect. It was barbarous to treat classical works as musical wallpaper, fit only to be used as background to restaurant meals. As to muzak in elevators and other public places, it drove him crazy: partly because it was rudely intrusive, but mostly because it was drivel.

He switched on the eighteenth century, and its supreme genius; and settled in to listen.

An hour later, as the last note dies away, he rejoins the twentieth century, a little reluctantly. As he does so, the solution to seventeen across comes unbidden to his mind. This has happened to him often before. He will give up, temporarily, on a clue that has baffled him, and will occupy himself exclusively with other matters. Somehow, though, his subconscious works on the solution while his focus is elsewhere; and the answer pops up without his even trying to figure it out.

So now: he has the answer. And not only does it solve the crossword completely, but also it gives him an idea for solving the problem he's been working on as a detective.

This is going to be interesting.

XXIV

SUNDAY MAY 22, 9.00 AM

In Tathwell Abbey, the community is in the choir stalls, for the short office of None, to be followed by Pontifical Mass for the Feast of Pentecost. They have chanted the prescribed Gregorian psalms antiphonally, women to the left and men to the right; and they finish the office with a polyphonic setting of the final antiphon, "Alleluia, deduc me Domine", by their composer-in-residence, Michel Lemoyne.

The Mass follows.

Devout in her stall, Sister Nancy Pringle sits and listens attentively as the Prioress reads the Epistle, from the second chapter of the Acts of the Apostles, the account of the first Pentecost. Multilingual herself, thanks to diligent study, she marvels at how a handful of northern Israelis, with Aramaic as a mother-tongue and perhaps a few words of Koine Greek and official Latin, suddenly by divine inspiration became fluent in all the languages of the, to them, known world.

"… and began to speak with other tongues, as the Spirit gave them utterance. And there were dwelling at Jerusalem Jews, devout men, out of every nation under heaven. Now when this was noised abroad the multitude came together, and were confounded, because that every man heard them speak in his own language. And they were all amazed and marvelled saying one to another, 'Behold, are not all these which speak Galilean. And how hear we every nan in our own tongue, wherein we were born? Parthians and Medes, and Elamites, and the dwellers in Mesopotamia, and in Judaea, and Cappadocia, in Pontus and Asia, Phrygia and Pamphylia, Egypt, and in the parts of Libya about Cyrene, and strangers of Rome, Jews and proselytes, Cretes and Arabians, we do hear them speak in our tongues the wonderful works of God.' And they were all amazed."

Then all stand for the Sequence, chanting "Veni Sancte Spiritus" to a melody almost as old as the Church itself.

***

In the visitors' narthex, Marge Lang is in attendance, as on most Sundays. It is a fixture in her life. This particular Sunday, though, is special. Catholicism was built into her early, and she has always been observant. But after her husband died, she was overcome with grief and something like despair. Only two things had kept her going: her son, and her faith. She needed to raise him without a father, and to give him what comfort she could in his distress. And she needed to find in her religion a source of consolation that she could not find within herself. That she was able to do so gave Pentecost a treasured place in her soul; for this is the Feast of the third Person in the Trinity, the Holy Spirit the Comforter. To whom, this year as every year, she kneels to give thanks.

With her in the narthex, today, is her son. He does not usually attend, for his vocation lies elsewhere. But he knows how important Pentecost is to her, so he comes this one Sunday if he can. This year he easily can, for no race or workout gets in the way. Tomorrow is the race he has trained hard towards for months; and the only run he will do today is a light jog in the afternoon.

As he sits there, he listens to the reading of the Pentecost narrative – this with a certain detachment, for he does not believe in miracles, either on the track or anywhere else. He is well aware that the world of religion, like the world of politics, has always had its myth-makers. But it seems to him there is probably a very simple explanation to the phenomenon of intercommunication between the apostles and the polyglot visitors to Jerusalem: famously, the Jews of the captivity and the exile had clung to their faith and to their understanding of the Hebrew scriptures, even though they became fluent also in the secular languages of their domiciles; arguably the apostles, too had a good grasp of scriptural Hebrew, and that will have been how they were able to speak to their foreign co-religionists and to be understood. Only later, when an official version of the story was to be circulated and written down, only then perhaps did the myth-makers latch onto it and give it a multilingual twist, thanks to miraculous intervention by the Holy Spirit.

There was, of course, an extraordinary parallel in modern times. Jews of the diaspora, like their forebears, had also clung to their faith and their scriptural Hebrew. So that when they came home (which was how they thought of it) after the State of Israel was founded in 1948, not only did they bring with them a fluency in the vernacular tongues of their upbringing, such as English or Polish or Russian, but also they had a rooted familiarity with enough Ancient Hebrew to catch on to its modernized version as the official language of the new state.

For Ross, there is another and interesting parallel. International athletes, like international pilots and flight-controllers, use English as a lingua franca. When they assemble, from around the world, for major competitions, they rely on English, however fractured, to communicate with each other and with the press. So tomorrow in Toronto, as in the Jerusalem of antiquity, there will be a convergence of nine runners and six mother-tongues on the starting line of his two-mile race. They will have far more on their minds than idle chat. But there will be, at that moment, a camaraderie that transcends any burning zeal to come out on top.

Marge will be in the stands. She knows what racing means to her son, and she has been proud of his every success. But she is large-hearted enough to know that all his rivals answer to the same vocation as his. So tomorrow, if she offers up a prayer at all (and she is by no means sure that track is a proper subject for prayer), it will not be that her son may defeat his rivals, but that all of them may run the best race of their lives.

The Mass concludes. They go home to their usual Sunday light lunch: broiled trout, whole wheat bread with cheese, cranberry juice, and a markerie salad.

XXV

SUNDAY MAY 23, MID-AFTERNOON

A few years ago, when the Prior of Tathwell Abbey had been murdered, on the premises, it had been necessary to conduct a homicide investigation within its walls. This required a special open-ness of mind, since it is not easy to figure out the nuances present, implicit or overt, in a wholly unfamiliar way of life. Coggin and Sump, assigned to the case, were able, quite successfully and soon, to see through the monastic exterior to the ordinary human beings within, full of individual foibles and strengths and weaknesses. At least, that had been true where the monks were concerned. But Tathwell was a double community, with monks and nuns leading, back then, strictly separate lives. That created a logistical problem of access. If two male detectives, using warrants, forced their way into the female half of the Abbey, it would create outrage and it would ensure that many of the nuns, if interviewed, would be disapprovingly uncooperative.

Adding Detective Constable Nancy Pringle to the team had solved the problem. After she became a nun, Coggin replaced her with another woman, Detective Constable Lorna Doherty. At the time, he had been glad to do so, on principle. Right now, he was pleased that he had, for practical and tactful reasons. If he took her with him, along with Sergeant Sump, there was a better chance that things might go smoothly on an informal visit to the Hertling mansion. What they need to do, if they can persuade the Hertlings, is have a thorough look at the mahogany furniture from Belize. Apparently, the whole consignment was destined for the master-bedroom; and a request to examine it, coming from a couple of men, might not go down very well. Conceivably, at least one of the drawers might contain intimate female garments. And even if they were folded away with the utmost neatness, the mistress of the house would probably balk at the idea of having some male stranger rifle through them. That's where Constable Doherty will come in useful.

He hopes so, anyway.

XXVI

MONDAY MAY 23, 6.00 PM

Conditions ideal: temperature 20 celsius (68 fahrenheit), low humidity, no wind.

They are bidden to the starting-line. Kippax, as designated rabbit, has the inside lane. The other eight stand to his right, poised, eager, variously nervous.

The gun goes off. Kippax, effortlessly, moves to the front. The others dutifully slot in behind him, in no particular order. At this stage, nobody is going to make any significant move. They coast around the curve into the back stretch like a disciplined phalanx, orderly, patient.

Fred Sump, in the stands, stopwatch in hand, sees nothing going on other than what he has expected to see. But one small detail catches his eye right away. Kippax, moving smoothly at the head of the pack, is carrying a lightweight stopwatch in his right hand. Is this a tribute, Fred wonders, to the immortal Nurmi? Back in the nineteen-twenties, the great Finn marched to his own drum, stopwatch in hand, relentlessly executing his own time-plan, regardless of anything his rivals could do, and left them helpless in his wake. What now did Kippax have in mind? He was an athlete with an experienced sense of planned tempo. Surely he, if anyone, could trust his own pace. Fred glanced at his own watch as the first lap ended. Sixty seconds, right on. Good for the Aussie! That's what rabbits are for: to set up the field, precisely, for a record attempt later – unselfishly.

Seven laps to go.

On the backstretch of the second lap, something unexpected happens: al-Hafid, the young Moroccan, decides to go out on his own. He charges to the front, at what looks like quite reckless speed; and by the end of the lap, he has a lead of almost forty metres. Unperturbed, Kippax lets him go, and notches another sixty-second lap, the rest of the pack staying with him. Time and experience, they reckon, is on their side. After all, al-Hafid is only nineteen years old and has presumably given way to impulse: if he thinks he can hang onto a lead like that with the world's best eating away at it for another mile-and-a-half, he's got another think coming. It was a risky, inexperienced maneouvre, sprung far too early, unlikely to pay dividends. Indeed, by the end of the third lap, clocked yet again at sixty seconds, Kippax and the others have started to reel him in. And at the end of the first mile, which Kippax has run in exactly four minutes, as requested, al-Hafid is back in the pack and will not be heard from again. Such is youthful folly.

Meanwhile, in the pack, there have been various levels of ease and unease. Three men, from Ethiopia and Finland and Japan, are essentially 10k and 5k specialists, who have dropped down to the two-mile distance for this event: they would have preferred a slower first four laps, to conserve energy for their finishing kick; they've been led through a four-minute mile, for starters, and cannot let themselves lose touch with the front, but they are not comfortable tactically. Two others, from Britain and Germany, are essentially specialists at 1500 metres, who occasionally move up to a longer distance: they are absolutely comfortable with a four-minute mile to begin with, having regularly gone under 3.50; but only time will tell if they have the stamina to match what Lang and M'bongo may throw at them in the end.

It is Lang's strategy, at this point, when Kippax drops out, his rabbiting done, to run the second mile with constant, gradual acceleration. He will begin with a fifty-nine second lap, and turn the screw tighter with every lap that passes. This, he calculates, will effectively deny M'bongo the hope of still being able to charge through a devastating last lap in forty-nine seconds, a coup de grace that would only be possible if the intervening laps were more relaxed.

To knowledgeable spectators like Fred Sump, everything seems to be panning out as one might expect. Kippax will run wide, to let the others by, and will jog to a contented stop with a nice cold Australian lager in mind. And Lang and M'bongo, the real class of the field, will fight it out.

Not so.

Kippax runs the fifth lap in fifty-eight seconds, and shows no sign of flagging. And it occurs to Lang now that this wily veteran from Down Under may, yes, have signed on to be rabbit at a requested tempo (which he has conscientiously fulfilled), but he may also have had an agenda of his own: something along the same lines as Lang himself has planned. Who knows what iron regime he has inflicted on his legs and lungs, down there in the Antipodean summer, while his rivals in the northern hemisphere have struggled through their fall and winter? Only M'bongo, in Kenya, has enjoyed a similarly helpful climate, along with the now out-of-it Moroccan.

And Kippax runs the sixth lap in fifty-seven seconds. Lang and M'bongo are hanging on. But it is Kippax who is dictating the race. If he can maintain this drive, his chances are clearly as good as theirs. Perhaps better.

The arithmetic is daunting. The third half-mile has gone in 1.57. Even if there is no further acceleration, the second mile will go in 3.49. That should be enough to win: add it on to the four-minute first mile, and 7.49 will be a new world record. Even if...

Kippax accelerates again. He knocks off the seventh lap in fifty-six taking a quick peek at his stopwatch. Lang, right on his tail, sees this. Is the man thinking he may have over-extended himself? Or does he still have something left, something that should be launched now perhaps, or perhaps not launched until the home stretch? All that Lang knows is that his role now, at least for the next half-lap, will only be to react. Then we'll see.

Three metres behind him now, and starting to falter, M'bongo is losing contact. Fred, in the stands, can see his shoulders tightening, his rhythm getting sloppy. Farewell, finishing kick. M'bongo is out of it.

Astonishingly, Kippax accelerates yet again. It is not a sprint, it is a surge. If he can keep it up, it will give him a last lap of fifty-five seconds, respectable enough at the end of a single mile, let alone now.

Lang digs deep and matches him.

Down the back straight they go and around the final curve, in lock-step and oblivious of all else. As they come off the turn, Kippax summons up, God knows how, one last mighty effort and starts to sprint.

But his nemesis is not to be denied. With ten metres to go, Lang hurls past him and wins by a stride. It is small consolation to Kippax that he, too, has smashed the previous world record by a huge margin. It has been the race of his life. But runners-up are a footnote.

$$***$$

Urine tests and blood tests are duly administered to Lang and Kippax, and to Denegal, the Ethiopian, who has roared out of the pack, twenty metres back, to pass M'bongo and take third.

XXVII

WEDNESDAY MAY 25, MIDDAY

It has preyed on her mind, having the damned gun. Simply having a lethal weapon like that around is enough in itself to make her nervous. But there has been the further anxiety, too, that her having taken the gun, however innocently, might connect her, in some guilty way, to Pilch's murder: police forces have been known, on occasion, to manipulate evidence in order to frame someone else, when the real perpetrator cannot be nailed. Unlike some young women of her generation, or of an earlier one, she does not subscribe to the counter-culture's belief that all policemen are chauvinists. As an actress, she refuses to deal in stereotypes: true characterization is the stuff of her trade. Furthermore, as a writer, she objects to the chauvinist slur, not only on the grounds of its bias, but also because it is an insult to the exact use of language: presumably its utterers mean "male chauvinists"; but without the "male" modifier, the noun is imprecise and meaningless.

As a stickler for good usage, she equally objects to people saying "like you and I." Unbeknownst to her, this makes her a kindred spirit to Inspector Coggin, who is repelled by solecisms like "How fun is that!"

Inspector Coggin, though, she has found hard to read. His awkward demeanour is too reserved for any quick appraisal. Sergeant Sump, on the other hand, has struck her as more obviously human. And she is genuinely grateful that he has taken the trouble to phone her and tell her, if she had feared being somehow implicated in the murder, to forget her fears, because the murderer's identity is now known. Thankful for that, she feels that the only honest thing to do is to come clean with him: to tell him, that is, of her having taken the gun and why, and of having been too timid to own up to having done so; as a sign of good faith, she will also send him the gun – and that will get the bloody thing off her hands.

She writes him a covering letter, explaining this, and stuffs it, and the gun, into an empty shoe-box, wraps the package in brown paper, addresses it to Sgt F. Sump, Homicide Squad, goes downtown to Police Headquarters, gives it to the front receptionist, who is busy on the telephone and leaves without a word.

***

Naively, what Amy has not foreseen is the commotion that follows. In a world infected with paranoia about terrorism in general, and about anti-police hostility in particular, the Headquarters on College Street does not take kindly to receipt of a suspicious package with no sender's name and address on it. Instant alert ensues. Two bomb-disposal officers who fortunately happen to be on the premises, take the package away, rather warily, and x-ray it, revealing it to contain only a revolver, an unloaded one at that, not some infernal machine. The gun, in due course, is duly identified as having been registered to Oscar Pilch, and there are only two sets of fingerprints on it: his, and those of a third party (Amy's) which do not match any of those in the large number available for computerized comparison.

***

The gun shows no sign of having been used for ages. This corroborates what is already known to Inspector Coggin and Sergeant Sump, that it was not used to kill Pilch. And it is an ironic footnote to Amy's story that the gun, being unloaded, would have been useless to her, if she had needed it, for self-defence.

They conclude that there is virtually nothing for them to act on in that aspect of the case. Amy may have committed a minor offence in purloining the gun, and in perhaps hindering the police in their inquiry by holding on to it. But she had come clean about it. So why should they do anything about it?

Nor do they have any reason to look further into what Pilch had been up to. Probably he was guilty of having blackmailed Boyle, but since he is now dead, he can hardly be faulted for that. And since his killer is also dead, from a police gunshot, he too cannot be arraigned – the cop who shot him will be cleared, beyond doubt, as having acted in self-defence.

There remains, therefore, only the matter of Boyle. If he is guilty of smuggling drugs into Canada by hiding them in mahogany furniture shipped to a Toronto customer, he will have planned to retrieve them from the warehouse by night. But that plan will have gone awry: a new coded access system has been installed, rendering useless the old key in his possession. In all probability, the Hertlings, like most multi-millionaires, have their mansion so burglar-proof that Boyle has had no way of getting at his stash: it must be still sitting there unsuspected, a fortune awaiting discovery.

If Coggin and Sump, with Doherty's help, can discover it, then Boyle can be nailed.

XXVIII

THURSDAY MAY 26, 10.30 AM

On time for their appointment, Inspector Coggin, along with Sergeant Sump and Detective Constable Doherty, in plain clothes and, not to embarrass the proprietor or to arouse the neighbours' curiosity, arrive in an unmarked car at Number 7, Massey Road. Architecturally, the street is a bizarre hodge-podge of styles and tastes. All that the mansions have in common is obvious wealth and a conspicuous display of size. Number 5, for example, is a giant version of Mock Tudor, complete with tall brick chimneys, decorative but non-functional. Number 9 is ostentatiously modernist, all glass and concrete, but devoid of warmth. Sandwiched between them, Number 7 is Baronial Bavarian: one expects obsequious gardeners in lederhosen and perhaps a discreetly hovering bodyguard with duelling scars. In a bygone time, there would have been stables at the rear, and a coach-house. Instead, tacked on at one end of the Herrenhaus, and a glaring cultural anomaly, there is a Rosedale-style three-car garage. All this is visible through massive and elaborate wrought iron gates, locked and only openable by buzzer.

Coggin presses the buzzer and identifies himself, and the gates swing open.

They park at the front door, and it is already open for them. The manservant who admits them, however, is no character from extravagant Heimweh: conventionally attired in a black suit, he perhaps doubles as butler and chauffeur. At the far end of the stone-flagged hall, seated on a throne-like Stuhl, is Graf Nikolaus von Hertling, who now rises and advances across the hall to greet the visitors, joined by his wife, the Grafin Katherina, who has come into the hall from the wing on his left.

Inspector Coggin, in German, introduces himself and his colleagues to them; but they respond in English, saying that they are quite comfortable in English, and that perhaps sticking to English would be more convenient for the Herr Inspektor's colleagues.

"Thank you," Inspector Coggin says. "That's very considerate of you."

Civilities are exchanged. Coffee is offered but declined. And Inspector Coggin comes directly to the point of their visit.

"Thank you," he says again, "for making the time to see us. Let me begin by reassuring you there's nothing to worry about in our appearance here as the police. We simply need your help in an investigation of something criminal that has nothing to do with you personally, and that you can't possibly know about anyway."

Help: it was a simple word, deliberately chosen. Coggin hates the stilted parlance of people given to what the immortal Fowler called *genteelisms*. In the detective world, suspects are said to be "assisting the police." And at suburban dinner-tables, hostesses offer to "assist" a guest to more potatoes. These things, he thinks, are a crime against language, to be ranked only a little lower than crimes against persons or property.

"But how, then, can we help," Hertling asks, "if it is, as you say something we do not know about?"

"Let me explain, sir," Inspector Coggin replies. "We have evidence that someone has tried to smuggle a quantity of illicit drugs into Canada, concealed in a shipment of regular imports. Ordinarily, the drugs would be retrieved on arrival, by an accomplice who knew where they were hidden. But something went wrong with that scheme; the drugs were not retrieved and the shipment has been delivered to the customer with the drugs still in it. Now this is where you come in – quite innocently, of course. The shipment concerned is the mahogany furniture you ordered, which I understand has now been installed in this house. Some of the pieces may have secret compartments in them, too cleverly constructed for anyone to spot them. So it is entirely possible there's a cache of illicit drugs on the premises, unbeknownst to you."

"Bitte," the Grafin interrupts, "*unbeknownst*? Dieses Wort kenne ich nicht."

"Unbekannt," Inspector Coggin translates, "das heisst, es ist möglich Sie haben an etwas unbekannterweise teilgenommen."

"Jawohl, natürlich!"

"So," Inspector Coggin resumes, in English, "if you'd be willing to help us, what we'd like to do is just take some measurements of your new furniture, to see if maybe there really is a secret compartment that could have been used for hiding packages of drugs."

"I see no objection to that," Hertling says. "How about you, Liebling?"

"Of course. As you perhaps know, Herr Inspektor, we come from a country with strong liking for – how do you say in English? – an die Regel und Ordnung."

"Law and Order."

"Danke! Yes, so we co-operate. All this furniture is up the stairs, in my bedroom. You like to see?"

"That would be very helpful. And by the way, we will, of course, try to leave everything neat and tidy, the way we find it. Sergeant Sump here will help me lift anything away from the wall, without disturbing the carpet, so that we can examine the back side of it. And we've brought Constable Doherty along to help: you'd probably rather have a woman look through your drawers than one of us men."

This negotiation has all gone quite smoothly, with minimal language blips; and the three Officers of the Law are dutifully led up a wide, sweeping flight of granite stairs, with wrought-iron banisters, to a tapestried corridor linking the west and east wings. The ceiling is vaulted in dark oak, and the two mullioned windows, to left and right, boast ancestral coats of arms in stained glass. After a journey of some twenty richly carpeted metres, they are ushered into a large, high-ceilinged bedroom, where the decor is in striking contrast to what they have seen so far in the rest of the house. Sergeant Sump, whose wife has taught him a thing or two about interior decoration, guesses at once that this is milady's domain, and that she has been given a free hand to indulge her own taste, rather than conform to the ponderous chauvinism so insistent elsewhere.

It is not as though the room will win any awards from *Canadian House and Home*. It is, if anything, conventional and unimaginative. But at least it shows a certain independence of spirit. There is deep-pile broadloom in a muted beige. The wallpaper is of a pretty but unobtrusive floral design, and is graced with four modest landscapes by Krieghoff (quite possibly originals), well lighted. There is a large mirror, framed not in Art Shoppe gilt, but in thin mahogany. And that is in keeping with the rest of the furniture, which is unanimously of mahogany: four-poster bed, with headboard; a small dresser; two side-tables with matching Milanese lamps; and two elegant chairs – this is clearly a room for sleeping in: two inner doors lead respectively to a dressing-room and a bathroom.

The three members of the Force put on latex gloves and set to work, while their two hosts sit down on the two chairs and watch them. It does not take long.

First, they move the bed away from the wall, to examine the back of the headboard: it proves to be quite thin, too much so for it to contain any hollow space within it. Then they strip the four-poster bed, with Constable Doherty taking careful note of how it was made up, so that it can be remade with scrupulous accuracy; while it is stripped, Inspector Coggin and Sergeant Sump test the frame and the posts for any hollows that are detectible. That done, they remake the bed and push it back to where they found it, flush against the wall. Apologetically, they ask the Hertlings to stand up so that they can inspect each chair for a hidden opening in its joinery. While they do so, Constable Doherty opens all the drawers in the dresser and compares their depths with their outside measurements, to determine if any of them have false bottoms.

They are about to give up in chagrin, and in some embarrassment at having bothered the Hertlings, when Inspector Coggin remembers how he solved the last and tantalizing clue in the magazine crossword. He remembers, too, how his grandmother slept in a four-poster bed, a much more old-fashioned one than the Hertlings' one, with knobs on top of the posts like this one here. Fortunately he is tall enough to reach the top of these posts without drawing any particular attention to his doing so. Reaching up with both hands, he exerts considerable pressure on one of the knobs, counter-clockwise. Nothing happens. Then, as he pushes even harder, the knob starts to turn. He unscrews it, carefully – after all, it is valuable wood, and he doesn't want to damage it, if his search is unwarranted. Slowly he unscrews it, and it comes away in his hands, off the top of the post.

The grooves, exactly matching the grooves on the top of the post, are clearly the work of a master-carpenter. But the knob itself is not a solid mahogany sphere: it is hollow, surprisingly light in his hands. Inside it, in sealed cellophane, is a batch of white powder.

By this time, although Inspector Coggin began inconspicuously enough, everyone present has become aware of what he is doing. They gather around and are aware at once of what he has discovered, and what its likely significance is.

"Mein Gott!" exclaims Mr Hertling, jolted into his mother tongue.

"Well, sir," says Inspector Coggin, "I can see that this has come as quite a shock to both of you."

This is said as much from politeness as from any wholly unqualified belief in the Hertlings' innocence. But Sergeant Sump, who reads people's voices and facial expressions and body language far more adroitly than Inspector Coggin, has no doubt at all of the husband's innocence. And the same goes for Constable Doherty, who reads the wife with a similar acuity.

"I'm sure you understand, sir and madam, that we have to take this package with us. And if you would like to make a signed statement that you were totally ignorant of its presence here, we'll be happy to enter that in the case-file on your behalf. Right now, though, you'll have to bear with us while we remove the other three knobs and see if there are other packages in them, too."

There indeed were. And when the three of them leave Number 7, Massey Road, they take four packages with them for testing in the Narcotics lab.

XXIX

FRIDAY MAY 27, 2.37 PM

      e-mail from Bio-Med Laboratories Inc., Toronto, Canada
      to World Anti-Doping Authority, Geneva, Switzerland.
      all three finishers tested after 2-mile race in toronto may 23
      pronounced clean. no disciplinary action required.
      cc canadian track and field association, ottawa, canada
            ross lang, toronto
            tom kippax, sydney, australia
            haile denegel, addis ababa, ethiopia
      blind copy pm foundation toronto
      blind copy sgt f sump, metropolitan police, toronto

***

In other words, Fred Sump says to himself, there has been no infraction of the official rules banning the use of performance-enhancing substances. So, equally, no criminal law has been broken that prohibits the importation of or trafficking in such narcotics.

XXX

FRIDAY MAY 27, 11.04 AM
Telephone call to Inspector A. Coggin, Homicide.
"Andrew, Ted Ainslie here. I've got the report back from the lab, about the four packages you found in that Jerry bedroom."
"Yes?"
"They're not what you might have thought. They're icing sugar."
"Icing sugar?"
"Yes as in 'If I'd known you were coming I'd have baked a cake'."
"Well, that is a bit of a surprise."
"I thought so, too. So I guess we've been chasing down a crime that hasn't been committed. Or at least, if someone was trying to smuggle some stuff in, he got double-crossed at the far end. Anyway, I thought you'd want to know right away."
"Thanks, Ted. See you."

***

Coggin hangs up. What an irony! he reflects. Goes to show, amateurs shouldn't get involved. So Boyle goes to a lot of trouble and runs a lot of risk, to organize some stuff, probably heroin or coke, and bribes the carpenter in Belize to hide it in the bedpost knobs; and when the furniture's ready to be shipped, the carpenter simply substitutes sugar, peddles the stuff for a small fortune, and sits back with a nice, tidy nest-egg. Result: Boyle's innocent – or at least I'm not about to charge him with illegal importation of icing sugar. That, we can let him get away with.

And what's more, he's admitted to virtual murder – or, that is, to wanting to kill Pilch, because he was being blackmailed. Only, someone beat him to it. No charge there, either. How lucky can a man get? Well, he is out of pocket for ten grand. So I guess Fred would say he's had a kind of punishment for criminal intentions.

The real irony for us, of course, is that this may very well be our last case, since we're putting in for retirement. And after all these years of running down villains, we've spent a couple of months working on a crime that didn't exist. Case closed. And this time we won't be saying, what's next?

275

XXXI

SATURDAY MAY 28, 9.10 AM

Three days in the octave of Pentecost – that is, in what is called Whitsun week – are called Ember Days, the Wednesday and the Friday and the Saturday, set aside for reflection and repentance. On this Ember Saturday, as on every day, the Tathwell community is gathered together for Mass. And there is a passage in the Ordinary of the Mass which is fortuitously apt to the purpose of reflection and repentance: it involves the chanting of seven verses from the twenty-fifth psalm.

As always nowadays in Tathwell Abbey, the chanting is antiphonal, with the monks on the south side of the choir and the nuns on the north taking turns in the chant, verse by verse.

Sister Nancy Pringle, in her choir-stall, attends scrupulously to fitting the syllables of the text to the inflections of the psalm-tone.

"I will wash my hands in innocency, O Lord," she chants: "and so will I go to thine altar."

"That I may shew the voice of thanksgiving," the monks respond: "and tell of all thy wondrous works."

Thanksgiving is indeed high on her list of devotions: gratitude for having found her way back to this heart's home.

"Lord," she resumes, "I have loved the habitation of thy house: and the place where thine honour dwelleth."

As the psalm goes on, she is able, like any practised religious, to give her mind attentively to the immediate outer demands of liturgy, but also to heed whatever inner duty is hers of reflection and repentance So today, as the monks chant the next verse, "O shut not up my soul with the sinners: nor my life with the blood-thirsty", memory goes back to her days with Homicide. She had been a good cop, much concerned with the idea of justice. But her heart had been elsewhere: first and sadly with a man who was now dead; and then, unbeknownst to her, with this vocation here, which had seized her and not let go. Being here, doing these things here is for her, she knows, absolutely right. And this she confirms out loud, chanting the last of the seven verses prescribed: "My foot standeth right: I will praise the Lord in the congregation."

XXXII

Lester Boyle has complied with a request that he come to Police HQ for an interview. And now he sits in an interview-room, facing Inspector Coggin and Sergeant Sump. They switch on the tape-machine and record the obligatory opening statement, noting the date and time, and stating who is present.

Boyle is clearly nervous.

"Mr Boyle," Coggin begins, "we've asked you to come in and talk to us, in connection with a case we've been investigating, which involves both murder and drug-smuggling. Both of those are serious offences; and if you were guilty of either offence, we would have to press charges against you. I think you understand that."

"Yes."

"Let's begin with the death of Oscar Pilch. It was, in fact, a murder. And you have been suspected of having committed it. Moreover, you have admitted to us that you contemplated killing Pilch, because he was blackmailing you. Correct?"

"Yes, but I also said –"

"I know: you also said that when you went to see Pilch in his office, you found him dead there, apparently murdered by someone else. Now, you must admit that perhaps that claim would sound a bit thin as a defence, if you were charged, without any corroborating witnesses."

"I suppose so," Boyle replies, lamely.

"Well, fortunately for you," Coggin goes on, "whatever your murderous intentions may have been, we happen to know it wasn't you who killed Pilch. It was somebody else. So you can rest easy on that score."

Boyle sighs, with obvious relief. "Who did, then?"

"That, sir, is really none of your business. However, it doesn't put you completely in the clear. There's this other matter of drug-smuggling. Strictly speaking, it wouldn't ordinarily involve us, in the Homicide unit, so much as our colleagues in Narcotics. But in this case, the two things are hopelessly intertwined. We were working on Pilch's murder. But Pilch was also part of the drug-scene; and you had hired him to investigate the use of performance-enhancing drugs by track-athletes. That, by the way, was of special interest to Sergeant Sump here: in private life, he's a well-known track-coach. Sergeant?"

"Thanks, sir. Of course, I do try to keep the two halves of my life separate. I can't let my track activities affect my work as a policeman. In this particular case, I have to keep two things disentangled. First off, there's the question of drugs in sport, involving you indirectly as Pilch's employer. Then on the other hand, there's the question of you being directly involved in the smuggling of drugs, other drugs, on your own account. On the whole, we're putting the sports-drugs to one side for the time being – though we have thought it only right, now, to keep Mr Morales fully informed about developments, seeing it was his Foundation that got Pilch involved, through you, in making inquiries. What he makes of it is up to him, not us."

"He already has, damn you," Boyle throws in angrily. "He fired ne yesterday."

"Did he indeed?" Coggin remarks. "Some might call that a kind of poetic justice. But never mind me. You were saying, Sergeant?"

"Just this, Mr Boyle. A lot of evidence, including what you've admitted to us, points to your having organized a little heroin caper of your own – or was it coke? You were in Belize, allegedly on vacation. You had the opportunity to bribe one of the carpenters there, to tinker with the next mahogany shipment and hide a stash in it. Once the shipment arrived here in the warehouse, you figured you could retrieve the stash from it after hours: you used to work at the Emporium, and you still had a key, or keys, to the premises. So what went wrong? Simply, you didn't know the Emporium had installed a new, foolproof security system. And there was no way you could retrieve the stash now, unless you could figure out how to get at it in the Hertlings' house after the furniture was delivered there. That's maybe something you've been working on. But I have to tell you we got there first. So your neat little packages, all four of them, are now sitting right here, in this building. That amount of heroin or coke or whatever would probably be good for seven years in the can."

"Except, of course," Coggin interjects, "that's not how it's going be at all. For the truth is, your little packages are pure as the driven snow – literal snow, not the slang kind. You may have spent a couple of grand in Belize, getting hold of drugs at source locally, that would be worth a couple of hundred thousand on the street up here, but your side kick down there double-crossed you. All that the packages contained is just icing-sugar."

Lester Boyle, hearing this, is a picture or utterly crestfallen defeat.

"The good news is," Inspector Coggin adds, sardonically, "there's no law prohibiting the importation of icing sugar. So actually no crime has been committed. No crime, no charges. We might send you a bill for the cost of the lab test. But my opposite number in Narcotics says, why bother?"

Boyle shifts uneasily in his chair, but makes no move to stand up.

"It's alright, sir," Sergeant Sump says. "You're free to go."

"And by the way," Inspector Coggin adds, "on your way out, stop off at the reception desk. There's an envelope for you there, containing your passport. And if you do go back to Belize, I'd strongly recommend you don't try and do anything about the carpenter there who tricked you. If I may say so, you're quite a bit out of your depth, playing with the pros."

The door closes.

"Amateurs!" says Sergeant Sump.

EPILOGUE

In the summer of 1988, the Seoul Olympics yielded no gold for Canadian distance-runners. Ross Lang had been widely regarded as a shoo-in for double gold in the 5k and the 10k, with a speculative chance of replicating the great Zátopek's triple in both and the marathon. But sadly in July, when out shopping, he was hit by a drunk driver, suffering irreparable injury to his right leg. He had blazed like a comet across the athletic sky. But his short and illustrious career was over. He enrolled in the school of graduate studies at the University of Toronto, aiming for a doctorate in international affairs; and from then on, he applied his formidable talents, and his stamina, to more intellectual pursuits.

Fred Sump, too, had retired, as intended. He took the job he had been recruited for, as senior distance adviser with the Canadian Track and Field Association. And his only subsequent connection with homicide was to attend, in 1990, the premiere of Amy Barton's starring performance, funded by the PM Foundation, in the two lead roles of "Two Women", her study of two historical murderesses. It took him back to former days on the Force, when there had sometimes been women among the killers he brought to book. In all those years, he had been exposed, depressingly often, to the seamy side of life. He had been a good cop. But that was over and done with. Now he was engaged, full time, in something he loved and valued. He was a happy man.

Andrew Coggin, also retired, found a way, bit by bit, into the world of his beloved Bach. He attended Bachian concerts whenever there were any of decent quality in Toronto. He joined the committee of the Greater Toronto Bach Choir, and served as a volunteer fund-raiser for it. It was not as though there were no other composers worth listening to. He basked in the warm humanity of Mozart. He respected the originality and skill of Beethoven, despite the man's unappealing emphasis on self. He relished the spiky volatility of Bartók. But all these, on the musical map, were just foothills to the Himalayan range that was Johann Sebastian Bach.

In 1990, he went to Europe to take in Bach performances in Leipzig, notably in the Thomaskirche, where Bach had been Cantor and had composed many of his greatest works. From Leipzig he went on to Prague. This, like his Bach journey, was almost a pilgrimage. Six years ago, when the city was still in the grip of a neo-Stalinist nightmare, he and Fred had been there, on a visit; and the two of them, with no official standing, had helped solve a murder committed by a member of the secret police, who had infiltrated a group of dissidents opposed to the Communist regime. The two Canadians had got away safely, but all the dissidents were rounded up and imprisoned. Among them had been Jan Štefek, their leading spirit, who happened to have been an old friend of

Andrew Coggin's. He was released from prison in 1989, when the regime released all such prisoners of conscience, hoping to stave off the fall of Communism. Little the worse for wear, Jan was delighted to see Andrew again, and immediately asked to be remembered kindly to Fred.

It was an emotional reunion for both men. It is hard to maintain a loyal friendship in the face of adverse circumstances. But there was more to it than that. There was a kinship of ideals. Štefek had stood for justice and truth, first during the dark years of the Nazi occupation, and then during the dark decades when Czechoslovakia was tyrannized by a puppet government of Moscow's, run by a gang of thugs and liars. Coggin, for his part, had served the cause of truth and justice twice also: as a young man in postwar Germany, he had done his best to help cleanse that country of its Nazi stain; and as a police officer in Canada, he had pitched in to protect the citizenry from criminals who were, granted, not political tyrants but who were, in their own way, a serious danger to society. In his long career, Andrew had been, in the end, a justified man. Equally Jan, in his long devotion to freedom, had been, in the end, a man justified by history.

As Andrew flies home to Toronto, he switches on his pocket-size archive of Bach cantatas. Number 184 seems somehow especially apt to the scene of liberated joy he had just encountered in Prague, the Prague of the Velvet Revolution. The introductory recitative established that quite pointedly. "Oh longed-for light of joy," the soloist sings (in German with Coggin listening fluently), "breaking forth with the new covenant! We, who wandered in the valley of the shadow of death, now know that God has sent the long-desired Shepherd to us." He does not need to be a Lutheran to appreciate the suffering of people under the sword of villainy, or their gladness at any kind of deliverance, whether sacred or secular; and the tragic transcendancy of the *St Matthew Passion* is overwhelming to Christian and non-Christian alike. He does not need to be a keyboard artist, himself, to fall in love with the *Well-Tempered Clavier*, or a dancer to move in spirit with the dances of the orchestral suites. As a detective who excelled in the sorting out of complicated evidence, he reveres the contrapuntal mastery of *The Art of Fugue*, which is richly eloquent where so many practitioners are drily academic. Along with that abstract reverence, though, he responds deeply to the Bach who is, above all, the greatest harmonist ever, the peerless matcher of astonishing dissonances and resolutions, the reconciler of conflict and peace.

If in his professional years spent in the world of crime and punishment Andrew Coggin had found a way to make the best of an often brutal existence, so now in the world of sound, as rung by Bach and by those who knew to make his notes relive themselves, he finds a way to spend the rest of his days in a life of good order and surpassing beauty. And when his time is come to bid all that farewell, he will certainly be able to say, like Bach, a simple, heart-felt Amen.

APPENDIX: SOLUTION TO THE CROSSWORD

ACROSS
1/ Repeats
5/ Rotor
8/ Shooting pains
9/ Tapes
10/ Last leg
11/ Rising
12/ Discus
15/ Sprints
17/ Knobs
19/ British tennis
20/ Evens
21/ Reladen

DOWN
1/ Reset
2/ Prompt service
3/ Artisan
4/ Single
5/ Ropes
6/ Triple crowned
7/ Resigns
11/ Risible
13/ Inkwell
14/ Esther
16/ Nails
18/ Susan

JOHN REEVES is a Canadian author, born in British Columbia and resident in Ontario. His books include detective novels, plays, poetry, writings about religion and music, and a study of Central European history. An award-winning producer of radio documentaries and features, he is also a composer of modern classical music, much performed at home and abroad. In younger years, he was an international gold-medallist as a long-distance runner.